The Measurable World

. . .

For Peter —
With accumulated
years of admiration —
Kate

Western Literature Series

The Measurable World

■ ■ ■

KATHARINE COLES

University of Nevada Press

Reno   Las Vegas   London

Western Literature Series

A list of books in the series appears at the end of this volume.

The paper used in this book meets the requirements of
American National Standard for Information Sciences—
Permanence of Paper for Printed Library Materials, ANSI Z39.48-1984.
Binding materials were selected for strength and durability.

Library of Congress Cataloging-in-Publication Data

Coles, Katharine.
The measurable world / Katharine Coles.
p.   cm. — (Western literature series)
ISBN 0-87417-273-X (alk. paper)
I. Title.   II. Series.
PS3553.047455M55   1995
813'.54—dc20   95-17114
CIP

University of Nevada Press, Reno, Nevada 89557 USA
Copyright © 1995 by Katharine Coles
All rights reserved
Jacket design by Erin Kirk New
Printed in the United States of America

2   4   6   8   9   7   5   3   1

For Miriam Magdalen Wollaeger Wilcox

1906–1995

Acknowledgments

This book was made possible in part by a New Forms Project Grant from the National Endowment for the Arts and by assistance from the Salt Lake City Arts Council and the Utah Arts Council.

It is almost impossible to acknowledge everyone who supported me in the writing of this novel, but I would like to thank my editor, Trudy McMurrin; Fiona Webster, Franklin Fisher, Patricia McConnel, François Camoin, Barbara Rodman, Douglas Unger, and most particularly Kenneth Brewer, all of whom who read the manuscript; and my family, especially my husband, Chris Johnson. Thanks also to Larry Bringhurst for the gun tips.

Though many of the events in this novel occur in real places, all of the inhabitants and habitués of those places are purely invented. In particular, Salt Lake City's Hole-in-the-Wall Saloon, which was already gone by 1991, when the novel begins, has been altered radically here; and though I never knew any owner of the old Hole-in-the-Wall, I assume that none bore the slightest resemblance to Ralph.

Contents

Prelude *1*

PART ONE ▪ *Storm Watch*

Chapter 1 ▪ January Thaw 7

Chapter 2 ▪ Storm Watch 37

Chapter 3 ▪ A Charm from the Sky 59

Chapter 4 ▪ A Little Two-step 91

Chapter 5 ▪ Working on the Dead 113

PART TWO ▪ *Still Life, With Grace*

Chapter 6 ▪ With Someone Like You 129

Chapter 7 ▪ Voice Lessons 148

Chapter 8 ▪ The Air of the Dream *165*

Chapter 9 ▪ Still Life, With Grace *179*

PART THREE ▪ *Overlooking Eden*

Chapter 10 ▪ Paying for Love *209*

Chapter 11 ▪ Sweet Dreams *225*

Chapter 12 ▪ A Breath of Air *239*

Chapter 13 ▪ Overlooking Eden *255*

Chapter 14 ▪ The Problem with Distance *281*

Prelude

February 1991

Grace Stern's grandmother, Imo, hasn't been to a funeral in over twenty years, though she is eighty-four and her friends have died one by one. Her husband of five decades was buried two years ago without her attendance or her blessing. Since the Park Service carried the body of her own daughter, Grace's mother Julia, off the mountain on a helicopter, Imo has not believed in death—or has believed, rather, in only one death, that of Grace's father, which has not yet occurred. As far as Imo is concerned, her loved ones are still here, not even ghostly, but solid and everyday. They are always about to walk in through the back door, shouting, stomping the snow off their boots.

Now it is snowing again, enormous flakes making the kitchen window a fast-moving screen. To Grace the house feels muffled, under water, though Grandma Imo, who has never learned much about economy, has turned on all the lights, even the fluorescent ones under the cabinets. Imo sets down her teacup and leans toward Grace across the table, her finger poking the air at Grace's chest level. She says, "At some point, you have to become responsible."

Grace says, "For what?" She couldn't agree with Imo more, but as Grace has passed into her thirties, she has become decidedly more fragile, less definite and certain rather than the opposite—not so much physically as in what she would avoid calling her soul. Now she doesn't know what to say about Pascal, can't tell whether it would be kinder to let Imo believe the impossible, that he could walk through that kitchen door smelling of blizzard and take Grace off Imo's hands again, or not. She says, "Pascal didn't love me for who I am, any more than a man ever does a woman."

Imo puts her fingers into her hair, which, without one of her ex-starlet wigs to hold it, threatens to flutter right off her head like some untidy gray pigeon. "What did you expect?"

"Something else," Grace says, and Imo puts her slippered feet up on a chair and bites into a shortbread cookie. Imo's ankles are trim, her stockings tidy. She raised Grace from nine years old, with the mixed blessing that Grace hears Imo's voice wherever she goes, her own private Greek chorus gone a little mad. Grace has given up trying to shake it, though it can't help her now.

"You never did understand the nature of love," Imo says.

"True enough," Grace replies. "Who would have taught me?"

Imo purses her lips and reaches for the sugar bowl. She adds two cubes to her tea, making a total of five.

As for Grace, impractical all her life and no more likely than Imo to become practical now, what she has always wanted is to be tough, independent and hard-talking but still soft, like in the songs, like a cowgirl version of her mother the

way Grace remembers her. This woman who is not Grace can
sass a man and drink him under the table, then jump on a
horse, careless of what she's leaving, and ride away under a
high, endless western sky. Her talent is that she has no memory: whatever she turns her back on vanishes. Grace closes
her eyes and sees her, framed against the light of a single
breathtaking mountain. Though the woman is supposed to
be going somewhere, Grace always freezes her in that still
shot, on her way but not actually moving, so that she has no
definite future either, with its sure tragedies, but only hope
caught in a static moment.

Her grandmother says, "Someday you'll really hurt yourself." Grace knows from experience: it's her own daughter's
ghost Imo sees when she talks, and Grace's father silhouetted
on the western horizon, casting a shadow so long it still chills
Imo across twenty years.

This desire, this imaginary woman, is one thing both Rita,
Grace's first best friend, and Ralph, her second, know in
Grace. Their knowledge doesn't always overlap. Through the
passionate school years, Rita and Grace never slept together;
they let all the moments when that seemed possible pass with
just a flush, a disturbance like air moving over the skin,
though after pushing each other up cliffs and peeing in the
woods together, maybe they were still more familiar with each
other's bodies than any man ever could be.

"What I wanted from Pascal was something familiar,"
Grace says.

"Another thing you didn't understand. You married for love.
Comfort is something else."

Grace sighs. "The first time I saw him—" It was up at Pascal's cabin. His cowboy hat was tilted back on his head, and
the aspens shivered behind him in the wind. The sun was
shining over his shoulder, so Grace couldn't see his face,
couldn't see his hair was a red dark as blood. But his shape

had reminded her of something solid, something she hadn't known since childhood. She runs her hand over her own black crew cut and says, "I thought, 'This is it.'"

"Anyway, he was from Houston," Imo says. "He'd never been on a horse in his life."

To Grace, just hearing his drawl was like walking into her favorite myth. And later, she could think of him as he would have been twenty-five years before, a teenager drifting in the Gulf of Tonkin on the deck of the *Coral Sea,* the stars in the black galaxy above crossed and recrossed by reconnaissance planes. How both her parents would have disapproved of him, if only they had known. It seemed for a while, in spite of what Ralph and Rita said, as if she could get what she wanted, an orderly life with just that little bit of disorder.

Grace doesn't want to think about this. She reaches to turn on the radio, but Imo lifts one long finger and says, "Remember the rules. Not until it ends." She means the Gulf War, whose news has taken over her favorite station, barking in on the old, romantic songs. "I can't stand it."

"At least it may be quick this time," Grace says, but she wonders to herself, Quick for whom? If Pascal were alive, she thinks, he'd be there, in the desert inside the radio, and she'd still be sitting here with Imo, waiting for him to return.

Imo says, "You could be doing something about it. Like Rita."

Grace sighs. "Sound and fury. Nobody's paying any attention to her. This is a happy war, remember?"

"You *did* get what you wanted. You just have to be more careful what you ask for."

"You're talking in clichés," Grace says.

"Just because it's been said before doesn't mean it isn't true." Imo lifts her thin nose and looks down it at her terry-cloth scuffs, white in the flickering light.

PART ONE

■ ■ ■

Storm Watch

CHAPTER 1

■ ■ ■

January Thaw

Ralph filled the shot glass. To Grace, squinting through the lens of a little more tequila than necessary at his big hands and feet, his long arms and legs, he looked like a cartoon spider, but with a familiar face in which everything seemed too wide to be quite perfect—prominent eyes and mouth, thick nostrils—and was therefore deceptively friendly. Even in his familiarity, he was the best-looking man she knew, every beautiful feature exaggerated beyond danger.

"Are you sure this is a good idea?" he asked. "Have you ever seen a dead body? You've always been a little squeamish."

"It's the idea of death I can't stand. I want to know if the reality is different." Grace shut her eyes but could see her mother's face only as she remembered it, alive and in motion, the kind of face no photograph, no single moment, could describe. Grace reached for the shot, then shook her head and said, "No. I have to teach early tomorrow." It was a Monday night, and she wasn't used to drinking more than a beer or glass of wine with dinner, but she didn't want to go home. Grace and Pascal had been split two months to the day, and without him the condo felt colder than ever, though not so cold she could bear to think of letting him come back. He had left little bits of himself behind—ragg socks, a leather vest—and she kept coming across them just at those moments when she had stopped thinking about him. "It's a lab," she said. "Trees and Shrubs. My hands have to be steady."

The evening had felt too comfortably like the old days. Grace was starting to spend too much time at Ralph's again, was suspended between two pasts, each defined by love, or at least by desire. She was perhaps asking for trouble. She and Ralph weren't sleeping together yet, but he clearly thought it was only a matter of time. There was something about his shoulder against hers, the snap of desire in the air, the chance to punish Pascal once and for all, that she didn't want to fight, though she was ashamed enough of her impulses and her motives to have resisted them so far. She leaned over and turned up the stereo—Lyle Lovett—and started to sing along, harmonizing above Lyle's tenor, her voice just skimming the highest notes. Some mixed mythology, about loading a pony onto a boat and heading out to sea.

Ralph turned down the stereo. "You may be my first love, but you still listen to too much country."

She looked up at him sideways and said, "You're only my boss on Wednesday night." She sang on Wednesdays for a piece of the gate in Ralph's little beer bar downtown, the Hole-in-the-Wall Saloon—not much money in it, but Ralph had always loved the way she came up under a note, had taken her on out of fondness even though she wasn't the best around. Ralph was one of the few who knew: through their adolescence, Grace had dreamed of becoming Patsy Cline and dying in flames. In junior high, whenever Ralph could escape to Imo's house, the two of them would stand together in front of the mirror in the basement bathroom and sing "Sweet Dreams" and "Crazy," using deodorant bottles like microphones, gazing into each other's reflected eyes. Since then, their tastes had diverged. He'd moved through Anthrax and Kiss, on to the Grateful Dead.

Grace said, "My nostalgia is no more sentimental than yours."

"Give it up," Ralph said. He rubbed his hand over her hair, dropped it to her shoulder. She laughed and twitched her shoulder away, and he put his hand back on his own knee.

"I forgot: you eat logic for breakfast," she said.

"Get off your high horse." He drank the shot of tequila himself. He looked away from her, then back. "You're the scientist. How much of sentimentality is hormonal?"

"I study plants. But only a man's brain deals out its tasks like cards."

Ralph shook his head. "I've got to stop drinking with you."

"You only just started. Anyway, I saw these pictures in *Omni* of brains with the cortical hemispheres lit up, different colors for speech, analysis, fear. Damage to the right penny-sized group of cells and a man will never speak again." She reached out and touched his head over the place where his brain kept speech. His hair was as straight and coarse as she remembered. She shut her eyes. Though she had always styled herself an intellectual, objective and detached, her first response to everything—a display of pollen-laden anthers against red petals as much as walking from shade into bright sun—was immediate and physical. Mostly, she fought it. Now, she thought of those photos, brains lit up in colors glowing like jewels spilled on a dark cloth.

He grabbed her fingers and held them softly, though he could have the hardest grip she knew. She thought of him as containing some great violence under a surface he strained to keep gentle and even. He said, "Do you always have to think like a scientist?"

She opened her eyes. "Less and less," she said. Then, "So he wants to dangle a woman from his arm when he goes out."

"Why not?" Ralph poured another shot and handed it to her.

"A charm, for luck." She waved her wrist at him and sloshed a little tequila onto the couch between them. He wiped at it with his fingers, then moved over onto the stain. She shouldn't drink tequila. It got her going. She put the back of her hand to her forehead. "That's the real world, where women learn to starve and shellac themselves for love."

Ralph laughed. "We could all use a little more luck," he said. "Anyway, at home men are looking for something else." He put his arm around Grace in a way she still considered safe, but he was giving her his big-eyed soulful look, from under lashes so long she was jealous of them.

"The angel in the house," she said. "That's exactly what I mean."

He shook his head at her. "Nobody would make that mistake with you."

"Thanks a lot. Anyway, I can show you. I have the *Omni* at home."

Grace has never claimed not to be a product of the myths of her culture. Or of her geography. She knows even science has its own occult power: Like a fundamentalist religion, it can refuse to see itself as another organizational mode, a way to justify calling what it can quantify and study *reality* so it can disregard the rest. And like any religion, it requires an absolute faith only of its lesser followers. Though Grace herself is not destined for greatness, she knows there never has been a great scientist who wasn't, like the best of saints, riddled with doubt. As Ralph pointed out, that woman Grace wanted to be isn't any more real than a Barbie doll.

"But she's more interesting," Grace said.

"Maybe to you." Ralph still had his arm around her, was holding her so gently she almost didn't have to notice. For a man who'd grown up working outside, building fences, herding cattle from the back of a horse, he could have a light touch.

Grace has always lived in town, but town's a different idea in the West. When she walks out onto what she still thinks of as Pascal's balcony, which wraps around the corner of the Bench Towers Condominiums' twelfth floor and lets her look either up into Emigration Canyon, cutting toward her through the mountains, or out across the valley where, on clear days when the copper works aren't running, she can see the sun glinting off a windshield for fifty miles, her heart closes for a second. She could drive a fast hour into the mountains or the desert and be lost in a wilderness. Grace's girlhood weekends on Ralph's family ranch overlooking Eden, that bowl of golden grass and sagebrush edged by granite peaks, became as much a part of her as the life she lived in Imo's elaborated house, coded indelibly into her memory. No wonder all the myths are of people—"Men, usually," Grace's grandmother Imo always says—riding into the land alone while the sun welts the sky red in front of them. What you see, you want to give yourself up to. Or like the miners and hunters, like the local pioneers who dragged across the Rockies their handcarts and the dead weight of their glorious hallucination of God, you want to clear the land of Indians and trees and tear it open and make it surrender what it holds.

So Ralph said, "Maybe you do need a little adventure." He lifted his hand off Grace's shoulder and touched her neck, only for a second, but a second was long enough.

"Not that kind," Grace said, though she felt herself leaning toward him. She'd reached that age when her body seemed to be telling her something about four walls, a fenced yard. An age she'd never imagined for herself. She shivered, whispered, "I'm trying to be fair."

He started to stroke Grace's neck. "You don't believe things could change?"

Even approaching intimacy, his touch had a deference, a courtliness. If it had been only slightly less thoughtful, Grace might have felt safe, even honorable, turning into it, into the warmth traveling from his fingers through her rib cage. Now decisive, she said, "The biological force behind culture is winging through our veins. Don't let it catch you."

He dropped his hand back to her shoulder. "Why don't you ever just say what you mean?"

She shut her eyes and turned her head away. "I don't know. Sometimes, after I open my mouth, I could kick myself for what came out."

"That's okay," he said. "You can kick me instead."

"No, really. Do you ever feel as if you have two people in you? One who stands out on the front walk, cracking jokes with passersby, and one hovering just inside the house, peeking through a crack in the curtains?" The tequila bottle was almost empty. Grace poured herself another shot, then rummaged around Ralph's couch cushions for the salt. She found the shaker, sprinkled some carefully into the little pocket of skin at the base of her thumb, licked it, threw back the tequila. Ralph's hand was there with a wedge of lime. She brought his hand to her mouth, bit the lime between his fingers, pursed her lips.

"Where's the Polaroid?" she asked.

He tilted his head in the direction of the stereo cabinet.

She nodded. The motion set the room spinning around her. "We need a photograph."

"Stop seeing yourself as an ornament," Ralph said.

She nodded again, grabbed for the arm of the couch. Then she lay down very carefully, her feet in Ralph's lap, and gave herself up to the whirling dark.

After teaching her morning lab, helping her students look through their microscopes at the tissues of heartwood, the rings of cells where springwood and summerwood merge, Grace let Ralph drive her, her bicycle, and her broken heart to the embalming lab at Shady Oaks. It had been her own idea after all, to confront death, as it were, in the flesh, and, the night before, it seemed a fine one. She had shut her eyes on the images she carried in her head of her mother and her grandfather alive, and concentrated instead on picturing the closed coffins that had held them. They were both gone, but she'd never seen any evidence that they had left their bodies, and she hoped seeing any empty body would help her imagine their deaths. She hadn't told Ralph she also wanted to see what could happen when Pascal's scalpel in a person's heart couldn't save it.

So in the morning when she walked out of the lab, Ralph's red Jeep Cherokee was pulled up in a NO PARKING spot, its driver's side door still open, as if to indicate the car wasn't really parked there but was just waiting for somebody important. It was the kind of fine logical distinction Ralph thrived on. Ralph was standing on the grass in his shirtsleeves and gray trousers, his gray lawyer suit coat draped tidily over the handlebars of Grace's chained-up yellow bicycle. On the sidewalk he'd set up a stool to which he had superglued a stripped-clean steer skull. He kept the stool and skull in the back of the Cherokee in case he ever had time to kill.

Grace stood and watched him. His sleeves were rolled up and he was twirling a lariat. Ralph had more energy than anyone else Grace knew; the rope seemed an extension of it, a displacement of nerves turning over his head. It looped and shimmied, graceful; Ralph paced beneath it, eyeing the skull. Then he let go. The rope turned once more in the air, opened, and fell, light as air, around the skull's white horns. Ralph yanked at just the right moment, and pulled the loop tight. Watching him, Grace felt that his arm described a larger circle, private to himself, representing some tragedy or gap she knew but didn't understand. She thought of him up at the ranch, his arms shoulder-deep inside a cow in trouble giving birth, and wondered how he'd ever ended up in the city at all.

Ralph didn't practice law anymore. In the end, in spite of

his love for distinctions, his own sense of justice had turned out to be too rigid for the negotiations and compromises required by the legal system. He had begun as an idealist, a trial lawyer who set out to defend the downtrodden innocent against a system gone lax and cynical. He'd found himself working to free clients he knew in his heart were guilty, and though he also believed in their right to a vigorous defense he became unsure he could provide it. Then came the client he'd been waiting for—a black teenager accused of raping and stabbing a white cheerleader at his high school, in the heart of one of the whitest communities in America. When police learned that the girl had been secretly dating Ralph's client, the trial was, as Ralph said, all over. Ralph's client was reprieved in the end, and a local football hero, white, was arrested in his place, but the boy had been sentenced to death in the meantime. As Ralph told Grace, a soul never recovers its innocence after that. He meant his own soul, Grace suspected, as much as his client's. The football hero would be eligible for parole in another five years. Ralph bought the Hole-in-the-Wall Saloon and never took another case. Still, he wore the uniform of the profession, as if, after all those years of training, he couldn't let it go.

Grace heard, "Doctor Stern?" As usual, she was being dogged by a student. When she saw who it was, she smiled. Dan wouldn't be interested in clarifying the difference between a corm and a bulb or a marginal spine and the major vein of a leaf—these were concepts he incorporated easily into his worldview. He wasn't even interested in Ralph's display, though a cluster of undergraduates had gathered on the grass to watch. They clapped while Ralph loosened the rope from the horns of the skull and set the stool upright again. His white shirt was still pristine, his necktie straight and fixed with an onyx tack, his black hair smooth against his skull.

Not that Dan had ever made explicit what he wanted: he'd told Grace about his idea for a perpetual motion machine and his patent on equipment to help the blind navigate obstacles located with sound waves; he'd told her about his mysterious fevers, his brother who'd stepped on a land mine in Vietnam and lived for minutes from the waist up, his fiancée's—Bliss's—miscarriages; he'd described the Tarot deck he and Bliss had designed around western motifs. He'd taken classes from Grace three semesters straight. She was becoming wary of his too-concentrated attention, but he interested her. He worried her only when she thought he was making sense.

Today he was talking about the stars. Their figures, that is, and their predictive powers. He bent closer to Grace. "When were you born?" he asked. "I'm interested in your future."

She frowned at him. "There's no evidence for astrology at all. None." He was closer to forty than to eighteen, though a face cratered with acne scars made it hard to tell very nearly. His tight brown frizz reminded Grace a little too much of a Barbie doll she'd had as a child whose detachable head she'd put through the dishwasher. He was all bone and hard angles.

"Bliss can see the future in anything," he said. "It's useful, even if only as a metaphor."

This was better, though in Grace's experience, astrologers were usually more devout. She said, "Does Bliss see astrology as a metaphor?"

"She's a woman. She tends to be literal-minded."

Grace shook her head. This felt like a setback, though she knew she should be happy just to have a student who knew such words—*literal, perpetual, frequency, metaphor*—who understood about the human mind's need to see structure and clarity whether it was there or not. She should be gentle, should lead by example. But at the moment Dan unnerved her. He stood so close that she was in his shadow. "Excuse me," she said, and pushed back her shoulders, walked past him to Ralph, and lifted her lips, waiting for him to lower his cheek.

Ralph did exactly what she should have expected: he put

his hands between her shoulder blades, drew her against him, and kissed her on the mouth. She thought, Why not?, though she knew she was wrong. She put her arms around his neck and shut her eyes. It felt like a long time since she'd been kissed.

By the time she opened her eyes again, Dan was walking backward down the path, waving good-bye. "Where were you born?" he called.

Grace leaned against Ralph's chest and breathed in. "Right here."

Dan said, "I'll have it for you by next Monday."

"What?" Ralph said.

"He wants to predict my future," Grace said.

"So do I." Ralph let go of Grace, fumbled in his suit jacket pocket, and handed her a Polaroid: herself asleep on his couch, arm curled around her head, mouth open. With her eyes closed over their careful expression, her face looked slack and young.

"At least I wasn't drooling," she said. "I'll add it to my collection."

Ralph patted the seat of her bike. It was locked to a rail. "Toss her on the rack. Let's go."

"I feel a little woozy." All morning, since waking up under an afghan, Grace had been tasting tequila in the back of her throat. "I've got to quit living like this," she said.

"You just started. Anyway, you've got to live somehow."

Rita raised her scalpel and said, "Observe."

Grace, regretting her bravado—and what she now admitted was mostly curiosity, however motivated—was trying hard to look straight at the corpse before her and not go pale, and, most of all, not lose her stomach. It didn't help that Wendy, the latest in Rita's line of red setters of the same name, was whining, scrabbling at the other side of the door. Grace understood why Rita had become a vegetarian. She was thinking hard about it herself.

Not that she hadn't been around corpses before. She'd grown up friends with Rita, the family business right there attached to the family house, where Rita now lived and kept a separate office stacked with flyers attached to various causes, the foremost now being the Gulf escalation, the building possibility of war. When they had played in Rita's yard there had almost always been a body a wall away, cooling under a sheet. Rita had even sneaked Grace in one Saturday when Rita's father was outside pruning the funeral home topiary into the shapes of the more majestic and patriotic birds, and they had gazed in silence at a gurney holding a sheet shaped like a body. Later, Grace's father had phoned Rita's in a white fury, but by the time he'd hung up the phone he'd been laughing. He'd said, "The guy's right. It's just life."

This was different. Grace had, then, never known anyone who had died. That shape, that Halloween ghost lying down, wasn't real to Grace, even in dreams, was no more real than the Vietnam body counts on the nightly news, while the corpse now on the table she'd seen just two days before, in the hospital, alive if only barely. Grace had poked her head into his room, looking for Pascal on his early rounds. They were one of those couples who, separated, still needed to see each other nearly every day, if only to remind each other they weren't getting along.

A woman had been sitting by the man's bed, where she must have been waiting all night in case he woke up. She held his hand in hers; her head rested on his stomach and the early-morning sun washed out over her cheek—Grace could see only half her face—and light ashy hair. His hair had looked oddly askew and unnaturally dark against his pale, still face: now, looking at his bald pate and the toupee on Rita's equipment cart, Grace knew why. She wondered if it was for that woman he'd worn the toupee even in his hospital bed on the last morning of his life. She had looked young to be his wife. She'd been asleep, her features calm, slackly composed around the slightly open mouth. Grace had just stood there by the door watching until she felt a hand on her rear end and Pascal's mouth against her ear, saying, "Looking for me?"

Part of Grace, the one she should have known to obey, had wanted to lean back into him, let everything be forgotten, put her hand on his cheek and ask him to come back home. But she still couldn't tell the difference between her heart and her body. Both had whispered, "Abandon," but each with a different intent. Abandon herself or him? She had let go of the door and turned fast, one hand on her hip—a favorite posture of her grandmother's, and one she'd been catching herself in all too often lately. If she closed her eyes, she could remember her mother in it too.

"Just checking up on your latest project," Grace had said. Since their separation, she'd been overgiven to such small impulses toward cruelty, followed, as in this case, by immediate regret. This time, the regret had made her less generous rather than more. She'd kept on, pushed by spite she couldn't seem to get rid of, like a bitter taste in her mouth. "Looks like you've lost it."

The heavy eyebrows had gone up. In a flash, she'd seen Pascal's leanness, the pallor under his dark red hair. If she'd known him as a younger man, before he put on his surgeon's confidence like a lab coat, she might have thought him gangly, clumsy as a boy, and wanted to protect him. But then, she wouldn't have loved him.

He'd said, "Some things deserve a second try." He'd reached out and touched her shoulder with his beautiful, pampered hand. He was flushed down to his stethoscope—even his oversized earlobes with their horizontal creases, the only extra flesh on his body, were a bright red that clashed with his hair.

She'd moved her shoulder out from under his fingers, and he'd let his hand drop.

"Glad to see you haven't gotten sentimental," he'd said, turning away.

What she'd wanted to say—"Good luck"—it was too late for, and he would only have replied, "Luck has nothing to do with it," and glanced down at his hands in that habitual gesture, as if to check that they were still there, still beautiful and charmed.

Now the poor man was naked except for the rag Ralph had dug up in deference to Grace, who he believed in spite of a lifetime of evidence might be as delicate as she looked, to cover the genitals. At the moment, though, they hardly seemed the most obscene thing about the body. Though the man had been dead only a day, already all his blood had pooled into his back, where it showed a deep purple through the skin; his face and torso were a tepid gray. Grace thought, Mortal clay—language she'd always passed over as hopelessly archaic, something her grandmother would have said in a certain mood, folding her hands under what was left of her bosom in the most self-aware possible demureness.

But what drew Grace's eye the hardest, the reason she was there, was the livid, L-shaped wound on the chest where Pascal had cut it open in his last effort to save the man's life— the kind of heroics that had attracted her to Pascal originally, before she decided the strut and posture were just that. Even now, with the blood drained away, the cut in the man's chest was so brutal and explicit that she could barely imagine it was originally meant to save him. The one time Grace had seen an open-chest surgery, the things that made her want to turn away were the saw humming through the rib cage; the split second of carelessness spinning off the finest film of blood and bone to spray the shoulders and arms of the surgeons; the cold force of wrist it took to pry the chest cavity open. The beautiful organs, laid open to her eyes. She thought of her own scalpel opening the stems of plants to graft one to another—how tidy those green bodies seemed next to the violent beating of human muscle and fluid.

After the heart was revealed for the first time, unnaturally, to light, Pascal had lifted his hazel eyes above the surgical mask and looked at Grace where she stood above him, hands pressed against the operating theater glass. She wasn't supposed to be there, at least not under any strict interpretation of the rules, but she had wanted to see for herself what Pascal did. Meeting hers, Pascal's eyes were not cold or aloof or even intent, but amused at some sign only they could read.

That patient had lived. But in the case of the man on the table in front of Grace now, Pascal hadn't gotten to take bows. This man had never awakened from the anesthetic, had drifted on the table, moored to machines. Then, just as the violence was finished and they were ready to sew him up, he had pulled gently loose. It was his second open-chest surgery, and behind the fresh wound was a sort of echo, the scar from the first operation. After the surgery, Pascal had said to Grace on the phone, his voice distant and watery, "There's more than life to lose."

"Like what?" she'd said, and crossed her arms over her chest as if to protect herself.

"You should know, of all people," he'd said. "You don't think so, but you've led a sheltered life." His voice was softer than usual, and strained.

"You don't know anything about my life."

He'd said, almost in a whisper, "That's just it, isn't it, sweetheart? Are you going to throw the baby out with the bathwater?"

Grace flushed, remembering. She had been too hard. Ralph saw her blush and readjusted the cloth over the man's crotch, then took her elbow, as if he thought she might need his help to stay upright. At the moment, she was glad to have a friend who believed in her fragility.

Pascal would have said, "So what? We're all dying," and made a joke worse than any Grace could have thought of; then he would have ruffled her hair, pulled her in under his arm like a child—a gesture she ached for, a feeling of shelter.

Now Grace said to Ralph, "I just want to see firsthand what

his mistakes mean." She thought she might understand Pascal if once she stood close to where he lived, at the painful center of things. She'd know why he had to send his mind somewhere else, too far for her to get to it; why he'd thought it shouldn't matter if he used another woman's body to make that escape. When she thought of Jemma, his redheaded nurse, she felt panic opening another part of her, and she wanted to persuade herself that a final separation was the only possible end to risk, to justify a closing inward that she didn't want to resist.

"Pascal's only a technician," Ralph said. "A glorified plumber. He has nothing to do with the real questions." But though Grace understood the analogy, she couldn't compare the pipes under her bathroom sink with human arteries, the interactions of flesh that could be so sweetly or so fatally complicated by food, by air, by love. Even in the botanical gardens, two researchers could plant two apparently healthy plants side by side, and one might live while the other died. The problem could be in the plant, the soil, the human touch.

She said to Ralph, "A washer is a washer. And if it fails, it doesn't much matter."

"And a scalpel is a scalpel," Rita said, spinning hers in her hand. She was happy to have an audience, something she'd missed since she stopped cross-country ski racing. She wore green hospital scrubs, a little too short, and her copper-wire hair was knotted at the back of her head.

"I'm going to make an incision here," she said, pointing with the blade to the artery on the right of the man's neck, "and then another one here." She indicated the place where the leg and groin came together. Grace understood about connections in the body, about how a kiss on the neck can make everything tighten, all the way down.

Ralph said, "Out goes the bad, in comes the good." The tubes started to sputter.

Grace's problem: what to do with her eyes. Her queasiness was beginning to pass, but watching this seemed like plain bad manners. The man's blood drained out of one tube almost black while into the other flowed an obscenely pink liquid.

Rita said, "Pepto-Bismol."

"You get to see him without his toupee," Ralph said.

"We'll get him fixed up, all right." Rita rummaged through her cosmetics caddy.

"Christ," Grace said, but now she couldn't keep from looking.

"It's my job to make him beautiful," Rita said. She checked a photo of the man alive, then leaned close to sew his lips together, his mouth going from slack to firm, from emptiness to the slight, knowing smile in the picture. Grace waited for blood, but of course there was none. Though Rita hired cosmetologists when she had a backlog, this was still her favorite part of the job, making bodies look alive, as if they could sit up and swing their legs out of their coffins. She brushed rouge onto his cheeks, over his browbone, then stood back to look at her work. "I feel as if I'm on stage," she said, and rolled her hips and shoulders in a kind of burlesque.

Grace blushed again. She couldn't help it: she glanced from the man's face to Rita's, the cheerful, fleshy moon that could never have inspired the trust of the grieving if Shady Oaks hadn't been the oldest funeral home in the city, in the family for over a century.

"Now I know why I work with plants," Grace said, but she couldn't stop looking. The man was recovering before their eyes; his cheeks filled with the liquid and turned pink, and Grace could see what a woman her age might have admired in him: a strong chin, a full-lipped mouth.

Rita buffed the man's hairless scalp, then she reached for the toupee, put it on his head, and stood back and looked, her head tilted. She adjusted the hairpiece, stood back again. "I always thought it was a shame to bury perfectly usable things."

Grace reached out and laid her finger on the man's arm. It felt cold and rubbery, nothing like the arm a man might put around her or offer to help her off a curb. When she took away her finger, its impression remained. She stared at it until the skin began to plump back. She wiped her finger on her jeans. This hadn't accomplished what she'd wanted from it: now, Rita's illusion complete, Grace kept expecting the man to open his eyes, restored to himself, as if he could walk right back into the arms of that woman who had loved him enough to lay her head down on his deathbed. Who would do that for her, she wondered? For whom would she do it? She resisted reaching a hand to either side of her, one to Ralph, the other to Rita.

"You want to donate his toupee to the poor?" she asked Rita.

"Why not?"

Ralph shook his head. He looked a little pale himself, though he still held Grace's arm.

"Needless to say," Rita said, "you won't tell anyone you were here."

"You didn't tell me this was illegal," Ralph said.

"Like you couldn't figure it out yourself," Rita said, her eyes as cool and clear as water. "Given that you keep the Utah Code behind the seat of your car."

Grace hadn't considered this either. "What's his name?" she asked.

"It wouldn't fit behind the seat," Ralph said. "Too many volumes. Anyway, figuring out and knowing are two different things. Let's go, Grace."

Rita was pulling off her thin rubber gloves. "We call them all Joe," she said. "It's easier that way."

Ralph and Grace walked under the columns, down the mortuary's marble steps and into soft air, a sun that felt almost like summer. Wendy sniffed at their heels, then ran ahead of them over the lawn, her wispy fur pantaloons waving behind her.

Ralph put his arm around Grace. "You okay?"

"I was thinking about that kiss." It had been a long time. Two months since Pascal moved out. And the three months before that, when Grace wouldn't let him touch her. Before she'd met him, it had been years since she had been involved with anybody. But the body can get used to love so quickly, can begin to remember how it needs to be held. She turned out from under Ralph's arm and walked toward the dog among the topiaries. Wendy was checking trees and shrubs for evidence of intruders—a secret wilderness in the middle of cultivation. Since Rita's father had died and left Rita the business, she'd hired Grace to design the garden, and they'd taken on the pruning between them. Under their shears the shrubs had grown into shapes that seemed right at first glance but then, on closer look, were a little off: a pterodactyl hanging out prehistoric wings where once there had been a heron in flight; a buzzard hunching its shoulders where before an eagle had perched; two ragged cormorants, looking as archaic as the pterodactyl, in place of the seagulls that had once, in honor of a Mormon miracle having to do with crops and crickets, flanked the front steps.

Every year Grace would say, "You know, the simplest science explains it perfectly well." Rita, who didn't believe in miracles either, never argued.

And every spring when they finished the pruning, Rita would let her loppers drop and say, "Looks like home."

Grace planned out Rita's larger vistas, too. This, Grace figured when they started, was between the two of them, what they could do instead of touching. For years, Rita, like Grace, had taken no lovers, had been faithful to what Grace allowed between them, the shaping of a green, only partly metaphorical landscape.

The mortuary was in a prime spot, set high up above the foothill cemetery. Rita's family had been in the business there from the beginning of the city, when her great-grandfather and his three wives unloaded their wagon and set to the labor of making the desert blossom. There was plenty of work for the undertaker then, too. The Old Patriarch, as Rita called him, was buried practically in the front yard, under a ten-foot obelisk, with his wives' flat stones, and those of the children who died before marriage, ranged modestly around. Rita's own father was less prolific: Rita, his only child, came late, years after he and his one wife had given up on having children at all. The result, Rita always said, with a smile and a toss of her wrist-thick braid, was that her presence made her father smile and her mother pray. Now that her father was dead, embalmed by Rita's own hands, her mother and another widow were cruising Mexico in a motor home.

Sharing the view on one side of the mortuary was the cemetery mausoleum; on the other side was a small clapboard house owned by Rita's uncle and his sons, with a red neon sign reading MONUMENTS flickering above the front door. In its little fenced yard were carved samples of headstones, some simple, names and dates only, others soaring toward the heavens in elaborately carved versions of celestial temples or hovering angels or straight-backed children with their hands on the heads of lambs. The fence was low, but nobody ever stole the merchandise. That day, a nearly finished stone featured a carved baseball mitt with two bats crossed under it like bones. It said, "Ricky, Keep Your Eye on the Ball."

Rita called Wendy and waved from the front door. Grace waved back, then walked across the street and leaned on the cemetery wall. Below her, the groomed lawn fell dizzyingly away down a hillside studded with graves. She thought about Joe, filled with a fluid meant to preserve him even underground—how we resist what we make such a show of at funerals, resist giving what we love back to earth, to the intelligent life of soil and plants. Another wilderness, alive under our feet. Grace could see, about halfway down, under a line of blue spruces, her parents' double gravestone, erected at Grandma Imo's insistence, though the grave was inhabited only by Grace's mother's pine coffin, which was empty.

Julia's body was burnt and broken already before her

cremation. And Julia had said time and again, "I want to go up in flames. I want there to be nothing left but smoke and ash." In fact, the way she did go—struck by lightning on the peak of a mountain called Temple—might just have had enough of instant glory in it to satisfy even her. Though Julia's ashes were stored in an enameled urn on the top shelf of the closet in Grace's old room, no logic could persuade Imo not to bury that casket. Rita's father tried, but he could not convince her that Julia's freed soul, dizzied by the vastness of a universe that seemed almost too small for her when she was alive, might not want in death to take up residence in a box the size of the body she had finally escaped. Now, as always when she looked at the grave, its marked emptiness, Grace could feel a space just that shape inside her, also empty, implying about her mother both absence and a terrifying freedom.

The two dates under Julia's name reduced her life to the size of the chiseled dash between them, while under Grace's father's name was still only the date of his birth, a dash, and empty possibility. Imo's wish: that his death would come soon and painfully. He mattered to Imo as someone to blame for Julia's death, his body only something that, if there is justice and a hell, would eventually give him agony even on the other side. To Grace, he was merely absence. Oddly, his was the only face she could picture boxed in wood and satin, contained.

At the bottom of the graveyard the city took over, on that day looking scrubbed and shiny enough even for its population of saints, covering the whole valley floor from mountain range to mountain range. Grace could see, nestled into the foothills in the west, the enormous open pit of the copper mine, a funnel opened in the earth as large as the mountain that used to stand there. The mining company touted it on local television ads as the eighth wonder of the world.

"I need some coffee," Grace said over her shoulder. She still felt a little green. "To get this taste out of my mouth."

"You'll be fine," Ralph said, but he put his hand on the back of her neck, steadying her. "You never could pass up a dare."

Grace was leaning on the wall as much to stay upright herself as for comfort, still surprised at how shaken she was. She said, "That never prevented you from making one."

Ralph put his hands in his trouser pockets and looked at Grace sideways. "Why? I never thought you were afraid of anything."

"I'm afraid of everything. I'm sensible."

"The guys used to say you had balls."

"Balls I didn't need. I had adrenaline." And the desire to keep up with Rita, who did everything headlong—climbing sheer cliffs ropeless, skiing glaciers on the tight edge of control, mouthing off to police at campus demonstrations, her long legs planted and her hands resting on her muscled hips.

"That's what I mean."

Grace thought of Rita next to her on her balcony the summer before, how Rita had flexed her whole athlete's body going freckled from the sun and said, "I'm losing it. There are things I just can't do anymore." Grace had felt the push of tenderness, the desire to put Rita back in her flesh. A softening under the roof of her mouth. She'd thought, Even her. She'd thought, Not her. Not for the first time, she had steeled herself against something that might have been love.

Before Ralph could move to help her, Grace turned and lifted her bike from the roof rack on his Cherokee. "I wanted to see it once," she said. "What it really means to be inanimate."

Even Grace's yellow bicycle, so much a part of her, reminded her of her life with Pascal. She'd chosen this one over fancier brands because she liked the name, liked the idea of riding a Giant Iguana. Though when they had shopped for a bike, Pascal had spent a good half-hour fiddling with brakes and derailleurs on more expensive brands, he finally carried this one out of the store for her, and as she pedaled out of the parking lot on her test ride he ran alongside, cowboy boots clomping, hand on her back as if she needed steadying, until he was unable to keep up and she rode out from under his touch.

After leaving the mortuary, Grace steered her bike headlong down the steep, narrow streets of the Avenues toward the University district, then leaned it against Ralph's parking meter in front of the Broiler, tugged on the lock to check it, and stood up and turned toward the sidewalk tables.

She saw a thin chest in a blue shirt. Dan was standing next to her, so close she'd almost turned right into him. She tilted her head back and shaded her eyes with her hand.

"I just need to tell you," he said, "I'm really sorry."

Grace looked at him for a clue. "It's okay," she said.

He shook his head. "I've been at your star chart all afternoon."

"That was fast." She had let things go too far. She said, "Dan, I'm all for entertainment. But I am a scientist."

He paused, shook his head again, as if to clear it. His eyes in that light were the uncluttered blue Grace associated with children too young to talk. "I have to say," he said, "I'm a relative beginner at this. But something's about to change. Bliss knows."

She shifted. "I'm meeting somebody, okay?"

"Oh." He glanced over at the outdoor table where Ralph was already sitting watching them. Then he looked down at Grace. "I just wanted to let you know. It's not good."

"Whatever." With those blue eyes on her, Grace felt a chill of superstition.

"Metaphors are as real as anything else," he said.

Grace thought this over. She wasn't sure if she would call metaphors real or merely useful. "I'll keep that in mind."

When she sat down across from Ralph, he asked, "What's his deal?"

"I don't want to think about it," Grace said. So they sat, soaking up the unseasonable sunshine through their sweatshirts. Grace took a big gulp of coffee and caught herself wondering if it was too early to switch to beer. She could still taste the chemicals, acrid and oily, that Rita had been using to preserve the body. She wiped her hands over her cheeks and then lifted her face to the salt breeze coming off the lake. In stronger weather, wind would whip up a stink from the lake bottom, but that afternoon the air felt fresh and clean.

"I suppose a person would get used to that kind of work," Ralph said.

"You couldn't get used to lawyering." Grace turned her eyes away from him, to look at the mountains jutting up to the east of the city. Their peaks were still white and frozen, though the air tasted of the faint, frothy green of the false season. "A person is either suited to a profession or not."

"You're pale." Ralph was leaning back in his seat, looking at her closely.

"I have a broken heart." She smiled, though it was true. She leaned over the table, took his hand. "Believe me, you don't want me like this. I am not to be trusted."

But the brush of his eyes on her cheeks, her lips, was almost palpable. He said, "You don't think I should be allowed to take my chances?"

Her heart hesitated, then beat hard once—a compensatory beat, Pascal had called it, his hand flat between her breasts, brought on by stress, nothing to worry about—and she pulled her hand away. She wiped her palms on her jeans, thought, Don't. She said, "Do you think fidelity is possible anymore?"

"As much as it ever was." He took a sip of his coffee. "My parents were faithful."

"That's even more frightening than the alternatives."

Ralph pressed his lips together. "You could give them a little credit."

"I'm sorry," she said. But in her memory she saw Ralph's bare back crossed by the belt. He still never went without a shirt.

"What are you going to do?" he asked.

Grace looked down at her empty mug. "I'm going to order a beer." He was looking over her shoulder. "Don't you start," she said. "Please." Her hand rested on the table next to her mug. He took it and leaned toward her, but he was still half looking at something behind her.

She glanced back just as Pascal came even with the table. I should have known, she thought. The woman with him looked familiar, but Grace guessed they all would. For a city of over half a million, Salt Lake feels like a small town, or several small towns, arranged like a series of overlapping circles, sets and subsets, a mathematics of connection that puts everyone within touching distance of everyone else.

Grace said to Pascal, "I can't go anywhere anymore."

Pascal was steering the woman in front of him, one hand between her shoulder blades. In the other hand he carried what must have been her purse, a gray envelope of patent leather. She was lean, wearing a slim, light-gray dress that reached nearly to where her silver metallic sandals looped, Roman style, around her ankles. Her pale hair was tied under a black chiffon scarf sprayed in silver with scientific impossibilities: crescent moons holding stars in their dark centers. She wore cat-eye sunglasses, framed in plastic that looked carved from marble, and a teardrop-shaped silver peace medallion, the kind that had appeared in trendy boutiques after the troop buildup in the Gulf started. It all looked as if it had cost a lot more than it was worth. Her skin had the kind of transparency that made Grace feel her own face must look gray and drawn.

Grace leaned back in her seat. She tried to let go of Ralph's fingers, but Ralph held on tight. She pulled again and he let go.

"Well," Pascal said, lifting his cowboy hat, an amber-tanned leather to match his eyes, and looking down from his great height. Still tucked into his hatband was a sprig of the eucalyptus that Grace had preserved from her wedding bouquet

and put there the week after they married. "It's always a plea-
sure to see you too, Grace." He nodded at Ralph. Grace
watched Pascal for some sign of strain, which she saw only
when he looked her in the eyes—his, usually readable, were
flat, more yellow than their usual soft gold. She felt a painful
tenderness when she couldn't tell what he was feeling. She
loved that sense of privacy in him, and of invulnerability.
Though it came between them now, she didn't want him to
drop it—had even, in the past, stopped him from doing so. He
was humming something between his teeth, but she couldn't
make out the tune.

"Hello," she said. She tried to keep her head still while she
spoke. She imagined she was the heroine of a Victorian novel,
trained in self-control, and gave a tight smile she figured
Pascal could take as he wanted. Then she looked past him at
the woman who hovered behind him, but he didn't introduce
her. The woman's silver earrings, mobile versions of the star-
swallowing moon, shimmered against her cheeks. She was
looking off into the sky. Her features were small and precise.
Grace felt jealousy flare in her stomach, though she knew
she'd sent Pascal away and into such promising arms herself.
And she knew that it was her own stubbornness that prevented her from calling him back even now.

Grace looked at the peace medallion and said to the
woman, "Are we going to war? What do you think?"

The woman turned her head and pointed her dark glasses
at Grace.

Grace caught herself on the verge of a nod and stilled her
head again. "Nice to meet you," she said, and held out her
hand. The woman put hers in it to be shaken, then drew away.

Pascal was still smiling and humming. He'd curved his
shoulders to bring his head down nearer to Grace and Ralph,
and his body looked like a comma, his very presence like an
emphatic pause in a sentence. Grace could go foolish again
at any moment. Pascal put his hand on Grace's shoulder and

said to the woman, "I believe Grace and I are still married. Unless she's done something I don't know about."

Ralph said to Pascal, "Grace can keep whatever company she chooses. Like you." He nodded toward the blond curls. Ralph was still smiling a fixed smile. His eyes, turned away from Grace now, looked hard, almost metallic where they caught the sunlight.

Pascal hooked his shoulders over even farther and lifted his hands as if to push something away. "I never said a word." He looked at Grace. "Did I say a word?" Even from a foot away he smelled like surgical soap and faintly, underneath, clean eucalyptus. He rocked back on the heels of his boots. He was the only one giving the impression he was enjoying this conversation. If Grace had been the one standing up with him, she, too, would have been immune, would have been able to slip her arm through his and smile and let him take care of everything. It was all she could do not to get up and touch him somewhere, one of the old, confiding gestures.

"You've been very good," Grace said.

Pascal glanced at the woman and said, "Yes, my love, I have," and whether or not he meant it as a kind of reassurance, Grace felt her stomach muscles relax. Humming again, Pascal made a little bow toward Ralph. "I've never questioned her taste."

Ralph looked up from his hand, which he was clenching and unclenching as if in time to his heart. "It had to improve."

Grace identified Pascal's tune: "Amazing Grace"—what he'd sung after the first time they made love, standing naked at the foot of the bed, hands cupped over his heart in a bad parody, a cross between Pavarotti and Joan Baez. It had been no special skill on her part but rather what had happened between them that had been remarkable. She started to smile at him, then stopped.

Pascal caught it, smiled back. "So we might have figured," he said to Ralph.

"Pascal," Grace said, "you never were original."

"I just follow directions. Preferably yours." He bowed a little. "See you tomorrow night, Grace. You too, Ralph." He put his hand on Grace's neck, just on that spot he knew was the right one for turning her inside out, and, almost in a whisper, he added, "I still make house calls."

"What about your equipment?"

"It travels with me. Sing a song for me tomorrow, Grace." And he walked away through the tables, brushing none of them in spite of his size.

"What an asshole," Ralph said. Then, "You didn't have to be so mean to her."

Grace said, "Oh, sure. People are going to start dying any day, and she's making a fashion statement."

Ralph rolled his eyes up toward the blue sky. "Maybe she really believes it."

"You just think she's pretty. Look at her. It's sexual nostalgia all over."

"That sounds like jealousy to me. I take it as a good sign." But he'd been watching when the smile passed between Pascal and Grace, and he looked at her closely now.

The woman had settled into her chair and was reading her menu. She'd crossed her legs, and the delicate cocked arch of her dangling foot moved even Grace. Grace sighed. Pascal had made it only halfway across the patio, where he leaned over a table of four women.

"Look at him," Ralph said. "He's probably slept with at least two of them."

Grace shut her eyes over the tears that rose suddenly.

"I'm sorry," he said. "I have just never understood what you see in him. Look at what he's done to you."

Pascal would have said, "It's not important."

Imo had said to Grace after the separation, "Some things a woman has to ignore." Then a wink: "A man, too."

Grace said out loud, "You don't know what I've done to him."

"At least when my father made a promise he kept it."

"He might have promised not to beat your mother bloody. And you, too."

"What?" Ralph's voice wasn't raised exactly; it was more as if an edge of it had lifted.

"I'm sorry," Grace said. "You do know about forgiveness. But maybe you know too much. There's such a thing as using it all up in the wrong places."

"That's what I'm telling you."

Grace was still watching Pascal. Even when he sat down, his head and shoulders were visible over the heads of the crowd. His hair blazed maroon in the sun. Watching him with the other women, graceful and composed, Grace wanted him back. Was this why Ralph wanted her, because she desired somebody else? Pascal turned his head their way, and she looked down at the table, then finally up at Ralph.

Ralph reached his long arm across the table again and took her hand. "Grace. You're the only real beauty in this restaurant."

"Knock it off, will you?" Grace couldn't help it. She glanced again across the patio at Pascal, who still looked back with a half-smile on his face. She wondered what she would see in his eyes now if she were the one sitting across from him. She realized she might never be immune, even though she knew she had invented at least part of what she loved in him.

Imo would have said, "That's the nature of love."

"Ralph," Grace said, "not now."

"Of course not." He let go of her hand and raised his index finger at the waitress to order Grace a beer.

When Grace woke up late that afternoon from a long, dreamless nap, she had to move Ralph's arm off her chest before she could get up and put on a robe and go into the kitchen to make coffee, good and strong to jump-start her heart. When she'd shut her eyes and moved against him, even after all these years, she hadn't been able to imagine she was

with anybody else. The body is just that intelligent, that tuned
and specific. So what she had wanted—simply a broad back
under her hands, skin that didn't dissolve into air as she woke
up—she hadn't quite gotten. There were too many memories,
too many ties. She had no complaints, only regrets that she
couldn't stop things where they were. It was after four, and
she flipped on the radio: news of the buildup and of the military might of Saddam Hussein. The president's voice came
on, boyish, talking tough, and Grace shut her eyes and tilted
her head back for a second, then she turned the radio off.

She imagined telling Imo about Ralph, imagined Imo shaking her head, making a small hissing sound between her
teeth. She would say, "Why are you telling me?" She would
look at Grace through eyes that were, those days, always watery. Sometimes Imo saw clearly what was right in front of
her, but more and more her brilliant past made the present
look dim and distant. When Imo faded, Grace wanted to
reach out her hand and drag her back into the solid world.
"Your generation never figured out what beauty was for, anyway," Imo would have said.

Ralph followed Grace into the kitchen a little later; he'd
pulled on his jeans but left off his shirt, and when he put his
arms around her she leaned her head against his bare chest
and shut her eyes. She could smell herself on his skin. The
smell was rich and almost sweet. Grace took a few deep
breaths.

He said, "Where are the towels?"

"Ralph," she said. "Hello there."

"I guess I should apologize."

Grace looked up at him. "Maybe not."

"You're right. Maybe *you* should."

Grace rested her head against Ralph's chest and said, "Yes,
I should."

"I'm not sorry." He had his fingers in her crew cut.

"I'll remind you that you said that." Grace pulled away and

poured coffee for each of them. "Let's just call it a draw for now, shall we?"

He opened his mouth to speak, but she picked up her mug and moved toward the bedroom. He followed. She dropped her robe on the bed, holding her stomach tight, watching him watching. He reached for her, but she walked past him and pulled her long johns from a drawer.

"Put on your jacket," she said. Then she led him out the sliding glass doors onto the balcony and sat down next to him on the old-fashioned glider she had asked Pascal for as a wedding present. All around, the potted plants that had made the balcony a small jungle in summer were withered back to gray earth. Below them was the city, its lights coming on and constellated but evenly, regularly, in blocks and long strings and plats, unlike the still unapparent stars, which, when they came out, would dim in competition, as if they were only vague, disorganized reflections of what stretched out at their feet. At the western horizon were the shreds of red from a brilliant sunset, courtesy of the copper mine. The wind was beginning to pick up in gusts, warm enough to warn that a storm might follow, tomorrow maybe, tomorrow night at the latest.

"Do you believe we can predict the future?" she asked.

"I believe we can make predictions come true."

She stretched. "That guy. Joe. The corpse."

Ralph rubbed his cheek against the top of her hair and said, "Soft."

"What do you think he died of?"

"What would be usual, under the circumstances? Heart failure. Anesthetic."

Grace said, "Surrender."

"Some people just never wake up."

He reached out and pulled her over so she was leaning against him, both his arms around her. Right then, his body felt warm and comfortable. His face was mostly in shadow, only the edge of it lit by the lamp on the other side of the sliding doors.

CHAPTER 2

■ ■ ■

Storm Watch

The valley was awash in sunlight, but in the west over the flat, aluminum lake, wispy gray clouds were beginning to clump up. Through the picture window, the scene looked like a painting set into motion, the land's enormous scale caught from above, reduced to fit the frame. Any minute, Ralph was going to come around the kitchen table and put his arms around Grace, and the longer he took about it, the more nervous she got. Yesterday, weakened by mortality, Pascal, and a kiss, not necessarily in that order but cooperating in a sort of alchemical mix, she would have leaned into Ralph, put her head against his chest and listened. But this morning, in bed, he had come to her again and, afterward, closed his eyes and made himself as small as he could against her breast. Grace hesitated, but then she put her arms around him and rocked. He smiled, and she felt a shudder run through her—of nerves, of contempt, as if she'd seen a weakness she hadn't wanted to know about.

But she had known it for years, since she was barely seventeen and Ralph was about to turn eighteen. The sun was shining that day, too, pushing its heat down, as Grace jingled her car keys in her hand, about to walk through Ralph's back door. Midsummer. Usually Ralph would have been at the ranch, but he had come down for a week to shop the back-to-school sales with Grace. She was daydreaming, not looking at anything, or she would have seen through the sheer kitchen curtains that something was going on. She put her shoulder against the door, twisted the knob, and turned into the room.

Ralph stood shirtless at the door to the dining room, his hands raised, pushing against the frame. His father stood between Ralph and Grace, his back also to her. It took her a few seconds to understand: Ralph's father held a belt in his raised hand. The welts were already rising on Ralph's back. Grace had never quite realized how white his skin was until she saw the red flaring against it.

She stopped, her hand still on the doorknob. They both turned toward her. Ralph's father dropped his hand. The end of the belt slapped against the linoleum.

Ralph's face was as pale and empty as sky. They all stood there for what seemed like minutes; then, slowly, as if willing himself to do it, Ralph turned to his father and held out his hand. His father stared at Ralph, but Ralph didn't drop his eyes. There was no air in that room, nothing for any of them. Then Ralph's father handed the belt to him. Ralph stretched it between his hands and raised it, and his father and Grace both flinched, but Ralph smiled and laid the belt down on the kitchen table, pulling it straight and flat down the table's length. As if there were no hurry, he picked up his shirt from where it was draped neatly over the back of a chair and pulled it on. Grace waited for him to wince when the cotton moved over his back, but if anything his face became more still. He tucked the shirt in, taking his time. Then he walked past his father, past Grace. She followed him out the door into the sun.

He stood, looking into the yard toward the back fence. He said, "This fall I'll be eighteen."

She was looking at his profile. His face was quiet, no expression. She wanted to know what he'd done, what his father believed he'd done, but she decided not to ask. It could have been nothing that deserved what she'd seen. She was thinking of all those summer days, neighborhood football or pickup basketball games, Ralph raising his hand, calling "Shirts," though it would be so hot the boys on Ralph's team would shake their heads and groan, and the other team's members would peel off their shirts in obvious relief. He'd worn a T-shirt swimming. Even at the ranch, he had never removed his shirt, just unbuttoned it, left it drifting against his shoulders and back. Grace had always assumed it was because his skin was so fair and the desert sun, at this altitude, so searing. He'd spoken about his father hitting him, but in a way that was so offhand it seemed he was talking about the kind of symbolic slap all kids received occasionally in a time when spanking was accepted.

"I never asked," she said. "I'm sorry."

"I didn't want you to know."

"You'll move out?"

He lifted one shoulder. "I may." He clenched his fist, then unclenched it and put it in his pocket. "My hand's asleep. I have to hold on to the door frame as hard as I can."

"Yes."

"Not for the pain. It's all I can do to keep myself from turning around and punching him." Ralph smiled and shook his head. "From the time I was a little kid. I stand there and think about how it would feel. How I would put my weight behind it. The impact."

"You're bigger than he is. You could do some damage." She bit her lip.

He nodded, looked down at the concrete. "Now I am."

Grace opened the car door for him. Without saying anything, she drove the car away from the house, away from the downtown stores full of new fall clothes, through the hot streets and their rippling mirages, onto the freeway, then off again at the exit for Millcreek Canyon. Still silent, without even pushing a tape into the stereo, they wound up the narrowing road between pine trees and rugged canyon walls. At the trailhead where the road ends, Grace took the blanket from the trunk and led Ralph through the woods. In a small clearing where they had never been together, where the leaves filtered the sun into a green, watery light, she took off his shirt and ran her fingers over the welts. They had broken open and bled. She pushed on them, but Ralph did not move. She turned him around to face her, and she put her arms around him, her fingers hooked in the ridges of damaged flesh on his back. Then he opened her blouse, and they lay down. Grace shut her eyes, but, still, the tears came. That was the first and only time they had made love, until now. Since then, they had been tender with each other but had used that very tenderness like a barrier between them.

Now Ralph picked up a teaspoon and examined it minutely, as if for a flaw in design or technology. Finally he said, "What next?"

"I have a paper to finish, but no classes today. Nothing scheduled until tonight." She had a light load this quarter and in March would start a three-quarter sabbatical. There was a bird circling the city, high up but practically on eye level with the twelfth-floor windows. From the shape of its wings it looked like some sort of hawk, but it was too far away to tell. Grace tried to catch Ralph's eye, but he was still watching light slide along the spoon's bowl as he turned it. She wasn't sure who was being more evasive, Ralph or herself. It was an old dance.

"You tell me," she said at last.

"You're thirty-one years old."

"Don't remind me," she said, though age was not high on her list of worries. She expected to sail into each new decade with aplomb, and she'd passed thirty more with relief than anything else, believing her life would begin to come clearer as she entered late youth. Still, she felt there was something she should have held on to but had let slip out of her grasp.

"Isn't *this* getting old?" He waved his hand around the kitchen, at the floor-to-ceiling window, the city that looked far away but was really at their feet. "Aren't you tired of being alone?"

"I haven't always been alone. There are worse things." She wanted to pull the curtains and lie down again, by herself this time. "I'm not sure how to tell anymore, but maybe we've made a mistake. How do we know the difference between what's past and what we really have?"

He reached his hand across the table. "It wasn't a mistake. We were just too young to know what to do."

"Not too young," Grace said. "We made love for all the wrong reasons."

"The right ones. The wrong reasons stopped us doing it again."

"The first time you were hurting. This time I am." Grace looked away from him, out the window. "What happens when neither of us is in pain? We make our own?"

"Grace, people learn. You can't protect yourself indefinitely." He looked exhausted, his skin, which had that thickness that wears so well in men, pale.

"Mice and computers learn, too. They're still just rodents and machines."

"That's exactly my point. Now we're even. Can't we just start here?"

Grace considered picking up her coffee and walking into the bedroom and locking the door, but what if Ralph went away? She didn't know what she wanted, didn't know what to do next, so she sat still. He gazed at her. The hawk was riding a downdraft into the canyon, his eye on some small movement below.

She still hadn't taken his hand. Ralph pulled his chair around the table next to hers. He said, "You're the married one, Grace. The ball's in your court."

"Separated. That's the point. It's supposed to be a time of reckoning."

"So, reckon." He took her hand, and when she didn't actually resist he started rubbing her fingers. She could still see the dent and white line from her wedding ring. It was taking longer to fade than it had to develop.

"You're one of my best friends." She held her arms open for him to come into them, but he shook his head. "Now I could lose you both," she said. "Pascal and you."

"You could anyway. You've been working on it pretty hard."

It wasn't a threat. It was a simple fact. The phone rang, but they still sat there. "I have to answer that," Grace said after the third ring.

"Saved by the bell?"

"Not for long enough."

He smiled at her and said, "Be careful."

It was Bliss on the phone. When she first heard the name, Grace's mind drew a blank. "Who?" she said, but as she spoke it came back to her—Dan's girlfriend of the Tarot. Bliss's voice was small, whispery, not at all what Grace would have imagined from Dan's descriptions.

Grace said, "How did you get this number?"

"It's urgent," Bliss said. "Dan is ready to walk. He's halfway out the door."

Grace thought of Dan dogging her from building to building. It was already too late. She had liked being mistaken, when she walked into class the first day, for another student, but at this moment she regretted her blue jeans and cowboy boots, that she had never learned to close down her face. She should have worn academic tweeds and shabby twills, should have cultivated the distant, dreamy look of so many of her colleagues. She was a scientist, for heaven's sake.

Before she could think better of it, Grace said, "The one who had the miscarriages."

Bliss didn't answer, but Grace could hear her breathing. Grace said, "I'm sorry. I'm an idiot."

Ralph got up and went out onto the balcony.

"Whatever's going on," Grace said, "it has nothing to do with me."

"It does. You're everywhere."

"I'm only Dan's professor." Grace picked up the phone, walked over and locked the balcony door, then made a face at Ralph. "Dan's learning to make connections," she said. "He's excited. It's easy for students to believe too much in their teachers." Ralph shook his head at Grace and lifted his fist against the glass between them, and she flipped the lock open again.

"No. I mean, you're in the cards. The Queen of Pentacles. First it was just when I read for myself. And now Dan too— he turns it every time."

"Look. Bliss. Do you really believe in this stuff?"

"I predicted the invasion of Kuwait. I predicted the president's election." Bliss paused, as if for effect. "We're going to war, you know. Soon."

"You and everyone else," Grace said. "That card could be anybody."

"But it's not."

"Take the card out of the deck." Grace kept her voice gentle and even, as if she were reasoning with a child. "Bliss, I can't help you."

Grace was remembering the time in college when Rita had briefly been given to reading cards. She had carried the deck with her everywhere, to the Village Inn and the Women's Resource Center and the polite, thinly attended protest marches against apartheid and for the ERA she'd kept organizing in the late seventies and early eighties, a block of years she still refers to as the Black Hole of Political Conscience. Imo calls the same era the Return of Civilization, because it was when department stores started selling evening gowns again. Rita had also carried a copy of *A Feminist Tarot,* an instruction guide that had more or less reversed everything in the traditional Tarot as a way of upending the mythology of patriarchy.

Or so Rita had said. She'd mellowed since, for practical reasons, but for a while she adopted the uniform of female revolution: fatigues, no bra, unshaven legs and armpits, in a town where even in the seventies women dressed to be known as women. Rita took to kissing her female friends—all except Grace—on the lips in front of the student union building. Grace had envied her a little, but though she had let Rita drag her up sheer mountains, Grace had never been brave enough to follow Rita into the radical new world, even if she'd been sure she wanted to.

Rita had used the Knight of Swords to represent Grace, but they were both twelve years younger then, and they were living in a dream. Even if Grace wouldn't kiss Rita in public, she had believed that members of their generation could live their lives as if the old loves and hates between men and women, the old restrictions on both and symbols for each, could simply be replaced at will. With what, Grace never knew, and Rita ventured to explain the future only so late at night and after they were both so fogged with cheap wine that, however good utopia sounded at the time, Grace could never reassemble it in the morning. Now, holding the receiver against her cheek, she shut her eyes and pictured herself on horseback, riding wildly toward some foe, her metaphorical sword raised over her armored head. But she knew, suddenly, that the person she was seeing in her mind was Rita after all, and that she and Rita were not the same. She still wondered what someone who didn't know her might glean from a deck she'd laid her hand on. But neither Rita nor Grace had ever really believed in what the cards had said: Rita had used them mostly as another way to make jokes, her own countermythological puns and revisions.

Bliss was quiet. Then she said, "It's not that simple," her voice edged with urgency.

Grace leaned against the kitchen counter and thought for a few seconds. She still saw Rita's head bent to the Ten of Swords—a figure lying on the ground, head averted, impaled ten times; Rita's red hair lit up in the window behind her, her face lifting to say, "No doubt about it. Sometime in your life, you're going to get screwed."

Grace smiled. She looked at Ralph, still outside, at how narrow the balcony was, with bars around it. The paper could wait. "Look," she said to Bliss, "if it really matters to you, I'll come."

"It matters to both of us."

"Meet me at the Hole-in-the-Wall," Grace said. "I have to check some amplifiers before tonight." An excuse, but she couldn't go out in the face of a storm just to have her fortune told.

Ralph would stay downtown to get ready for the evening bar rush, and the storm was coming in too fast for even Grace to want to ride her bike, so they took separate cars. In just an hour, the sky had grown steel gray, the clouds not soft anymore but abrasive-looking, as if, if you touched them, they could take the skin right off you. They could tell Grace nothing except that when she drove back home to get ready for her first set, she would likely be driving through snow. And in spite of nonlinear dynamics, chaos theory, the whole burgeoning study of complexity, science couldn't tell her what path a single flake would take through the drafts of air to earth, much less what she would want when she woke up tomorrow and looked out her window on the valley frozen white. Ralph, all tenderness and pain, with which her own pain resonated too exquisitely? Pascal? Something else?

She slid out of her pickup truck in front of the Hole-in-the-Wall. Inside, the lunch rush, such as it had been, was over, and though the air was still heavy with cigarette smoke there were only three men sitting at the bar, their shoulders bent around their beers.

Dan was already ensconced at a table with a bottle, three glasses, and an oversized deck of cards in front of him. Somehow he'd managed to twist himself cross-legged into the wooden chair, and he looked like a Buddha gone inexplicably anorectic before his altar full of offerings. On the table, next to his right elbow, lay a Colt automatic pistol, ugly and serviceable; Grace recognized it because Pascal had one like it, the sidearm he'd brought back from Vietnam, which he had taught her to use at the firing range, showing her how to lock her wrist and brace against the kick. Dan's, she noticed, had its magazine in place. She hoped the safety was on. Ralph was stocking bar glasses and talking to one of the waitresses.

The bar was in an old hotel. Ralph rented rooms by the week to those who moved back and forth across the thin line between meager shelter and the streets. He kept the rooms in order, the plumbing and heat in good repair. There were shared baths on every hall; in the shabby but clean lobby, old men in stained sweaters and hookers tired out from the demands even of such a tidy and virtuous city passed time smoking cigarettes and telling stories about the nonexistent past. Ralph kept an office off the lobby, with a bulletin board over the desk where he'd tacked liquor regulations, his business license, and, in the upper left corner, like a sun illuminating it all, his tin sheriff's star from childhood. It still looked as shiny as it had the first time he pinned it to his T-shirt and called his imaginary posse to chase Grace, red bandanna masking the lower part of her face, through the blue sage and golden grass on the hillsides above his family's ranch. The only other pieces of furniture were an antique oak swivel chair and a scarred bookshelf where Ralph kept the Utah Code, his old texts from law school, and, piled in front of it and around it, what looked like every magazine and newspaper he'd ever read.

The hotel had once had a kind of grandeur, and over the saloon's scuffed oak floors, once polished and laid with fringed rugs, high tin ceilings still arched above a molding so darkened by smoke you could barely make out its elaborate patterns. It couldn't be long, Grace thought, before someone would offer Ralph enough money for the building to persuade him to move on; they'd kick out the geezers and the over-the-hill whores, shut down the bar, and renovate the place for tourists and the lawyers who did their business in the court complex up the street. Ralph would put his money in the bank to accumulate and go back to the ranch where he belonged.

Next to Dan, in chilly profile, sat a pale woman in tight black leggings, an enormous black sweater, and black cowboy boots with very high heels, fashionable rather than functional. Her hair was tucked up under a black felt cowboy hat with a long purple feather slid into the band. She turned her head toward Grace. She had half a dozen holes in each ear, and from each hole dangled a colored crystal.

"You must be Bliss," Grace said and held out her hand.

"That's an understatement," Dan said, but the woman didn't smile, just turned her shoulder in a way that, though it was only the slightest gesture, seemed to exclude him altogether. She barely touched Grace's palm. Though it wasn't cold in the bar, her fingers were protected by purple angora gloves. It was like trying to pet a small rabbit, not exactly nervous, just more fur than body. She tilted her head at the pistol. "You can see why I worry," she said. Then, as if she'd seen Grace looking at the multi-hued stones dangling from her ears, "Each crystal channels a different energy."

Dan touched the cards with a bony index finger. "We've been fighting over them all morning." He picked up the deck. "We'll read together, if you don't mind."

Grace straddled a chair. "It's your show," she said. Though she wouldn't have admitted it, she felt a tightness like excitement, as if it were her real future they would be telling.

Dan pulled the Queen of Pentacles out of the deck and

handed it to Bliss, who rubbed it between her angora hands. It wasn't a deck Grace recognized—the queen in this representation sat astride her throne, actually a ladder-back chair, and instead of a crown she wore a cowboy hat tilted back on her head, its band elaborately jeweled. The card had been hand-drawn and colored with Magic Markers. Grace remembered what Dan had told her about his western Tarot. The figures were drawn with a lively precision. They weren't Dan's: he had trouble rendering magnified cells of a stem that bore any relationship at all to what he saw under the microscope.

Grace said to Bliss, "You're talented."

"We think it'll sell," Dan said.

Ralph was leaning up against the bar behind Dan, his thumbs hooked in his front trouser pockets, navy pin-striped this afternoon. He stood close enough to hear every word, though Dan's body would still be blocking his view of the gun. He smiled at Grace and half closed his eyes like a cat waiting to be scratched.

Grace said to Dan, "I don't see why not."

Dan laid his finger across the card. "And this is what keeps coming up. A woman with black hair."

"How can you tell, under that ten-gallon hat?"

His finger traced the images around the figure. "Vines, ripe fruit, verdant fields." In Rita's deck, Grace was pretty sure, black cows, slightly comic, did not spot the background, and there was no saddled horse tethered to a rail fence. Dan looked at Grace with an intensity that made her shiver. "This is a woman who works the earth. Fertility."

"Lots of women work the earth." Grace touched the rabbit escaping the rough hutch drawn in at the woman's feet. "Why don't you find someone with too many children?"

He looked sideways at Bliss. Bliss held steady, her eyes on his. He looked away, then he laid the Queen of Pentacles in the middle of the table and shuffled the rest of deck. He asked Grace to think of a question. She thought, rejected the obvious and, reluctantly, the jokey. She cut three times and Dan dealt the cards out onto the table. Bliss, who had been leaning back in her chair with her arms folded, now bent forward, her lips moving.

"The great love of your life has red or fair hair," Dan said. "He is impulsive." His voice rose at the end as if in a question, but Grace was determined not to help him.

Bliss put her fuzzy purple hand over the card covering Grace's: the Knight of Wands, also wearing a cowboy hat, sat astride a horse with a western saddle—clearly a working ranch mount, not a heraldic steed. "You can't be too careful," she said. "Any card but the King could refer to a woman." Even though Grace had heard it on the phone, Bliss's voice surprised her again—it seemed too infused with air to be coming from such a precisely shaped head. Grace wondered what Bliss saw in Dan. Bliss didn't seem the type to appreciate either intelligence or eccentricity.

"Still, you have the strength to get through any trouble he may bring you," Dan said. In this deck, Strength was a woman in blue jeans bending to stroke the head of a cougar. Grace was encouraged by this card, in which she could finally recognize something she might want.

"Sometimes courage can come in a daring move toward love." Bliss was sitting straight now, her eyes only half open, her purple angora palms facing up on her lap. Her act was a good one, but that wispy voice spoiled everything. Did she really believe, or was she pure charlatan? Did it make any difference? Grace loved her own work, but she couldn't say she would have the character to keep doing it, full time, if she didn't need the money. Even the singing had the potential to become just another job, if she ever made any money at it.

"You haven't said anything that couldn't be true of half the people I know," Grace said.

"All stories are universal. That's why it works." Dan leaned forward, almost smiling.

Grace said, "I will think about it."

"The cards can be as specific and true as your breakfast cereal," Bliss said. "Your cynicism about love, on the other hand, may be earned."

"Maybe I'm not cynical. Maybe it's something else."

"You've been prodigal," Dan said. "You've wasted your gifts."

Grace said, "No kidding."

"You're just hiding," Bliss said. "When the right time comes, you will emerge from your cocoon." Her purple hands fluttered up like wings.

"Right." Grace had had enough of contradiction. "I can tell this is an inexact science."

She looked up at Ralph. He still leaned against the bar, now with a cup of coffee at his elbow. He lifted it and smiled, and Grace curled her lip at him.

Dan touched the card at the top of the cross. "But that's behind you. Now you're learning sympathy, charity."

Ralph came over with the coffeepot, three extra cups dangling by their handles from his little finger. He pulled up a fourth chair and sat down. He saw the gun, paused, then nodded at it. "What have we here?" He tipped his chair back and rested his hand on Grace's shoulder, trying to appear cool. Grace was glad for his touch, familiar and, at least for the moment, true.

Bliss tapped the figure in the card, a cowboy dropping coins—pesos, no doubt—into the hand of a beggar wearing an enormous sombrero. She said, "You can't buy your way out."

"The gun's only illegal if it's concealed," Dan said.

"In a bar, maybe not," Ralph said. "I'll have to check the Code." He brought his chair forward again, but he didn't get up.

"He should know. He's a lawyer," Grace said to Bliss. She touched the card. "You might want to reconsider the sombrero."

"It's not the kind of question you run into every day." Ralph looked as if he might be about to embark on a sea of case law.

"In your future is a dark-haired man," Dan said. "He may be duplicitous, cruel. Don't trust him." Dan looked at Ralph again. He'd given his stare a baleful edge.

"A man would think so," Bliss said. "This man"—she touched the card, reversed, a seated cowboy with a bowie knife resting on his lap—"is not on their side anymore. It's no sin for him to change his mind."

"Whose side?" Grace was turning her head from one of them to the other. "I don't know what you're talking about. This is obviously between the two of you."

"Only up to a point," Bliss said. "Just go with it."

"And this gives me the creeps." Grace touched the barrel of the gun.

"It has sentimental value," Dan said. "My brother was wearing one like it when he was killed."

Grace thought back to the classroom, trying to figure out whether Dan had been carrying it there. She couldn't decide—he toted a backpack like everyone else. Grace had assumed it was full of books, but he could have been stashing anything in there—a bomb, stolen VCRs, forged Rolex watches. It would never have crossed her mind that her students might actually be armed.

Bliss laid her hand on the cards. "You don't want men to mess with you anymore."

"What about you?" Grace asked.

Ralph cocked one sarcastic eyebrow at Bliss.

Dan said, in a high, mincing voice, "Any card but the King can refer to a woman."

Bliss lifted a black wool shoulder. "Anyone can be too masculine."

Dan clenched his hands on the table. "Bliss and I use different methods." He'd gone red in the face, and shiny over the flush. He'd had some sort of plastic surgery, dermabrasion maybe, to reduce the acne scarring. His skin looked artificial.

"I guess." Grace was thinking of Rita brandishing *A Feminist Tarot* and her unforgiving wit. Marriage and Death—the same card. The whimsy of mathematics and chance. "Symbols," she said, "are what you make them."

Bliss stuck out her tongue at Dan. Even that gesture looked delicate. She rested her elbows on the table, tapped it with gloved fingers. Her cheeks were pinker, as if the room had warmed up, though it hadn't. She said, "You need to understand more about your situation. The right path will become clear. The past will tell you."

Grace leaned back in her chair and looked at the spread. Like Rita, she could read into it almost anything, which was maybe its use—for the subject to teach herself something about her life, to organize it, even around an arbitrary structure. Why not this one? Under the microscope, she knew, she saw what she saw, but how she fit it in was another question. And in the garden, she could shovel a whole bed under and start anew, but she never knew for sure what seeds she might turn to surface, what a shrub or flower would do for her once it was in. The real lives of plants, how they flourished or failed, had become chancy enough for Grace.

When it came to herself, she wanted a loophole, to know that she really could decide, at every moment, who she would become. The evidence was piling up that an almost arbitrary reaction of cells and chemicals determined everything: who she loved, what she read, whether she or anyone else was inclined toward order or fated to a career in mayhem. How, then, could she blame or praise? Would this knowledge increase human compassion, or would we, human that we are, take some easier, crueler way? Scientists, honest and passionate ones, or so they believed themselves, had come up with eugenics. The electric chair. Every kind of controlled explosion—another oxymoron. Most of the tools of war.

Grace said, "Do you two feel better now?"

Dan and Bliss looked at each other. Ralph reached over and took Grace's hand under the table. She pulled it away.

"I feel weird," Dan said.

"She didn't ask the right question," Bliss said.

Didn't Grace get to decide that? "What question would that be?" she asked.

Bliss lifted her shoulder again. "Something our presence would answer."

"You're fulfilling your own prophecies just by being here," Grace said. "I mean, aren't you also begging the question?"

"I only know that when we read for ourselves, you're there," Dan said.

Grace waved at the table. "Where are you, then?"

"Maybe here." Bliss touched the Knight of Wands. Another possibility Grace hadn't thought of. She glanced at Dan just to be sure.

"Couldn't the answer be simple?" Grace recognized Bliss now, and Bliss knew it: the woman from the Broiler the day before, the one who had been with Pascal. Yesterday's sunglasses and today's hat had thrown Grace at first. Today the face was showing, but the blond curls were completely covered, and the row of earrings marching through delicate cartilage had distracted Grace from Bliss's features. Did Bliss think she was in disguise? Grace wondered whose messenger she really was. Now *Grace* wanted to warn *Bliss*, but she figured it could wait until they were alone.

She said, "I can't believe I'm having a serious conversation about this."

"It could be simple," Bliss said. "But that doesn't mean it will be clear."

In the women's room of the Hole-in-the-Wall, Bliss took off her hat and her purple gloves and leaned into the mirror. She fluffed out her hair, then pursed her lips and dabbed at them with an ice-pink lipstick. Her hands were tiny and short-fingered and covered with streaks of different-colored Magic Marker, but her nails were filed and painted in the same pink she wore on her lips. Grace leaned against the rough brick wall and watched. Grace had Imo's movie-star bones and skin, but she still felt, in her blue jeans, her crew cut and scrubbed-clean face, boyish, underdone.

Bliss twisted the lipstick back into its tube, then, not turning to Grace but just catching her eye in the mirror, said, "Thanks for not saying anything about Pascal. Dan gets a little jealous."

"It's not my place," Grace said, "but I think it's kind of weird."

"This?" Bliss waved her hand around at the bathroom walls, but she was talking about the reading, about bringing Grace out in what was sure by now to be a blizzard to tell a future that might after all have nothing to do with any of them, that was probably all in Dan's mind.

Grace nodded. "And you and Pascal. I mean, doesn't your"—Grace hesitated—"friendship with him answer your question?"

By now Bliss had taken out a very pale powder with bits of glitter in it, which she was applying by pouring it into the palms of her hands and slapping it onto her face. Then she pulled a big, soft brush from her bag and began to buff her cheeks. "You may think it has nothing to do with you. All I know is, there's something going to happen." She stood back and looked at herself, then started to buff again.

"If you believe it, then it will. You can't help influencing what you observe. It's called the uncertainty principle. As soon as you look at something, it becomes something different."

Bliss turned and leaned against the counter and looked right at Grace. "I don't have much use for theory. What I want to know is, what are your intentions?"

"Regarding?"

Bliss folded her arms. "Pascal." She jerked her head toward the door. "Him."

"I don't see what Dan's got to do with me," Grace said.

"Maybe I didn't mean Dan."

Grace let her breath out. "Ralph and I are old friends. We can work things out."

Bliss snorted.

"Maybe when it comes to Pascal," Grace said, "I should be asking the questions."

Bliss looked into one of the toilet stalls as if there might be some graffiti in there that had a message just for her. "For Bliss, call any number." She said, "I know what it looked like. But there was nothing, like he said. Pascal tried to save my father, is all. And when he couldn't, we both needed someone to talk to. I mean, where were you?"

Grace sensed there was something Bliss was keeping back. She felt a burst of irritation at Pascal. "It didn't work out," she said. "That's all."

Bliss shook her head, then shut her eyes against what must have been tears, and then Grace saw another image, a silver head resting on a hospital bed, the patient's toupee askew, dark against his white face. It was his daughter Joe had wanted to look young for.

"You must have loved your father," Grace said. She wanted to apologize for seeing him there, on Rita's table, but she stopped herself, unsure Bliss would understand. Unsure she would have understood, in Bliss's place.

"He never gave me any choice." Bliss lifted her eyes—they were so light, Grace kept thinking that from the proper angle she would be able to see right through them to an empty sky. "My mother left him when I was a baby. I was all he had."

"I'm sorry." Grace put into the words all Bliss didn't know, though she also wanted to tell Bliss how grateful she should be, how lucky she was to have had any parent at all.

"It wasn't Pascal's fault. He did what he could."

Grace touched Bliss's shoulder, then let her hand drop. "He's the best." She still wanted to give some warning. "The best surgeon, I mean."

Bliss nodded, her eyes still shut. "The truth is, he asked me to call you."

"Pascal?" Grace wasn't surprised after all—or was surprised only at the gratification she felt, unrolling like a warm washcloth in her stomach.

"It wasn't totally unethical," Bliss said. "I mean, your card did keep coming up. But it could be, you know, that you're on his mind and he's on mine. That could be it."

Grace had never thought of Tarot readers as having a professional ethic. Bliss opened her eyes again. Shutting them hadn't done her any good—her glittering cheeks were streaked with tears. There were tears, black with mascara, puddled under her eyes. "But it never hurts to be certain. The cards were confusing. For sure you're going to have to make a decision."

"About what?"

"For one thing, about your husband. He still loves you. I didn't need the cards to see that." Bliss raised her eyes to the ceiling, as if it held images she could read. "And you love him, too. How much simpler could it be?"

Grace pulled a paper towel out of the dispenser and started tearing it into little shreds. "Much simpler. For example, he didn't have to sleep with his nurse." She put a handful of shredded paper towel into the trash can. "I never expected to find myself married at all. Anyway, what business is it of yours?"

"Love is my specialty. It's not something that's just in the air for you to catch, like a virus." Bliss smiled with one side of her mouth and said, "If he broke some promises, so did you." She rummaged around in her purse, pulled out a business card. It said, "What does the future hold for you? Call for Future Bliss," and had a toll number 1–900–FUTURES. She turned it over and scribbled a local number on the back. She handed it to Grace. "I know. You won't call us; we'll call you."

Grace said, "Sure."

Bliss was looking at Grace's face, her head tilted to one side. "You know," she said, "with the right makeup you'd be really pretty."

"Thanks."

Bliss said softly, "He misses you. What he did—was it really so bad?"

It wasn't a question Grace had been able to answer for herself yet. It was like a wall she couldn't quite see over the top of. "I hate to say it," she said slowly, "but I'm not sure it has that much to do with his infidelity, as such."

"I'm closer to his age. There are things we can remember together. I had friends in Vietnam, and a cousin who was killed. For a few years, we lived as if there might be no tomorrow. That's how it felt." She waved her hand. "I could see how it could get to be a habit."

"I tend to think about his life before me in an abstract way."

"The way you do about your parents, you mean?"

Grace smiled. "They're not abstract to me at all. Just gone."

"Dan wasn't drafted," Bliss said. "After his brother was killed, Dan was the only son left in the family. There was a rule about that. It almost killed him. Sometimes, he believes he was there. He has dreams about holding his brother in his arms, except in the dreams all that's left is a head."

"I'm sorry."

"Though that's close enough to the truth. You're too young to know what it was like."

"I may know more than you think."

"There's knowledge and knowledge. Pain and grief—it's weird how they can't be shared. Not like happiness."

Bliss turned back to the mirror. She put her hand up against her cheek where it was wet and said, "Oh, shit," and flipped on the taps. She filled her hands with water and rubbed them over her face. Then she glanced up into the mirror. Grace was still there, watching, fascinated. Without the foundation and powder, Bliss's skin did look older, not wrinkled but delicate, as if it might tear, like white tissue. There was a scar, still new, running a red line through her lower lip all the way to the cleft in her chin.

"I'm going to be in here a while," Bliss said. "You might as well just go on out without me."

CHAPTER 3

■ ■ ■

A Charm from the Sky

That Wednesday after she'd said good-bye to Bliss and Dan, tapped the dude-ranch version of the Queen of Pentacles with her finger one last time, and lifted her lips to Ralph's, Grace went home to soak in a bubble bath and put on her show-biz clothes. She would line her eyes with kohl and mousse her hair with maroon-glittered foam, a ritual saved for Wednesday nights, when she treated herself like the kind of woman whose real life is in her body, in being watched. Ralph would be there, and, even since their separation, Pascal still came by the Hole-in-the-Wall every Wednesday night when she was singing. Grace thought he did it more to drive Ralph crazy than out of love, though perhaps the two reasons were so entwined as to be indistinguishable. He'd listened to her before he knew her, he said when they separated, and he wasn't stopping now. Under his certain surface, Pascal may have been no more sure than she was how to mend the fabric torn between them, may simply have found comfort in sitting in the dark while the spotlight lit her up, in leaning back as her voice washed over him.

Driving home, she longed for him again in a way she hadn't almost since their first meeting, the first time she saw him standing on the stone porch of the cabin with his hands on his hips. She'd pulled her truck under the pines in front of his cabin and turned off the stereo and the engine. The summer of 1989. He wore blue jeans and cowboy boots that looked as if they'd been made out of at least one endangered species and a necktie with Van Gogh's sunflowers on it, and the first thing Grace thought was how she would describe him to make Rita laugh. She would say, "Cardiac cowboy."

He lifted up his cowboy hat, then he leaned against Grace's truck door and told her through the window he'd heard her sing. She looked at his face. With his height, and that red hair so dark it was almost maroon, she should have remembered him, if she'd ever seen him clear through the lights. In the sun, his skin looked fresh and rosy, like a boy's, though maybe because of the set of his jaw, the barely perceptible thickening of a boylike thinness, the easy tilt of his pelvis, this brightness didn't feminize him, didn't complicate the issue of his masculinity. Grace looked pointedly at his elbow on her truck's new paint.

Pascal said, "You aren't too bad."

"Be nice," she said, "or I'll sing right here." He opened her door and she slid out of the truck and looked around. As a sideline she did landscape design for people with too much money to think about it themselves. It let her get outside, get her hands into the growing life of the earth. It provided a contrast to the clean surfaces in her lab. And it paid better than teaching because people would write checks for almost any amount if the yard looked right when she was done. She had to get the money right away, though, before they realized how much work they would have to do to keep things that way, perfectly groomed, all the shrubs proportional.

She told Pascal, "You change much, you'll find out you've got nothing but weeds."

"They'll move in?"

She tilted back her head to get a look at him. Also to show him the fine bones in her face. "They're already here. They get in the way of what you want, they're weeds."

"Maybe a little lawn?"

"If you really think so," she said, breathing in the native smells of the canyon, plants raw and rangy and not meant to be cut.

He took her out back. A creek lined with scrub oak, willow down to the water. Though the day was hot, it was cool under the trees. There was a redwood picnic table with a model boat on it, not new, its odd, flat deck a little the worse for wear. Grace walked in front of him, talking her way through the landscape. "Maybe some steps down through this grove. Stone, native. There's a lot of granite around here." With her hand, she described a low wall where the ground sloped up away from the house, wildflowers spilling over it. He pointed at the picnic table, and she shook her head. "A stone table," she said. "And benches."

"No lawn." He was looking around as if seeing, for the first time, possibilities in what was there. "Well, you're the boss."

"I'm the expert. You're the boss."

He laughed. "In medicine, they're the same thing. Pity the poor patient." He looked through the scrub oak up the mountain. "There's something to be said for leaving well enough alone." He picked up the boat, and Grace followed him down to the creek, which widened into a little pool. He set the boat in the water, and they watched it turn and drift, then speed up as the current caught it.

He had built the boat himself. "It looks like a toy," he said, "but it's an exact replica." His fingers, long and tapered, traced in the air a structure so precise Grace could see its internal details. The boat lurched in an eddy. He leaned down and picked up some pebbles, squinted out over the little creek as if it were a vast body of water. He tossed one of the pebbles at the boat, then another. They ticked against the sides but didn't knock it free into the current.

He handed a pebble to Grace. She rolled it in her hand, nervous to show him how badly she threw. It splashed into the water almost at their feet. He handed her another, less a pebble than a rock. She hefted it, aimed, and threw, and the rock landed flat on the boat's deck. The boat rolled, swamped. Grace watched, hoping for the best, but Pascal was laughing.

She started to laugh too. "That was a fluke. I promise."

"I shouldn't have let that first throw fool me." He sat down on the bank and pulled off his boots, tucked his socks into them, and handed them to Grace, then he waded out into the water. The rock had punched through the boat's deck, but not through the hull. Back on shore, he dumped the water and shook the rock out through the hole. "Not a fatal breach." He handed the boat to Grace, rolled one sock on over his wet toes, then stuck his foot into a boot.

Grace's body was feeling more and more awkward. "It sounds like you've spent some time on the water."

"More than you can imagine." He held his still-bare foot clear of the dirt and looked into the creek. He paused, as if he might change the subject, then he started to put his second sock on. "I was on an aircraft carrier in the Gulf of Tonkin. The *Coral Sea*." He pulled his boot on, then he lifted the model from her hands. Its undamaged hull said "*Coral Sea II*." He said, "I keep trying to sink the thing. You almost succeeded"—he tilted the brim of his hat at her—"where I have failed. I would consider it an honor, ma'am, if you would try again."

She could see, now, wrinkles around his eyes, a coarsening of skin. He still didn't look old enough to have been in Vietnam. But now that Grace was out of her twenties, it seemed that everyone between, say, twenty-eight and fifty looked the same age.

He caught her looking and said, "I'm forty-five."

Her father's age the last time she saw him—the age he still inhabited in her mind. Would forever, she guessed, while she aged, moved past it. This year, she realized, she'd be the age her mother was when she died.

Suddenly, forty-five seemed the perfect number. It had been a long time since she'd thought about romance, almost a decade since she'd decided it was easier, and in every way safer, to keep people beyond touch, to save passion for living things that don't talk, that are purely themselves, not made of words. Both Rita and Ralph had pushed against this resolve from time to time, but with no success, and since they understood her they didn't push hard. So Grace was unprepared to feel now, looking at something as simple and safe as this man's dark red hair curling under a hat and against a white neck, a liquidity in her stomach that signaled danger.

"Pilot?" she asked.

He shook his head. The boat caught on some low-hanging branches and stalled in the almost still water. "Nothing so romantic. I was a crewman. A red shirt." He'd been scanning the ground, and now he leaned down and picked up another pebble, which he handed to her.

She tilted her head.

"I loaded bombs." He glanced at Grace sideways. "When the planes came back empty, I loaded more." His matter-of-factness didn't make him seem cold. She imagined him at night, looking out over the water, watching the stars. When one moved, it would be a plane—U.S., since North Vietnam had no air force. He was everything she'd been taught to disapprove. And then there was her body, bathed in its own electric charge. She rubbed the pebble between her hands.

"All I wanted was to get off that boat."

Grace was hugging herself. Behind her eyes ached the unrelenting light of ocean.

"I don't talk about it much," he said. "It's in the past."

"You're talking about it now." She didn't want him to stop but couldn't hold back the part of her that believed in her dead parents. At some point while he was on that carrier, she would have been riding her father's shoulders above the crowd at a march against the war Pascal was fighting. She thought what Rita would say. "Did you ever think about where those bombs went?" Grace asked.

He smiled. He was rubbing two remaining pebbles together between his fingers. The air was still. There was no indication, that July, that in less than a year the country would begin mobilizing toward war.

"You were drafted?"

"We were poor. I was just an enlisted slob." He took aim at the boat, but the pebble fell short again.

She shook her head.

"I came home, went to college on the GI Bill, then to Baylor Med, in Houston. It was my only chance." He lifted a shoulder at her, not accusing, still dealing with simple fact. "It's the kind of thing you wouldn't understand."

She was looking into his eyes now, and he was looking straight back. A shadow—leaves flipping in the breeze—kept moving over his face, and his eyes seemed to brighten and darken as if to an inner beat. He grinned, but there was a tightness in his body that never eased.

"Let me guess," he said. "You never knew anybody who fought in Vietnam."

"How do you know?"

"Your posture gives you away. A sort of"—he moved his hands over her shoulders, but without touching her, describing her with his fingers as he had the boat, so that she saw herself clearly—"decorum, maybe. It was a poor man's war." He spread his hands—this was the first time Grace saw him do that; his hands were the most active, the most eloquent she had ever seen—and looked at them, then out over the creek. His face was very still. "Don't worry. I'm not going to snap and start shooting up fast food restaurants." He looked down again at his hands, holding them still. "It made me want to be a doctor. I hardly know how to tell you." He smiled. "It's like holding someone's soul in your palm."

Grace shivered, though she hadn't seen him yet with his fingers inside a human heart. She would never hear him talk this way again, as if what he did was anything more than a matter of the right touch, a valve adjustment here and a stitch there. He was offering her something.

"At first, it scares the shit out of you," he said.

"And then it becomes, what? Routine?"

"Never that. It's science. Like what you do."

Grace sensed something in him closing, a corresponding door shutting in herself. "I cut up plants, not people."

"They're alive, aren't they?"

She smiled. "Not when I finish with them."

He lifted his hat at her. "The stakes are a little different. I've never lost one yet. Not on the table." He laughed again, softly. "They all go eventually. The question is, of what?" He had been leaning toward her, but now he stood up straight. "When I left the States, sixty-four, there was nothing going on. When I came back, it had all started. I grew out my hair. I even went to a few protests."

Grace pulled a blade of grass, began to tear it into long pieces. "Did you believe in it?"

"I believed in lots of things. They didn't always square. Back then, if I'd told you where I'd been, you wouldn't have gone out with me."

Grace gave him a slow smile. "Back then, I was six."

He looked her over. "This is hypothetical."

"You think I might go out with you now." She tilted her head at the same angle as his and returned the look. She wasn't avoiding, only prolonging, the slide.

He tossed another pebble, not aiming this time at anything. "I took to school like some of my Air Force friends took to heroin. It dulled the pain, kept my mind from filling with ghosts. And it saved my life. Late at night, when I was done studying, I used to drive out to Galveston. If it was warm enough, I'd swim into the Gulf." He reached over, set the boat back in the creek. It floated back out into the same eddy. He squatted down and picked up more pebbles. "Then, I used to dream about signing on with one of the big tankers. I knew they were out there, drifting in that same water I was touching. Some of the crew were asleep. Others were watching the water and the sky."

"For danger?"

"All they had to worry about was the weather." He hit the side of the boat with a pebble, another. A flake of paint chipped off into the water. "That's where the stories come from. The Bermuda Triangle. Monsters. Lonely men in the middle of nowhere, giving shape to nothing. Me, too. I would think about letting the water take me. But I always swam back to shore. At the hospital, people were dying. I could help them, even if I couldn't bring all of them back."

She couldn't help herself. She said, "It was like that in Vietnam, too." She lifted her pebble and tossed it. It hit the boat with a crack.

"Another good shot," he said. The boat's hull swung out into the main current and started bouncing downstream. He held out his hand. She put hers into it, and they picked their way after the boat. It was stuck again—this time caught in scrub at the water's edge.

Pascal said, "Your turn." He tucked his hand into the waist of Grace's jeans and she leaned out over the stream, his knuckles pressing her spine. He lowered her until she could reach the boat. She untangled it from the scrub and picked it up by its stern. "Careful," he said. He pulled her back in and she handed the boat to him. They walked with it up to the house.

He set it back in the center of the picnic table and looked around. "You're right. The place isn't bad as it is."

"Maybe you've just got too much money."

"You've got to work on your sales pitch," he said.

"Don't be fooled. Nature isn't cheap either. You'll see when you get my bill." They stood, shoulder to elbow, breathing in the smells of fresh water and light, and she felt no charge or pull then, just a kind of stillness, as if her skin had opened to let the air move through her.

Before running her bath, Grace turned her back on the winter outside the window and went to her orchids. After Grace and Pascal married, it was his idea for him to move down from the cabin and her to move up from her little rental house surrounded by garden into the high-rise condo on the foothills. Middle ground, he had called it, though there was no ground at all. He had persuaded her that she didn't need a garden of her own when she planned a dozen gardens a year anyway. They'd stepped out on the balcony, the real estate agent hovering behind them, and he'd waved his hand at all the backyards below as if she could own them all.

The orchids had been his idea too. The day they moved in, he set up the table and sun lamps along a wall of her study, her potting table before the floor-to-ceiling windows that filled the whole west side of the room. She laid out her tools, not the dainty miniature tools of the indoor hobbyist but a sturdy outdoor hand hoe and a shovel and mattock that would have no earthly use up here so far from the ground. There was dirt still clinging to them; some of it crumbled off onto the white carpet. Grace thought, We're tired, is all: a week of packing, of moving on their own the things they loved most— the tender new orchids and Grace's computer with her drafting program and designs, and Pascal's stereo, western art collection, and medical etchings. Her mother's wedding china. The rest they watched movers bang against walls and woodwork. Grace's muscles ached more from clenching against the thuds and scrapes than from what she'd hefted herself. Her whole body hurt with it.

But Pascal was right about the orchids. Grace loved the process of sowing seed, how everything had to be sterile for the orchids to grow. She was planning to divide her sabbatical between the experimental gardens at the arboretum, creating flowers to grow in the high, dry desert, and her work with orchids. Three quarters, a growing season, to spend with living plants in her hands.

Now, she added the agar-nutrient mixture to distilled water and set it in the pressure cooker to boil. She'd better leave time to eat, she reminded herself, before going back to the bar.

That other evening, they'd ordered pizza and sat on the balcony floor in the breeze. They hadn't been able to find the glasses in the pile of boxes in the kitchen, so they passed the bottle of champagne and watched the sunset, vermilion, through the railing. Grace felt between them some coolness, a formality, and she watched Pascal, wondering how handsome he would be without the ease that came with his skill with the knife, with money, with the power people give those who cut open their sick bodies to save them. Handsome enough, she decided, though she'd lost her objectivity and was perhaps seeing a certainty of mind that she mistook for beauty.

She'd wanted to look at him constantly: his hands, yellow eyes that clashed with his hair and gave him a look of watchful, feline serenity. Sometimes, when she was to meet him after work at a cafe, she would arrive early and wait in her car so she could watch his tall figure move toward her, graceful, leaning forward with purpose. She liked to think it was the prospect of seeing her that gave his body its urgent slant. She would open the car door and stand on the sidewalk waiting for him to notice her, watching his face for the moment of recognition and delight.

She would have moved anywhere for him, she thought, gripping the balcony railing and looking out over her new view, but why here, so far from the earth? He picked up her hand, turned her palm to his lips and kissed it. She wanted then to empty herself of will, for him of all people, the man who wanted her with her will intact.

He took another swig from the champagne bottle, then handed it to Grace. "You'd be surprised how real dreams can become," he said. "Good or bad."

Remembering, Grace looked up from her vials, gazed out the window at twilight signs of industry and at the houses where couples might be just leaning, now, to give each other habitual goodnight kisses. Some would grow into passion, others stay cool and dry on the lips.

And their lovemaking that night had been cautious, as if, sharing the same rooms at last, they'd had to make a new kind of distance to keep between them, a courteous tenderness. She'd planned to give herself over to him fully for the first time that night, to fold herself into his hands and become his, and when the moment came she couldn't tell if she was holding back or he wasn't receiving, or if the problem was her expectation that they could have become one in some real sense. They'd shuddered, and held each other, and spoken each other's names, but they'd remained separate bodies beating against the dark. She had feared that so many betrayals of love over the years—not least her own—had unsuited her for what she wanted from him, had made her unable to trust any affirmative.

This she was certain of: seed and root, stem and flower. She measured calcium hydrochloride with a dropper into a vial, then she sterilized a knife tip over the gas flame and used it to add a bit of *Cattleya* seed. She felt rather than heard Pascal behind her in the doorway, but she didn't turn around.

Behind her, Pascal said, "Are you going to talk to me?"

Grace lifted the vial of seed. "The timing is critical."

"It is." He was leaning against the door frame, his thin hips tilted forward and shoulders curved in, fingers tucked in his blue jeans pockets. "Are we really going to do this?"

"I thought you weren't going to use your key anymore."

Grace held the vial between her thumb and forefinger, shaking it by turning her wrist from side to side to disinfect the seed. "Shouldn't you give it to me?"

"Not yet." She looked out the window, and he said, "Why don't you look at me?"

"The snow is really coming down," she said. Then, "Are we living the same life here?"

He spread out his hands. "What life are you living?" He walked over next to her, reached out and touched her breast. He put his face close to hers. She could smell toothpaste. He must have brushed just for this, with the kit he kept in the glove compartment of the Jaguar. He was a good doctor, not just technically good but compassionate. But he also liked the toys his surgeon's salary allowed him. "Where are you?" he said. He pressed his cheek against Grace's head, put one arm around her, and began to dance her around the room, his other hand still on her breast.

"I don't know," she said against his chest. "I don't know where I want to be."

He curved his shoulders even closer around her. "I hope you want to be here."

"That's just it. I do. But only if I can rely on it."

"I'll give you your privacy." He leaned back far enough to smile down at her. "I'll even do my best to be faithful. But we can't go on like this forever."

"What if I can't forgive?"

He stopped dancing and put both of his hands on Grace's shoulders. He was so much taller, he could have been a father leaning over his child. She moved the vial, which she was still shaking, out of his way.

He said, "Who?"

She was trying to keep the tears away. She shook her head. Pascal had never had the trick, like Ralph, of melting his eyes. It was as if he was transacting business—cool, the tension vibrating but always under the surface. That made it easier to refuse him. Grace turned out from under his hands, went into the bathroom adjoining the study, and poured the seed chaff off the top of the vial. Now she had to work quickly. Pascal leaned against the wall again, watching.

She glanced at him over her shoulder. "If I don't do this now, it will be ruined."

He smiled. "Sure. I can wait." But his eyes on Grace made her hands shake.

She lifted a flask from the pressure cooker and put its stopper in a bowl of Clorox. She said, "Is this a trick you learned in the war?"

"I didn't learn everything there."

"No." Grace put the dropper in the vial and squeezed its rubber bulb, blowing a bubble of air into the liquid holding the seed to set it spinning, then took up a few drops of seed and fluid.

He put his hand on his head, turned around once. "Can't you see what you're doing?"

She smiled, steadied her hands. A point for her. "I'm growing something." She measured four drops of seed onto the agar, moving the dropper in a circle in the mouth of the flask.

"Yes, but what?"

She took the stopper from the bowl of Clorox. She shook it to get rid of the excess, but her hand was trembling again, and a few drops landed on Pascal's green cotton shirt. It was his favorite. They watched the white spots emerge on the placket. He reached out his hand to her, and she flinched.

He said, gently, "What were you expecting? A perfect life? I don't know how to do that." He took her wrist, removed the stopper from her fingers, put it back in the Clorox.

She looked at the stopper. "It will be ruined."

"Are you saying this is it?"

Grace looked away. "I don't know if I can risk it again." She put her hand on her chest. "It's like there's a locked box inside me." She knew where the key was, but she didn't want to open it. She tested its hardness, pushed against it, found it unyielding. She smiled and said, "I've read the Pandora story."

He shook his head. "I know I've been a pig."

"Maybe it's for the best," she said. "Maybe it's just not in me to be married. I'm just glad I found it out in time." She was still waiting for him to find some magic word that would prove her wrong, that would let her relent and open her arms.

He was smiling, but Grace couldn't read his eyes. "In time for what?" he said. "Not to spare us."

"Spare *me*." Grief or rage—she couldn't tell which—was rising in her, choking her like smoke. To contain it, she smiled wider, baring her teeth. "Do you think I like what I see when I think of you? Do you know that whenever you touch me, I see Jemma's mouth on you?" She swallowed hard on the lump in her chest, still rising. "I know it's pride. But I don't know how to get rid of it. Or even if I should. What would I be left with?"

He reached out and chucked her cheek, not hard enough to qualify as a hit but too hard to be affectionate. He said, his voice as even and cold as a scalpel, "Who knows? You've already lost your sense of humor, sweetheart."

"Maybe it's you who's not getting the joke," she said, but she was regretting her words already. How long had it been since she'd laughed? It would take only one word, one gesture from her, to tip things in either direction—toward resolution or disaster. She wanted to ask, How many?—but what if he named a number higher even than she had imagined? Was that what reconciliation would mean, a kind of unbearable honesty? A constant grief instead of the kind she was used to, coming one loss at a time. She was afraid of becoming pathetic. If she yielded now, she could lose herself.

He said, "All this time, I thought we were alike." Before she could say anything else, before she could say, "We are, more than you know," and tell him about Ralph, he turned and walked down the hall to the bedroom. She exhaled, fished the stopper out of the Clorox, and closed the flask with it, but she hadn't shaken the bleach off. Two drops held, fell into the agar. She clenched her fists, then she took the flask with its ruined medium out the sliding door onto the balcony. Below was only white hillside, sagebrush rimed with snow, sloping away twelve stories down, all of it blurred by blizzard. She leaned over the rail, held the flask for a second, then let go, and watched it fall until it shattered against a snow-covered rock. She felt the impact in her stomach, how it opened there, and, in a matter of seconds, came out of her mouth as a sob. This time, she didn't want to hold anything back. By the time she turned to go back inside, snow had already covered the broken pieces of glass.

Grace rinsed her face in the bathroom, then she opened the door to Pascal's study. She went to the top drawer of the desk and took out his unloaded Colt. She found a full magazine hidden under files in the back of the filing cabinet, and she slid it into the handle of the gun. She took the gun back into the living room and set it on the coffee table. She sat on the couch and looked at it, its seriousness, her fists clenched in her lap.

When Pascal came back out of the bedroom, he carried a shoebox full of brushes and bottles from his bathroom cupboard, things he had left behind when he'd moved back up to the cabin. He set it by the door.

Grace said, "Is that everything?" Her voice was shaking. What would it be like, when everything his was gone from here? Was it possible? She still touched, every day, objects that had rested in her parents' hands. A wineglass. A silver hand mirror.

He smiled up at the ceiling. "I'm not that rash. No matter how you look at it, this is a step in the wrong direction." He came over to the couch and took her head in both his hands and tilted it up toward him, and she could feel in his palms he wasn't speaking only out of tenderness. "The cabin's awfully cold this time of year." His hands tightened against her cheeks.

"What's the punch line?" She looked at the gun, imagined its heft in her palm.

He loosened his hands. "Why do you have to understand everything?"

"I don't know."

"Try this," he said. "I did it because I wasn't supposed to."

"You still aren't."

"I'm not so unlike you. I wasn't used to this. I couldn't tell if it was real." He looked at her from under his deep, red eyelashes. His eyes were the color of fallen leaves with the sun on them. Not even a fool could resist him. "I'm sorry," he said. "I won't do it again. Will you?"

The picture of herself and Ralph together flashed into her mind. Was that really what she had wanted for Pascal? Grace said, "I'm no fool. How am I supposed to know what to believe?" She felt the cold blade of loss. "If I forgive you, I have to admit we had something to lose, and that it's gone now." She wiped her face on her sleeve.

"My love, it's not gone." He put his hands under her elbows and lifted her until she was standing on the couch. Then they were just the same height. He put his arms around her, pulled her close. "So, you haven't lost your sense of humor altogether. But you're in serious danger."

"You're right," she said. She relaxed a little and smiled at him. "I am. But I'm not done punishing you."

"Fair enough. You want to be courted for a while. I can do that. Then when I get tired of it, you can court me." He held her chin, leaned into her, and barely brushed her lips with his. "I can think of worse things. You let me know." Before he left, he held out his hand, and she picked up the Colt and put it in his palm. He looked at it, then slid it into his jacket pocket.

Grace, feeling foolish, laughed. "I don't know why I took that out."

"That's the problem, isn't it? I'll see you at the bar."

While she got ready, Grace flipped on the radio news as always, and in the middle of a usual story, the kind she would listen to with half an ear and then forget, the report came through, the voices on the speaker both authoritative and confused. The first full-scale war of her adulthood had started, and though Grace had watched it coming she still wasn't prepared. She braced herself against the dresser, imagined all the people alone in rush hour, imagined the flow of cars on the freeway coming to a stop as everyone leaned closer to their radios and listened. She flipped on the television and sat on the end of the bed, her mascara open in her hand, trying through those remote scenes—a dark airfield, bomber planes taxiing down the runway—to bring the idea of it closer, to make danger tangible, coax it near. But these were not the explicit images of her childhood, of tangled bodies and elaborate, pulsing jungles. And as she thought about the people she knew, it occurred to her for the first time that her immediate generation had escaped. They'd been too young, barely, to go to Vietnam; now they were too old to be called to the Gulf, at least against their will, unless the fighting lasted a long and bloody time. She remembered a boy from high school, skinny then, with glasses but already straight-backed, who, last she heard, was commanding a tank somewhere in California. But though they had been in college when draft registration had been reinstated, and though Rita had organized everyone to march against it, especially against a draft that would take only men, they had slid without noticing through a fifteen-year keyhole to the other side of youth, losing on the way the stupid courage so precious to war. They were mortal and, therefore, useless.

Grace watched a young aircraft technician raise his fist into the air. She was weeping, but it was still for the anonymous, as she had been taught to weep as a child for people—American and Vietnamese—she had never met, and for the abstract difference between justice and self-interest, the iniquity of her country and her own safe and selfish heart. The faces of her parents, young, her mother's so like her own and her father's blurred oddly with Pascal's, rose in her mind. How we spend our passion, and on what. The technician's face was smooth, would have been childishly sweet without its sheen of bloodthirst. Grace turned off CNN and waited until she knew her tears had finished, then she washed the makeup off her face and started over, careful, bracing one hand with the other. She had no time for dinner. She descended in the elevator to the underground garage and drove her old pickup out into the blizzard-lit night.

When Grace got to the Hole-in-the-Wall, later than usual and still hungry, Ralph had CNN showing on the TV over the bar, and Rita was watching from one of the old stools, drinking a Diet Coke and eating a pickled egg from the jar next to the old cash register. Grace was surprised at how crowded the place already was, as if people hadn't been able to get themselves to go home from work to watch the beginning of a war that might end in no time or last for years—nobody knew—alone in their houses, in those walled-off islands of civilized light. People were clustered at tables, leaning toward the screen, or just huddling together, holding hands, stunned and remote.

Rita looked disgusted, and she had her shoulder pointedly turned against Pascal, already sitting as usual at a table right up front. In front of him was his bottle of Jack Daniel's; next to him sat Grandma Imo in her best cascading blond ex-minor-film-star wig with a powder-blue pillbox hat perched on its teased top, darker cornflower-blue pumps, and a matching cornflower purse that she held on her lap.

"Shit," Grace said. This was the first time she could remember seeing Imo in a bar. Imo was looking around, her eyes bright, head cocked to one side.

Grace looked up at the television and reached one hand to Rita and the other over the bar's polished surface to Ralph. Ralph said, "It was inevitable."

"Not until it happened." Rita shook her head. "I can't believe it."

"You did what you could," Grace said, her hand in Rita's hair. "You organized everything."

"The world has changed. There was hardly anyone to organize." Rita looked pointedly at Grace. Grace put her arm around Rita's neck and held her.

"Nobody has a sense of commitment anymore," Rita said.

Thinking of her students, Grace said, "Maybe there doesn't seem like much to commit to."

"You should know." Rita turned back to the television.

Pascal had seated himself and Imo facing the stage, with their backs to the television. Grace looked longingly at the pickled eggs, but said to the side of Rita's head, "I guess I'd better face the music."

At Pascal's table, she leaned down and kissed Imo on the cheek. "What are you doing here?" she said, her voice light.

"Lovely. Reminds me of Prohibition." Imo meant the temporary look of the bar, as if everything but the fixtures could be folded up and removed in a matter of minutes. She leaned over and whispered to Grace, "Everybody speak easy," then giggled.

"Ralph didn't have much to start with," Grace said, "but you can bet it's all legal."

"Don't be sarcastic, dear." Imo clasped her hands over her purse and smiled. She looked right at Grace's chest—Grace was wearing no bra and a gold silk-satin blouse, behind which her nipples glided like well-greased ball bearings—and said, "Isn't this nice." Not that she believed Grace should wear a bra for support—she'd just always figured, she would say, that somebody with a figure like a floor lamp could use all the art that extra padding could provide.

Grace waved toward the television. "What do you think?"

Imo ignored her and Pascal shook his head, one small shake full of tenderness, indulgence.

Grace looked away. "I can only sit for a second. I'm late, and I still have to warm up."

Imo was drinking a Manhattan. She reached over and put her hand over Pascal's on his shot glass. "Don't worry. He's taking very good care of me. He got me extra cherries."

Pascal smiled and lifted his glass. "Anything for you, darling."

Grace couldn't tell if he was really being good or just trying to prove a point. "That's nice," she said.

Pascal said, "Don't be so suspicious."

Imo wouldn't take off her pale blue hat with the flowers dyed a bit darker and wouldn't put down her matching bag, but she kept on smiling, as if she thought someone might sneak up and take her picture. When she was in the movies, she'd once told Grace, an aide from the studio escorted her everywhere with a huge portable floodlight. She always stood under its glow, lit for the cameras that followed wherever she went. For weeks after that, Grace and Rita had played film star, taking turns following each other around with Grace's bedside lamp, a ceramic ballerina—the lightbulb shaded by her tutu—that matched the Degas ballerina wallpaper in Grace's room.

When Grace got up on stage, she had nothing more than usual in mind, though she felt jittery, with a dangerous tentativeness in her throat. She began with her planned set, easing into "Walking after Midnight" and launching from there into

"Ford Econoline," but though her voice strengthened and solidified as she kept on, she found herself leaving out songs with any silky suggestion of dirtiness in them, any temptation toward throatiness, hip-grinds, caressing of the mike. Though Grace couldn't see her through the spots, she knew Imo was down there, something familiar and resistant beyond the brightness of the lights.

Then she found herself faltering, with space to fill. She fiddled with her guitar for a few minutes, improvising, then realized she was picking out on the strings a song she didn't recognize at first, it was so familiar, one her mother had taught her years ago on the protest lines, its rhythm as intimate as Grace's own heartbeat. As she sang "The Cruel War," two tables full of drinkers got up and walked out, then a third, but, though her stomach clutched, Grace kept on, until one voice, then another, joined her from the audience. She followed with a song everyone would know, "Where Have All the Flowers Gone?" She had never liked its roundabout sentimentality, but she wanted to hear other voices raised with hers, which they were, and again for "This Land Is Your Land" and, finally, Country Joe's raucous countdown to war.

Imo sat with her feet together, her hands on her purse. To end the set, Grace sang "Home, Sweet Home" for her, for the evenings at the piano when Grace played and Imo and Grandpa sat on either side of her, the piano light and the glow from the fire illuminating their cheeks and fingers, and for the nights when Imo played while Grandpa spun Grace slowly across the wooden floor.

When Grace finished the set, Imo said, "You were like an angel, dear," and she leaned over and patted Grace's hand the way she had after Grace's childhood piano recitals. Imo looked around again at the smoke, the dim yellow light. "But this isn't Lawrence Welk. Don't you think you'd better spice it up a little?"

Then, her head next to Grace's, "'Home, Sweet Home' was

one of your grandfather's favorites. But I always did hate that song."

Sitting there, her eyes closed against the house lights, Grace could still feel Ralph's fingers on her skin. They seemed to remember from half their lives ago what her body wanted; and her body still wanted the same things. Ralph's had taken on the harder definitions of adulthood, but it was still white, knotted with muscle; and on his back were still carved the grooves of his father's old belt for Grace to lay her fingers in, one simple fact among others. Grace wondered why the two of them didn't know better, why she wasn't steadier in her purposes.

She had said, her finger pushing on the shirt button next to his heart, "You have to make your own decisions," but she knew as well as anyone it wasn't that easy. Now there was her promise to Pascal, that she would keep trying, made possible because she had taken Ralph to bed, had that sin uneasily on her side.

And Grace realized that it wasn't just war that bothered her, a war, after all, that might end as no more than a historical footnote when all the reports were in, but the loss over, say, fifteen years, of a certain spirit and its replacement with another, more violent and vengeful, a national idea that bloodshed was something to celebrate, as long as the blood was somebody else's and shed at an antiseptic distance.

She and Ralph and Rita, growing up, had begun to understand, as if in their bodies, that they, too, might die. But as their mid-twenties, the age of mortality, had approached, along with the middle of the eighties, that corrupt decade, they had also begun to feel there was after all no essential order waiting to reveal itself—the social and political revolution of their childhood had faded with all its bright banners and promises, and its leaders, just enough older to have been heroes to Grace, were making fashion of necessity, preaching patriotism, what Grace considered the most self-indulgent possible religious philosophies, and the very self-control they'd never mastered until they were too tired to keep up the excess.

Only a few, like Rita, kept faith. Others, Ralph's lawyer friends among them, rode the older generation's coattails to riches. Ralph fell back on old-fashioned virtues—honesty, plain hard work. And Grace, who had reduced her world to the illuminated circle inside her microscope and the controlled wildernesses of her gardens, who had thought that through smaller structures she might comprehend a whole, realized that even science kept changing its mind. It could offer no single permanent idea she might rest upon, though the plants she studied had intricate intelligences, though each seed, like our own bodies, contained both the history of the universe and any number of possible futures. Even Rita, after repairing, as much as she could, the surface of a young man killed in a car accident or knife fight or a young woman raped and beaten to death, would call Grace up and say, "All causes are natural."

By eleven, all the tables were crowded, and the air in the bar was redolent with smoke from clove cigarettes. Imo finally took her handkerchief from her purse and held it over her mouth. Now, leaned up against the bar or moving between the tables of people who still hadn't made it home from work, were kids wearing string ties over black shirts, cowboy boots and holey jeans, their spiked hair washed with pink or blue or orange, their conversation more intense than usual, like a wire pulled tight in the air. Ralph had turned the television's sound off, but he'd left the picture on: a reporter interviewing one of the pilots cleared by the Army to talk to the press.

Grace looked around the bar, from face to face, trying to decide which of these boys poised on the lip of the future were young enough to be called if it came to calling. These would be the kids who had been protesting since last August, who had a personal stake; Rita, now revived, moved from table to table, greeting patrons Grace didn't recognize. She had organized them, had taught them how to go limp as bored lovers, if necessary, in the arms of the police. Grace saw one of her students, a woman a decade younger, laughing with Rita, tilting her chin for a kiss, blowing blue smoke up toward the ceiling.

Grace felt a twinge of jealousy. She worked this moonlight job partly to recall something of her old life, so much like theirs; to see the messy human world in the present tense, solid and real. But now she remembered a movie she went to years ago with Ralph and Rita. She couldn't recall the title. The screen showed, silhouetted against another screen, the heads of a fictional movie theater audience gripped, enraptured, by what they were watching above them: a larger-than-life, impossibly endowed female chest billowing, it seemed, right out of its own image toward them, and toward the real audience as well; and only the real audience could guess that a car full of desperate and funny men was about to rip right through that bosom and pile its ton of metal and grinding axles into their—the fictional audience's—laps.

When Grace started in on songs about good love and bad— "Stand By Your Man," which she sang with a self-ironic twist; "Two Cigarettes in the Ashtray"; "It Wasn't God Who Made Honky-tonk Angels"—she tried not to look at Pascal or at Ralph, though she could feel each presence vibrating through her with the music. Instead, she sang to Rita, who turned her back to the bar and spread her long arms along it like wings.

Pascal sat next to Imo, drinking his Jack Daniel's and looking from Ralph to Grace, making sure Grace saw him do it. She knew he'd found something changed in the gravity between Ralph's body and hers, however far apart they stayed. As Grace got up from her stool and reached for the glass of water Ralph was handing up to her on stage, Pascal caught her eye, then he nodded, slow, not smiling. It was an accusation as direct as any he could have made with words. The idea that she had hurt Pascal, the very idea that had sent her, she admitted to herself, into Ralph's arms in the first place, made Grace long now for forgiveness, the terrible sweetness of surrender and reconciliation. But it was exactly that desire for surrender she hated in herself, that kept her from reaching out and touching him. She couldn't find a way to do it without sinking.

She thought for a moment that Pascal would turn, pick up his leather jacket, and walk out the door, and if he had she would probably have jumped right off the stage and gone after him; but when she lifted her hand, as if to say stop, he nodded and stayed where he was, his hand on his glass. Imo, who never missed much of what she wanted to see, watched the whole exchange and twirled her swizzle stick in her drink.

During the second break, Grace sat back down at Imo's and Pascal's table, and Imo said, "Pascal says you're usually more fun to watch." The volume was back up on CNN, but fewer people had their eyes on the set. More were huddled around tables with their heads together, smoking and talking in voices pitched high.

Pascal shook his head, smiling. "I think you're holding back, Grace."

Grace shook her head back at him, a warning, but out loud she said, "Yes."

"You know," he said, "you could give your grandmother a little more credit."

Grace wondered why he couldn't be as nice to her as he was to Imo. "Whose grandmother is she, anyway?"

"This may surprise you, but I'm an old-fashioned guy. If she's yours, she's all mine." He leaned over and put his arm around Imo, who snuggled in under it. "You will be too, when you're eighty-four."

"Who will you be sleeping with then?" Rita pulled out a chair and sat down next to him. "Hmm?" she said.

He cocked his head in a perfect imitation of Imo. "I don't know. What about you?"

Rita tossed her unraveling braid back over her shoulder.

"That's the question," Imo said. Then, "Maybe Grace wants you to take me home now."

"If you want to go," Grace said, "go." At first, she thought Imo could at least have declared her loyalties. Then she realized she wasn't sure where those loyalties would have been.

"Aren't you going to kiss your husband?" Pascal leaned over Grace's chair, his face next to hers. Imo was watching with her eyes opened wide, but Rita turned her head away.

"Not here," Grace said. She had made up her mind, but she wanted for the moment to keep Ralph at bay, to keep everything as quiet as possible. Imo looked from Grace to Ralph. Ralph started toward the table, but one of his cocktail waitresses caught him by the arm and he bent down to listen to her, his eyes still on Pascal.

Pascal put the tips of his fingers under Grace's chin, lifted it, and kissed her, laying his lips firmly against hers. Imo pressed her lips together and nodded, as if she, at least, had finally seen what she came for.

"I'll be back for the last set," Pascal said. "Don't go away."

"Oh," Rita said, "don't you worry. We'll be right here." Then to Grace: "Getting rid of him was the smartest thing you ever did."

Pascal turned around. "She's not rid of me yet."

Rita smiled her sweetest, most innocent smile. "There's plenty of time," she said.

"Less than you think." Pascal blew another kiss to Grace, then followed Imo out.

With Imo gone, Grace's throat opened, and she found herself able to put her body back into the old songs, which seemed now to well up within her, though earlier in the day she wouldn't even have known she remembered them. "I Can

See Clearly Now," sung with an edge of sorrow; some Dylan, some Ian and Sylvia, Cohen's "Bird on a Wire." Whenever she sang well, when her voice sounded fuller the farther it rose up toward the smoky tin ceiling of that old hotel saloon, she knew that what was happening to her was happening at the same time to her audience. We may all be discrete organic systems moved by hearts that, Pascal would have said, shaking his hand as if to flip something sticky off his long fingers, are mere machines for our lives, but for a moment or for an evening everyone in that room could feel the same emotions rise through their chests to their throats like hot air balloons that first filled them and then carried them up and on. Finally, Grace stepped down from the stage into the audience. She sat on a table and strummed and listened to all the other voices rising around her.

Before she got back around to singing "Home, Sweet Home" again to end the evening (this time, an undercurrent of throat, of something less sweet than what the Victorians might have had in mind), she didn't know what or to whom she was singing—to Ralph or to Pascal, stationed as they were now at each end of the bar as if, between the two of them, they were keeping it tacked just where it was; to Imo, who by now had murmured her goodnights to Grandpa's ghost and settled in under her eiderdown with a celebrity magazine; to Rita; to any of Grace's own versions of a childhood or a future in which she glowed in a soft, artificial light, that charm illuminating her way to a Victorian illusion of safety and comfort. Though in the first set she'd been singing the song for Ralph and Imo and to serve her own construction of the past, now she looked over at Pascal at the bar and said, "This is for you, straight from the hypothalamus," and he grinned and laid his hand on his chest.

She let go of the last note, bowed her head, then opened her eyes and looked out into the room, but not at Ralph or Pascal or Rita, just at all those young faces shining at her like too many moons. Then Grace smiled and turned around and walked back up onto the stage to turn off the equipment.

Pascal was there to hand her down, but Ralph said, "Excuse me," with the authority of a man on the job, and, after a second, Pascal stood aside.

Grace gave her guitar to Ralph and said to him, "I'll see you in a minute."

Pascal looked from Grace to Ralph. "Excuse *me*," he said. "I'm trying to talk to my wife. If you wouldn't mind letting me in on things, is this temporary?"

Ralph said, "Not this time. Not on your life."

"Ralph," Grace said again, "I'll see you in a second."

Ralph leaned between Pascal and Grace, gave her a tidy, quick kiss, then slung the guitar over his shoulder and backed up to Rita's table.

Grace said, "Pascal, I don't know. I messed everything up."

He smiled and looked past her at the wall. "It may be you've done exactly right. Though it complicates matters."

This was too much. She looked him in the eye. "You started it."

"That depends on how you look at it. Anyway, no woman but you ever wanted me for good. Certainly not Jemma. But he"—Pascal jerked his head toward Ralph—"isn't just going to fade away."

"Isn't that exactly the point? The question is, What did you want Jemma for? Because I wasn't good enough? Or so I wouldn't want you for good?" This was what Grace had been afraid to say. Now it had slid out. She was almost ready to lean up against Pascal, but she couldn't see clearly through her stubborn pain to what he needed to say for her to put her arms around his neck. On the other hand, it was the first time she'd seen him unsure. She thought she had plenty of time to play this out, to learn her own next lines.

"I wanted to separate action from result," he said.

"You know better than that."

"Apparently you don't," he said. "So I guess we're even."

"How could we be even?" She had her back up against the bar wall, and Pascal leaned over her, his hand on the wall above her shoulder. She could feel his heat down the front of her body. He was looking at her now as he might have at a child who had gone astray.

"Okay," she said. "Say we're even. You've been waiting for this, and I gave it to you."

"I promised never to do it again. How about you?"

"I could."

"Would it change anything?"

"You tell me." She was looking not in his eyes but at the shirt button right at her eye level, the white bleach spots next to it. She lifted her hand and covered them. "Ralph's waiting for me."

He put his hand where her fingers had been on his shirt. "So am I. You have some promises to think about yourself."

For a second, she didn't know which way she'd go. There was still some wall in her she couldn't push through. Not quite. She touched her lips with her finger and raised it to his lips. "Not yet," she said. "I can't. Maybe later."

He grabbed her hand and held it at his chin level. "How much time do you think you've got?" He stood there a second longer, then he dropped her hand and pushed away from the wall, gestured for her to precede him.

She felt the air between them tear. She kept her head down as she turned to go—she was trying hard not to weaken, not to let any tears fall. Testing her own strength, as if something important relied on it.

Then he touched her on the shoulder, and she turned back to him. He said, "I just wondered if I could count on you when I go over." He was smiling, but the edges of the mouth were too still for the smile to be casual.

"Over?"

"It helps if you know someone is waiting. In your own bed,

not someone else's." He jerked his head toward the TV, and she felt her heart yank in her chest as if it were attached to his chin by a thread. "I'm in the reserves," he said, "but it would have taken a while for them to get around to me. So I signed the papers this afternoon. After I left the condo."

"Today?"

"I figure they'll need all the help they can get."

"You're leaving me now? In the middle of all this?"

His head was cocked, but his eyes were soft. "I'd rather have fixed this"—he gestured between his own heart and hers—"without telling you I was going away."

"How did you think you were going to manage that?" Grace closed her eyes and put her hand back on his shirt. She was trying to recover her breath. She could feel his pulse speed up, but it wasn't her touch that did it. It had more to do with where he was going, far away and unimaginable.

She got some air into her lungs and said, "You're going to fight?"

He laughed. "Oh, sure." He flexed his arm. The sleeve over his bicep barely changed shape. "They'll need surgeons." He wrapped his hand around the back of her neck and said, soft, "I can't undo anything. But I can do this. I'd hoped we could be okay before I left."

He had offered her a faulty reason to lay aside her hurt, but he had offered it alongside the right reasons. And her desire to hold on to her hurt was, it seemed to her, equally flawed, equally obscure. This was almost irresistible, coming as it did with the chance to be noble and stalwart in a number of directions at once: to stand by him, tolerant, both with and against her own beliefs; to wait alone for his return, re-creating in her memory an image of him to love, unimpeded by his stubborn, solid presence. She touched his cheek, then she tilted back her head and stood on her toes and kissed him. She recalled their first kiss, a world of meaning withheld, and put its recollected force behind this one. He wrapped his arms around her.

"You old fool," she said, and he bent down and kissed her again. Into his lips, she said, "I thought Rita was the only one who still acted out of belief." In the corner of her eye, she saw Ralph moving toward them. He could really cover ground when he wanted to. "I love you," she said. "But tonight I have something to take care of."

"That's okay. I have a date, too." She put her fist against his stomach, and Pascal smiled and lifted his hat.

"Call me tomorrow," she said.

"You call me."

This was fair. She nodded. She rolled her eyes upward to keep the tears from falling. "I'm such a sucker."

Behind her, he said, "Quite the contrary. You won't believe even what's right in front of you. It's one of the things I've always loved you for."

Grace stayed where she was, leaning against the wall by the stage. Ralph lifted her fingers to his lips. "It had to be done," he said.

"We may be talking about different things here," Grace said. She could still feel Pascal's heat on the palm of the hand Ralph held. "Ralph," she said, "I still don't know how to do this."

"I'll help. You tell him to get lost. You aren't doing him any favors, stringing him along."

Grace started again. "Ralph, we've been friends for a long time. Forever."

Ralph still held her hand against his cheek. He leaned over and looked into her eyes. "Oh, for Chrissake," he said, "I can't believe it." He moved his head, impatient. "Then why did you start this?"

Grace looked down at the floor. "Give me a break. I was

wrong to let it happen. I told you that last night. But I hardly started it."

Ralph wrapped his arms around her shoulders and drew her to him. He put his mouth in her hair and said, "Last night."

"I told you."

His breath was warm against the top of her ear. "You were talking to my mind."

"Now who sounds like a country song?" She couldn't explain to Ralph at the moment, though he held her and looked into her eyes with his most serious expression. "I'm meeting him tomorrow," she said. "That will be that."

"All right, you two." Rita's head appeared over Ralph's shoulder. "Break it up."

"That's exactly what we're doing," Ralph said.

Ralph and Grace moved apart just enough to let Rita in.

"I'm taking you guys dancing," Rita said. She shuffled her feet in a quick waltz, then grabbed Grace by the arm and spun her out into the room. "A little two-step, I think."

CHAPTER 4

■ ■ ■

A Little Two-step

When they'd climbed up the blare of music at the Barb Wire and walked into the smoky, dark room at the top of the stairs, the first thing Grace saw was Pascal bent over a woman sitting at a table. Grace could see only the back of the woman's head, but she recognized the ashy curls. There was a man there too, at least a man's shoulder, just visible beyond Pascal. Grace had known Pascal might be there, and she had already forgiven him for almost anything, but this she wasn't sure about. The woman tilted her head back, laughing at something Pascal had just said. Then he held out his hand and she took it and he pulled her up out of her seat. The band was in full swing, playing a country waltz; there was no sign here, in this room smelling of sweat and beer, that the country was at war, unless it was a sort of tightness under the noise that seemed to pitch everything a little higher than usual for a Wednesday night.

When Pascal turned, he saw Grace watching him. He only smiled, tipped his hat, and gave the woman his arm. Bliss was wearing her black cowboy boots and a black, loosely crocheted minidress with—quite obviously—nothing underneath. Even from a distance, Grace caught a glimpse of nipple through one of the holes in the pattern. Bliss waved at Grace with the tips of her fingers, then they moved away from the table.

Rita said into Grace's ear, "Oh, my. Who is that woman?"

"Forget it," Grace said. "She likes men all too well."

Ralph, also watching Bliss, said, "That's never been something I've been able to predict."

"She ought to be arrested," Grace said, and Rita cocked an eyebrow at her.

Dan stayed at the table, watching Pascal and Bliss through the haze. And others were looking at them, too, Bliss's pale goldenness against Pascal's deep red, her body moving like a clapper inside the bell of dress, both light on their feet on the dance floor. When Pascal lifted Bliss's arm to spin her under, the dress rose so high against her thighs that Rita and Ralph both leaned forward, expectant, lips parted. "Damn," Rita said, when the turn was done. "Not a thing."

Dan glanced back at Grace, and she lifted her fingers in a perfect parody of Bliss and waved, with a flippancy she would later think back on and regret. He pulled a flask from his back pocket and poured from it into his water glass. The Barb Wire was a beer bar. Grace frowned at him.

All night, Pascal and Bliss stayed on the dance floor, where he held her not with polite abstraction but with his most real hands. Bliss leaned into him full body. Grace watched, reminding herself of what Pascal had said earlier in the evening, trying to trust the promises between them. She and Ralph and Rita took turns dancing together in any combination, even one silly three-way waltz in which Rita and Ralph battled for the lead and Grace let them spin her between them, her head turned so a cheek pressed against each of their chests.

At one point, when Pascal had gone to the bar for more beer, Rita asked Bliss for a dance. From a distance, all Grace could see were blond curls shaking side to side, emphatically. Later, she said to Rita, "I told you."

Rita raised one rusty eyebrow. "A girl's gotta try."

When Dan asked Grace for a two-step, his eyes were focused not on hers but on the dance floor behind her. Grace put her hand in his and stepped out with him. He was a good dancer in spite of arms and legs that seemed too long for his body, but he kept steering her close to Pascal and Bliss and bumping her into them, and his grip on her shoulder was tight enough to hurt. When he pulled her near, the gun tucked in the waist of his jeans below his leather vest dug into her ribs, but by now she was used to the idea of it. Every time they bumped, Grace said, "Excuse me," and Pascal nodded and Bliss glared over at Dan.

Dan said in her ear, "Were the stars right, or what?"

"I'd be tempted to blame it on the stars, too. But this looks like your problem, not mine."

"It's hard to tell," he said. "It's only been a few hours."

Out of what she thought of as kindness, she said, "Look, I wouldn't take this too seriously. It's just dancing."

After their dance, Dan returned alone to his own little table and Grace sat back down with Ralph and Rita. Before long she saw Dan drinking right from his flask. Ralph put his pin-striped legs and cowboy boots up on the table and cited the liquor codes Dan was violating, chapter and verse, until the waitress came by and swatted at his toes with a damp rag. Later, Bliss followed Grace into the ladies' room. "Cowgirls," it said on the door, with a silhouette of a woman in a short skirt, boots, and hat, turning a lasso over her head.

Bliss said, "Dan thinks there's something between me and Pascal, but that's not it. I always knew you two would try again."

Grace pulled from her Levi's pocket the lipstick that matched the burgundy mousse still in her hair. "You don't have to tell me." She cocked an eye at Bliss in the mirror. "Though I can hardly blame him. You two seem"—she paused—"comfortable enough with each other."

Bliss leaned toward the mirror with her old familiarity. "He wants me to leave Dan."

Grace stopped her lipstick, held it in midair. "What?"

Bliss paused a beat, long enough to see the panic take Grace's face, before she smiled. "Not for Pascal. He's made that clear enough. For my own good. Dan keeps cracking me open." Bliss touched her lip where Grace had seen the scar under her makeup. "Why do you think I had those miscarriages?"

Grace's stomach turned. Dan had talked about Bliss as if something were wrong with her, as if she couldn't carry a baby to term. As far as Grace could tell, Pascal was talking good sense. She didn't know Dan that well, but he frightened her more the more she thought about him. Bliss's lip, the gun— those were only concrete signs, the ones she could put her finger on. There were others, a sort of tension in his body that felt electrical, explosive. "Aren't you afraid?"

"Some people can't be happy without an edge," Bliss said. "Danger's part of the appeal. If you don't see it, you don't."

"I see it." Grace recapped her lipstick. "Where there's an edge, there's a blade."

"But it's gone way too far. Pascal's protecting me." Bliss met Grace's eyes in the mirror. "I was right. With lipstick, you're a knockout. It's the same face, but without the paint a woman is invisible."

Grace lifted a shoulder. "Speak for yourself."

As the evening wore on, it became more clear: Bliss was enjoying watching Dan sliding down in his chair, his eyes measuring her every spin and turn. Pascal kept leaning into her on the dance floor.

"You're taunting him," Grace said to him during a break. "So much for professional ethics."

"My professional relationship with her is past. I'm just trying to be a friend."

"You think you're being a friend to her? Look at Dan. His knuckles are white as paper. What do you think he's going to use them for when he gets her home?"

"He won't get her home. That's what I'm working on."

"What would you do if social workers started to take up heart surgery?"

Pascal shook his head. "You're talking mortal injury. This is different."

Grace wasn't so sure. If they hadn't been at first, by the end of the night, Bliss and Dan, whom, because of his stringy build, Grace had never quite seen as a moonlight cowboy in spite of the new Tarot, were fighting in bitter earnest. Once, Dan followed Bliss all the way into the Cowgirls' and dragged her out by the arm, flushing a fluttering covey of booted, fringed, and hatted women, but before he could say a word to her Pascal had spun him up against the wall, his lower arm crossways across Dan's shoulders. Grace thought of the gun in Dan's waistband and put her head down on the table.

But Dan raised his hands. "Okay, okay. There's no need for that."

Bliss, still enjoying the show, all the more so because of its serious currents, turned her crocheted back on Dan, put her arm through Pascal's, and walked back toward the dance floor.

Grace leaned back in her chair and addressed herself to her long-necked beer. She felt lightheaded and remembered she still hadn't eaten. She was trying not to pay attention anymore, but she couldn't help glancing toward the dance floor.

When she realized she hadn't been able to spot Pascal, Bliss, or Dan for ten minutes or so, Grace grabbed Rita's sleeve. "Bliss should know better," she said. "Where's Ralph?"

Rita stood up, looked around the room. "Maybe in 'Cowboys.' I'll go in after him, if you want."

"I'm not in the mood for another scene," Grace said.

"I won't do anything to their little weenies."

"Looking at you," Grace said, "they'd never believe it." She peered through the smoke, still looking for a sign of Bliss or Pascal. "I have a bad feeling about this."

The waitress came by in her little fringed skirt and said, "Last call."

Rita dropped a five on her tray. "Honey," she said, "we're out of here."

It took Grace a few minutes to find Pascal in the parking lot's far shadows. He stood next to the open door of his Jaguar, but the dome light illuminated only his side, lining with a gold glow his shoulder in its Levi's jacket and his arm, outstretched as if to take something from somebody's hand. The snow had stopped. Above him, headlights flashed by, but under the freeway girders, just beyond his fingers, it was so dark Grace couldn't see into the shadow, or rather could see only what seemed a deepening of shadow in human shape, maybe more than one shape.

She let go of Rita and put her finger to her lips. Above their heads the freeway whined, and a car backfired, accelerating out of tune. She heard it again, a popping that sounded as if it couldn't hurt anyone. Something flashed in the shadows under the freeway, but so briefly she wasn't sure she'd seen it.

Pascal spun to one side, staggered, and fell to his knees, struggling to stay upright, his hand to his head. His hat lay next to him on the pavement. Between his fingers gushed more blood than Grace would have thought possible. She paused, as if what she was seeing was just an image, flattened on a screen. Then her heart beat once in her throat, and she pushed Rita toward the lit-up pay phone at the Barb Wire's entrance, then took off at a run across the parking lot.

Then Ralph was next to her, saying, "Shit. Where did you guys go?" He took off his suit jacket, stripped off his shirt and gave it to Grace.

"Rita's calling for help," she said. She knelt over Pascal and wrapped the shirt around his head, where the wound bled so heavily she couldn't tell anything about how serious it was. She wiped his forehead with the shirt's sleeve, breathing hard, trying to keep her hands steady, her voice quiet, the way Jemma did around patients. Grace went so far as to wish that Jemma was there. She sat down on the pavement and pulled Pascal's head down into her lap.

He looked up at her and tried to grin. "So this is what it takes."

"Quiet," Ralph said. "Don't talk."

Pascal said, "Don't worry, pal."

Grace picked up Pascal's wrist and held it as if she would know something from feeling where his pulse should have been. "This is temporary," she said. She put her fingers, then her lips to his mouth. "Only until you ruin my jeans. No more promises."

"You don't make much of an angel of mercy." Pascal was struggling to breathe now, air and fluid catching behind the words.

She blinked, trying not to weep. "Count on it." She tried to smile back at him, tried not to let him see how frightened she was, but her lips were shaking. There was blood everywhere; she was sitting in a pool of it and she could taste its salt. There was blood on Pascal's mouth.

Ralph had pulled his suit coat back on over his bare shoulders. He put his fingers on Grace's head, as if he could steady her, but his hand was shaking. "Are you cold?" she asked.

Ralph said, "How is he?"

She dropped Pascal's wrist and shook her head. "I don't know what I'm looking for. There's a pulse, but it seems uneven."

Pascal whispered to her, "That's normal under the circumstances."

"What circumstances? What the hell happened?"

He said to Grace, "Why don't we just forget about it all?"

"This?"

He paused, working to draw enough breath to speak. "The infidelities. Just the ones we've accomplished. Then we can concentrate on more important things. Like our future infidelities." He just managed to lift the corners of his mouth.

Grace looked at him. Was he confessing or accusing? "Is it that simple?"

"It could be."

She didn't believe him, but she didn't have to. She leaned over and kissed him just as the sirens came within earshot. "Don't talk, love," she said. Two police cars pulled up, lights flashing, and the pulse of the ambulance siren broke over them in waves. Rita came up behind Grace and touched her shoulder.

A uniformed officer, very young, Grace thought, looked at the crowd lined up behind Pascal, and at the shirt wrapping his head. It was wet through, red with blood.

Pascal touched the cotton, his hand shaking, and whispered, "Scalp wounds. They bleed."

The officer gave him a blank look.

"I'm a doctor. My pulse"—Pascal made a show of lifting his own wrist the way Grace had—"is a little fast, but no faster than you might expect. I've had a tense evening." The last words were barely audible. Grace had her hands on his chest. She couldn't tell just where all the blood was coming from.

The officer wasn't taking any chances. He said to Grace, "What happened here?"

"I don't know," she said. "I couldn't see. He was standing here, then I heard the shots." The flashing lights were making Grace sick to her stomach. She knew she needed food. She felt suddenly as if she were looking at everything from a great distance. Outside their little circle, a crowd had gathered, mostly drunk, stunned into quiet.

The officer grasped Grace's shoulder. He looked at her blue jeans, soaked with blood. "What happened to you?"

Pascal laughed out loud. "She should have been a doctor herself. She has the heart for it."

She was the only one who knew he was insulting her. "Thanks a lot," she said. His shaky laugh seemed born more of panic than anything else. The paramedics laid Pascal on the gurney and loaded him into the back of the ambulance.

Grace stood up. "I'm going along."

The officer said, "I'm afraid not." Grace tried to pull away, but he still held her by the shoulder.

Ralph came up beside Grace. He held out his hands to the uniform, as if for the cuffs. "Let her go," he said. "She's his wife."

Grace swatted at his outstretched hands. "Ralph, the police don't take hostages."

"Wipe your mouth," he said. "It's covered with blood." She touched her lips with her fingers.

Ralph said to the officer, "She needs to go to the hospital."

The officer looked at Grace's bloody jeans. "Are you hurt?"

She looked down at herself, unsure, then shook her head no. "I feel a little faint." She looked toward the ambulance again. They were fastening Pascal in.

He said, "You're his wife? Do you know what happened?"

"She was with me," Ralph said. "We didn't see anything."

"I saw him fall," Grace corrected. "It was dark." The rest confused her. She was dizzy. She felt Ralph's hand tighten on her arm, a warning. Where had Ralph been? She knew she had to think quickly, when in fact she didn't feel able to think at all.

The officer pushed his hat up by the bill, then pulled it back down over his forehead. He looked about the age of her younger students, but he already seemed more tired even than she did herself. A man in a rumpled suit appeared at the officer's shoulder.

"Look," the rumpled man said. He reached into his suit and pulled out a badge. "I'm Detective Flint. We just need to figure out what the hell happened here."

"I should have seen it coming," Grace said. She held on to Ralph's arm to keep from falling.

Ralph said to Grace, "Shut up." Then, to the detective, "I'm her lawyer. She's not to say anything."

The detective shook his head and looked at Grace sadly. She supposed it was his job to want things as simple as possible. He jerked his head toward the ambulance and said to the officer, "Where's the gun?"

The detective and the uniform huddled in conversation. Grace said to Ralph, "Where were you?"

"Just say I was with you. It will make things simpler. I'll explain later."

"What about Pascal? What about the *law*?" Grace looked into his face, trying to read it.

"Forget the law," Ralph said. "Let's talk about love."

"This conversation makes no sense." Grace steadied herself, then walked away, toward the ambulance. She leaned in and touched Pascal's hair, wet from blood, but he was unconscious now, or unable to respond. She began to climb in beside him, but the paramedic stopped her. "He'll be fine," he said.

She lowered her lips to Pascal's hair, whispered, "I won't be long." Then the officer took her arm and led her to the cruiser. Ralph and Rita followed. The crowd parted to let them by.

The offices in the police station were so ordinary they seemed almost studiedly so: flesh-colored linoleum, flickering fluorescent lights, the utilitarian municipal architecture of the fifties, in which the function of everything was made clear so nobody would be tempted to look for anything frivolous or merely decorative. Grace couldn't tell if the linoleum was that color on purpose, so it wouldn't show dirt, or if it was in fact dirty. In the duty room, a small black-and-white TV was tuned to news, the same images over and over of runways and the flash of bombs. Grace stood and looked for a moment before she remembered what she was seeing. The war now seemed just a fact, and a distant one.

The officer turned them over to the rumpled detective. Under the lights Flint looked as if he'd been sleeping in his clothes when the call came. His shirt was wrinkled, and his necktie was flung around his collar but left untied. He brought coffee for Grace, Ralph, and Rita, then took them one at a time into a bare room with a table to ask them questions. While Grace sat on an orange molded-plastic chair in the hallway and waited for her turn, she thought about Dan's long, nervous fingers, about the gun in his belt, about his dreams of holding his brother's head in his lap. What did such details prove? She didn't know.

This is what she told the tired-eyed detective. "I don't know," she said, when he asked her what had happened.

He leaned toward her over the table. "Look," he said, "I'm sure you want to cooperate. We'll sort it all out. But you understand things don't necessarily look good for any of you."

She lifted her head to look at him. It had never occurred to her to be afraid, in spite of Ralph's posturing. Even now, Flint's voice was gentle. She liked his face, which was narrow and sad, but with the promise of humor playing around its edges, like something you catch out of the corner of your eye.

"I mean, take a look," he said.

Grace didn't need to look. When they'd reached the warmth of the station Ralph had wrapped her in his suit jacket, which hung to her knees, but she could smell Pascal's blood on her, could feel it drying into her jeans, stiffening them to the shape of her legs. Even so, the others sitting lined against the hallways had paid no attention to her, as if it were normal to sit in a dingy police department hallway covered with blood. Another wave of nausea overtook her, and she lowered her head to the desk again, thought of Ralph, no shirt, no jacket, his bare, scarred back livid under the station lights.

Detective Flint said, "You're a college professor. I'm sure this isn't your usual attire."

Grace raised her hand to her glittery maroon hair, lifted her head and shook it. He kept his eyes on hers. She felt he was somehow looking inside her, into her brain. She tried to keep it blank, though she felt his presence in her head as a gentle one, oddly kind. "I must be exhausted," she said, closing her eyes, "but I don't know." She felt herself drifting, though she didn't know for how long. She was warm, and she could smell Pascal's blood.

His voice brought her back. "I don't necessarily think you had anything to do with it. Not necessarily. But you've got to help us out here, you know?"

With difficulty, she opened her eyes and looked at him. "Why wouldn't I help you? He was my husband. I told you. I was with Rita." She paused. Was one witness enough? She closed her eyes again. "And Ralph was around too." It wasn't exactly a lie. Why couldn't she remember? "They'll both tell you that." It was 3 a.m. Grace pressed her fingers to her eyelids. She wanted to know what Ralph and Rita had said; she wanted to sit down with them and construct the evening, to learn what had actually happened, before she said anything more. She waited, her stomach churning, for Detective Flint to close in on her. "Isn't there anything to eat?"

Flint bounced the eraser end of his pencil on the table. "Look. All we need is the facts. Whatever you know. It's the only way to find out. Don't you want that?"

Grace nodded, still silent.

Detective Flint said, "Look, you're a botanist, right?"

Numb, Grace nodded.

"It's like science. All we want to know is the truth."

She wanted to lie down. She wanted to turn back the clock, just three hours, hardly any time at all, but those hours were irrevocable, an untraversable abyss.

"That's what I want, too," she said. "But even in science, truth's not always so simple."

When Grace woke up in the morning, still groggy from the sleeping pill she'd taken from Pascal's medicine cabinet the night before, Rita was standing by the dresser, her arms folded over her chest and the local section of the newspaper in her hand. She shook the paper at Grace and said, "This is what you get when you hang out with cowboys."

Ralph, who had spent the night on Grace's couch, leaned against the bedroom door frame. He had already showered. He had brushed his black hair carefully against his head, and he wore one of Pascal's bathrobes, a jewel-toned paisley that would have looked wonderful on him if he hadn't worn it with such gingerly unease. He snorted. "This is a city, and Pascal's no cowboy." He lifted the hem of the bathrobe as evidence and curtsied clumsily.

"Maybe I was talking about you," Rita said.

After the station and the detective's questions, after they had picked up their cars from the empty Barb Wire parking lot and gone to the hospital and been told by a tired resident with little hope in her eyes that Pascal had been given blood and was resting in Intensive Care, to go home and get some sleep, Ralph had followed Grace back through the snow, thickening again, to her place. It was the second bullet they had to worry about, after all; it had gone in under Pascal's upraised arm and through a lung to lodge next to his heart. There was no use, the resident said, in operating until he was stable. Grace could picture him there, machines humming around him, doing the work of his torn-up body.

Grace had said to Ralph, "Please. I don't even want to try."

"Don't worry. We'll talk about it in the morning," Ralph replied. And he held her until she fell asleep against him; then, apparently, he carried her to bed.

Now, Rita opened the drapes. Squared in the glass was the complete, painfully bright whiteout of blizzard. Rita was still covered with snow from walking through the parking lot to the front door; Grace could see the individual flakes against her black parka, each holding its shape until all at once it melted into water. Rita waved at the bed. "Is this your only revenge?"

"Against whom?" The possibilities multiplied before her. Grace sat up and tucked the sheet under her arms.

"You don't have to hide anything from me." Rita eyed the sheet covering Grace's chest.

Ralph looked from one of them to the other. He put his hand over his eyes and said, "Rita, I spent the night on the couch. Anyway, I thought you were on my side."

Rita looked at Grace. "At the moment, I'm on nobody's side but my own. Don't you think it's time you started making some decisions?"

"Maybe," Grace said. "You aren't the only one to suggest it." Pascal would have laughed to see this. He'd have said, Even your best friends.

Rita wanted to go down to the station and tell Detective Flint exactly what had happened and let him do his job. But as Ralph pointed out, they had already lied.

"I said you were around, which was true," Grace said. "But I can't remember. Where were you exactly?"

"Good question," Rita said. "Not with us."

Grace closed her eyes, tried to reconstruct the evening. "I remember we decided to leave," she said.

Ralph put on his let-me-explain face. "We're dealing with law here. All its intricacies. We have to make plans."

"And whose idea was it to lie in the first place?" Rita said. "And why? You're the one who believes in the system." She snorted.

Grace looked from one of them to the other. Her impatience and exhaustion gave way to tenderness for them both, there with her on this frozen morning. Their bickering had more weight now than usual, but it was still familiar, warming. If not for them, she thought, she would feel as cold as the snowy air beating against the window. "Rita," she said, "we have to stick together."

Ralph said, "The law isn't a matter of simple facts. It's what you do with facts, which are never simple. We have to decide on our angle. You don't know how dangerous this is."

"I know right and wrong," Rita said. "I never liked Pascal, but he's lying up there with a bullet next to his heart."

"I'm your lawyer," Ralph said. "You should take my advice."

"I don't remember hiring you. But I'll make you a cup of coffee anyway. Grace will want to get to the hospital."

Grace looked at her watch. "Shit," she said. "I have a lecture this morning."

"I called your department secretary," Rita said. "A grad student's filling in for you." She walked past Ralph and down the hall toward the kitchen.

While Ralph was getting dressed, Grace showered, then leaned over the kitchen counter in her robe, with her hands around a mug of coffee, while Rita buttered a piece of toast for her. The front page of the paper was there, blazoned with headlines about the Gulf. Grace glanced at them, but she felt no more than a distant curiosity. None of that seemed to have anything to do with her anymore. She nodded at the paper, said to Rita, "I thought you didn't believe there was real justice in this country."

"You don't get it. That's what I have to believe. It may not always work, but it's all we've got." She put her elbows on the counter, wrapped her hands around Grace's on the mug. "I wonder what Ralph knows that we don't?"

"Rita. Don't start this. We have to stick together." Grace freed a hand and bit into the toast. "I didn't realize how hungry I was."

"There are people whose job it is to figure it all out. You can't protect him."

Grace swallowed, took another bite of toast. She said softly, "I would protect you."

The phone rang. At that moment, Pascal was still alive, but he would not last long enough for Grace to pull on a sweatshirt and jeans and let Rita drive her and Ralph through the abandoned, snow-filled streets to the hospital.

Grace recognized the doctor on duty only slightly from Christmas parties and hospital picnics, but it was enough. He took both her hands. His name tag said "Dr. Craig Mills." The name suited. He was young, just out of his residency, and looked as if he scrubbed his very white face several times a day. He told her some people pull through things that look impossible. But not Pascal. That morning—he raised his hands, shrugging—Pascal's heart had gone haywire, into fibrillation, then given up. A chaotic motion. Myocardial infarction. It was no surprise. Even one bullet, he told her, could do a lot of damage. Shock would implicate the whole system.

Though Pascal was more than a decade older than she was, Grace had never imagined the world without him, had, in spite of their trouble, thought she would have years with him before she'd have to consider the possibility of this kind of loss. Now, she had a vision of him leaning over her potting table, scoring larkspur seeds for her one by one with a razor blade, his movements almost magically precise, economical, his concentration complete. There must have been somebody he could have trusted to have used that kind of care on him. He had chosen Grace. "Lord help him," she said.

To Craig Mills, Grace said, "Thank you." He kept her hands. She wanted, suddenly, to confess how she had failed Pascal, but she just let him squeeze her fingers once more before she detached herself.

"He was planning to go to the Gulf," she said. "And he gets shot down in a parking lot."

Craig Mills shook his head. "Not with that heart, he wasn't. There was weakness there. It might not have emerged for years, not without some trauma, but it was definitely there. They would have spotted it when he took the physical."

Pascal hadn't liked to go to the doctor, hadn't gone in for years.

Dr. Mills asked if she wanted to see him. Grace took a second to compose her face, which had fallen into little uncontrolled convulsions around the mouth, like sobs centered there instead of in her chest. If she didn't look at him now, she would never believe in his death.

She stood at the doorway to Pascal's room. The doctor went in alone and pulled down the sheet, then he left. Someone had closed Pascal's eyes, but his mouth was still open in a grimace that looked too much like pain. Though his face had been wiped clean, a crust of brown blood lined his forehead and matted his hair. His skin already had that gray, emptied-out look Grace remembered from the embalming. Without his heart to keep it moving, his blood, what was left of it, must be pooling along his backside. She walked into the room, pulled the visitor's chair over to his bedside, sat down, and laid her head on his chest. Silence. As if some essential pulse had vanished from the universe.

She closed her eyes and said, "'Bye, Joe."

Craig Mills said from the doorway, "I want to know if you will be all right."

Grace lifted her head. "Thank you. I've seen enough."

The doctor took Grace back out to the waiting area, where Rita and Ralph sat, uneasily turned away from each other, shoulder to shoulder. Rita went to the cafeteria to get everyone coffee. There was a big window at one end of the room, and the glare of the storm filled the area. Ralph opened his arms, and Grace walked into them and put her head on his shoulder. When Rita came back, she put down the coffee and wrapped her arms around both of them, and they stood, lit by the storm, swaying in rhythm to Grace's sobs.

During the rest of that week while Grace waited for the police to release Pascal's body for burial, the world stayed frozen. In spite of the earlier thaw, this was turning, day by day, storm after storm, into one of the worst winters on record, and Grace moved through the weather slowly, as if a sudden motion would shatter everything—the sleeves of ice and what they encased, her own heart. At the police station, which Grace entered with Rita and Ralph holding either hand, Detective Flint was gentle with her under the flickering lights, and she told him about Pascal and herself, about Dan and Bliss, the Tarot, the gun on the table, the two-step.

She was still less clear about the actual shooting, that moment in which some details, the whine of traffic and the orange cast of the light over the parking lot, were so clear she believed she would never stop seeing them in her sleep, and other details would not fall into place. When she closed her eyes, she could see Ralph standing there next to her, next to Rita, and she could no longer say for sure, even to herself, if he'd left the building with them or not, if she had heard his shout when the shots rang out. The invented version had entered her imagination as if it had happened. She didn't remember being without him. But a member of the band, Flint told her, had seen Rita and Grace leave together, had thought of following them because they were, in Flint's word, "unescorted," and while she sat at the flesh-colored table in the flesh-colored room, Detective Flint pushed at her. Grace felt sorry for him, for his faded eyes and the weariness in the lines around them. If his face had had a different shape altogether, she might have called the same wrinkles laugh lines, but the pull of gravity was too clear.

She said, "He must have been mistaken."

"He seemed to recall you very clearly," Flint said. "You and

Rita make a pretty distinctive pair." His hands were folded, a fist inside a fist, on the table in front of him. He wore a plain gold band, and Grace wondered if he went home every night to children, a woman who looked out into the snow whenever he was late, worrying, and who took his coat to hang it up for him in the simplest gesture of love when he finally got home. Grace hoped so.

"He must have been waiting for us in the foyer then. I'm sorry; I just don't remember."

Flint changed the subject again. "Okay. After the shooting. You were sitting on the pavement with Pascal's head in your lap."

Grace nodded. Of this she was sure. She still had the jeans to prove it, lying on the floor of the laundry room at the condo. She had no idea what to do with them. They would never wash clean, and she couldn't yet bring herself to throw them out.

"You didn't ask him who shot him?"

"I asked what happened. But he seemed to think there were more important things to say." At this moment, she realized he must have known he was dying, and the tears welled up. And then, she told Flint through the thickness in her throat, they had thought he shouldn't talk.

"Who thought so?" Flint was still speaking softly, still trying to be patient, but Grace noticed that he'd begun to bounce the eraser end of his pencil on the table again.

She considered. Had it been Ralph who had told her to keep Pascal quiet? "We all thought so," she said. "We told him not to speak."

"But he did speak."

"Personal things. I told you, we'd been having trouble. He told me"—Grace looked at the fleshy wall over Flint's stooped shoulder and blinked—"he loved me. He wanted to put every-thing behind us."

"What everything?"

Grace blinked again, kept her eyes on the wall. "I told you, we'd had some trouble."

"Like?"

"He'd been sleeping around."

"And you?"

Grace lowered her eyes to Flint's faded gray ones. "Me too. The night before, for revenge, I'd slept with Ralph."

Flint's pencil was still. He kept her eyes. "I see. And Ralph was content to be your revenge?"

Grace glanced away, then back. "Not exactly."

He dropped his eyes to his pencil. "I don't imagine. And where was Ralph just before the shooting?"

She remembered Ralph had taken off his shirt to bind Pascal's head, an act of tenderness. She knew she was wrong not to push herself harder, beyond the story fixed in her mind. She was starting to wonder if she was helping Ralph this way, or only focusing attention on him. But she'd made up her mind: Dan had shot Pascal, and Ralph was the one who could help her. She let those facts obscure the smaller details, the smaller doubts, because she didn't have the strength to ask questions, much less answer them. She let her mind drain, her body drain, into the blankness that surrounded her. It was a relief.

She said, "As far as I can remember, Ralph was with me."

Ralph called Friday morning to make sure she was up before he came by to drink coffee with her, but he didn't try to touch her. He drove her to campus, waited outside while she stood in front of her students, clutching last year's notes, trying to put together the words. Her students sat before her quietly, turned in their lab reports in silence, whispered their questions. Ralph never said anything about where he was in that ten minutes before Rita and Grace walked out to the parking lot, and she didn't ask. She let his imagined presence next to her continue to grow, to take solid hold in her brain.

Nor did Rita touch Grace, though she was there all the time, producing cups of coffee or bouillon steadily all morning until lunchtime. Starting in the afternoon when, though it hadn't stopped snowing all week, Rita would look at the ceiling and declare the sun to be over the yardarm, she switched Grace to shots of bourbon. At times Grace was tempted to throw herself at either of them, to dissolve into somebody's arms and weep, but she didn't know whose. With all her old instincts, she suspected a sharp, firm touch might bring her back into a world she could recognize, if only briefly. But Ralph and she were standing on a middle ground made even less certain than usual, and Rita would have said to Grace, "If it's guilt or grief instead of love, I don't want it." She would have been right.

So on Sunday morning, the day before the funeral, when Detective Flint dropped by the condo, carrying his coat and a paper sack, they were all three there, surrounded by a *New York Times* they had unenthusiastically dismantled but, unable to concentrate on the intricacies of Persian Gulf attack and counterattack, not read, and by the usual crumbs and debris of bagels and coffee. Flint accepted a raisin bagel and went to work on the cream cheese with the first real vigor Grace had seen in him.

After he'd taken a bite, he leaned back in his chair and said, "We have a problem. I don't mind telling you." He looked around the table at their faces, Rita's structurally cheerful expression creased by worry and the tiredness they all felt, Ralph's eyes as steady and impassive as a lawyer's in the courtroom. Grace felt pale and bruised, as if from the inside. "We've got Dan's .45," Flint said. "He let us search the house, and we found it." He looked at the bagel. "Among others."

"So what's the trouble?" Rita asked.

"The trouble is, it isn't the gun that killed Pascal. For one thing, it hasn't been fired in a while." Flint licked a dab of cream cheese off his finger. "You might be able to help us sort this out. Maybe you can tell me if this is the gun he had with him that night." He opened the paper sack and lifted out a clear Ziploc bag containing a handgun. He laid it on the table.

Grace looked at it. She couldn't say it was the one he'd had at the Barb Wire, the one she'd felt against her ribs while they'd danced. But it was a Colt, the same make and color as the one he'd had in the Hole-in-the-Wall.

Ralph agreed. "But that doesn't necessarily mean anything, does it?" he asked.

"That's right," Grace said. "How do you know he doesn't have two of those?"

"We don't know. It was the only .45 we found in the house, and it's the only one registered to Dan. But we don't imagine he would keep a murder weapon around for us to find."

"Still," Rita said slowly, "if this is the same gun, it was your primary basis for suspecting him."

"I don't get it," Grace said. "There are plenty of those around. Pascal owned one himself. He took it out of the condo that very evening."

Flint sat up straight, his mouth full of bagel. "Why didn't you tell me before?" he said around the cream cheese.

"I didn't think of it," Grace said.

He swallowed. "You can see how this might complicate things for us, can't you?"

Grace and Ralph and Rita looked at each other. "What about motive?" Rita said.

"There are others with motive," Flint said.

Rita looked around the table. "Yes," she said. "That's what I meant."

CHAPTER 5

■ ■ ■

Working on the Dead

Rita and Grace leaned on the wall across from the mortuary and looked out over the valley. Everyone else had squeezed Grace's shoulder or hugged her and then gone, as if she'd stuck by her husband until the bitter end. The only one who hadn't come to the funeral was her grandmother, who had said, when Grace told her Pascal was dead, "Don't worry, dear. They usually come back, if you forgive them," and who had told Grace she was always welcome to move back home with her in the meantime. The view was sharp and cold and painful: there was still a thin sliver of sunlight on the peaks of the mountains, but the wind was gusting hard enough that they held their skirts against their thighs, and, toward the west, where the sun was going down and the storm was coming in fast, clouds pulled their snow like a blowing curtain over the lake.

The hillside fell away in a white sweep blown smooth and

brittle. The cemetery staff had chipped out paths to the new grave, opened in the refrozen ground by power drills and saws. Below where she and Rita stood, mourners of a different tragedy, clutching themselves against the freezing wind, followed a coffin down, and the bearers set it over a newly cut grave, in the apparatus for lowering it into the earth. Its bronze top was obscured by an enormous wreath of yellow and copper chrysanthemums. The leaves were already turning black from the cold.

Grace hadn't been able to stand the idea of feeding Pascal into the fire; though he had never said he wanted to be cremated and there was nothing about it in the will that his lawyer had recovered from the safe deposit box, she felt this as her failure. She had considered, briefly, scattering his ashes over the ruined, sacred pool of Chichén Itzá, where they had spent their honeymoon, to mingle with the remains of sacrificial virgins, but she was tired of ironic gestures, wanted instead to see him lying back against satin cushions, made up and peaceful, his mouth stitched into the slightest smile.

All of which Rita had taken care of with her own large, oddly precise hands. After the police had finished with Pascal, after the autopsy, after the hospital had removed what remained of his heart for its medical students to cut into to see what heartsickness looks like, Rita had picked up his body in the hearse and brought it back to the mortuary. She mended his flesh and painted him, brought Grace headstone designs to look at; she suggested the plain oak coffin.

Pascal once said to Grace, "When it comes to the action of the heart, nuance is everything." Grace almost turned to Rita at that moment to say she'd changed her mind. About what? It was too late. She whispered to herself, "Corpse," and Rita put her arm around Grace's shoulders.

"What did you call him?" Grace asked.

Rita looked away. "The ones you know are the hardest."

"It's spreading." Grace meant the cold in her stomach. "I think I'm going to throw up."

Rita put her hand under Grace's elbow and said, low, in her ear, "If you're going to be sick anyway, you might as well tie one on."

Ralph had gone to get the Jeep, and now he pulled in next to them and opened the car door for them to climb in. Grace turned her back on the view and said, "Ralph." Dry, heated air gusted out the open door over the static from the radio. Grace could tell just from the announcer's tone of voice, a mix of deep seriousness and high-pitched excitement, that he was talking about the war. She felt as if she were looking at everything through water. She wondered which of the frozen trees had lost buds started by the too early warm spell. She couldn't keep her mind from wandering to objects other than the pertinent one, which she forced her thoughts back to in-termittently, pressing at it like a bruise to see if it was still true, if it still hurt. The night before, she had dreamed that all the gardens of the city had opened into bloom, with a kill-ing frost, the last half of winter, still to come. She had stood in her old yard with a pitchfork and a truckload of straw mulch, knowing that no matter how deeply she covered the flowers over there was nothing she could save.

Rita said to Ralph, "Grace will stay here with me."

"You going to hang out?"

"Yeah," Grace said. She wanted to sit between the two of them the way she had in high school, comfortable and un-shaped by anyone's hands but Imo's.

But Rita said, "I'm going to put Grace to bed." She squeezed Grace's hand, an old signal.

Now Grace looked at Ralph's face above the stiff white col-lar of his shirt, and she thought, Maybe it's for the best, and kept quiet. She hadn't learned to be angry at him; but now, in the lethargy brought on by sorrow, she thought if they couldn't offer each other what they wanted, maybe they should offer nothing at all. The blizzard had started up again in a sudden gust of white wind.

Rita, still preoccupied by the details of her craft, said,

"Thank goodness it stopped snowing long enough to get him into the ground." She put a gloved hand on Grace's shoulder, kicked off a shoe, and rubbed her toes with the other hand.

"Rita, for Chrissake," Ralph said.

"It's okay." Grace liked this ordinariness, that death could be routine.

Rita pressed her fingertips to her forehead and said to Ralph, "Oh, shove it. It's my job."

Grace had been shivering, had been so cold it felt as if her toes were iced together, when she and Rita stepped into Rita's house attached to the mortuary, so Rita turned the thermostat up to 75 degrees and lit the gas fire in front of the couch. Now the open curtains revealed a white sky. It looked as if it could snow for weeks.

They sat on Rita's white couch in their black wool dresses—Rita's one of many she had for funerals, what she called her "dress for success" wardrobe; Grace's bought for university parties and other somber gatherings. Rita leaned over to slice a lime on the cutting board she'd set on a stack of *Vogue* and *Sports Illustrated* on the coffee table. The swimsuit issue was on top, on its cover a lithe, big-breasted woman with her back promisingly arched. The point was not the swimsuit, which looked as if it would fall away at the slightest breeze. Grace tapped it and said, "Where are your politics?" Rita rested her fingertips next to Grace's on the woman's tanned stomach.

They had both kicked off their low-heeled black shoes. Having dispensed with the relative if not entirely sober gentility of the past five days, they were drinking tequila straight from the bottle. Rita fed Wendy canned dog food by hand, scooping two fingers into the can and holding them out for the dog to lick. It was the only way Wendy would eat, whether out of love or out of revenge Grace didn't know. Rita had pulled the pins from the coil of red hair on her neck, and the loosening bun was hanging lopsided over her shoulder. Grace reached over and tugged at the coil until it unraveled down the front of Rita's dress.

"How do you feel?" Rita asked.

Grace's chest felt tight. "I missed my paper deadline," she said. "At least I managed to teach my Friday class. I don't remember what I said, but I must have said something." She handed over the bottle, and Rita put down the knife and took it. Grace got up and grabbed the afghan off Rita's pioneer grandmother's ladder-back chair, then brought it back and put it over both their laps. Rita was shaking her head, her lips pursed from a bite of lime. Wendy pawed her knee, and Rita gave her another fingerful of food.

It would be a while before Grace knew what to say to anyone. "I thought you were used to this," she said after a moment.

"Usually I'm great with the abandoned." In the light from the snow, Rita's eyes were the palest imaginable green. She pursed her lips again, recollecting the sourness of the lime. "I still wonder how I ended up here. It's harder when you know them, even just."

"Like you said. Not just another Joe." They looked at each other. They both started to laugh, then to cough. They had to wipe tears from their cheeks with the backs of their hands, but Grace kept gulping after Rita had stopped. Wendy whined, laid her head on Grace's knee.

"I'm usually efficient with the bereaved," Rita said. "With you, I feel helpless." She handed Grace the tissues. "Now I know why doctors don't treat their own families."

"You'd think I'd be done with this. I cried for three days when he left."

"You mean when you kicked him out. But you never gave him up." Rita was looking not at Grace but at the window, its maelstrom of white on white. With her head still turned away, she said, "You're getting thin."

"I'm always thin."

Rita held her arm up to Grace's. Her wrist was winter-pale but substantial, the forearm under the black wool firm and muscled. It was true: next to hers, Grace's arm looked like a miniature, like a doll's arm, fragile—as if it had been whittled out of a substantial block, until it had become attenuated to this. "All our lives," Rita said, "I've wondered how you don't just break."

"I'm getting old, is all," Grace said. She really felt it that day, for the first time since she was a child and knew once and for all that she would be alone. She had resigned herself, perhaps too thoroughly. She blew her nose and said, "I don't know what I'm going to do."

Rita patted her own thigh. "According to the experts, you have exactly six months to feel sorry for yourself. So come here."

Grace lifted Wendy's head from her legs and stretched out, her head on Rita's lap. It smelled like her mother's lap, and like Imo's, but with the faint overlay of Rita's perfume, an Oriental overtone, more sophisticated than patchouli.

"You're too spicy for an undertaker," Grace said. Rita spread the afghan over her. Grace sat up for one more shot of tequila, then she lay back down with her cheek against the swell of Rita's stomach, and while Rita stroked her lips and cheeks Grace cleared her mind until all she saw behind her eyes was the white swirl of the blizzard, and then, at last, blackness.

When she woke up, it was dark in the room, the only light coming down a short hall from the kitchen. Rita's grandmother's afghan was still tucked around her, and there was a needlepoint pillow under her head. Next to the couch, stretched out on a Persian rug just her size, Wendy snored gently. On the white kitchen counter Rita had left a carafe of coffee and a note: "Gone for Chinese. Back in a flash."

Grace showered and put on Rita's purple bathrobe, which was hanging on a hook on the bathroom door. It, too, smelled of Rita's perfume, deep and rich. A good five inches of its hem dragged on the carpet. Grace thought, Aren't redheads supposed to avoid purple? Another too general rule. Rita was stunning in purple, against which her skin turned a soft gold. Grace was trying not to think about the place in her gut that was half numbness, half ache, as if she'd had something removed and the anesthetic was starting to wear off. The absence was physical, visceral. There was nothing she had done or said that could be remedied, no new touch she could try on Pascal that might work. Still, she felt him the way she would a limb that had been removed, its ghost still stretching when she stretched, cramping when she sat too long.

Grace carried the hairbrush back into the bedroom, Wendy now ticking along beside her, and set it down by the phone. She lifted the receiver and dialed Pascal's cabin. At the click, she pulled in her breath. It was the machine. His own voice repeated the number, normal, as if he really would walk through his door in an hour and push the button for messages, would stand there with his right hand behind his neck and his head cocked toward the little electronic voice, talking back to it. Grace hung up the phone, hit redial, listened again. After the beep, she said, "Call me."

She pulled the tangle of red hairs out of Rita's brush and used it. Then she set it on the bureau and opened the top drawer, looking for a pair of the thick wool socks Rita always wore skiing. In the drawer were scarves and evening purses and jewelry still in the velvet jeweler's boxes. Where did Rita wear this stuff? Grace had never seen it. The middle drawer held lace slips and camisoles and a little pile of garter belts. Grace held one up, then another. Both were exactly the same as the belts she owned, which Pascal had ordered from the Victoria's Secret catalog in all the jewel colors over the brief course of their marriage. In the pile right next to them were

Rita's matching bras and the merry widows, bright silks and lace and chiffon and even crushed velvet. All just like Grace's but bigger, larger than her life.

Even if she hadn't had warm socks as an excuse, Grace would have kept going, like Goldilocks testing each chair and bed in turn. In the bottom drawer, next to the socks, was a little pile of black bikini Jockey shorts like those Pascal wore, like the ones Grace still had in her own top drawer. She picked them up and held them to the light. They were stretched and worn, the fabric slightly thinner, in exactly the same spot Pascal's always were. Grace put them down, seeing now what she had refused to see months before.

She wanted physical evidence, something of his actual body. She took the tangle of red hair out of the trash and went back into the bathroom. She looked in the medicine cabinet for Rita's tweezers, then she laid the nest on the counter and started to pull at it. Her vision seemed to her preternaturally sharp, her concentration absolute. She separated out three short, dark-red hairs from Rita's extravagant, tawny ones. Rita had always had the kind of hair Grace herself loved to dig her fingers into. The shorter hairs she lined up together on the vanity; she dropped the tangle into the wastebasket under the sink. She leaned over the toilet, finally, and threw up. Then she went back into the bedroom and took out one of the garter belts, a deep-green silk one, a matching bra, and a pair of Rita's good, thick socks, and she put them on under the trailing purple bathrobe.

By the time Rita got back with the Chinese food, Grace had found the Pepto-Bismol. She was half through the coffee and hard into the tequila again. Rita grinned when she saw Grace on the couch, bottle in one hand, coffee mug in the other, Pepto-Bismol on the coffee table. From the long liquor store sack she had in her oversized purse, she pulled out another fifth.

"I'm getting a vision for a whole new funeral," she said.

"You're just reviving the old-fashioned wake. A return to traditional values."

Rita put down the sack on the table and started unloading cardboard cartons. They said, in red, "Long Life Vegi House." Rita touched the cartons one by one. "Eggplant with garlic. Fake chicken with cashews. Broccoli tofu. Egg rolls."

"You don't know what I've been thinking," Grace said. She walked over, reached up, put her arms around Rita's neck, and buried her face in Rita's shoulder. She needed Rita's warm body next to her, that kind of comfort, without what was about to come between them. Rita had an egg roll in each hand, but she crossed her wrists around Grace's back and started to sway. Then, when Grace was ready, she said, "Come here." She pulled away and led Rita down the hall into the bathroom.

Grace showed Rita the three short red hairs lined up on the counter, the knot of long ones in the wastebasket. She opened the bathrobe. The bra sagged open over Grace's small breasts; the garter belt hung on the very widest part of her hips.

"Oh, darling." Rita laid the egg rolls on the edge of the vanity beside the hairs and put her arms around Grace again, this time in earnest. They were both crying.

"Why do I have to see him everywhere?" Grace asked, and Rita said, "I'm sorry. I forgot." She put her lips on the top of Grace's head, stroked up and down Grace's back. "It's been over," she said. "I promise."

Grace raised her face, but she couldn't bring herself to let go of Rita. "I can't believe you would do this. You didn't even like each other."

"That had nothing to do with it. He came to me to talk about you."

Grace put her fingers flat against Rita's lips and pushed. She wanted to hurt, to draw blood. "I don't see how the rest follows."

"Look," Rita said, hooking her finger in the satin bra Grace was wearing. "He only bought me what you already had. It was a way of making you solid."

"Excuse me." Grace swept her hands down her body. "This *is* solid. Not as solid as you are, maybe, but nonetheless." She wanted to ask what Rita's stake had been, but she was afraid. Whatever might be lost between herself and Rita, she couldn't bear right now to lose the rest, firm and warm in front of her. Grace said, "You told him about you and me?"

"He already knew." Rita's finger was still hooked into the front of the bra. Grace pushed her fingers harder against Rita's mouth. Rita opened her lips, and her tongue moved against Grace's fingertips. Then Grace, half with revenge on her mind, half for comfort, raised up on tiptoe, tilted her head back, and shut her eyes.

It was Rita who stopped, who first closed her mouth to Grace and then stepped away, out of reach. "Not like this," she said, shaking her head.

Grace, dazed, sat down on the floor and buried her face in the purple folds of the robe. Rita was right. Grace didn't want it either. Sobs rose in her, moved through her like little storm fronts. She said, choking, "You were always the one who was good."

"Darling," Rita said, "we are none of us as good as we should be."

Grace taught her Tuesday classes, but otherwise she spent the next two days in Rita's bed—they slept and listened to Lyle Lovett and k.d. lang and played their extravagant childhood gin rummy game and looked through photograph albums and yearbooks from high school. Grace thought occasionally about reaching out her hand, but she never did. Then, on Wednesday night, Rita walked her into the Hole-in-the-Wall. Grace had her guitar just as usual, but there was already another band up on stage, four big guys in cowboy hats warming up for the first set. Grace had seen them around. She could feel the thrum of their bass like a reliable pulse behind her eyes.

Ralph got up from his bar stool and came over to meet them. He didn't look at Rita at all, just took Grace into his arms. Into her hair, he said, "I tried to call. You were always sleeping." Then, "You smell like a distillery." Grace stepped back, grabbed his wrist for stability. He held her by the shoulders and looked her over. She was trying to look straight back, not to cry or go belly-up, though for the last week she'd felt always on the imprecise edge of dissolution.

"I hate it when you cry," he said.

Grace said, "That's what men always say," though Pascal never had.

Ralph took her guitar. "I'm sorry. I thought you'd want to take some time off."

"She thinks she needs to keep things normal," Rita said.

"Like a pint of tequila a day is normal?" he said. Then to Grace, "I should tell you. That set you played last week—it really struck a chord, as it were." He tested a smile on her. "People have been asking when you're singing again. But I don't want to push you."

Grace was silent. She knew she couldn't sing those songs again, not right away.

Ralph shrugged. "How about a warm-up set? See how it goes."

Grace nodded. Ralph went over to talk to the guys up on stage, and they waved at Grace, then started unplugging their guitars. Rita took Grace to the ladies'. There was a poster for Cowdaddies on the door: a cowboy couple, the man's arm around the woman's waist, dancing off a moonlit butte and into a sky full of stars. "That's what I want," Grace said.

"Don't forget about gravity," Rita said.

"Gravity is exactly what I want to forget."

In the bathroom, they stood with two very young women in front of the mirror. Rita laid Grace's makeup out on the counter. The young women wore all black, and each was putting on yet another layer of black mascara. Though their makeup was pale on their cheeks, dark enough around the eyes perhaps to fool people their own age, they couldn't hide from anyone older that they weren't weary with experience after all. The circles around Grace's eyes, on the other hand, looked exactly as real as they were. She was wearing an authentic beaded belt she'd bought for two dollars at Little America, Wyoming, in 1977, when these two were in grade school.

Rita smiled and winked at the others in the mirror, then went to work on Grace's face. When she was finished, Grace looked something like the younger women—as if she were trying to hide the kind of pink glow she got from a good day of skiing.

"You learn a lot of tricks from working on dead people," Rita said, and the two young women stopped their teasing and spraying and stared at Rita in the mirror. Rita smiled back.

Grace sprayed her hair with glitter and ran a comb through it, then she tuned up in the office and carried her guitar onto the stage. The lights felt good the way a hot shower does on a cold day, and for a second she shut her eyes and felt the heat entering her body. She hooked the guitar around her neck and started to play the opening chords for "Sioux City Sue."

She said into the mike, "This is a variation on Willie Nelson's variation." She played the opening chords again, then again. She opened her mouth, shut it, opened it. The words— "I'd swap my horse and dog for you"—hummed through her brain, and she was trying, but nothing would come out. There was something between her and her voice, a thin membrane keeping her from it, though not at her throat where her voice would usually catch—her throat was as open as a bird's. Something had emptied from her sinuses through her chest, and all the way down to the bottom of her pelvis she could feel only cold, closed space. She opened her mouth one more time, then she stopped playing, unhooked her guitar, and walked off the stage.

Ralph offered to take her home, but Grace shook her head. She handed him the guitar and walked past him, past Rita, out the door into the blizzard.

Grandma Imo opened her front door and looked at Grace, shivering on the porch, white with snow, her cowboy boots soaked through and her jeans wet from where she'd fallen, trying to climb through drifts on the boots' slick heels. It was three miles from downtown to Imo's house; Grace's feet were blistered and numb with cold.

"You don't ever have to ring," Imo said. "I knew you were coming." She held her arms open. Grace didn't even shake the snow off her hair and coat. She made herself as small as she could, walked into Imo's arms, and stood there, rocking, her head on Imo's shoulder, until Imo said, "Shut the door, dear. We'll both catch our deaths."

In the morning Rita brought Grace's clothes and all the books on the list Grace had given to Imo. Rita gestured Grace back inside. She unloaded the back of the Range Rover herself in the blizzard and set the boxes and suitcases down in the front hall.

"I don't know about this," she said.

"I need a little time," Grace said.

"You can't go back."

Grace knew this. She just wanted to pretend for a while. Imo came up from behind and put her hand on Grace's shoulder. She said, "Why don't you lie down, Gracie?" Ice cracked the air between Rita and Imo, and Grace was right in the fractured middle.

Rita reached over and took Grace's hand. When she felt how cold it was, she lifted it to her lips and blew on the fingers. "Call," she said.

Grace said, "You know I'm not going anywhere."

"That's exactly what I'm afraid of," Rita said.

PART TWO

■ ■ ■

Still Life, With Grace

CHAPTER 6

■ ■ ■

With Someone Like You

When she wants to, Imo forgets her own beginnings—her father's little family store, her own frail, blond good looks, her older brother's death from gas in World War I, her run from her father's dingy little small-town grocery to California and the moment, only weeks later, when she looked up from the head she was shampooing in an upscale Hollywood salon and met in the mirror the eyes of a producer, who said, as if in self-parody, "You ought to be in pictures." This was the studio version, and Imo had never denied it.

"I gave it all up for your grandfather," Imo says now, though Grace knows the movies—the long hours under hot lights—never did live up to Imo's ideal of romance. Neither did marriage: while Grace's grandfather went exploring for oil in the forests of Asia and South America, he left Imo behind in the cities to clink champagne glasses with dull diplomats and the minor royalty of vanished principalities, in whose fragile marriages she found wicked entertainment, at least until the birth of Julia, who enraptured her from the beginning. Now she lives in a house on a hill, bigger than any her mother ever dusted; she has a service coming in twice a week to polish the furniture and the silver and keep cobwebs from growing in the corners.

Meeting her, Pascal bent over her hand with the same gentleness with which he had first taken Grace's, but with, Grace assumed, none of the precisely placed pressures that had traveled through her body instantly. Although who knows: Imo blushed and looked around, saying, "Where do you think your grandfather's got to now, Grace?" It was still less than a year since they'd buried him, the man with the white hair and narrow nose who had taught Grace and Rita to dance in the lamplight of the living room.

Pascal, to whom Grace had explained everything, bent down to take Imo's arm through his and said, with even more of Texas in his voice than usual, "Let's wait for him in your kitchen, shall we? Grace says you're liable to have a cup of tea to give us."

She beamed back up at him, her pretty little face flushed. Grace rolled her eyes at Pascal when Imo wasn't looking, though a blossoming of love made her want to put her arms around him. She was beginning to realize that this side of Pascal was authentic, a contradiction but not created for the moment. She followed the two of them—Imo talking up at Pascal in her near whisper and Pascal lowering his head deferentially, tenderly down to hers—toward the back of the house.

Later he said to Grace, running one finger down her breastbone, "She's got years, that old bird. It's just as well she keeps him with her." Grace had never thought of it that way and was surprised at him. They were still at that stage when all responses were erotic, and she took his finger and kissed it and then, keeping his finger in her mouth, brought her lips up against his.

Imo says now, as if it explains everything, "After all, Gracie, he saw death every day." His scalpel cutting into a patient's muscled heart might either have held the end off or have brought it right down to enter the flesh that had been given with such desperate faith into his hands.

"They only trusted him because they had to," Grace says. But she really wants Imo to keep going, to tell her all the good things, the mythic things, about Pascal. She imagines herself and Imo, suspended in that house, re-creating the beloved past. Come back to her grandmother's house to grieve, all Grace wants is to sleep. She thinks about it during the day, while she teaches and grades lab reports, while she eats her supper—that moment when she can climb the stairs to her old childhood room and close her eyes and drift. If she's careful, she can block out the visions of silver cylinders falling, her stomach dropping with them as if she, too, were floating with such apparent lightness toward the occupied houses below, toward women huddled with their children in basements, in bathtubs. She concentrates, until behind her eyes she can see only the high country—Ralph's family ranch, the whole bowl of that little valley going gold under Indian summer, the sky deepening its blue. If she reached out her hand, the ranch would be hers, and with it Ralph, his fists closed tight around whatever bothered him. She could slide so easily into that life, into the past, leaving behind all questions of passion or of will.

Around her now, the city is crystallized, sheeted in ice, and the mountains circle it, also frozen, serrated and remote as knives. Their peaks seem impassable—the freeway drifts over, and airplanes, their wings iced, hesitate and descend. The passengers lie down in the snow and go to sleep. Under the snow, Grace tells herself, plants are already swelling, their roots spreading like hairline fractures through the soil.

Usually at this time, she can't wait to get her hands into the dirt, but when she looks out she sees only what the cold has frozen into place.

Imo clicks her fingers in front of Grace's face and says, "Snap out of it."

"You're one to talk," Grace says, but Imo just grins.

Grace goes out only to teach her classes. She's a good teacher: meticulous, attentive, coming up even now with occasional mild plant jokes, easy puns on "root" and "stem." For the freshmen, she distinguishes between them, showing that the distinctions are trickier than her students with their desire for clear categories expect. She complicates for them the differences between thorn and prickle and leaf. Every day she looks for Dan, anxious. He has not been charged—no witnesses, no weapon—but since the week after the shooting he has stopped coming to class, and though Grace is grateful not to see him, his absence is as palpable a reminder of him as his presence would be, full of all the disasters she can imagine for their inevitable meeting. He is not the only absentee, but she knows where the others are, the young men, at home with their families, with their sudden, even younger wives, waiting for the call to war. Their names she crosses out in black ink. But she marks Dan's absences in her roll book, a line of red diagonal slashes and zeroes for missed quizzes and lab reports across the blank squares of days.

She thinks about going to the Hole-in-the-Wall. She would walk in and sit down, and Ralph would bring over the coffee-pot and a blue-plate special with its ice cream scoop of mashed potatoes. After the lunch rush ended, he would sit down next to her with the calm old confidence, knowing to be quiet unless she spoke. She misses his silences, misses knowing that if he did speak he would say what he meant, as far as he knew it, even if half the time what he meant would be some instruction that would drive her crazy. She doesn't know, at the moment, how to make her way back to any plea-sure. Whatever she gained with Pascal was tenuous, and now it's gone.

Instead she stays stupidly at home between classes and stares up into the wintry hills and thinks about sleep. She is smarter than this, but at times even the distance between the living room and the kitchen seems more than she can cross. She tries to tell herself jokes about her own immobility, but she can't find it in herself to laugh at them. It may be just as well for her mood that the thaw, so promising, has ended, and real spring will come late, if at all. But Pascal hated the cold.

It is a gray morning, not snowing but threatening to snow, when at last Ralph comes to visit her. Grace has been drinking coffee in the living room, and the doorbell seems to chime from such a distance that for a moment she doesn't realize what it is. Ralph blows in, gusting cold air, takes off his over-coat, and sits on Imo's Victorian divan. He leans his elbows on his knees. For a moment, even in his gray flannel suit, he is reduced to cowpoke by worn, dark green velvet and carved walnut, but when he asks her how she is, he puts more nose into his voice than usual. Grace has forgotten this side of him, what she used to call the Latent Attorney. She smiles and shakes her head.

After she brings him tea in a painted cup too small for his hands, he says, "Rita thinks you've made a bad choice here." He drinks half the cup of tea in one gulp, looks around the room again. The curtains are drawn, and his face is mostly in shadow. "She thinks you ought to go back home."

"To the condo?" Even after the separation, Pascal was pal-pable in those rooms. Now, she doesn't know what she'll find. His presence, a kind of ghost. Or, worse, nothing at all. A red toothbrush stood up in a glass on the sink. She shivers and says to Ralph, "What do you think?"

"I said I would talk to you. I'm not supposed to tell you it was her idea." Ralph looks around at Imo's high ceilings and valanced windows. "I can't imagine going back to childhood. It's an understatement to say I wasn't close to my parents."

"I wasn't close to my parents, either."

"It's sort of hard when they're not there." He smiles and shakes his head. "But you had Imo. I guess if this is what you need, it's where you should be."

Grace leans back in Imo's green chair and presses her fingers to her eyes. Ralph has always reminded her there are worse things than being without parents. "I don't know what I need. I had just decided on one thing"—she reaches out, as if to pluck an apple from the air—"and it was gone. As if my desire made it vanish. How can you want anything, after that?"

Ralph grins at her. "After a while, you won't be able to help it. For now, there are people who would be happy to tell you what to do. But you won't get the same answer out of any two."

Grace moves over next to him on the divan and whispers, "I'm so glad you came."

He wraps his hands almost completely around her head. He massages her scalp, the back of her neck, and she bends her head forward and gives up to the pure sense of his fingers moving.

"I need to talk some business with you, too," he says.

"Talk away," Grace says into her turtleneck.

Ralph waits, then he stops rubbing behind her jaw and tells her to look up. When she doesn't, he leans over her and speaks into the back of her head, his breath on her scalp. "I wish I could be your lawyer, now more than ever."

Grace's head pops up so fast it cracks against his chin. He has always been her lawyer, from when they played together as children, when she was the outlaw. After he had, in the role of sheriff, caught her and jailed her in the shed, he would unpin his tin star, bail her out, and defend her against his own testimony. They always won, the two of them together using invented law against invented forces.

He rubs his chin. "I wanted to tell you in person. You may have to testify against me. It's a clear conflict of interest." His ranch twang is almost gone. He sounds like a lawyer again. "But if you think of something you need," he says, "anything, you call me."

"What if I need a lawyer?"

"We'll cross that bridge when we come to it." Ralph sets his cup down on the Chinese cabinet that serves as an end table. He takes both her hands and leans toward her, his wide mouth serious and still. "I want one favor from you," he says.

Grace sits up straight. "Give me one reason—"

"It's not what you think," he says. "I want you to go see Bliss."

Grace curls her fist against her thigh. When she thinks of Bliss, she sees only pale curls, a stray nipple. "What is it with her? She's the one who caused all this in the first place."

Ralph takes Grace's hand, slides it around his ribs to rest on his back. "I know what she's been through. You can't imagine." He is right. He holds her arm around him, but when she doesn't relax he lets go, wipes his hands on his trousers.

At the front door, Grace says, "I'll talk to her. But I can't promise it will help."

"Watch out for her," he says. "Take care of her."

"Why don't you, if you're so worried?"

"Think about it. If I get involved, it will just cause more problems."

Grace looks out the window. "I don't know why everyone is so worried about *her*."

Ralph takes both her elbows. "We're worried about you, too. But she may be in danger, Grace." He looks around at the front hall, its marble floor, its woodwork and high ceilings from another age. "In a way," he says, "you've never been safer."

Grace lifts her chin and smiles. "That's what's got Rita in a twist."

"There's my Grace," Ralph says. He leans down, kisses her lightly on the forehead.

Later, when Rita phones and asks, her tone even and casual, what Grace and Ralph talked about, Grace imagines her voice, an electrical spark sliding down the wires like a finger over a string from the mortuary to Imo's house. Maybe the lines are faulty; maybe it's the miles of heavy weather between them—Rita's voice sounds feeble. Grace doesn't know what to say to her.

Still, Grace has learned: she really can change things in her head, in the "if onlys" she runs through at night just to make sleep possible. "I should have planted the new lilac in the corner," she used to think, and in her mind she could see it there, exploded into flower on the edge of dream. And the next spring, before its buds began to swell, she would dig around its roots and lift it out and carry it the way a father carries his sleeping child from the car to bed, without the child ever waking. It has nothing to do with mysticism, but only with how she persuades herself to action. She hopes she is storing her energy for something, but she isn't sure enough what that something is to bring it to mind.

And maybe what Grace is giving in to now is more serious, even dangerous, though Imo has years since surrendered to such revision entirely, continually rewriting what was into what might have been. Increasingly, Imo inhabits a world of possibility lost and regained. Grace tells herself it's not senility; it's merely a question of where Imo wants to live, that the past holds more promise than the future. The flowers are bigger and brighter, the people more lifelike, their conversations dazzled with wit. Imo is still beautiful, and she wields her charm like a sword. In her presence women guard their husbands, as if that will do them any good.

To Imo, Grace's grandfather never died, and she converses with him as intrepidly now as ever she did when he was alive, as if it's still not too late to change his mind about what to have for supper, which animal—strutting rooster or staid cow—the new weather vane on the garage should sport, whether to plant string beans or wax beans in the garden come summer.

Grace tilts her head as if considering serious matters and says, "Turkey Divan, copper whale, string and wax beans both," and Imo says, "We'll wait and ask Luther."

And who is Grace to say it's not all the same? If Imo has a way to keep him near, the man she stepped down from the silent screen to promise her life to, why should she stop listening now for his voice from the other room? Taking her place next to Imo at the kitchen table or in the front parlor, where nobody may sit in her grandfather's empty chair, Grace is tempted to listen for his voice herself, and for Pascal's, deeper, gentle as he bends his head. She could make everything up to Pascal, if only she would give in. She could raise him from the dead. There's nothing she couldn't do better, if she had it to do over again, sitting motionless in a comfortable chair.

Now, Grace sits at Imo's kitchen table and lets Imo do it all.

"There's never been a divorce in our family," Imo says.

"And there won't be now," Grace says. "But it was never for want of reasons."

Grace wonders why Imo believes she's staying here, where in her invented order she thinks Pascal might have got himself to. Imo thinks it would have been better for Grace to have killed Pascal herself in a betrayed, barehanded, female rage than ever to have let their separation blossom into divorce. But the issue is settled. Grace says, "You were the scandalous one."

"Scandal was different in my day. It took hardly any effort at all."

"Not in your case. I have photographs." Grace reaches over and takes Imo's cup, lifts the blue-and-white padded cozy off the old painted teapot from China. "I think we have enough wood to last," she says. It is nearly March, though it's still plenty cold; finally the sky outside is blue again, and at worst it should have only three, maybe four big snows left in it. But below the blue, the mountains and even the foothills are the color of winter, and the wind is blowing hard from the north. "As soon as it warms up, I'll call the man to take down the storm windows."

"Pascal is too busy?"

Grace smiles a little, as if testing. "Yes." She likes this way of looking at things, sees in it a kind of absolution. She, too, can barely lift a hand, she's so busy.

Imo folds her hands in front of her on the table. Grace wraps hers around her cup, though it's bone china and Imo looks at her with a little pursing-up of the mouth. But Imo says only, "Your grandfather would prefer to do it himself."

"Yes, Imo."

Imo says, more emphatically, "He would prefer it." She leans a little closer to Grace. "He's a good man. But he's just got too damned old." For years Imo barely spoke to him at all. No wonder it makes no difference to her, this dying of his. He's never been more than an idea.

Grace says, obediently, "Not so old, Imo."

Imo sits back. "Well, I'm glad you finally found someone respectable." She looks at Grace and nods. In her head parade the musicians, artists, house painters, would-be philosophers, truck drivers, and pool sharks Grace never brought home through the years. They leer at Imo now, in her inventive memory. Still, even they would have been better than nothing, than Grace alone in lamplight, her head bent to her book. Imo never had much use for studious women.

"We were worried, your grandfather and I. But now—a doctor, no less." Imo nods.

"Well. Maybe a little less, by now," Grace says.

Might Pascal and Grace really have reconciled? Would that sense she never lost of his hand on her chest, his palm right between her breasts, have returned her to him? Pascal knew that the only real difference between that place under his hand and the same spot on any other woman was in what moved behind the ribs. Not, of course, mechanics only too familiar to him, the nuance of pulse and the body's electrical charge, but the thing the cardiologist can't quantify, what opens a heart in hope, closes down breath in sorrow and defeat. What both Grace and Pascal turned to science in the first place to avoid thinking about. They were, after all, alike. Pascal always said the reason Grace liked botany was that she got to bring nature into her own hands and rearrange it. He put his mouth right next to her ear and whispered, "Fibrillation. Chaos." And it's true that she would create a hybrid just to see a new flower open for the first time, would put a plant in one year and rip it out the next to know how one set of leaves looked beside another.

She'd say, "Some of the gardens I only plan. Then I leave them to others."

He would raise his eyebrows. He would say, "The seat of emotion isn't the heart. It's the hypothalamus." And Grace would nod and touch his ribs lightly with her fingers.

Grace and Imo sit together after tea, waiting for Detective Flint to arrive. Imo is darning one of Grandpa's old socks. The sock is gray, but the thread she uses is bright red. Grace is daydreaming her first kiss from Pascal. They stand outside the cabin on the day they met. She feels the shadows of aspen trembling over her skin. She waits for his hand on her shoulder. He turns her around, takes her hand, touches her palm then her inner wrist to his lips. She shivers.

"In my day," Imo says, "a gentleman would never have kissed your palm like that. And certainly not your wrist.

Certainly not. Not on first acquaintance. Your grandfather never would have." She looks up at Grace from her needlework, her thin eyebrows lifted, and grins.

"Just how many gentlemen did you know?" Grace hears Pascal's voice saying, "Mmmm," his breath moving against her wrist, the breeze under the trees. The chill travels all the way up her arm, lifts the hair on the back of her neck. Their eyes are locked, and every time she feels the shiver ripple through her, she can see its echo in his pupils. And it's something Grace could never explain to Imo: it's not so much the physical effect of his touch as the fact of it. Grace says to herself, This is the past. She makes a good effort, but she gives in again.

Imo rests the sock on her lap. "The back of the hand maybe. Although it would have been a tremendous impertinence. Tremendous," she repeats almost dreamily, as if she is remembering something. She turns the sock briskly, runs her finger over the darn to check its smoothness. "There are many, many sensitive nerve endings in the hands. It's a scientific fact. It's a wonder it all turned out as well as it did."

Grace doesn't think Imo's talking about her anymore, but she believes her anyway. About the nerve endings, that is. If anyone would have known about this, it would have been Pascal, who might have used his medical school education to discover just such facts. Grace still feels the tingle on her shoulder as if someone has barely finished touching it. As for the rest, of course, Imo's missing something. In her mind, the story is a comedy, ending with the wedding.

Imo ties a knot, bites off her thread. She has an unlimited supply of Grandpa's old socks and shirts. She never mended his things while he was alive; she hoarded them all her married years as if just for this. He's over two years gone, and she reaches into her work basket every night and finds something of his to stitch back together. She wields her needle mercilessly. She nods her head at the piano and says, "Why don't you?"

Grace shakes her head, though Imo is only trying to help.

"He has his good points," Imo says. "I'm not saying he hasn't. He's a charmer. But men these days have no idea." She shakes her head. "No idea at all what they're putting a young lady through." She peers at Grace again over her glasses. "Not that you were any spring chicken. I'd say you were lucky to get him, any old how."

"Like you." This is a button Grace pushes to keep Imo going.

Imo sits up straight, her shoulders back. "I was a sex symbol. All I had to do was get married before there were any obvious signs of disintegration." She rethreads her needle, knots the ends of the thread together. "Of course, in those days, our foundation garments were a real assistance to us. Not like now."

Grace nods and looks out the window. It's snowing again, and the yard is full of the stuff, clotted and thick.

"Where is that fellow with his shovel?" Imo says.

Still humoring her, Grace says, "Do you mean Grandpa or Pascal?"

Imo peers at Grace over the needle. "Don't be a fool, dear. I mean the boy. The boy who shovels our walks."

The first time Pascal and Grace made love, she kept waiting for him to touch her with enough force to make her take in her breath. She waited for fear, that sharp edge she'd learned to associate so closely with passion she didn't recognize passion without it. She still didn't realize it was never her own heart, always somebody else's, that evoked it. She closed her eyes and conjured up Pascal's history of violence-from-a-distance. When she opened her eyes again, he was looking right into them, his own eyes not fierce but softened, like honey, moony and rich. Grace reached her hand up to his cheek, and he closed his eyes and turned his lips into her palm. The tenderness took her by surprise; she had no time to avoid it, to turn and let it go by. Not his tenderness, her own: a wave of softness through her stomach that almost felt like nausea. Concentrating on small violence was a way of avoiding something bigger.

Now, Detective Flint sits with Grace at the kitchen table. Behind her, Grace can hear Imo fluttering around the teapot, waiting for the water to boil. Grace is amused—the masculine presence still brings out the plumed bird in her grandmother. Imo appears next to Flint with a plate of cookies, lays her hand, just for a moment, lightly on his shoulder, as if to smooth the furrow out of his jacket where it doesn't quite fit.

"We've searched the condo and the Jaguar," Flint says. He picks up a cookie—oatmeal studded with raisins and pecans. "And the cabin. We can't find any gun."

"He had it when he left that evening. Otherwise, I'm not sure I would have remembered it at all."

Imo pours tea for them, then lifts the plate of cookies and wafts it under Grace's nose. "She eats like a bird," she says to Flint. "Tell her she needs to keep up her strength."

"You tell my grandmother," Grace says, "she needs to eat something besides sweets."

Flint smiles at Grace. It's as if a little light goes on behind his eyes. "You seem plenty strong to me."

"Really?" Grace says, surprised.

"In my day," Imo says, "women had something to them."

"She's obsessed," Grace says to Flint.

"And they didn't talk about their elders as if they weren't there."

Grace lifts her hand helplessly, palm up, and begins to laugh.

"Grace has got something to her," Flint says to Imo. "I'm just not sure what it is yet."

"Men seem to see it," Imo says. "Some women, too. But I don't."

Any subject would be better than this. "What about Dan?" Grace asks.

Flint rubs his eyes so hard Grace thinks he'll tear the skin. "What do we have?" he asks. "Not a thing."

"But he did it," Grace says.

"We have to prove it."

"Dan, Dan, the straw man," Imo chants. She reaches over and plucks a raisin from Flint's lapel. She says, "I can reknot that necktie for you, if you'd like. I've tied Luther's every day of his life. He'll be so sorry to have missed you."

"Luther?"

"Oh," Imo says, placing the raisin on her saucer. "My dead husband."

Grace lies in bed now in Imo's house, shuts her eyes against the afternoon, and waits for Pascal to call her name, to push her head too far back for comfort, to lay his hand over her mouth, though he never did any of these things. It's the only way she knows to give him revenge, to let him at her. A way of bringing him back. It was simple tenderness that he always wanted, and that she was always afraid of, from the beginning, when he stood on the bank of the creek and looked into the trees and told her what he'd been. Not her quiet waiting, her acquiescence, but her hand reaching out. She had been learning. She had been planning to lift the phone as he'd asked, to call him, a gesture that would say she had decided this for herself.

A red shirt. Metonymy—taking a thing for a man. She is still looking for consistency, for a way to make things fit. She presses her own hands against her body, too hard, and takes in her breath. When she's done, she waits for him to get up and pull on his jeans and boots and say, "I'll get you home now." That meant, at midnight, a drive down the dirt road from the cabin, then down the dark canyon, Pascal's headlights sweeping the trees as they wound around the curves, catching, occasionally, the glint of a cabin window through the branches.

Instead, he touched her so gently she almost couldn't feel it—rather, she felt at first only the slightest ripple moving through her, before it gained force. It was a kind of touch she didn't know what to make of, meant to turn her outward to him instead of in upon her privacy.

He said, "Open your eyes." Then he lay that first time with his head on her shoulder. She wrapped her arm around his head, her fingers in his hair. It was coarse and curly; she couldn't pull her fingers through it without getting entangled.

"I'm just waiting for the catch," she said.

"There has to be one?"

The shadow tenderness casts: the possibility of grief.

He spread out his hand on her stomach. It covered her from side to side, from between her breasts all the way down to where his little finger curled into her pubic hair. He said, "Resistance is useless."

"I'll only fight if you want me to." With another man, this might have been an honest invitation, but she knew it would hurt Pascal. She turned her head to the wall and waited. In the dark under her skin under his hand, she could feel her insides dissolving. Finally, too late, she said, "Yes."

He rolled over on her again, careful to keep most of his weight on his arms, and this time, weeping, she gave up.

Grace is in the Food King looking for the prunes. She has Imo's list in her hand, and she can barely read the wavering handwriting. Storm tears the outside air, but there was a moment, sitting in the parlor after her nap, when all Grace wanted was to go out in it; when her only regret was that it wasn't more furious still, more wild, that it wouldn't strand the car and force her to abandon it like a great dying animal in a snowbank and forge on alone and on foot through the blizzard. She looked up at the window as usual, with the now-familiar languor, and it was as if the wind, made visible by the flakes it drove, blew for just one moment right under her skin.

All the two-mile drive to the store, she could hear the limbs of trees with their new leaves giving up under the burden of snow and cracking like shots. In the morning, when the storm passes, the lawns and streets will be littered with them.

She is experimenting. "Where are the prunes?" she says.

She hears, You remember. Canned fruit.

Then, "White bread?" and she feels the hand in the middle of her back, guiding her, the familiar breath on the top of her ear.

"Pop Tarts?" and the inevitable, the expected, *Pop Tarts?* Pascal ate bagels for breakfast, spread thick with cream cheese, though he knew as precisely as anyone what this would do to his arteries. She hears, "For that detective of yours?"

"Imo likes them," she says. "And Ding Dongs."

Part of the game: she can't look up. If she does, she will see nobody—just the store, almost empty because of the storm and far too brightly lit, the clean floors and abandoned aisles, and, in the awkwardly angled mirror over the butcher case, only herself, if she looks just right, gazing upward, big-eyed and distorted, her head twisted back on her neck.

"Once he was gone, you wanted to bring him back," Imo says. After the separation, which Grace asked for out of what?—despair? malice? Imo tells Grace it's not her fault, that Pascal was going to do what he was going to do.

Grace says from the sink, where she is peeling carrots, "I should have let him go or taken him back. Now I have."

"Taken him back?"

"In my way." In Imo's way, Grace means, but she doesn't say it. "What more do you want?"

"I wonder what's keeping them."

Grace puts down the peeler, opens the kitchen door, and looks out. It is almost evening. "I don't know," she says. "They're late." The snow has nearly stopped. It is warm in the kitchen and Grace leaves the door a little ajar. She has the kettle on the stove, cookies on the plate, the teapot full of hot water to scald it for the tea. The soup for supper is starting its boil in the pot. She adds the carrots, then goes to the cupboard. For the first time since she returned, she doesn't hesitate at all—she sets the table with four places, four cups and spoons and napkins and little cookie plates, and Imo watches her. When Grace is done, Imo gazes at the table for a long time, then she looks back up at Grace, her lips pursed, but she doesn't say a word. The room still feels warm and the kitchen's light is bright enough but soft on the eyes. Grace could sleep for a long time. She thinks, Three hours and I can go to bed.

Imo's hands are folded demurely, but she keeps squeezing them together as if she's pumping something out from between them. She looks up and says, "Dear, how old are you?"

"Thirty-one."

"You know," Imo says, "you have time."

"Yes."

"Not like me." Imo puts down the fork very gently. "He's gone. You've got to stop kidding yourself."

Grace doesn't want to have this conversation. Imo's eyes are blue and, at that moment, as sharp as ice. "It's my last chance," Grace says.

"For what?"

"To let him come back."

Imo hesitates. "Some things take more time than you get."

Grace looks back out the door. The yard is bare and dark. She feels herself emptying into it, into the darkness and cold. She is exhausted, though she's done almost nothing all day. "You're right," she says. "It won't do."

"Shut that door then. I'm eighty-four, and it's colder than hell in here." Imo cracks a little bit of a grin. "That's something they could tell us about, isn't it, your grandfather and Pascal?"

"Neither of them ever could stand the cold."

The sharpness fades. Imo waves her hand weakly toward the door. "Shut it, then, before they catch their deaths."

Grace says, "Yes, dear," and she closes the door. She stands for a minute looking out the window at the twilight, then she turns back to the kitchen, to the table set for the living and the dead, and she pours the tea.

CHAPTER 7

■ ■ ■

Voice Lessons

Imo has decided to give Grace singing lessons. After she teaches her last class, Grace sits next to Imo at the piano and opens her mouth, and the kind of squeak comes out that she made on the very top notes when she was first learning to sing. She makes a fist and hits the piano bench in a light rhythm. Grace is making progress, though she has a hard time seeing it that way. She wants to recover her old self immediately, but it's as if she's separated from that self, the self of passion and motion, by a deep canyon across which she can't quite see, by memories she can't quite bring up to traverse. She wants to get back to the other side, but it seems too far away. It's not only Pascal, but what he opened in her that had been closed for a long time.

"Your problem is," Imo says, "you never had formal training. You never understood how you did things, so when something else moved into that space in your brain it all vanished, like"—Imo kisses the tips of her fingers—"poof." Imo has always held instinct in contempt. She says, "Now, remember to make the space in your head." She drops her jaw way down and pushes her tongue against the back of her bottom teeth to flatten it.

Grace lays her hand on Imo's hand. "Thank you," she says. "I know I'm impossible."

"It's your father in you. I can think of places I'd rather hear you sing than in a seedy bar. But you always did just what you wanted. Like your mother."

In the kitchen, Imo pours two cups of tea through the silver strainer. Just watching her makes Grace tired. "Maybe I'll take a vacation," she says. "When my sabbatical starts."

"You're practically on vacation now," Imo says. "When was the last time you held office hours?" What Imo has wanted most has happened: Grace is under her roof again, reduced to a child.

Grace leans back. After all, she can't imagine what it would take to renew her passport and load herself onto an airplane. The year she was eighteen, she drifted around the world like a tide, but now she can't get up the energy to pack a bag and walk out Imo's front door.

"You're not a child anymore," Imo says. "You can't just do what you want."

Not as a child, either. Then when? Grace says, "No."

It is too beautiful to be believed, the world: fields and stalls of flowers, poppies and mullein and daffodils and lilies, gold and red and violet and the most astonishing blue blossoms piled in carts along the village streets; woods smelling of wet dirt and greenery; the dapple of light and shadow; the smell of coffee on a terrace in the morning, the smells of cinnamon and yeast; a yellow jug on an indigo cloth and a view over cliffs of a sea that works at its coasts without mercy, that yields also without mercy to any sinking body, then closes over it and resumes its shape as if nothing had ever disturbed it, as if there were no human history worth noting.

From the shores, mountains climb their own precipitous slopes to a cold sky or a warm one; or the beach fades into a desert that stretches out for hundreds of miles, too dangerous to cross, full of a light that won't distinguish itself from the land, that moves over the hills and valleys like skin over muscle.

This is what Grace sees when she leans her elbows on the kitchen table and shuts her eyes. In the seventeenth century, Thomas Burnet believed land was only a crusty froth, like meringue, adrift over the heavier element of a watery earth's core. When Grace was only eight, her mother told her Burnet wasn't a bad scientist as such. It was a matter of assumptions, of what an age permits a person to see. In Burnet's model, the waters could rise again anytime. And in Lyell's model, too, of deep time, except instead of water one layer of rock lifts over millennia while another sinks below the surface. The slightest shift, a city is shaken to rubble.

I lay my hand on a stone wall older than I can imagine and lean my face against the bark of an olive tree. I walk up a mountain road, past a cafe where under a rusted iron table two ducks copulate in a cackling glee I might take for pain or instinct, not wanting to see myself in them. At the top, I stop in a taverna alive with an ancient language. I listen for nightingales. In my own world, even the geography feels newer than this, and people still believe in the idea of frontier.

I will be like that cowboy, my own version of the medieval knight riding off into the unknown—only the quest will matter, the bright idea, terminal; along the way, each moment will wait to be rescued. Halfway around the world, a soldier brushes sand out of his eyes, his wrists rubbed raw with it. All night, shells bloom into his sleep. He peers out of his foxhole, afraid. In his heart, he fans the flame of an idea, fear an abstraction coming to life. When he faces real fire, his blood will hammer its walls until they give, a vein bursting open in his neck, next to his heart.

The past is wilderness, too. A constant arrival. Low fields of tulips, a cactus exploding into flower against a white wall, a rocky talus slope shifting under gravity or a bridge so old I do not dare set my foot on it to cross to the abandoned mill on the other side, however much I want to pick the roses there, gone wildly astray in the afternoon sun.

If you're not careful, the simplest things can tear the heart right out of you.

"You'd have sand in your bed," Imo says. "You'd have to wash your clothes in the sink."

Grace opens her eyes on the kitchen's fluorescent light.

"Fleas. Dysentery. Hepatitis. Malaria."

"There are vaccinations," Grace says. Upstairs under Grace's bed are the journals she kept in her youth, and all the maps her father ever drew for her, up to the last one, where she filled in some of the blanks herself: the red mountain, the long hike back down in black.

Imo finishes her tea and folds her hands on the tablecloth. "Only for what they can predict."

Grace's father traveled the West for the Geological Survey, charting bumps and dips of land, the mesas and the hollows and mountains and deep canyons, which he explored, often on horseback, looking at nothing but topographical features, the curve of a canyon wall something not to be admired but to be recorded faithfully on graphs.

Grace could imagine, watching him, how scientists get their reputations for de-animating the world, flattening it, turning it into disconnected fragments, a merely quantified reality—an impression her mother failed to give merely by the way she dressed, by the urgency with which she fluttered her hand when calling Grace to the microscope to observe the structure of a crystal.

"They're constructed like snowflakes," Julia would breathe, and for a moment the heaviest matter would seem the lightest, as if rocks could float down from the sky in a gentle storm.

But the maps Grace's father drew for her were different—bright color, intimate places named after people she loved. Imogen Gulch. The Valley of Ralph. And there were the other maps he brought home—maps of towns and of galaxies; replicas of medieval sea charts that showed monsters curling their tails beyond the known edge of the earth; a photograph of the oldest map of the world, a stone disk with Babylon at its heart.

On vacations he would bring Julia and Grace back to the places he had charted; he'd tilt back his head and point to fields of pelicans rising off the lip of a river as if pulled free by the wind, to a cleft between rocks that may have provided Butch and Sundance themselves with a route to ride on a wild escape from order.

And Grace would tilt back her head at the same angle, would fill her chest, the way he did, with the bright air.

In Paris, of all places, Grace, barely eighteen and emptied of everything but nerve, tried touch. He was tall and lean. Grace smoked his cigarettes, Gaulois, rough in her throat. She let his fingers trickle down her neck, toward the low vee of her man's T-shirt. She looked at him from under her hat brim. She wore cowboy boots.

He smiled, cocked his finger like a pistol, and said, "Le western. Bang." On the bed in her little room he glided over her. He was clean and skilled; it was about time she had a lover who would teach her something she could take into life. She and Ralph had been completely innocent. Now, she could have been anyone. Was this what her mother had been looking for?

Rita finished a year of college without Grace, won the women's collegiate national championship in cross-country skiing, but nothing else changed. The August Grace returned, the city looked small and dry. Heat rose in waves from thin skins of concrete and asphalt, as it would have from the desert floor. Later, showing Rita her snapshots, she, too, looked at them for clues.

"Why can't you stay put for a while?" Rita asked.

But Grace didn't know. At night she had rinsed out her underwear in the hotel sink. Down near the drain, grains of sand had collected in wisps like pinwheels.

Rita reached for the photo of the Paris hotel room, held it up. He slept on tousled sheets under the window, one hand stretched over his head, his ankles crossed. Grace's cowboy hat lay on the bedside table next to him. Around him the sheets made a landscape of shadows, and he himself was only a beautiful body, an outstanding feature. You could see from the light it was morning, that the man in the bed was a stranger who would wake and smile and reach out his hand. He would want Grace to put some part of herself into the broad palm lying open on the pillow. Grace touched the hat on the bedside table and said, "That must be where I left it."

Oh, heart, where are you now?

When she hears her father's voice, Grace knows it immediately, even after twenty years, even though she is expecting a call from Flint, or her department chair, or Ralph—any number of other men who might ask her, Where have you been? This is the voice she can't resist. Against reason, it will ravish her. It will drive other voices away, all the ones she invokes to send her to sleep at night, even Pascal's, which ripples over her skin like water. Her father's voice is like the tremor that precedes the disaster. She presses the phone against her ear, and his voice asks again to speak with Grace, though its lift in tone tells her he, too, knows who he's talking to.

Grace wants to be dreaming. As a child, she used to tell herself jokes in her dreams, ones that, reassembled later, would make no sense, though in her sleep she would laugh until she laughed herself awake. But it's been a long time since she has slept so lightly.

She says into the phone, "Are you sure you've got the right number?"

"Grace," his voice says. "I didn't expect to find you there."

She waits for it to sink in. "I still drop in from time to time," she says. She is embarrassed to be caught back in her childhood home. She pauses, listens to the phone. "So. How are you?"

"I know this must be unexpected. I think about you all the time. More and more."

She wills her voice to be airy, smooth. "Since when is thinking not enough?"

He's quiet. She presses the phone into her ear. "I know this can't be easy," he says. "But there are things you don't understand."

"True enough." Grace leans up against the wall in Imo's foyer, tucks the phone between her shoulder and chin, puts her hands in her pockets, and waits. On the wall across the little hallway is an old convex mirror, meant to hang over a dining table, to distort the room so the hostess can see all her guests. On its gold filigreed frame tiny cupids sport through ornately carved roses and fruits. From among them, the glass bulges out like a bowl. In it, Grace's body recedes into a reflected distance, while her face protrudes forward, round and taut. She brings her face close to her reflection and watches her nose swell, her cheeks plump out, and her eyes and chin vanish into almost nothing.

The air is silent but still open, full of space and possibility she's not sure she wants to be confronted with. She was just getting comfortable. She starts swaying toward the mirror and away, watching her face bulge and return almost to normal.

Finally the voice says, "I'm calling from California. I thought I might come and see you. *We* might. My wife and I."

This makes it easier, though Grace knows it shouldn't be a betrayal. "Your wife is dead," she says.

"I think this is enough for now." His voice sounds heavy, weighted with sadness and patience that Grace still recognizes, all this time later, though she doesn't want to hear them.

"I know it's a shock," he says, "after all these years. I'll call again soon."

Grace pauses. "Okay," she says. She waits, listening for the click. The air is dense. The line is closed.

When Grace returned from abroad to start college, she became, briefly, an artist's model. Not for money, or even exactly for love, but because she'd never met anyone like Willem before. He had been a heroin addict in Amsterdam, then in Hong Kong—when Grace knew him he studied karate and wore his hair in a long braid like her own. Willem would have gone back to the horse in a minute, he'd said, except it was so expensive here. For such a country, where drugs are procured in secret and used in dark rooms with the curtains shut, he was filled with scorn. He walked as if he traveled through enemy territory, in which absolute silence, the lightest possible tread, was necessary. The first time she talked to him, Grace wanted to keep watching his brown eyes, the corneas fading imperceptibly into yellow, move over her face.

"This is the land of milk and honey," he said. "Everyone is rich. Everyone has what he needs." He had a slight accent, a careful shape to his vowels, a grammar too perfect to be native. He let out his breath. "I'm thinking of a painting. But I have a problem—the space where the woman is supposed to go." He raised his hand, sketched a crude shape on the air. "It's blank."

By this time Grace had surrendered the idea that sex could make her free, or even happy, but she hadn't given up on its redemptive power. She and Willem made love on a sleeping bag on his studio floor. After they were done, he wouldn't let her touch her hair or look in a mirror or use a towel to wipe his dampness from her thighs. He put her in an old green chair under the window, then he lit a joint. Grace draped her legs over one arm of the chair, and he posed her with her cheek leaning against the chair back. She looked up, through the window behind her, at the sky.

"Like you're dreaming," he said. That was easy. The smoke had already clouded her vision. She still had long hair like her mother's, and he fanned it over the back of the chair.

In the mornings, she went to class, read botany texts with their intricate drawings of cells and leaves, the types of which she memorized—entire, sinuate, crenate, serrate, dentate, lobed, double serrate—and also books of poems, Victorian novels, biographies in French. In the afternoons, when the hard desert light came through Willem's west window, she went to his studio. She believed she was learning something about the world. After they made love she sat in the green chair, looked out the window, and thought about the essential sexlessness of the rose and the pure, self-cloning garlic; of Proust's incurable nostalgia; of Eliot's Dorothea setting her chin against a future of darkness in her aging husband's house. When the light faded they went down to the Twilite Lounge and met Rita and Ralph and friends of Willem's.

Ralph would lay his arm over Grace's shoulders. "He has no future," he'd say into her ear. "He's a *painter*."

Grace would say, "I'm not looking for a future," and smile her sweetest smile.

Rita, too, had admirers. When she walked into the Twilite, her six-foot body moving so smoothly you might have thought she was gliding on snow, Marcus turned to look. When she leaned over the table to shoot, his eye traveled along the bend of her body.

"Rita may be asking for trouble here," Ralph said.

Grace said to Ralph, "Willem's a black belt. He could kill you with one blow." She lifted up her hand and chopped at Ralph's neck.

"There are some things you shouldn't joke about," Willem said. But this was a world Grace still couldn't imagine—though she was in it, even charmed by it—so distant was it from Imo's house and the bright meadows of her childhood.

With Willem, she believed, she could step from light into shadow without fear, with only a pleasurable chill.

Over Ralph's shoulder, Grace saw Rita looking down her cue, and Marcus's face, watching.

What a woman may not know is that a man, looking at her, is not thinking, "pretty," "smooth," words from the vocabulary of distance, full of unlocated longing. He is more likely thinking about contact, how to drive his way in. "Open, open," or "I'd like to shove her face into a pillow." It may be normal, even necessary for him to think these things.

She's been educated in pretty manners, how to show herself to advantage. Even if Grace's father had stayed around, all those years ago, there is knowledge he would have protected her from. He admits it when she asks him over the telephone. He would have praised her beauty, even knowing that beauty might as easily elicit violence as gentleness. He asks her what else he could have done, as if his presence at her entry into adulthood is more than hypothetical.

He has called her now perhaps a dozen times, each conversation longer, more intimate, than the last. He has told her he wants to get to know her again, wants to learn what her life has been like, but he is still only a voice in her head, no more substantial than her dead mother, her grandfather, Pascal, all of whom she talks to at night as she drifts into sleep.

She has told her father about her trip abroad, about summers riding Marley at Ralph's ranch, about walking into Ralph's kitchen under the snap of his father's belt. As she approaches the idea of her father, of allowing him to take on flesh and walk back into her life, she wants to test him, wants to learn how far she can go, how much she can hurt him without turning him away. She makes him laugh at Willem's dark seriousness, at his milky eyes, even at their lovemaking and the dingy carpet in the studio. Once his guard is down, she tells him the rest.

It was December. Rita was in training, her body strung tight, her mind turned inward on the image she was building of herself bent over her skis, pushing forward into her own harsh breath. She wouldn't drink or stay out late.

Marcus bought her one Sprite after another, but she was barely aware of him. Too focused on her body in motion to think about sex, Rita hadn't come out yet, but she'd never been more than merely friendly to men. And Marcus was both rough and attenuated. Everything about him was long. His jeans had been let all the way down to a ragged hem.

"Look at the poor guy," Grace said. "He's in love."

Willem said, "What does that mean to you?" and Grace shook her head and turned away to take a beer from Ralph's hand. She wanted to be loved, yes, but, against all her careful self-training, she was looking for the real thing, the love that would eradicate her, would render her mind superfluous and her body supreme.

Now, her father says, "It doesn't exist."

"You and my mother had it," Grace says. But now she's old enough to know they had it only for brief moments, an afternoon here and there, an exceptional week; that passion cannot be sustained against the daily demands of the world. So her mother had looked for it elsewhere, trying again and again to move back into that other sphere.

Grace was tipsy but not drunk that night when Willem took her home, late; they made love and he got up, as always, and left. She was asleep by the time Marcus knocked on her door. She was still naked; she pulled on jeans and a cardigan, then opened the door, leaned against the door frame, and looked at him. He seemed smaller than she remembered, forlorn. She could feel herself drawn toward him by romance, a man's tender yearning.

Marcus's voice was rough with longing. "It's Rita," he said.

"Is she all right?"

"I guess." He pointed to his car. "Let's go to my house. I need to talk. I'll make eggs." She looked back into the apartment, at the pile of books on her desk. Her coat was tossed across the couch. It wasn't a question of manners, of whether she could have looked Marcus in the eye and explained, counting on her fingers, the reasons she should be afraid. She didn't know what they were. It was only a question of comfort, sympathy versus the temptations of a warm bed.

At his house, he put the coffee on, came back into the living room. She stood at his bookshelves, fingering the spines of books. She didn't know what to say, kept looking through the titles—Marx, Kierkegaard, Dostoevsky—while he stood behind her.

Finally she said, "Maybe you guys aren't right for each other." Grace didn't want to put a name to Rita's desires, not for Marcus or any man.

He put his hands on her shoulders. "There may be a reason for that, too." He was looking into Grace's eyes. "You think no man has a chance. But he might. Being a man isn't so bad." Marcus took the side of her head in his hand.

"Of course not." Grace backed out of his hands, but she was still trying to be nice, trying to help, as if, if she relaxed and didn't fight the undertow, it would release her, pop her back to the surface. None of the possibilities she ran through her head were right.

He leaned over and kissed her. She backed away again, but his hand wrapped the back of her neck.

She said into his mouth, "Stop."

His tongue moved against her closed lips.

"No," she said.

Her father says now, "Too late." It is a sort of sigh.

Marcus had his hand in the neck of her sweater, a cardigan with pearl buttons, no shirt underneath, no bra. His fingers were cold. She tried to push him away, but he yanked down hard. The buttons hit the floor with a light clicking. He held her at arm's length to look, and when she folded her arms he grabbed her wrists and pulled them apart.

"A little skinny," he said. Then, "Why did you come here?"

"Because you wanted me to."

"Exactly." He took both her wrists in one hand and put the other hand on her breast, not gently, but grinding it into her ribs. She tried to pull her wrists free, but his grip tightened. She was learning what men know: how strong they are, how much control and tenderness they must exercise every time they reach out their hands.

She is careful to get the details exactly right. She speaks to her father in a monotone, as if her own voice can distance her. She does not want to spare him anything. Between them, they know it is part of his penance to hear this, to know that, hearing it now, there is nothing he can do.

Marcus turned her around and pinned her against him. She felt her jeans scraping over her skin. He said in her ear, "No underwear." He ran his hand over her hip.

"You gave me no time." She still thought if she said the right thing he would stop, say he was sorry, it was all a mistake. The coffeemaker burbled in the kitchen. He twisted her arm behind her, pushed her into the bedroom. She was crying.

Her father says, "No."

Marcus reached down and touched her, felt the dampness still left from Willem. "You're wet," he said. He knelt on Grace's legs, keeping them open. His knees ground against her thighs; every time she tried to pull her legs out from under him his bones rolled over her bones. He had her wrists in one hand again; with his other hand he unbuttoned his fly. He put his hand on her throat and said, "Quiet, now," then his fingers were at his fly again. Grace stopped struggling but she was still crying; she turned her head aside. The tears seemed to have nothing to do with her; she'd floated up to the ceiling to watch the struggle, his face against her breasts, her eyes open, staring at the ceiling where she drifted.

"You're so beautiful," he said. "I've always wanted you."

The ghost on the ceiling thought, "Here goes nothing."

"It's Rita you want. Please."

He bent down and kissed the woman on the bed, kissed her breasts, then lowered his body onto her. He whispered, "Ride 'em." His face was red.

The woman lifted her head and spat in his eyes.

Grace says into the phone, "Are you listening?"

Marcus pushed back up on one hand, wiped his eyes with the other, then lifted it, slapped her across the jaw. "You know who Rita wants, don't you?"

Her father says, "Yes."

The slap yanked Grace back down from the ceiling, and she was there, under him, when he entered her hard.

Grace tells her father that, when Marcus was finished, she went to his bathroom and threw up, then she called Yellow Cab and pulled on her clothes and went outside to wait. It was almost dawn. If the cabby noticed the blood on her mouth or the way she held her sweater closed with her hand, he didn't say. At home, Grace took a long bath, got out, scrubbed out the tub with cleanser, filled it again. She stayed in the second tub for a long time, rubbing at herself with a washcloth until her skin hurt. The bruises on her wrists and thighs were already coming out, but if she looked at them through the green surface of water, she could imagine they weren't hers.

"You shouldn't have bathed," her father says. "You should have called the police."

"Right," she says. It was what Rita told her when Grace called her later that morning. She tells her father, "I did it to myself." She knows where all her mistakes were, exactly at what points she went wrong. He asked for her help. His plea seemed to come straight from a damaged heart. "It was three in the morning," she says.

At the time, after Ralph and Rita had appeared together at Grace's door, Ralph said to Rita, "It was you he wanted," his voice thin with anger.

"Ralph, stop it." Grace put her hand over Rita's on her cheek where the bruise darkened it. "Have you ever been in love?"

Rita walked to the window, looked out at the street. She said, very low, "Yes."

"Are you in love now?"

"Yes. Yes, I am," Rita said, still looking out at the newly gray day.

"I am," her father says. "But it's different than it was."

The first painting showed Grace with a shaft of light slicing over her face and one breast, a glint of green eye, though her eyes in most light are blue, the rest of her barely visible in the shadow washed over with deep green. Two more paintings had followed; Willem was working on the fourth. In each, he composed her differently; in each, something different was lit.

That afternoon, he examined her face. She shut her eyes and imagined herself in a clearing with sun coming down through the trees. Then it was dark, and the trees had closed around her like walls. Willem put his brush down on the palette. Usually, nothing could break his concentration when he had a brush in his hand. But he loved Grace, if careful looking can be considered a kind of love. For Grace, her acquiescence was an acceptance; it would not have occurred to Willem that it was not necessarily a return.

He set down his palette, came over and sat on the edge of Grace's chair. "How can I work with you like this?" He opened her knees, ran his fingers over the bruises on her inner thighs. Then he took her face in both his hands, pressed his palm against her swollen lip. "What happened? You are so white." He pushed a thumb under each of her eyes.

She was too tired not to tell him, though she didn't want to explain yet again her disappointment, how her sense of failure was not a moral one.

He got up and walked to the other side of the studio. When he stopped touching her the cold rushed in.

"You should have known," he said. It was less an accusation than a plea. "It wasn't the first time. Didn't anybody tell you?"

"Who?" she said. She put her head down, looked at the hands folded over the mottle of black marks on her thigh.

He sighed. "Me." He brushed his forehead with his fingers, stood for a moment. "Don't worry about Marcus," he said. "I'll take care of him." He opened her legs, adjusted the light. He pushed his thumb against her cheek where it was wet and smeared the tears under her eyes.

"Don't move," he said. It was the only advice Willem had ever given her.

It was as if Marcus had never existed. He vanished from the bar and the restaurants where everyone ate, and nobody said a word. Grace concentrated, at night, on compressing the burning place until it hardened first into an egg, then a marble, then a pea. Then she would imagine it as frozen, a frozen pea joining the solid box shape of its mates. She had realized there were other peas like it, there behind her ribs, though she had no idea how many. As long as she kept them in that cold place, they would be fine.

One afternoon she didn't go to Willem's studio. Now she was afraid. Every day for a week Grace watched through the blinds as Willem walked up her apartment building steps, then she sat as still as she could while he knocked. She pressed her cheek to the wood, felt his pounding vibrate through it. She didn't know how to look at him and tell him to go away, that Marcus's vanishing wasn't enough. Or that it was too much.

Winter quarter, she cut her hair short, scrubbed her face clean. She wore her baggiest clothes, in grays and browns, as if within them she could make her body invisible. She stopped reading Baudelaire and Eliot; she gave herself over to cell structure, to organic precision, the demonstrable hypothesis.

She still remembers: Afterward, Marcus kissed her on her cheeks where the tears were flowing. "There," he said. "Was it so bad?"

She pushed her fist against his mouth. "Get off."

"You never even hit me," he said, then moved her hand and kissed her. She hadn't, until that moment, understood that hitting him had been an option. Her blood was on his lips.

He said, "You're as beautiful as she is, in your own way. But it's not the same."

CHAPTER 8

■ ■ ■

The Air of the Dream

Yesterday the ground war officially started, and though she must know that, in distant cities, bombs with her name—all our names—etched invisibly on their skins, however impersonally delivered, have rent thousands of bodies limb from precious limb already, it's the idea of soldiers fighting face-to-face, seeing what they're going to kill alive and then killing anyway, that awakens in Grace a more primal resistance, a fear she remembers. This is what Pascal would have been there for, just behind the front lines, waiting for young men to come in on stretchers with bullets or shrapnel embedded in their flesh, which he would have to open even farther with his scalpel to remove the foreign bodies, doing damage in order to heal.

Grace isn't sure if Dan's avoiding her or simply his life, whether he stays away out of consideration or out of spite. She wants to see him, though the idea of him repels her.

Doesn't he think of her? She should be thinking, Good riddance. Instead, she imagines him and Bliss in their small house, the heat rising. Part of her envies that heat, what she conceives as their passion.

The last time Dan came to lab, the week after the shooting, Grace lifted her eyes from the microscope to catch him looking, his scalpel held up between them like a sword drawn to some challenge. She had been describing a plant's epidermis and endodermis—osmotic pumps moving water across the root—and for a second her voice solidified in her throat. The class is still shrinking—one young man after another has come to Grace after lab to tell her he's enlisting: the Army, the Air Force, the Navy, the Marines. Grace wants to reach her hand out and touch each of them, the not-so-solid flesh holding in all that muscle and blood, the blue intestines, and say, "Are you sure?" She looks at the walls of the lab, their sleek hanging cabinets, tatty posters showing the cross-sections of stems. Her students can have no idea where they are really going. But then, neither can she. She wants to say, "Remember, you're mostly water. You could just dissolve."

Bliss comes and stands outside the lab door before class. When Grace arrives, Bliss touches her arm and hands over Dan's lab assignments. "I tried your office hours," she says. "But you weren't there. These are for you."

Grace can tell just turning through them that Bliss has been doing the drawings: even when she tries to make her lines wobble, her rendering of the scattered vascular bundles of a corn stem glows practically into life. True to the stains on the slide, she's used a delicate watercolor wash in greens and mauves, and in her drawing each vascular bundle, afloat among the thin-walled cells, looks like a small Martian face with empty, wide-set eyes and ebullient hair. And her coloring of the vascular rays penetrating an oak's inner heartwood almost vibrates against Grace's eyes, the stains ranging from the same delicate mauve into a deep blood red, with green ringing the large xylem cells the rays traverse.

"You mean, they're for him," Grace says. "They're beautiful. Are you okay?"

Bliss blows a gust of air upward, lifting her curly bangs. She is wearing jeans with paint stains on them; she looks faded and puffy. "I know he isn't good for me." She still has the watercolor stains on her hands, faint traces of green and rose. On one wrist are quarter-sized bruises the color of plums. When she sees Grace looking, she covers them with her other hand.

Polite as ever, Grace turns her eyes to the drawings. "Tell Dan I want him to try again." She touches Bliss on her arm. "He'll feel better if he does them himself. But these are beautiful."

"Why do you even care how he feels?"

Grace passes her hand over her forehead. "I don't know. It's my job, I guess. Maybe if I just act as if everything's normal, it will be."

Bliss shakes her head. "It won't."

"Not ever." Grace stares at the wall and sighs. "If it will help, tell him he can relax. He can come and do his labs between classes. When I'm not here. I'll get a teaching assistant to work with him. He can come back fall quarter."

Bliss looks down at the drawings. "You don't really think he'll be here in the fall, do you?" In her eyes when she raises them again is a pleading hope.

In some ways, Grace wants to avoid that question. She takes a deep breath. "You know more about that than I would. It depends on what he's done."

"And on what the police find out."

Grace touches the hand hiding Bliss's wrist. "Tell him whatever you need to. He's a gifted student, and I'm a teacher. I don't know anything else to do. But you should be careful."

She waves her hand around the room, at the laboratory islands with their microscopes and instrument drawers adrift in fluorescent light. "I've always got this."

"Look. I'm not saying anything," Bliss says. "But don't cut him any breaks."

"You either."

"You can keep the drawings." Bliss holds her wrist as if it's too fragile to bear the weight of the hand at the end of it.

Grace's mother's hair was black and waist-length, her skin white. She was small, like Grace, though Grace remembers her as tall, her back so straight it looked as if she wore a brace of some kind—a tree, definitely, rather than a reed.

"A small tree, then," Imo says, willing to give her daughter only so much stature in death.

Grace is listening to country-blues, Mary-Chapin Carpenter singing about getting lucky. It's been a while since Grace has turned any music on. Imo usually would have questioned the choice, but now she presses her lips closed. Imo's opinions are strong, and such control takes considerable force. Grace tries to hum along, but all she feels is wind in her throat.

Sometimes her mother smelled of salt, the wind coming hard off the ocean; she smelled of snow, dry dust, grass. She smelled of the crowd. She would fling her arms out and say, "Today, I feel bright as water."

Mary-Chapin Carpenter has just won the lottery. She's sitting in a honky-tonk with Lyle Lovett's hand on her thigh. Imo sits on the edge of her bed with a box open on her lap. She holds out a photograph. Grace recognizes herself as a child, but the photo looks older than it should, as though it's been aged on purpose for effect. "I don't remember that dress," she says. Her throat is still empty of tune, of vibration.

"It's not your dress." Imo squares her shoulders, and Grace notices how thin they've become, little wings of bone.

When they get to more recent photos, shots of Julia shortly before the accident and of Grace as an adult, the likeness fades—habits of expression, maybe, or of thought, have shaped their faces differently. If Julia had lived, the resemblance might have persisted; Grace might have learned to register thought and emotion in her mother's lines. Now, her face has taken on some of the mobility of Imo's, without the slyness. But in that photo of Julia at twelve, it is Grace looking out through the eyes. Julia even has the same ringlets Imo gave Grace at that age.

As bright as water. This would be a good day: on a bad day, Julia was a cloud of wet leaves, formless as the piles they raked out of the flower beds in March.

Imo, who hardly ever talks about this, says, "It was a flaw in her character," though it has been only since Julia's death that Imo has imagined any flaw in her at all.

Carpenter has moved on to a sad ballad, and Grace turns the tape off. She smooths out the bedspread with her fingers. "The world hurt her," she says.

Imo comes so close her breath brushes Grace's cheek. "Let me tell you a secret," she says. "Your father is right about one thing only. The world hurts us all."

On a very bad day, Julia might say, "I can't face it." She would gesture toward the window's cloud-bound sky, bare trees, the street dull with rain.

"Face it," Imo says. "She was a baby." Imo stands up very straight.

Grace adjusts Imo's sleeve. "Your clothes are hanging on you," she says. "I need to take you shopping.

Grace and her mother would lie on the couch, each to an arm, and look up toward the sky at the mountains where their peaks vanished into the clouds. Grace would try, with drawings of horses and women, paintings of houses lined with tulips, to tease her mother out.

One morning, Julia rose to her knees and, using one of

Grace's markers against the glass, began to trace in green the routes she had taken up different peaks framed in the picture window. Grace knelt too, followed the green lines with her fingers. Up the broad foot of each mountain the marker mounted, to these cliffs here, up this crack, beneath this over-hang. Julia sketched on the glass a mountain from an entire continent away, one that, taking its shadowy shape on the window, engulfed and towered over the real peaks fading into background.

Grace shut her eyes and breathed the thin mountain air until it burned her lungs. Her foot scraped against the tiny alpine lichens. She moved to the edge, looked down at the remote world of people, tiny from so high, and at the distant, everyday business of life.

Then, near the peaks, only clouds, a soft dampness that closed around Grace until she could see only the next hand-hold, only the wet, slippery stone in front of her face. It was a kind of comfort, to imagine the mist could be substantial enough to hold a moving body to the cliffside.

Then Grace lay down over her mother's body, and Julia rubbed her daughter's back absently. But Julia was not sinking back into inaction; under Grace's thin limbs, the strings of her mother's body vibrated with energy. Julia was about to pack her ropes and pitons and haul herself up a sheer cliff face with only the friction of her fingers and toes against the rock to keep her from falling. Grace could see the green skirts of the mountain fanning out onto flatlands, and against them the shape of Julia growing smaller, her legs and arms spread as if to catch the air.

If she returned, she would return fully, with the force of a bird against glass, except the glass would dissolve, let her through, just as she hit it. Stunned, she would settle once more like a bird onto a perch, as if the glass had not closed again behind her, solid, impenetrable.

In labs, botanists have successfully germinated seeds from

before the time of Christ. Grace has seen those plants. But such long dormancies are still nothing, mere moments in geologic time. Now Grace understands the apparent unpredictability even in motions so slow they seem static, the dynamics determining the formation of a crystal as much as the opening of a flower or the inconstant curl of an ocean wave.

Julia is kneeling on a trail in her khaki hiking shorts, holding up a tiny piece of rock, explaining from this minor evidence geologic violence of a million years ago. She loves the rocks not for their precise beauty but for what they say about a wildness that originates in the core of the earth, a wildness she wants to enter, to ride. She gestures at the peaks in front of her, glaciers still scraping their flanks, heaving up boulders and trees. Her face is white with passion. She turns to the man standing closest to her—not her own husband, Grace's father, but someone else's. It makes no difference. She opens his hand, puts a rock into it, and says, "Fool's gold."

Any second, she told Grace, the earth could open and swallow us all into its blazing heart.

On the trail, her mother caught her looking and let go of the man's hand and knelt and drew Grace to her. Grace put her head on Julia's shoulder, closed her eyes against the light, against the jagged mountains where they were walking. She can still smell sweat and patchouli, grass, hair dried all afternoon in the sun. Behind her eyes, the grave peaks of the Wind River Range fall away to a coldly intimate meadow alight with tiny, buoyant alpine flowers, where Grace, her parents, Rita, that other man and his wife, Mr. and Mrs. Abrams, made camp on the banks of Clear Lake.

They fished for trout. Julia laid out on a tarp ropes, pitons, carabiners—hardware to keep her hooked onto the earth. She, Grace's father Byron, and that other man pointed out cracks, overhangs, possible routes up Temple to the sky. You wouldn't have known which man Julia was married to—she leaned first to one, then to the other, her voice low. As they packed up their equipment, her laughter rose from under her straw cowboy hat like bursts of small flushed birds; in the thin light, her face was pink with excitement.

The climbers left in a cold dawn. Wind ripped at the lake. The campfire was pale in the early sun. By noon, dark clouds massed over Temple, though at camp the sun shone intensely, as if compressed by the weight of the clouds. Thunder in the distance. Mrs. Abrams shaded her eyes and looked toward the peak, invisible behind clouds. Grace knew her mother would never turn back until she'd gained the summit. The violence of a storm would only spur her on.

That night, Grace watched lightning flash against the orange walls of the tent. At dawn, Mrs. Abrams went for help. The sky was clear again, and there was snow on the peaks; the meadow was frost-limned, and lupine and paintbrush glowed, frozen in the thin, clean air. When the sun hit the flowers, they would turn black.

Later, Grace read that lightning not only travels down but also leaps up, out of the earth. She imagined her mother's body's charge as so strong it pulled that fire through solid granite, through the bodies of two men at once, and sent it into the sky. But in spite of the clarity of these pictures, Grace still can't recall realizing her mother was dead. She remembers her mother in the morning, coming toward Grace down the trail. Julia is wearing her khaki hiking pants with all the pockets—they're dirty and wet to the knees where the rain-soaked grasses have brushed her legs—and the faded red anorak she got in college from the Seattle Coop, and she has her day pack slung over her shoulders and her red nylon climbing rope looped around her.

She turns around and points back up the trail—Grace can just see her father, his shadow at least, coming around the bend through the trees—and then Julia keeps on walking, down into the meadow alight with sun, Julia who was always careful to stay on the little deer paths now so happy to see Grace she's tromping the frost-burned alpine flowers, across the grasses and mosses, all so fragile that if you step on them or tear them out they don't grow back, not for fifty years or more—maybe, Rita and Grace had thought when they'd first arrived there, maybe not ever in their lives.

Grace is sitting at her old childhood desk at Imo's, going over her students' lab reports but thinking about a bracelet of bruises, about her promise to Ralph to watch out for Bliss. She has failed, has let herself sink into her loss. When she glances up she doesn't really see Imo, so it isn't until Imo says, too politely, "It's really nothing. I'm sorry to disturb you," that Grace realizes something is wrong. Imo's face is gray and there is a sheen of sweat on her forehead. She has a wig already on, slightly crooked, and her hand lies over her heart.

At first Grace goes still, then she says to herself, Move. She says in a voice that surprises her with its calmness, "Of course." She gets up and throws her sweater around Imo's shoulders and helps her down the stairs and out to the car. Imo's standing as straight as she can, but her face is still gray and her skin looks artificial.

Now, Imo sits on the examining table in one of those backless gowns, and Craig Mills runs the stethoscope over her chest, then has the nurse come in and hook her up to an ECG. Grace stands next to the bed while the nurse tapes the nodes to Imo's torso. She tries not to look at Imo's stark ribs or her breasts diminished by age, like envelope flaps. Though the equipment looks shiny, high-tech, the electrocardiogram works essentially the way it did when it was first invented in 1920 or so. Pascal used to have a photograph in his office of the inventor wired up, his foot sitting in a bucket of water to ground him, his dog looking up, all admiration. But Grace is furious for all the decades in between. Surely they could have done better by now.

In the hall, Craig Mills tells Grace it was a minor attack, but he wants to keep Imo for tests.

He looks at his watch, and Grace says, "Are you in a hurry?"

He laughs. "It's just a habit. Being around someone her age gets me started thinking about time." This is what Grace has been afraid of, ever since she moved back in with Imo and began to watch her drift through the increasingly blue air of her memories.

"You're living with her?" Craig Mills asks.

"For now. It's only temporary, until I'm back on my feet." It's not cold, but Grace has her arms wrapped around herself. "What shall I do?"

He touches her shoulder. "Think about getting your grandmother back on *her* feet."

"How?"

"There are good places. A little companionship might not hurt. People to talk with about the old days."

Grace smiles. "She hates old people. They can't keep up."

"She is one," he says.

Grace tilts her head back to look at him. She loves thinking about Imo this way, as if she's immortal, as if her body isn't vanishing into the air. "I won't tell her if you don't."

Grace goes down to the admitting office and finishes the insurance forms. While she waits for the elevator to take her back to Imo's room, she feels a touch on her shoulder.

Jemma stands behind her, her cap pinned into an improbable tousle of nut-colored hair, her eyes made up in shades of purple, her white uniform pulled tight over a blowsy bosom.

Next to her, Grace feels scrawny and underdone. She has no trouble understanding what Pascal might have seen in Jemma. So much, she thinks, for the clean-faced high ground. "Oh. Hello," she says.

"I wanted to tell you," Jemma says. "I was with him. You know. Before he died."

Grace raises one eyebrow.

"Oh." Jemma laughs. "I'm sorry. My job." She shrugs, apologetic, then lets her eyes move back up to the panel showing in green numbers that the elevator has just moved from the fourth floor to the third.

"Of course."

Jemma drops her eyes again. "I thought you would want to know. He was okay at the end. Even though he could barely speak. He was talking about heaven."

This time, Grace feels both eyebrows shoot up—and immediately hears Imo's voice say, "Wrinkles." She says, "Heaven?" Nothing could seem less likely.

"Well, he was talking about *grace*. I thought he was calling. You know. For you."

Grace feels a wash of tenderness, opens her mouth to thank Jemma.

Jemma says, "But then he started talking about, you know, happiness, about how good he felt, and I knew I was wrong."

Grace closes her mouth. Jemma's face is as blank as innocence.

"It was kind of weird. He was obviously in pain. It was sort of a struggle, you know, for him to talk. If he'd been anyone else, I wouldn't have paid attention."

Grace wonders how many last words have been lost on Jemma. Did Pascal ever actually talk to her? "And you think he couldn't have been talking about me?"

Jemma widens her eyes, then says, "Oh." She smiles. "Well, I guess. I just wanted to tell you. And that I'm sorry."

Grace believes Jemma is sorry, but not for Grace, nor for sleeping with Pascal. The elevator has come and gone. She pushes the button again. Jemma begins to turn away.

After all, perhaps she meant well. Grace sighs. "Jemma." When Jemma turns back, Grace takes her hand. "Thank you anyway," she says. "I appreciate your telling me."

Jemma looks surprised. "Sure. I mean, it seemed right, you know?"

When she arrives upstairs, Craig Mills is already leaning over Imo, but he straightens up when Grace comes in.

"Run along back to your schoolwork," Imo says to Grace. She makes eyes at the doctor. "I'm in very good hands." She still looks pale and tired, but it has been only with Flint that

Grace has recently heard just that undercurrent of purr. Imo's hardly been out since Grace came back to stay.

"I'll bring my work back here. And a dressing gown for you."

Imo considers. "The blue peignoir, I think."

"This is a hospital," Grace says, "not a movie set."

"And some magazines, if you please. *Cosmo.*"

The sun is shining, and though the breeze is chilly Grace stands in the driveway for a minute, her face lifted to the light, before she turns back to the empty house. She puts Bliss's drawings away under her bed, then she pulls down the folding stairs to the attic and climbs them. She hasn't been up here since she moved out for college. Even if she had been tempted since coming home, she would have been made nervous by Imo's eyes on her.

There are windows under the eaves, and the dust floats through the sunlight like motes of gold. Cartons, their labels fading from age and dust, are stacked between racks of clothes, hatboxes, old trunks. Grace looks around, then lifts the lid of the box closest to her.

An hour later, when her father calls, this is what she tells him: "I wanted to see what was there." Of her mother, she means, what of Julia Imo had boxed up to keep. But she's willing to let her father believe she might have been looking for something of him there, too, now that she's got it in hand. "I found your mandolin," she says. She has it around her neck right now—when the phone rang she was tuning it by ear.

He says, softly, "I thought you might want it. Someday."

"Listen." She plays a little riff into the receiver, but the strings are so old they stretch back out of tune as soon as her fingers touch them. Next to her is a pile of Imo's old movie posters tied with twine. In all of them Imo is big-eyed and clearly in distress.

Grace hesitates, then tells him about Imo's heart.

"I'm sorry," he says. "There's been too much between us, but I wish her no harm."

"She's at that age." Grace has to force herself to say this, to make it true. "It's to be expected. But it seems everyone is flawed just there." She pauses again, her hand on her ribs.

"You have to expect it. It's the most common cause of death."

"The doctor says it may not be what gets her. He thinks I should find a home for her."

"What did you say?"

Grace looks around at the attic full of memories. "I didn't." She lifts a framed photograph of a young Imo on horseback, black and white with all its glamour. Imo is wearing a glittering lamé drop-waisted gown and lipstick in so deep a red her lips look black. She's sitting sidesaddle; she is composed against a backdrop of lush jungle. The sun is just rising into her eyes, or just setting, but in spite of a sleepiness, or maybe a languor, in her body, she does not look ready for bed. She lifts a glass of champagne at the photographer, dangles a spangled mule off the cocked toe of one outstretched foot.

"She looks like some sort of commercial for the twenties," she says.

Her father laughs. "That's exactly what she was."

After they hang up, Grace sits looking at the photo, Imo staring back from an impenetrable past. Grace thinks whoever shot the photo was never Imo's husband, though Imo wears his ring; the eye is too tentative, too charged, its caress running up the lamé-draped leg too full of longing. Whoever was behind the camera watched Imo's figure emerge under the darkroom's red lights, then, as soon as it dried, ran a finger from Imo's toes to her squinted, heavily lined eyes.

Later, in her hospital bed, Imo touches her younger face and says, "Costa Rica."

"Who took it?" Grace asks. She fingers a card on a bouquet of daisies and is surprised to read that they're from Detective Flint.

Imo is looking at the far wall of the room as if it has dissolved. After a minute, she shrugs. "A girl I knew. We'd been at a party. We rode all the way up the mountain, just to watch the sun rise. I named your mother for her." She looks up at Grace sideways.

Grace says, "Julia." She wonders where her grandfather was—off in a primitive jungle, searching for oil. In the old pictures, he is young and skinny; he wears hats, smokes a pipe.

"Your grandfather was against the name, but I filled out the form while he was passing out cigars. Men don't understand what they do to make themselves peripheral. We left Costa Rica a few months later. I never saw her again." Imo puts her lips to her wrist and looks dreamily out the hospital window, and suddenly Grace knows that this woman, this faraway place, is more immediate to Imo than her own house, than the hospital bed and the tray with its uneaten red Jell-O still jiggling on the bedside table. Even than her blue peignoir, itself another door to the past.

This is history. Grace is having trouble connecting it to the little old woman in the bed. "You mean, the one who took the picture," she says.

Imo focuses on Grace. "Dear, do try to keep up."

In the morning, Craig Mills announces that Imo is going to be fine. "For now," Craig says. "But she's not getting any younger."

"Says you. I'm not deaf, you know." Imo smooths the long ringlets of the ash-blond wig Grace brought her over the pearl-embroidered breast of her peignoir.

"Just make sure she takes these"—Craig gives Grace Imo's pills—"and see she gets some exercise."

"I'm eighty-four," Imo says. "I'm entitled to a little rest."

He says, "When you die, then you can rest. Now I want you out and walking."

Imo lifts a skinny finger at Grace. "Don't think you're going to get rid of me too quickly," she says.

CHAPTER 9

■ ■ ■

Still Life, With Grace

Grace's work suits her. Even now, she can turn a corner in the greenhouse and come upon a flower that, yesterday, was only a secretive bud, and, seeing it open, ruffled and veined and breathing, she will stop short, her heart opening. In such an uncomplicated response, physical, even sexual, she finds her relation to the world. She knows the plant's cycle, the pang she will feel as the flower fades, how long it will be before she might coax another to open, and how the new bloom will be the same, yet individual, unique. Grace can nurture growing things, can splice a limb to another kind of tree knowing it will bear its own sweet fruit, can feel, among her plants, like a mother or a lover, all without any of the emotional un-tidiness that arises from human relations. These things are simple to her, clean and orderly, responsive to pruning and coaxing.

Earlier on the day Grace found Pascal with Jemma, she was

sunbathing with Rita on the condo balcony. They had taken off their bikini tops and turned onto their stomachs, drowsy with heat. Rita lifted the bottle of sunscreen, and Grace nodded. Rita's hands moved over her shoulders, her back, slid around to her stomach. Grace opened her mouth to speak, then stopped. She couldn't feel the difference between her skin and the warm lotion, what was melting into what.

Rita whispered, "It's okay. Turn over." Grace hesitated, then rolled onto her back, shut her eyes, moved into the touch. The radio was on, Jackson Browne from their school days, and Rita's hands moved to the drumbeat, the beat of Grace's heart.

The announcer broke in to say that Saddam had just invaded Kuwait. Grace opened her eyes. Rita said, "Shit," and her hands stopped. Almost grateful, Grace picked up her towel, slung it over her shoulders so its ends covered her breasts, and walked through the sliding glass doors into the study. She could still feel Rita's touch inside her mouth, at the back of her throat. She adjusted the shades, leaned over the case of orchids and breathed in.

Rita came in after her. She lifted Grace's towel from her shoulders. Grace didn't stop Rita, but lifted Rita's hand, put her face against it for a second, and said, "I'm sorry." They stood in the cool shadows of the room. Rita knelt. Goose bumps rose on Grace's arms; her whole skin tightened around Rita's first touch. When Rita said, "Now," Grace lay down on the floor. She could hardly breathe through the musk of orchids. She closed her eyes against the room, against the light coming in.

Later, waking on the floor in the sun with her head on Rita's shoulder, Grace said, "It's done." At that moment, she would still not have undone it if she could have. She could convince herself that the shape of this love, its pressures and obligations, was different from what she felt with Pascal. She had given in to necessity, which was now past. She felt an openness she wanted to carry to Pascal, to give him with her two hands. She would go and tell him; she would lay her head on his shoulder, and he would forgive. This would be a betrayal of Rita, but Rita, Grace believed, was prepared.

Rita touched Grace's cheek. "Is that everything, then?" She turned her face away, so Grace couldn't see her eyes.

So in spite of everything, Grace was surprised when she opened Pascal's office door that August day, quiet, in case he was napping with his feet on his desk, as he sometimes did after his morning surgery, and saw a white nurse's uniform leaning over him where he sat at the desk. Jemma had her hand on the desk and looked as if she were waiting for him to answer a question. His desk was a mess as usual, covered with charts; his tie was loose; his hair was too short to fall in his eyes, but he lifted his hand and smoothed it back anyway, a nervous gesture that tipped Grace off, made her look at Jemma's hair, its chestnut muss a little less planned than usual, and her full lower lip where the lipstick, the color of a ripe tropical fruit, was blurred at the edges—an image that obliterated what Grace carried with her that day, what she had gone there to tell him.

Now she says to Pascal under her breath, "Asshole," and Imo looks up from her *People* magazine, which she reads faithfully ever since they did a "whatever happened to?" profile of her in 1985, with the most sultry of the photographs from her heyday and one recent shot, Imo sitting with her hands folded in her lap and looking mostly prim in her blue-chignoned wig, except she has shut one eye in a delighted wink at the suggestion she's just made to the young photographer.

"There's no need to speak to him that way," Imo says.

Grace clears her throat. Again, she feels that empty space opening, yawning in her chest, a kind of cold, the rest of her constricting around it, closing up.

She didn't know, at first, how much more than that she was

able to contain; that she would be able to go for weeks, it would seem, without even taking a breath. And that the longer she went that way, knotting herself tight around her secret, the more impossible it would become to untie herself and open again into speech. All she needed to do was tell him, to put herself where he was, in the wrong, but she couldn't speak the words.

She says to Imo, "He knew all along."

She went to Pascal's window. The season had turned: fall was coming, imperceptibly as yet, but the day had taken on a stillness, the acute dryness of the last moments of summer. She couldn't decide what to do. She wondered if he could persuade her that whatever had passed meant nothing at all.

"Nothing," she says. She closes her eyes and calls up, as she did then, her mother's face, the mother lost to the most careless kinds of passion, and whispers, "Betrayal." Her mother's foot, raised, delicately arched, above the bare back of a man who is not her father; herself at six or seven or eight, her small face framed by the cracked-open door, her black hair escaping its braid.

Such a small thing, so close she couldn't see past it. The worst was that she hadn't expected this. She had let herself be taken by surprise. She kept looking out at the day, dull yellow, dusty, oppressively still. She let her left hand play moodily along her thigh, fingering chords against her jeans, all minors. She wanted the sky to open, that instant, into thunder.

For three months, she walked from window to window, looking out so she wouldn't have to observe anything close to her, watching the weather turn and the leaves fall and, finally, the first snow come. She stopped watering all her houseplants except the orchids; when the plants died, she dropped them into the trash, hearing the dull thud on the bottom of the can with satisfaction, and blamed their deaths on Pascal. She knew she was being ridiculous. Sometimes she would think she heard a woman's laugh in the other room, and she would go to the doorway, ready for the explosion, but there would be only Pascal sitting with a book under a lamp. He would pull off his reading glasses—he was vain, even around Grace—and look up as if hoping she had something to say, some accusation he could answer or be forgiven for. Some confession.

Grace wanted only to be sure of him again, and instantly. She wanted to be sure of herself. Emotional danger, then as always, frightened her more than the physical. But they were only human, after all. She would look at the long face that had made her think he was sensitive, the square jaw she had taken to indicate exquisite strength, trying to abstract them from the man, to learn from them. She examined her own weaknesses of heart. She put her hand against the window and watched steam collect around it. She didn't dare to ask: Was the trouble in him or in herself? Should she spend afternoons at cosmetic counters, looking for a lipstick to transform her? Would she find the seeds of their infidelity in her boyishness, her failure to open, to give like a woman until she was empty? In her fear? In her own lack of faith?

"In here," his voice says. Closing her eyes, she can feel his hand on her breast.

At night, Grace lay still as she could on the futon, trying not to move, not to brush her leg against his, however her desire built. In the mornings, Pascal would pour Grace's coffee and tell her what he had planned for the day, as he always had. Then he would pull on his jacket and leave, blowing her a kiss off the tips of his fingers as he walked out the door. She wondered who he would see, who he would touch. She screened her calls, avoiding Rita, letting the messages pile up, then trail off. With the same concentration that she brought to the minutiae of her work, that allowed her to be arrested by a single extravagant bloom, she forced herself to picture Pascal with other women, his limbs entangled with female limbs, anonymous, longer, more elegant than her own. She built elaborate pictures she carried in her mind, to the bar, into the classroom, of their bodies blooming into elaborate shapes.

The shapes her body had made with Rita's. Fingers and lips on bare skin. Not a simple case of a man taking his hunger somewhere else, of closing his eyes and swallowing what was fed him. Letting Rita touch her had seemed so uncomplicated. But Grace hadn't accounted for Pascal's inevitabilities, or her own inability to fit the pieces together. The way Pascal, without knowing it, would hold up a mirror and show her an image she couldn't bear, either in memory or in the present, and that she couldn't pass through. All this and more. Pride, for example—stupid, hypocritical, and unmovable. Purely human.

Rita said then, "I can't believe we waited so long."

Grace lifted her face and let Rita put fingers then lips against her mouth. Shutting her eyes, she can still taste the suntan lotion and salt.

Imo says, "Salt," and licks her lips, just as the doorbell chimes.

When Grace opens the door, Detective Flint is leaning on one arm against the door frame, slumped around his spine as always, as if the wrinkles in his clothes are cut deep into the body underneath. She's begun to think of him as the victim of some internal erosion.

"You're a regular metaphor for society," she says, and the smile he gives her is tired but edged with sweetness. She's beginning to like him.

From the living room couch, Imo calls, "You feed him, Grace. I'll just stay right here and give you two some privacy."

"Right," Grace says. "Your ears are still good, anyway."

At the kitchen table, over a plate of Imo's sugar cookies, Flint tells her Dan has vanished.

"I'm not surprised," she says. "I told you to arrest him. You're at least searching?"

"We're poking around. We still don't have enough to charge him."

"Bliss would know where he went." Grace checks the color of the tea, then pours.

"She says not. She says they argued and he took off."

"That's not the typical result of their arguments. Does she have bruises?"

Flint raises his eyebrows, snaps off a bite of cookie. "I hadn't thought to look. What else haven't you told me about?"

Grace brushes at the air with her hand, impatient. "It was obvious. Anyway, if he's run away, isn't that evidence? It couldn't have been anyone else. We all know that. And Bliss"—Grace pauses, tries to recall just what was said— "Bliss seems sure Dan will be in prison by the fall. That's what she said."

Flint leans his elbows on the table and talks around the cookie in his mouth, ticking off on his fingers: "One, Bliss says he was with her the night of the shooting, in the car driving home. Two, she says he was never out of her sight the whole evening, except when she was in the ladies'. With you?"

Grace nods. "Cowgirls', actually."

He smiles. "Three, we have no weapon. Four, he tested negative for powder."

"Gloves," Grace says. "How long did you guys give him to clean up, anyway?"

"Five. There was nothing with powder among his clothes. Traces in the van, but he says he's spent some time at the shooting range."

"He has."

"So. Not conclusive. Six, he has no more motive than anyone else."

"Than Ralph, you mean."

Flint leans back in his chair. He has tiny grains of sugar stuck in the stubble on his chin. "Or you. Even Rita, if I understand the situation." He looks at Grace, waiting, but she remains silent. She wants to lean over and brush the sugar off his chin, but she resists.

"Everybody accounted for," he says. "Including Ralph." He looks at her sideways. "Unless your memory changes." Flint dips another cookie into his cup of tea. "I understand that this has been a confusing time for you. A painful time."

"That's an understatement." Grace takes a breath. "You do understand I want to help. But why waste your time on my memory? It's not a matter of change, but of reliability. I'm working on it, but we both know who did this."

Flint looks her over, and she feels herself go red. She hasn't worked on her memory very hard. He says, "Why don't you think about it a while longer. Talk it over with Rita. Or your grandma."

This seems irregular to Grace. Shouldn't he be hauling her downtown, making sure she gets it right, doesn't square her story with anyone? Though it's too late for that. His gentleness embarrasses her.

"Great cookies, by the way," he says. He waves his damp cookie in the air. "I take it you didn't bake them?"

From the living room, Imo calls, "You take it right."

Grace notices the wedding ring is gone, and she feels a sudden, human sadness for him. A white dent circles the finger where it used to be, and the whiteness makes his hand, which is square and strong, look oddly vulnerable. Before she can think about what she's doing, she leans over and brushes the sugar from his chin with her fingers. "Are you having your ring cleaned?"

He looks past her out the window. "It was just a habit. We've been separated almost a year."

She feels herself blushing, leans back. "I'm sorry," she says. "Just sugar." The light outside holds the thinnest wash of sun. "Looks like spring. It's about time."

"It's an occupational hazard. The hours aren't real good for marriage." He rubs the back of his hand vigorously over his chin, then proffers it for her inspection. She nods.

"I shouldn't be saying this," he says, "but I wish you would think it over. What you say is no use if you keep changing your mind." He meets her eyes. His are gray, like rain clouds, and warm. Suddenly, Grace thinks that he likes her too. He says, "You have to be sure, or you can't help us. Give me a call at the station when you're ready."

It's been weeks since Grace was last in the saloon, and it looks larger than she remembers, dingier, like a warehouse. The same suggestive sunlight filters through the windows. There are damp spots on some of the walls. Ralph is behind the bar polishing glasses.

Grace slides onto a stool next to a big jar with a sign that says in careful Magic Marker, "Tipping is not a city in China." Ralph lifts the coffeepot, and when she shakes her head he draws a Wasatch Ale and sets it down with a bag of Cape Cod chips. He leans on his elbows and watches her take the first swallow of beer and smile.

"Oh," she says. "It has been too long. I've been awash in tea. Lapsang Soochung." She makes a face. "Tastes like my father's old fishing creel. And sugar. Cookies. Ding Dongs." She points with a chip. "Give me one of those pickled eggs? I'm desperate for salt."

"It's good to see you out," he says, and lays his hand on top of hers. Like his features, his hands and feet are broad, a little flat but shapely. He looks tired, his eyes redder than usual, and his hair sticks out in little flaps over his ears. This is the first time Grace can remember that he's ever visibly needed a haircut. Usually, he's regular as a calendar, every three weeks. She raises her hand to her own hair. She needs a cut, too.

"I'm sort of here on business," Grace says.

"I do business."

"Legal business."

Ralph stands up straight and picks up the dishrag. "That's different. You know I can't talk about it with you."

"I have only one question."

Ralph half smiles at her. "That makes it worse, I bet."

This time, it's Grace who captures his hand, and though it's enormous compared to hers he lets her do it, keeps his fingers quiet. She strokes his knuckles. "Ralph," she says, "I have to go in and talk to Flint."

He looks into her eyes, serious. "Of course you do. You should have done that a long time ago."

"What?" Grace speaks very quietly, but Ralph lifts his finger to his lips as if she's shouted.

"What?" she says again, this time louder. She tightens her hand around her beer. "I said what you asked me to. Now, what am I supposed to tell him?"

"Sweetheart, listen to me."

Grace nods. She's looking into his eyes, but they have a flat, ironic cast she can't see past.

"You have to tell him the truth."

She blows out. "That's great. I'm here as a favor to warn you, and you tell me we've been wrong all along?"

"Not all along. Just now."

"Well, I can't tell the truth. Not until you answer my question."

Ralph cocks an eyebrow at her and smiles.

"I think I know the answer," she says, "but I'm just not sure, you know?"

Ralph sighs, looks at the ceiling. Grace can almost hear his brain ticking, figuring advantages. For what? His eyes drop from the ceiling to the wall behind her. "I've got to have this place painted," he says.

She taps the back of his hand hard with her knuckles. He shifts his gaze to hers. "You tell them the truth," he says. "I wasn't with you. You don't know where I was."

She closes her eyes and the scene is clear, herself and Rita leaving the bar together, standing in the dark parking lot. "How am I supposed to do that? You want me to walk in there and say, 'Hey, I'm sorry I lied, but my lawyer—excuse me, my ex-lawyer—says it's okay to tell the real story now'?"

"Listen. You didn't lie. You were confused. In shock. You weren't sure what happened. Rita and I told you different things."

"But Ralph—"

"I told you I was with you, and you wanted to believe me. You were afraid." He puts his finger to her lips. It's cold, and she feels the chill run down her back. "Hush," he says. "It wasn't me. You know that, don't you?"

"I want to." His finger is still on her lips.

He holds her eyes, searching them. "I can't quite believe you don't."

She pauses, then says, "I do now." She lowers her eyes, raises them again. "I remember what you told me once. You told me innocence isn't always enough. And then you quit the law. What's out there now that's more powerful than innocence?"

"Maybe nothing. Maybe innocence will suffice this time."

"If I tell them everything, so should you. Whatever you know."

He looks at her closely. "You're so sure of me?"

Grace thinks. She wants to tell him the truth. All she knows is their childhood, the quality of his imagination, of his hands on her. As much as you can know about anybody. "If I can't trust you, I can't trust anyone," she says.

"Even though I lied?"

"When it's time, you'll tell me why."

"That's my Grace." Ralph comes around the bar and lifts her off the stool into his arms. She presses her face into his starched white shirt. They stand together, not like lovers but pressed together, just getting warm.

"Pain," her father says over the phone. "Right now. Isn't that what you want?"

Imo snorts. She's taken to listening in on her bedroom line, as if by talking to Grace where Byron can overhear she can say what she needs to without breaking her vow of silence against him. "You know, Gracie," she says, "some things we used to take for granted from men."

"Did it help?" Grace says. Remembering her father's hand on her bootlaces, she suspects maybe it did, but at what cost?

"Of course not. But we let them think so."

"Thanks a lot," he says.

"She always called you 'Grace's departed father,'" Grace says.

Imo says, "It wasn't a lie, exactly."

"No," Grace says. "But people generally took the word 'departed' to indicate something more permanent than a move to the Coast."

Byron pauses, then says to Grace, "And you went along."

In fact, though she is ashamed of it now, she was only too happy. By letting people believe her father was dead, she escaped questions, both on the playground and in her bed at night, which she clung to like a raft spinning her into darkest space. Where was he? She never had to say out loud that she had no idea, in spite of the postcards he sent from wherever, which she tacked to her bedroom wall, puncturing the Degas ballerinas that graced the wallpaper. By the time the cards arrived, she knew, he would be someplace else, somewhere she had no picture for. But she could close her eyes, like Imo, and envision that double gravestone.

She can't remember seeing him that day in the meadow. She can't remember if he left the path to walk toward her through spinning blue and yellow flowers and small flames of paintbrush as she so clearly sees her mother's ghost doing, can't remember his arrival at camp or the sun in his red beard. There are too many questions, and they are so much a part of her that she no longer knows how to put them into words.

Imo says, "You're still gone, as far as I'm concerned."

"She's right," Grace says. "You weren't here to tell me anything. You'll have to settle for what I invent." But she still wants to know his version, though she won't acknowledge it's any more real than her own. What she has are his postcards, his name on the backs, which she blacked out. The cards didn't make her feel small, but rather vast and unpopulated and full of constant buffeting drafts.

When Grace dismisses her Wednesday morning lab, Bliss and Dan are waiting together at the lab door.

"Bliss tells me you want to see me," Dan says. He holds Bliss by the elbow, as if to restrain her. Grace wants Bliss to pull away, but though she is clearly uncomfortable she's docile in his grip. Dan says to Grace, "You've lost weight. Let's get you something to eat." If anything, he's more impenetrable than before, but Grace also gets a sense of geologic wildness, something about to shift under his cratered surface.

Grace says, "I thought you'd disappeared."

"I'm still around. Just a little harder to find than I used to be."

"That may not be such a good idea," Grace says. "It makes you look guilty." Then she wonders to herself, Whose side are you on? She still has a hard time looking him in the eye and thinking of him as anything but what she knew before, still ordinary enough to be harmless. She forces herself to think of the taste of Pascal's blood, to think of Bliss's bruises, not abstract but painful.

"Looking guilty isn't a crime," he says. Then, "I'm starving. Let's go."

At the Broiler, Bliss asks Grace if she believes in ghosts.

"Maybe as figures of the mind," Grace says. "I can think of people who deserve to be haunted, but they're never the ones who are."

Dan says, "Don't be so sure." He's always been thin; now he looks gaunt, his skin screwed tight over his bones. "Believe me," he says. "I've lived with them all my life."

"No," Bliss says. "I mean real ghosts."

Grace says, "My grandmother's haunted," though she's

never thought of it this way. She likes this word better than Craig's: senile dementia. Or the one he won't say yet: Alzheimer's. She suspects Craig likes the distance that clinical terms provide, their reduction of a mind to a condition instead of a complexity, what a life constructs and then dismantles. First, connections fizzle. Then the figures of the mind lose flesh and substance. Eventually, they fade altogether away.

"We are all haunted," Bliss says.

Grace says, "But not in the sense you mean."

"How do you know what I mean? Anyway, that's like saying a rose and a daisy aren't both flowers."

Every voice Grace has believed lost has come back to her eventually, over the wires or in her own memory, sweeping through her body like a wind. She realizes that she has heard Pascal's voice less and less over the weeks, as if her father's has taken it over. She misses Pascal. She longs for his body as she longs for certainty, for explanations, though she will never settle on a permanent one. She says, "There are different kinds of death."

"Like how?" Bliss has her head cocked to one side.

Grace is looking at Dan. "Some are just losses. Some are thefts."

"It's good for you to get out," Bliss says, as if she hasn't heard. She smiles at Dan. His face doesn't move.

Grace says to Dan, "You could have come to lab an hour earlier and gotten credit."

Dan shakes his head. "The lights bother me." He leans over, looks carefully into Grace's face, so close she can feel his breath. She jerks back. He says, "It feels too much like an interrogation room." Bliss takes Grace's hand.

Grace feels trapped, hemmed in. "You mean you're afraid the police will look for you there," she says. "Or don't you want to face me?"

Bliss turns Grace's hand over and begins tracing the lines

in its palm with her small pink fingernail. "You've suffered a great loss," she says.

Grace has been accumulating patience for Bliss, but this is too much. "For Chrissake. You were there. You know more about it than I do." She takes away her hand and rubs her palm to get rid of the tingling, then she looks back at the menu.

"I don't mean Pascal," Bliss says. Grace notices she doesn't deny having been there. She pretends to ignore Bliss, runs her index finger down the list: fried scallops or oysters, Cajun catfish, tuna sandwich.

Dan smiles at Grace, and his scarred face seems to break open. It's been a while, she realizes, since she's seen him look happy. Maybe never—concentrated, maybe, but not happy. He looks at his menu and says, "Bliss has that effect on me too."

Immediately, Grace is sorry again. Bliss turns her head away from them both. Grace reaches under the table and rests her hand on Bliss's leg. After a minute, Bliss puts her hand on Grace's and squeezes. Then she turns her face back toward them, with the most composed smile Grace has ever seen.

After the waiter takes their order, they sit in silence. Grace has made a mistake coming with them. She doesn't know what she meant to accomplish. Twenty times a day, she re-members that Pascal is dead, feels the shock of grief all over again, fresh, and she forces herself to concentrate on the real-ity, the permanence of his absence. Getting used to it, the way she lets new shoes give her blisters that will heal into calluses. This lunch, though, is redundant, and therefore merely self-indulgent.

"Oh, look," Bliss says. Grace groans when she raises her head. Ralph and Rita have come in, and Rita is waving over the heads of the other customers. Grace waves back, though by now Rita's eyes are not on her, but on Bliss. Ralph and Rita make their way between the other tables. Both hug Grace, ask Bliss how she is. Dan raises his hand as if to shake with Ralph, but they ignore him. He sits back in his chair and smiles at everyone.

Even Bliss keeps her eyes averted. Rita has lifted Bliss's wrist and is tutting over its bruises, almost faded now, and casting dark looks at Dan.

Grace says, "Join us?" Her voice is weak. Rita waves toward the host where he's putting their menus down on an empty table.

"We're committed, I'm afraid," she says. Grace doesn't blame them—she feels, herself, like a traitor in the enemy camp, embarrassed to be caught out.

After their lunch arrives, Bliss picks up her tuna sandwich—not the old-fashioned kind but fancy, made with watercress and fresh tuna, guaranteed by the waiter in his blue shirt and long apron and bow tie to be caught by line instead of net. Bliss delicately knits her eyebrows, worried about dolphins. "Do you think eating any tuna at all does damage? Just by increasing demand?" She sets it down and lifts her glass of milk to her lips.

Grace looks at her plate of oysters, and her stomach does a little flip. "I can't believe you're worried about *dolphins*. As if nothing has changed."

Bliss gives her a blank, puzzled look.

Grief bubbles, moves from Grace's stomach to her throat; and for the first time, she can locate her rage, attach it to something personal. Pascal was wrong. Emotion is the abstract made physical, visceral, after all. It is no mere invention of society or the mind. Grace says, "Do you think you're on Oprah or something? Pascal is dead."

Bliss's hand hovers in front of her face with a piece of bread in it, her mouth open, pale eyes rounded into little O's.

"Sorry," Grace says. She feels her chin bunch up as it always does when she's trying not to cry. Her mother's did the same. Bliss is quiet. Her eyes are glazed with water. Dan reaches across the table and circles Bliss's wrist with his fingers—only a metaphor for restraint, since he doesn't tighten his grip.

Grace says, as if she's returning an objectionable gift, "Metaphors are as real as anything else," though Dan's gesture has given her an instance where this is only partly true. A metaphor, for example, raises only the idea, the specter of a bruise.

Bliss puts down her bread, purses her lips, which only shows more clearly how perfect they are, made to pout.

Grace says, "I keep dreaming about the murder. Except I'm the one who gets shot."

Dan leans forward. "Can you see who did it?"

"Only a shadow. Tall, slim. Dark clothes." She looks at him. He leans back in his chair. She says, "I see the bullets coming, feel them enter my flesh. My stomach, never my heart. Not with a tearing pain, but with a kind of—I don't know—sickness in the muscles, an ache. I put my hands to my stomach. They're covered with blood, bright red."

"You dream in color?" Bliss says, her hands cupping her own stomach.

Dan says, "We want to know exactly what you see in it."

"Then, I see Pascal as I saw him that last night, laughing, blood running down into his eyes, so red it makes his hair look like rusted metal. I reach out my hand and wipe it off his eyelid, and he grabs my fingers and looks at them. He is still laughing, as if he planned it all. I can't tell, now, if the blood on my hand is his or mine. And then I wake up, one arm wrapped around my stomach, the fingers of the other hand in my mouth."

The waiter comes, and while he refills the water glasses Grace falls quiet, looking down at the table.

When he's gone, Grace says, "I've had a long history you guys have no idea of. If I want to dream, that's my business." She points to Bliss's sandwich. "That's dead flesh, no matter how you look at it. The watercress too. But we make distinctions. It may not be right, but we do."

Bliss crunches her nose and looks away.

Dan drops Bliss's wrist and takes Grace's hand. She wants to pull it back, but she concentrates on letting it rest in his fingers, which are damp and cold. Whatever she does, she thinks, it will be Bliss who suffers, so Grace has to be careful. Dan turns her hand and traces the lines on her palm. Bliss has tears on her cheeks, but she does nothing to hide them or brush them away.

Dan seems relieved. "Believe it or not," he says, "the future looks good."

Bliss, still avoiding Grace's eyes, looking into the newly leaved trees, says, "Dan—"

He says, "But you've got to quit feeling so sorry for yourself."

"Don't you feel guilty? Aren't you afraid?" Grace wants to see pain, some evidence of regret. For the first time, she wants to see somebody punished.

Dan and Bliss look at each other, then back to Grace. Bliss stares, trying to tell Grace something with her eyes. "I didn't mean anything," Dan says. "Ask Bliss. I was with her." Then, "You may have seen more that night than you think. Your dream may be trying to tell you something."

Grace looks at him, first with horror, then with fear. "Do you mean, I could know?"

Bliss brushes at her eyes, which are pink around the rims. She looks at Dan quickly, then away. She says, "For God's sake, Dan. Of course she doesn't." Then, to Grace, "You aren't the only one with nightmares."

Grace and her father have established a routine. The phone rings every day between four and four-fifteen, soon after Grace brings Imo in from her walk. Imo used to be able to go around the block; now they walk only to the corner and back. Sometimes, when she hears the ringing, Grace thinks she won't answer it, but Imo always shouts, "Aren't you going to pick that up?" For both of them, always, in the end, Grace puts out her hand for the receiver.

Her father's voice says, "How are you?" and Grace shrugs, as if anyone can see her. She closes her eyes and pictures what's between them: salt desert, mountain peaks still frozen. Then the green coast, where he sits under a pool umbrella, surrounded by palm trees, talking into a cordless telephone. Imo's phone is the old-fashioned kind, black, heavy, with a rotary dial. Grace works on constructing a face for him, one she believes is close to the real one, at least as it was twenty years ago.

Today he says, "What are you doing in Imo's house?"

"How did you find me?"

"This was the logical place to start."

She looks at the small foyer, the walls needing paint. Everything is familiar and comforting. "This is temporary," she says. "I'm just putting things back together. Anyway, Imo needs me." She closes her eyes. Her picture of him wavers, as if it's under water. "You don't know the first thing about my life," she says. "Only what I tell you."

"There are things I can remember. A person doesn't just become somebody else."

"That's what I would have thought. But I learned."

They are quiet. Grace can hear breathing on the line—not a loud breath, or a labored one, just a gentle give and take so low she might be imagining it.

"The last time you saw me, I was a child," she says. It's as if he's standing behind a dirty window—she can see an outline, some faded colors, but no more. "I can't even picture you. To me you were dead."

"In a way, I was," he says. "Except I've always loved you. Isn't that evidence of life?"

"Yes," Grace says, though she's surprised. There are many things she could say, questions she could ask, rebukes, accusations, jokes she could make, but she doesn't. She touches her cheek with her fingers. They come away wet. She says, "I know. But if you're going to haunt me, can't you try a different medium?" She resists the twinges of sympathy that come over her, unexpected. She still does not plan to make things easy for him.

She hangs up the phone and stands for a long time looking into the gold-framed mirror. Then she reaches up and puts her hand over her reflected face. Her cheeks, distorted, blossom beyond her fingers. When she removes them from the glass, she sees Imo reflected behind her, still wearing walking sneakers. She's been listening in again, which is fine with Grace. Grace wants Imo to know what is going on, what she helped to create.

Imo leans on the wall next to the mirror, just the way Grace is leaning, her shoulders against the wall, her hands on her thin hips. "Sometimes, the most unexpected people pop back up," she says. "I'm not going to interfere. I just want you to understand the dangers."

"He's unexpected?"

Imo shakes her head.

"Imo," Grace says, "you kept us apart as long as you could. But this was inevitable, wasn't it?"

Imo looks away. "I don't see why. We were doing perfectly well without him."

"Byron can't hurt anything now," Grace says.

"You don't know that. You don't. As far as I can tell, he's got you hypnotized. Maybe brainwashed."

Grace feels a smile coming on and puts her hand over her mouth. "Over the phone?"

"These days, you never know. There's always technology." Imo folds her arms tight across this conviction.

Grace drops her hand and grins. "I'm sure that old phone isn't wired for brainwashing."

After a second, Imo smiles back. "You never know," she says. "It was made in the fifties."

Now Grace is laughing. "He sells insurance, for heaven's sake. All this time, I never knew how harmless he is."

"He should have started out that way and saved us all a lot of trouble. Traipsing all over the landscape, indeed."

"You're one to talk. Nobody did more traipsing than you."

Imo's nostrils narrow. "Nobody ever died through any fault of mine."

Grace doesn't know for sure if Imo's talking about Grace and Pascal or Byron and Julia. "So, you were lucky."

"I know people who've been haunted," Imo says. "It never ends. It's like something they carry inside." She puts her hands around her own belly, skinny but slack under her dress.

"I wanted not to blame her. That's all you want too. So you blamed him instead. I understand. I forgive you. But the time comes when you have to face things."

"Forgive me?" Imo's voice rises. "Me?" She waves her hand around the room as if at a bleak and ravaged landscape. "You'll be the death of me yet."

"I may." Grace takes a deep breath and grabs her keys and coat and walks out the door. Behind her, Imo calls her name once, but she keeps going. Her heart is beating hard.

There is one thing she believes she will not tell her father. Not because it will hurt him, but because she doesn't understand her relation to it, her complicity. The night after Grace kicked Pascal out, he was back and standing at the door with his hat in his hand. This is not a figure of speech; it was just the way he was brought up, in a flat, hot place where manners meant not everything but plenty.

"I thought you might want some dinner," he said. Then he stepped in from the hallway and got Grace's coat out of the closet and held it for her. She slid her hands into the sleeves, and he ran his palms gently over her shoulders before he stepped away and opened the door.

Over his hamburger, he said, "It's different now."

"Yes," Grace said. Her heart was beating as if they were courting again—after all, maybe it was distance she wanted, some perfect combination of privacy and desire.

"Last night," he said, "I kept wondering where you were, what you were doing."

She raised her eyebrows at him but didn't say anything.

"I got into the car and drove down from the cabin. I stood down below the building and counted up and over until I figured out which windows were yours."

She smiled. "All this time, you didn't know which ones they were?"

"I had no reason."

"They were your windows, too."

"If you lived in a house, I could stand in the yard and watch you." He was looking at her now. His lashes were very deep red, the sheen of freckles the same color as his summer tan. His eyes he made unreadable on purpose, so Grace couldn't tell if he was joking or serious, couldn't take from him her cues on how to react. Was this a concession, this offer of a house with, presumably, a garden attached? He leaned over, his elbows on the table, and said, smiling, as if the conversation were ordinary, "I want to know what you're doing." As if he were proposing the most common kind of cure, he reached over, ran his index finger down the side of her neck.

"So do I," she said. If she'd known what she wanted from him, she might have been able to read him. But in fact she wanted everything, not only all the protective distance in the world, but intimacy too, someone who knew her and would stay with her anyway. It was the last she couldn't believe in: she understood the power of physical beauty—even, to some extent, her own—but suspected that knowing each other's minds and hearts would more likely drive lovers apart than lock them together. She wasn't afraid of what she looked like in the morning, but she was afraid of saying, even of knowing, what she really meant at any given moment. So Pascal had looked to someone else. So she had looked to him, but from under someone else's hands.

She moved the fingers on her left hand under the rim of the table, searching the frets on an invisible guitar, a new progression taking shape in her ear. With her other hand, she reached for a french fry. "It's only been one night," she said and bit into the fry. "I went to bed with a book."

"Then I'm jealous of the book." He took hold of her fingers with the fry in them. "I'm jealous of the rest of this french fry," he said, then he ate it.

She watched him lick her fingers, then his lips. "Not anymore," she said.

"Let me come home with you." He leaned over, put his finger against her mouth.

She opened her lips, licked the salt off. "You want to have and eat." But a part of her knew this was what she wanted too, at least a part of what had taken her to Rita after all: romance, the frisson of courtship, the tension of not knowing exactly where the first touch would lead.

He ran his finger over her teeth. "Either one would do."

This was something she had never thought of before. She could give and withhold at the same time. She said, "Only to watch."

"Only to watch," he said.

Grace handed Pascal his key to the condo over his bacon-and-blue-cheese burger and half-pound of fries. And Pascal let himself in that night at ten, all bundled against the cold. He walked through the living room while Grace lowered her head to her book and pretended not to see him. He went out the sliding door onto the balcony that stretched across the whole front of the condo. She had left the curtains in front of the full-length windows in the bedroom, living room, and dining room open just enough. Her heart picked up as she laid her book aside.

Twenty-one mornings, she planned what to wear under her

clothes all day, just for the moment when she would unbutton her blouse that night, slowly, in front of the mirror. What if someone wanted to touch her, someone she didn't have to keep under glass? But Pascal's possession was written all over her. No other man would come near.

After three weeks, she said, "I can't do this anymore. Either you're here or you're not."

He touched her. "I'm here. It's you who's flickering in and out."

"What is it that's between us?" She meant both what held them together and what held them apart. Was it the same?

"Only the window," he said. "Clear as glass. Think about it."

It was not enough for Grace. It was too skewed, him on the outside in the wind, looking in, his eyes pinning her. It was too much what she'd been used to. She wanted to move, to take the initiative.

Mostly, Grace finally does tell her father, she didn't want Pascal to know she was outside his cabin, at least not at first, not until she figured out what exactly she intended. She parked fifty yards or so past the turnoff, then hiked in through the woods from there. She was wearing snow boots and a heavy parka. The cabin lights glimmered a long way through the trees; she sank into snow up to her knees, and by the time she reached the clearing, sweat trickled down her back.

The curtains were open. Pascal's was the only cabin on that road. He sat in front of a cold fireplace reading a medical journal. There was a miniature Christmas tree from the Food King, pre-trimmed with plastic candy canes and tiny glass balls and all, on the end table. If he'd set the stage to soften Grace, he couldn't have done it better. She stood at the corner of the picture window; the glare of light would obscure her, and even though the snow reflected light from a full moon, Pascal would have to press his face to the glass to see her among the junipers.

He stretched, seemed to look right at her, then padded into the bedroom. She followed, walking as quietly as she could through the snow, trampling the junipers she had recommended for planting the foundation. Faint music drifted through the walls—the Cowboy Junkies? In the bedroom, he took off his shirt, stretched; scratched his stomach, under his arm. His fingernails left red welts on his white skin. He went into the bathroom, came back out. He dropped his jeans, then pulled off his Jockeys and walked to the closet. He left his clothes in a pile on the floor.

The first night he had brought Grace here, he had rolled her off him when they were both done, then leaned over and tilted the lampshade so the light fell right on her body. The lamp was from his childhood: a porcelain horse, rearing, as its base, and a paper shade painted with cowboys spinning lariats overhead. On the bedroom walls were oils, pastels, and acrylics of the desert, its beautiful, difficult light, its impossible-to-paint vastness only suggested. He got up and put on his robe and stood at the end of the bed just looking at her. Grace reached for the covers, but he said, "Are you cold?" and then, "Please. Don't move."

Standing in the snow outside his bedroom window, Grace tried to decide why he was different now than when he'd undressed that night under her eyes. He came back from the closet still naked, with a robe in his hand. He threw it on the bed, stretched. His hands traveled over his torso—maybe this was the difference—lifting and letting drop, scratching. He patted himself on the belly, on the ass. His hand touched his penis, then his scrotum, but briefly, as if checking that they were still there and intact.

This wouldn't do. Grace wanted to start something, to feel what he felt looking in at her from the balcony, or at least something like it. Pascal looked right at the picture window, absently, as if he could see beyond the dark what the plate glass was supposed to frame: trees, the snowy vista. Almost without thinking what she was doing, Grace took off her gloves, lifted her left hand, and pressed it flat against the glass. With her right hand, she unzipped the top of her parka.

Immediately, Pascal's hands quieted. He looked at where her hand pushed on the window. She still wore the engagement and wedding rings he'd given her. He was perfectly still, not just self-conscious the way he was in their bedroom when he could reach out and touch her body instead of his own, or when she would cup him in her palm. Now he was frozen. There was something Grace expected, but he could see only what she wanted him to see: her fingers spread out on the window, and maybe, if he looked closely, the outline of her head and shoulders, her black hair standing out against snow-covered trees. Whatever she wanted, it was not, they both knew, the same thing he wanted from her when he stood behind the sliding glass doors, not the same tip of hip, not the same arch of back to expose the breastbone and vulnerable throat, the consciousness of a sexuality fixed, defined by the gazing eye. Not something, either, that Grace could see on any street corner, not the man in the cemetery below Rita's when Grace was a child, moving his fist like a piston then running away, as if his own act of aggression had frightened him off. This was something only Pascal could do, could give her to acknowledge her act of protest.

It was a full minute at least before he moved. His hands, unlike Grace's, were awkward on his body, but they did the trick, full of efficient business. He was looking not at the window but at the wall to one side. Grace put her other hand against the window to brace herself, but she kept her face carefully back, hidden in the shadows. This was the wrong time for any part of her but her two hands to be visible.

Her lips are pressed against the telephone. She would never be able to tell her father any of this in person. She is speaking to a ghost, to an electric voice. She is whispering into the dark.

When Grace got home, she took off her wedding rings and put them in the back of her mother's old leather case with Julia's jewels, which Grace had never worn. After that night Grace didn't go back to the window, and Pascal didn't call or use his key to let himself in until the night he died. Grace knew when she drove up to the cabin that he would stop coming over afterward, that this assertion of hers, however necessary, would change the balance between them. Still, she felt his absence like a dull ache, as if his body in front of the windows had kept the huge spaces of night out and away. Now those spaces were everywhere in the condo—in the shadows falling on the bathroom's white tiles, in the corner of the bedroom, opening in the flowers of Grace's orchids or in her own chest when she let go of her guitar and stared off into space. If Pascal ever stopped the car down below and counted over to her window anymore, Grace didn't know it.

PART THREE

▪ ▪ ▪

Overlooking Eden

CHAPTER 10

■ ■ ■

Paying for Love

After the long buildup and the briefest, bloodiest of fights, the war has ended. The finish was sudden, anticlimactic even, given what the generals have said about the strength and determination of the enemy. Did the end justify the means? Can one judge such a thing in retrospect, when results may diminish any larger questions?

Grace tries to engage herself, but it all seems so distant, reduced to the size of the TV she watches in her bedroom after Imo goes to sleep. She can't tell if this little war will be the barest blip on the screen of history, or if it's only a beginning, the start of a new series of alliances and devastations and betrayals. On television, she watches the troops moving across the desert and into ravaged cities, the refugees crossing one border or another, escaping toward something, or away. In her own country, people are celebrating in the streets over a war whose importance is distant and whose tragedies are local: there, women who were the enemy pick through the rubble, hold to their bosoms bloody bodies, not knowing to whom they belong.

The details we hang on are personal. None of Grace's boys, her students with their new beards, was hurt; for her, there is no new, specific grief. The quarter is ending. And the weather has broken in earnest, warm, sunny days between storms blowing in more fitfully, dropping rain that has melted the snow and moved on fast. The gardens are already greening; Grace spends more and more time in the arboretum greenhouses or pacing the experimental beds. The mountains release their snowpack into water, which flows down toward the valley, trickles of runoff joining to make larger and larger creeks. The West was in its seventh year of drought before the late storms came and kept coming, and though Grace looks to rain clouds blowing in and sighs, she of all people knows to be grateful. Finally the perilously low reservoirs are filling, ripples lapping higher and higher on their dry banks. If this weather keeps up they will be full again. If it keeps up another year, maybe two, the floods will come, but for now the ground is dry enough and the underground lakes empty enough to hold the year's runoff.

Rita calls every day, released by the end of war into her own life: the usual suspects, she says. When she's done with her day's work, she returns to the endless paperwork and pamphleteering of ordinary activism. "The trouble is," she says, "everything here is too small."

"Only for you," Grace replies.

Imo says, "Will that phone ever stop ringing?" but she nods, knowing Grace is being pulled by a kind of gravity back into the world. "You're young enough," she says, "if only barely. You could marry again." This is her first admission that Pascal isn't coming back.

"You're going to have to change your life," Rita says. "The

longer you wait, the harder it will be." Today, the sun is shining warm through the windows onto the front hall floor. Rita says, "I missed you on the protest lines. It would have helped you to be there. But I'm not going to hound you."

Any second it will be summer, full blown. Grace leans up against the wall in the little foyer and tucks the phone against her neck.

"Go home," Rita says, and, "That's no place for you," and, "I've watered and fed the orchids, but it's not enough. They need your touch."

"Let them go."

"I won't. But they'll go anyway."

"This is a place I could settle into for good," Grace says, but by now she knows she's lying.

What Grace needs is to be bullied a little. "You might as well just come on over and let me embalm you," Rita says.

"Rita," Grace says, "she needs me. Give me just a little time."

"You've had over thirty years. Don't you know how soon we'll be old?"

Grace is occupied. Her father's getting so close he frightens her. He almost has a body. When he calls, she says little. She listens to his breath, the improbable blood pounding in his veins, though she knows what she hears is the pulse in her own ear, meant to remind her of the flesh she lives in, not somebody else's.

"Don't you get it?" he says. "It's the same thing."

"Flesh of your flesh," she says.

He says, "I don't think you should tell me everything," though everything he missed is exactly what she tells him.

"Don't worry," she says. "It doesn't get any worse." She wants to give him her life, though whether as a gift or an act of aggression neither of them knows. What she doesn't want to talk about is the past they shared together. She is experimenting with distance, is tempted to try a charm to keep him at bay.

When finally he says, "Do you remember?" she says, "I think it's too soon to talk about this."

"You're a coward," he says.

She can't deny it. "So should you be. Do you still climb?"

But he goes right ahead. "The tarantula under the jar?"

"No."

"Your first rappel, the way the air held you like a hand against your back? Her hands on your head in the morning when she braided your hair? The way your hair and skin smelled like campfire until we got home and into our baths?"

Grace won't tell him about all those later climbs with Rita, the ones that looked impossible right up to the very summits. She doesn't tell him she's wondering, too, what happened to that girl who would do anything. She's sparing him as well as herself. She feels a growing tenderness for him, though she is still angry. It's the anger she cultivates. She remembers her mother: Courage isn't lack of fear, she said. It's that you keep going anyway. She said, You have to believe in your luck, even though you know it will fail.

"Doesn't this bother you?" Grace asks.

He says, "The moose?"

She hesitates, and then, after a physical effort around what feels like a glottal stop in her throat, she says, "Wind Rivers." These are words she hasn't put together for years, though separately she uses them all the time, almost without hesitation. The moose stood across the trail in front of them, brought his head with its huge rack slowly around to look, and they stopped, held as still as they could until at last he turned and moved on through the pines. Grace thinks of the map under her bed upstairs, the upright moose lifting his head under enormous antlers. With such a record, how can she not remember everything? Her mother put her hand in Grace's hair and said, "Shh." In a week, Julia would be dead.

Grace says, "Your map."

Her father lets out his breath.

"Your hand was so precise. They were like a web—the routes from car to trailhead, all the side trips. You had that moose standing on his hind legs, like Bullwinkle."

He pauses. "I wonder what happened to it."

"I have it. Remember, you drew your planned route up Temple in yellow?"

"We always drew the actual route when we got back. In red."

Grace remembers the light in her parents' tent was green, like glacier-fed lake water when Grace ducked under and opened her eyes. Grace found her father's cardboard map tube, brought it out, and unrolled the map onto the ground. While Rita watched, Grace took out the red marker and colored in the mountain. She said, "There they are."

Grace clears her throat, then she sings, very tentative, in a barely tuneful whisper, from "Last Night I Had the Strangest Dream." The last campfire, her father picking the tune on the mandolin, her mother's voice filling out the sound, tinged with both sorrow and joy.

He sings back the next lines, then Grace says, still whispering, "You might come around for a visit."

"I might." He hesitates. "I think that's enough." And he hangs up. It's the first time he's been the one to make this decision, that he hasn't let Grace tell him to go away.

She looks into the dead phone. "I think so, too. Asshole."

From the doorway Imo says, "Didn't I tell you?"

"Yes. You told me."

"Not that I'm always right." Imo looks up at Grace, who can't tell if Imo's sorry or teasing. She says, again, "Not that I am. But I've seen what I've seen."

Grace keeps thinking she should feel emptier, that she should be as vast and frozen inside as Antarctica, but completely uninhabited—without science stations, without the brief summer ephemerals, without even the comic penguins nose-diving off ice floes to play and feed in the frigid sea. But instead something inside her keeps swelling, expanding, threatening to spill. She doesn't know what it is, but she imagines herself opening into the spring air like a volcano ready to blow, a pot ready to boil, one of those Japanese clamshells that, when you drop it into water, blooms into a ravishing paper flower. Scarlet, ruffled like a poppy. She tries to keep a lid on it. Did her mother open her body to fire? Was there exhilaration in her final anguish? There's comic potential here, the possibility of a happy ending, and it feels—what? inappropriate?

"It sounds like self-pity to me," Imo says.

"No doubt." Grace closes her eyes, pictures a cold, enormous sky, and tries not to laugh.

"Why not?" Imo says.

Grace says, "Don't confuse me."

Grace watches the soil ball, then crumble in her hand. Everything is accelerating; the flower beds are ready to work, even in the shady places under the yews on the north wall of the house. She finds footprints in the dirt under the sprouting daylilies, big ones made with Vibram soles. Something is about to begin, has begun already. When she sets her own foot inside one of the prints, it leaves only a small, faint echo of the larger foot. She counts on her fingers, "Ralph, Dan, Rita, Bliss." Bliss's feet are clearly too small, and anyway these are only secondary possibilities. Only her father is courting Grace in this way, with the kind of diligence that would bring him to stand beneath her window while she sleeps, and he's in California. The rest are as evasive and noncommittal as she is. Even, she realizes, Rita and Ralph, both of whom wooed her fervently when she wasn't free to respond.

She's stepped back into the bed of lilies to see if she needs to separate them this year. Their green leaves have already pushed an inch, two inches above the soil. Now that they've started, she'll practically be able to see them growing. The footprints walk in from the driveway, over the low purple bar-berries and through where the gloriosa daisies will flare up in August, thirsty and wild. The boots that made the prints stood still under Grace's window long enough to sink down into the mud, though whoever wore them would have seen nothing from below but a patch of ceiling, then turned around and left the same way they came in. As far as Grace can tell, the boots trampled nothing, though in the dark this would have taken nothing less than a miracle of instinct and tenderness. But all the new shoots are clean and still standing upright.

Grace digs out the lilies with her spading fork, uprooting them with the greatest care, and pulls them gently apart, un-tangling one delicate set of roots from the others. She wraps half in damp paper towels and sets them aside, then replants the rest in the same bed, pulling the wet earth back over the roots up to the crowns. Then she moves to the annuals bed, loosening the soil with her fork, getting it ready for the rich compost she will mix in to feed the flowers into brightness. She pictures blue lobelia, rosy nicotiana. She pushes her fork in.

It stops, six inches into the ground. A rock, maybe, out of nowhere. But whatever is down there gives strangely under the tines when she pushes on the fork. Grace sighs and works the tool around until she finds the edge of the object, then she levers it out.

A red-orange shoebox, Nike, wrapped in a plastic bag from the Food King. Grace sets it down in the driveway and looks at it. Then she unwraps the bag, opens the lid of the box.

Inside, still clean and dry, is a Colt .45. Military issue, if she's not mistaken.

Into the phone, Dan says, soft, "I want you to come have a look at my yard."

It is not what Grace wants to hear. A voice from the world of green, yes, but his makes her brace herself, her hand on the wall. Back at the condo, the answering machine must be full of messages from clients. Gentle, fretful over beauty gone weedy or otherwise awry. Once the snow melts—overnight, faster than you ever thought—disasters manifest. Weeds already, impossibly, growing under the last crust of ice. Where are you? the machine will say; my forsythia hasn't bloomed, my lilac is failing, my lawn. What might have to be done: moving of earth, seduction and feeding of worms, coddling of delicate shoots. How tiny we are, on this planet spinning off through darkness and cold. How little such local care as Grace's means, and how much.

"I just told you I found a gun buried in my flower bed," she says. "What kind of person are you, anyway?"

He is quiet. Then he says, "I've begged Bliss's forgiveness. On bended knee."

"I've explained about flowers," Grace says. She thinks of them as themselves, in the way a scientist thinks, but they also live for her as extensions, metaphors for the human spirit. Who deserves a garden? Who, deserving or not, most needs one?

"Not everything," he says. "You have no idea how much help we need."

Grace's brain is clicking. What can she make of this? "You give me the creeps," she says. "Let me talk to Bliss."

"I've unmade my beds. She won't lie down again until I make of them a veritable Eden."

Veritable. Grace says, "She's the only one there with any sense."

"Maybe when it comes to plants. As for the rest—"

Grace can see him whirling his finger around beside his ear. He doesn't seem to realize that by sane standards she should be afraid of him, furious with him, planning bloody revenge. "I'll make a deal with you," she says. "I'll do it for free."

"And?"

"You tell the police everything. Everything." Is that enough?

He laughs. "How will you know if I've told them the truth?"

"I know more than you think. And let me make this clear. You are not to touch Bliss."

"In love?"

She shudders. "You know what I mean." Bliss and Dan in bed Grace does not want to think about, any more than she wants to think about Dan's hands coming down on Bliss's face, back, legs.

"You haven't seen the yard yet. It's a mess. I have a lot of catching up to do."

"So do I," she says. "We'd better get to work." She hangs up the phone, leaves her hand on it for a minute, thinking, then picks it up again and dials Flint's number.

She loads the panniers onto the back of her bike and fills them with tools, wrapped lilies, the gun still in its shoebox, then she pedals up to Rita's. At the door of the mortuary office, Grace holds out the thinned lilies, still wrapped in their damp paper towels.

"Peace," she says.

Rita opens the door farther. "It's about time. I was starting to think I'd have to hire someone." She gives Grace a slightly skewed smile. "Like paying money for love." She takes the lilies, puts them on the table. Her hand doesn't touch Grace's. "It wouldn't have been the same, to have a stranger digging out there," she says. "I'll get my boots."

While Rita pulls on her Wellies, Wendy runs around Grace

in circles, panting and whining. Every time Grace says the word "garden," Wendy lets out a bark and wriggles over to the door.

The three of them walk around the building looking for the right place. They settle on a spot in the back, a sunny corner near the fence, and Rita starts to dig with her fork, turning the soil, while Grace spades compost, rich and dark and fragrant, from the compost heap into the garden cart. She likes the feel of sun on her head, the tightness in her back and shoulders that tells her she's working hard.

"We're going to feel this tomorrow," Rita says.

Wendy runs a few circles, then lies down in the sun, close enough to protect Rita and Grace from any imaginable danger.

"My father's been calling," Grace says.

Rita glances up sideways, brushes back the stray coppery wisps of hair escaping her braid. "It was bound to happen eventually."

"I never thought so."

"You lost your faith in him. We could all see it happening. It was Imo's doing, you know." Rita has turned the soil to a foot's depth. She stands up and stretches with her hands in the small of her back.

"I know. But it's hard to blame her." Grace spreads compost over the soil with her shovel, and they both begin to turn the compost into the ground. "Now I'm afraid. It was all a long time ago."

"Afraid why?"

Grace blinks. "What if he isn't what I want? Or worse? What if I'm not what he wants?"

"You've missed the point. That may be why you need to see him. This may be your only chance to choose your family. If you like him, fine. If not,"—Rita lifts a forkful of earth, grunts at its weight, turns it over—"also fine."

"It feels strange. For me, it's a lifetime since he left." Grace looks out over the city, gray concrete and glimmering glass, the thin spring light tinged with green.

"Not for him."

Grace says, "No."

Rita sets her fork down and touches Grace on the shoulder with her gloved hand. "You're an adult. There are things you need to face." Rita squeezes Grace's shoulder. When she takes her hand away Grace can see the muddy prints from Rita's gloves on her sweatshirt. "I remember it so clearly," Rita says. "But you took everything that moved you and buried it somewhere."

Grace knows this is true. "What was I supposed to do? I could hardly wear my heart on my sleeve."

"No. It's not your style. But you have a history there. You're like Wendy. Everywhere you dig, you're going to find a bone. Your own or someone else's."

"Yes." Then, "Let's stomp this bed down." They should heel the lilies in for now and let the soil settle a few days, but Grace loves the feeling of sinking into freshly conditioned ground.

They hold on to each other's arms and step into the loose soil. Their feet sink with each step. "You know," Rita says, "I love your Imo. But she's an anachronism."

Behind Grace's eyes, Imo says, "Is that so bad?"

Grace thinks of that house with its gentle light. She waves her hand. "What about this?" The mortuary topiary looks scraggly, worn by the long winter.

Pascal would say, "You're wasting your time."

"This, of course, is a joke," Rita says. "I've been waiting for you." Grace is on her knees now, pressing dirt around the lilies' new roots. Rita says, "Come on. I'll lop. You take care of the delicate work." She hands Grace the clippers with their curved blades like the beak of a parrot. Their fingers touch on the handles.

"Any new ideas?" Rita says.

Grace shakes her head.

"I want you to know." Rita takes a deep breath. "I'm not sure, but I think I've met someone. I could fall in love."

Grace looks away. She wants to be purely glad. Or she could say something now, she thinks, to bring Rita to her. She could say, I thought you were in love already, and lift her beautiful face, an offering. But she knows it would be a temporary one. She forces herself to look down. They are still holding the clippers between them. Rita gives Grace a good twenty more seconds before she lets go.

When Grace and Rita get to Dan's, Wendy running behind them, but obediently, on the sidewalk, they lock their bikes to a pair of dead birches—borers, Grace says—on the parking strip and stand with their hands on their hips, shaking their heads. It turns out Dan wasn't exaggerating about the work. Even Rita can see how serious this is. There are husks of weeds years old decaying into Dan's front yard. Some of them from last summer are still standing, but bent in half by the snow. They must have been six feet tall, Grace figures. Among them, young weeds are already thriving, pushing toward the sky. Dan bobs through them. Wendy runs to meet him, her tail waving like a tattered flag.

"She has no discrimination," Grace says.

"Well, I'm glad you've got a project, anyway," Rita says, her hands on her hips. "Though I don't know why it has to be Dan's garden."

They've been through this. It took Grace almost an hour to convince Rita to come. "You'll see," she says again. "It's my way of keeping an eye on him."

Dan says, "The city says I've got to do something. The neighborhood is in an uproar." He flings his long arms out to either side.

"I don't pull weeds," Grace says. "I point them out and tell you to get rid of them."

He looks the weeds over as if for the first time. "I can follow instructions."

Grace says, "Get rid of them. Now, I have to see the lay of the land."

"I can understand that."

Bliss comes out on the front porch, shields her eyes with her hand, and waves. Rita waves back with, Grace thinks, inappropriate enthusiasm. Though the breeze can still be chilly in the shade, Bliss is wearing very short cutoffs and a white man's shirt unbuttoned, tied between breasts that look fuller than Grace remembers. She appears, already, to have a full-body suntan. Even from here, her eye makeup looks too dark. She takes her marbled sunglasses out of her shirt pocket and puts them on.

"This is a different look for her," Grace says.

Dan glances over his shoulder at Bliss. "They're all different."

"She looks great to me." Rita puts her hand over her heart and pats it, sighing, then gestures Bliss toward them. Dan tilts his head and looks at her.

Grace pulls Dan away. "Haven't you learned anything in my class?"

"This is trouble on another scale," he says. "These are not plants dying passively under the lens like ladies in the opera. This is nature asserting itself."

"Nature is no excuse." Grace is in the mood for starting over. She feels a buoyancy she hardly remembers. "At least there's nothing left to save."

"The garden was always my ex-wife's doing."

"If you neglected her like you do this," Grace says, "I'm not surprised she left."

"She was a bitch, anyway," Dan says, and rocks back on his heels.

Grace feels a chill travel her spine and is glad of what she's doing. She resists looking over her shoulder down the street, and instead leads the way around back. She waves her hand at the yard. "Leave the maples and the spruce. Everything else goes." She allows herself one look around. Behind Grace and Dan, Rita stands in the driveway, too close to Bliss, bending her head down to hear what Bliss is saying. Even Wendy seems entranced. She pushes at Bliss's hand with her nose, then she lies down in the weeds and rolls onto her back. The street is still empty.

Grace pushes her way toward the back fence. She feels in control, a small ship under sail. She can make this take as long as it needs to. Dan follows in her wake.

"Everything's got to go but those three trees and the dirt. Bring in some topsoil."

Rita and Bliss walk toward them, rustling across the weedy lawn. Rita steers Bliss with a hand on the back of her neck.

"What about the junipers?" Bliss asks.

"Choked. You'll be lucky if you don't have a manroot down there."

"Manroot?" Rita raises her eyebrows.

"Bindweed. Wild morning glory. Actually very beautiful. But it can grow a root about ten feet down, the size of a man's leg. You have to dig up the whole bed to get rid of it." Grace makes a leg-size circle with her hands.

Bliss looks at the ground as if she can see the root thickening under her feet. "What do we do with it?"

"Take it to the dump," Grace says.

Behind them, Detective Flint says, "It sounds like something out of a late-night movie." Even Grace jumps, though she has been listening for him. His approach was absolutely silent, and she's let the bindweed, the idea of that root growing out of sight, distract her. She can see no car parked at the curb.

Dan looks down at Grace, his eyes as flat as ever, like china plates. "What a bitch," he says, his voice cold.

Grace flinches. "It was part of our deal. I'm just making sure."

"You could have trusted me."

"I don't see why."

Bliss's eyes are wide with panic. Rita wraps an arm around her shoulders. "It will be okay," she says. To Grace she says, "I didn't know you had it in you."

Flint tells Dan not to worry; it's just a matter of a few questions. Grace lifts the shoebox out of her pannier and hands it over, its cellophane bag still crusted with mud. Dan presses his lips together when he sees it.

After Flint leaves with Dan, Grace unlocks her bike from the dead birch. She feels a fragile but definite exhilaration.

"Clever," Rita says. "Why didn't you tell me?"

"It seemed simpler not to. I wasn't sure I could keep from giving it away if you knew."

"Yes." Rita looks back toward the house, where Bliss breathes somewhere behind the closed curtains. "What's he like these days, your dad?"

Grace shrugs. She's not at all sure she wants to talk about this. "I haven't seen him yet. He's a voice on the telephone. He has no body."

"Or he has a body made of electricity."

Grace smiles. "That's what we all have."

Rita shuts her eyes, as if calling his face to mind. "Is he what you remember?"

"I was an American girl. What I remember is a hero."

Rita cocks her head. She looks uncannily like Wendy, who sits beside her with her head at the same angle.

Grace says, "Tanned. Muscular. Enormous. Able to leap tall mountains."

"I remember him that way too. When I slept over, I used to think about how he was just on the other side of the wall."

"When he didn't save my mother and bring her back, I knew he was dead. By the time Imo told me, I was already certain of it. Now I'm not sure I want him alive again."

"Your mother too," Rita says, her voice even. "I don't see how you can stand it."

"What?"

"Didn't you see? Bliss. All that makeup."

"There's no harm in it. It's just for show." But as she says it, Grace realizes the makeup's not for show, but for the opposite. She remembers the scar on Bliss's lip. Grace's small joy flickers, goes out. She has, in comparison, so little to hide. She touches her own eyelid, pushes as if she can make it hurt. She can't bring herself to push hard enough.

"Don't you see?" Rita says. "He's going to kill her. If they don't hold on to him, we have to do something. Ralph thinks so, too."

"They've got the gun. They only have to prove Dan used it to shoot Pascal." Grace looks at Rita, says, "Here's the thing about my father. What if he's only life-size?"

Rita pulls Grace against her. "Just a few feet away, both of them lying there in the dark."

Grace is picturing Bliss from a distance. "You leave my mother out of this," she says.

"You go on ahead," Rita says. "Bliss won't talk to you. Not after this. But I'm going to see what I can do."

CHAPTER 11

■ ■ ■

Sweet Dreams

Though she was never an orphan, not in the strictest sense, Grace has been pleased to think of herself as one—even the loved child's fantasy, to be such a reproachful object of condolence—almost until the last moment, through the years of postcards, even through the phone calls, until now her father appears in the irrefutable flesh on Imo's front porch and says, "Forgive me."

She could always demand a blood test. "What, for showing up?" she says. Watching pain flick its whip end across his face, she reproaches herself, but she doesn't go so far as to take it back. He still has, after all, some things to make up for. A few phone calls could hardly balance the account.

Grace leans against the doorjamb. A flutter in her pulse could be nerves, fury, joy. Behind her father is a spring sky—heavy clouds, patches of blue to raise hope—which she looks at because the first glimpse of him has almost undone her, and she does not mean to be undone. The ground looks grimy, but there are flowers and grass. The breeze is warm, and soon enough will come the leaf-crackling heat of summer. Grace pictures herself swinging up onto Marley's back and riding off over the chemical-green front lawns of the neighborhood, toward the desert.

After what she hopes feels like a long time to her father, she lowers her eyes. He doesn't say anything more. He's wearing jeans, a sweater, and a tan canvas jacket.

From back in the kitchen Imo says, "You're making a draft."

Grace is trying to figure out what she has been expecting, why the man in front of her is a disappointment, as if all she really wanted was the voice, mysterious with static, with no real body to make it solid, troublesome. She's already embarrassed at the things she's told him. She's forgotten: she herself has grown, has changed immeasurably since she last saw him. He's no longer bigger than life, but only the size and shape of any other man his age, still fit but going a little loose around the belly and neck. His nose has grown, too, bulbous and fleshy. She's not going to cut him any slack. He's got a lot of nerve, though this was once a quality she admired. There's still red in the curly gray hair; the beard is more precisely trimmed than she remembers.

Wasn't it better for her to think of him as dead? When his postcards arrived, she blacked out the signatures with indelible Magic Marker and pinned them to her walls. When she returned from her trip to Europe she entered what she thought of as adulthood, wrongly believing adulthood would be a secure place, unlike childhood's shift and countershift, and before moving into her own apartment she took the postcards down and put them away in a cardboard gift box with a gilt lid, which she slid under the bed next to the roll of maps. She always read the cards not as messages from her father but as clues to something larger about her life.

Watching him, she remembers him suddenly as a man

whose appeal is in the mobility of his face, the way emotions flicker through it like pictures across a screen. She is too nervous to say anything quippy, though she would like to.

He shifts his weight and puts his hands in his pockets. "Well?"

She has to squint. He's too bright with the spring sun behind him. She puts her hand over her eyes, thinks about escape. At last she says, "I need to take a nap now."

"I can understand you might want some time. More time." He enunciates the last two words very precisely.

"You haven't been here. You don't know anything about me." She keeps her voice even, reasonable. She concentrates on feeling the door frame against her shoulder, solid, part of the measurable world. "You have no rights," she says.

"But it's been years. And you invited me. Remember that."

"I've never forgotten for a second." She's surprised at the amount of bitterness she spins out behind the words.

Imo says from the hall, "You know she's lost a husband."

Grace likes the way this sounds—as if she's set him down someplace and forgotten where. She puts her hand on her hip.

Her father reaches his hand out toward her, pulls it back halfway. It's square-fingered, freckled and dry, a strangely masculine, larger version of her own, and for a second she sees those fingers holding a match to dry tinder under a Boy Scout–tidy teepee of twigs. She has never thought she had any gifts from her father. She was her mother replicated, but smaller in spirit. Suddenly, she thinks of his maps of the land and her own of the bodies of plants, how the differences are mostly of scale.

"But don't worry," she says. "It's not as if I've never lost anything before."

He says, "I'll call you."

Grace shuts the screen door between them.

"Sweet dreams," he says, then he turns and walks down the

driveway to the rental car parked at the curb. She goes upstairs to the Degas ballerinas. If she looks at them closely, she can see where they've been punctured with pushpins. Instead, she lies down under her pink canopy. She once read about an experiment in which a prison painted its walls pink, hypothesizing that the color would enervate the prisoners, make them passive and easy to control. Grace can't remember the results, but she stares up at the canopy, hoping it will quiet her. She would like to lose her nerve completely.

When she was a child, Grace would pretend the canopy was clouds in a fairyland where every gesture followed the arc of perfect grace, or that she was a princess on a hundred feather mattresses with a pea at bottom. However hard she tries now, she can't imagine a story that would have the same mythic power, but that may be because she can't remember herself in motion.

Back then, Rita would say, "You can't escape," and in fact the life of the princess was no life Grace would have wanted. After only minutes of play, of lying as still as she could on coats piled up on a peanut, she would be twitching, ready to get up and move on. But she wanted to be the person who would want such a life, the person Imo thought she was creating out of lace and air when she slipped ribbon-trimmed dresses over Grace's obediently upstretched arms. Grace wanted to be everything to everyone, so that nobody would ever want to turn away from her again. It never crossed Grace's mind: the mattresses have always been second-rate, rocky with sprung springs. It wasn't the princess's sensitivity the prince was testing. What man wants a woman's back impossibly mottled with bruises from a single, harmless pea?

As Grace drifts off, Imo says through the door, "This isn't what I expected either."

"You never have had a lot of foresight," Grace says into her pillow.

She feels rather than hears Imo lean against the door. "I

suppose that's mostly true," Imo says after a second. "But I did have the sense to marry your grandfather before it was too late."

Grace is almost gone, into a warmth, like an affection, she's almost forgotten. "The sense of humor, you mean. There's one lesson I learned from you."

She dreams her father calls on the phone. In her dream, this is the first time he calls. Imo's knock brings her out of a deep sleep. "It's *him*," she says.

Grace is so fogged with sleep, she can't tell if she actually saw him on the porch this afternoon, or if that was a dream as well. She stands in her underwear in the little hall in front of the mirror. Her eyes droop and it looks as if someone has rubbed a thumb over the skin underneath them and smudged it. She's lost weight; her ribs and hipbones stick out.

"Do you ever have trouble distinguishing your dreams from what's real?" she says. It's the kind of thing you ask someone who has carried you from the wrong kind of dream into the right night after night, his hand on your forehead or between your shoulder blades. "Forget it," she says. "Never mind."

"All the time," he says.

She remembers the warmth of her sleep. "Okay. I'll be right there." And just on the chance this is real she runs a comb through her hair and pulls her jeans back on and gets on her bike and rides down to the Broiler, where she dreamed she told him to meet her, all the while biting down on her cheek in case he doesn't appear. But when she reaches the top of the Broiler's stairs, the same tall man she dreamed was at Imo's front door stands halfway up and lifts his hand. She shuts her eyes, opens them: he is still standing, his smile a little too wide, his hand in the air.

He has his wife with him in a booth by the window. Grace thinks, "new wife," though they've been married, he tells Grace, his arm around the woman's shoulders, for fifteen years. Happily, he says. They've ranged themselves on one bench of the booth; Grace slides in across from them. The new wife is around Grace's father's age, a decade older than Julia would have been. She looks nothing like Julia. She is weathered, but it's the kind of weathering a woman gets from lying at poolside, not from squinting into the sun to track the one possible route up a cliff face. And she is "done," if gently—blond bobbed hair, a broad red mouth. Brown eyes with the liner smudged so nobody will be afraid of them. She is wearing a white felt cowboy hat, its band worked in silver and turquoise, and white cowboy boots. Grace is sure the woman has never been on a horse in her life. The woman's name is Miranda.

Maybe by this time Julia would be wearing lipstick in broad daylight too, but the possibility does not occur to Grace. She says, "Miranda?"

"Like in *The Tempest*," Miranda says.

"Do you enjoy reading Shakespeare?" Grace doesn't mean to sneer, but Miranda flinches and looks away.

Grace's father says, "You never got real big, did you?"

Grace looks at Miranda's long legs. "I'm the same height my mother was. You liked small women. So you said."

"You like what you're used to." He looks out the window at the mountains. "If Julia had been taller, she could have been the best woman climber in the world. I've often mentioned this to Miranda. Haven't I, honey?"

So Julia has a presence in his new life. There is no secret Grace can use against him, however he may deserve it.

Miranda looks around. "Isn't this nice," she says. She is sitting so close to Grace's father their arms overlap.

"You must be the best woman climber in the world," Grace says.

It's a weak effort, and Miranda has recovered. She looks at Grace and smiles. She rests her fingertips on Byron's arm. "I leave the heroics to your father."

Grace flops against the back of the booth and crosses her arms. "You're jollier than you used to be," she says to her father. "But maybe you're just pretending."

He says, gently, "I'm happy," and takes Miranda's hand.

Miranda narrows her wide eyes. "Cut him a little slack, will you?"

Grace looks at her more closely. She may, after all, be a force.

Miranda waves her hand at the restaurant. She almost hits the waiter, who has come up behind her with oysters on ice. Miranda pats the waiter's arm. "Here we are," she says. Her fingers are long and brown; each one has at least one silver and turquoise ring on it, even the thumbs. Grace turns her own rings on her fingers—an art deco sapphire from Imo's mother, her wedding rings, which she's taken to wearing again, but on her right hand—and considers slipping them off and into her pocket.

Her father says to Grace, "That's quite a sapphire. Ceylon, if I'm not mistaken." This was something her father from the old days would never have known. "Miranda and I are in California. We'd like you to come visit."

"Whenever you want," Miranda says. She puts her hand over Grace's. "You can sit by the pool. Let us spoil you for a while. We've never had any children of our own."

"If we all get along, you could come live with us," Grace's father says.

Grace is still looking at Miranda's rings. They are so new their metal seems to squeak against the air, and she's wearing so many she can't bring her fingers together.

"If you wanted," her father says.

Grace says to Miranda, "I am his own." She's already beginning to think of Miranda as "That Woman," as though Miranda has broken Byron's marriage to a mother who is still alive.

"We could all get acquainted," Miranda says.

"Of course," her father says. "That's not what Miranda meant." He looks over at her. "Sometimes Miranda doesn't quite say what she means, right, honey?"

Miranda smiles at Grace's father. "I'm more a doer than a talker."

"I am an adult now," Grace says. "I have a job. It's too late for all that."

Her father looks at her, his eyebrows raised. "You're on sabbatical, right? You have until next winter."

"Sabbaticals are about work." She feels a twinge, thinking about the projects waiting for her. "Then there are gardens. But you wouldn't know about those, would you?" Grace pauses, closes her eyes. "I'm just wondering. Where have you been all my life?"

Miranda takes in her breath. She looks out at the traffic.

Grace's father says, "That's a fair question. The question is fair enough."

"This morning, I thought I recognized you. And before, on the phone. I didn't want to know you, but I did. But for the last fifteen years you've lived with her." Grace nods at Miranda. "No offense, but you're a stranger to me. Why is that?" Grace tugs at her rings.

Her father leans over the table and touches her cheek and then her hair where it is just getting long enough to make bangs. His eyes have the same smudged look her own did in the mirror. "You're so much like her," he says.

Miranda says, "She's like you, too, Byron."

He brings his hand up over Grace's head. "I don't know what the hell you did to your hair, but other than that, it's amazing."

Miranda gathers up her purse—white suede and fringe—and says in a chirpy voice, "I have a little shopping to do." Byron lifts his hand for the check, but Miranda grabs his

raised fingers in hers. "Why don't you two stay here? Get reac-
quainted." She turns to Grace with a smile so bright it looks
laminated. "He just gets in the way. You know how men are
on shopping trips."

This is an act of such tact Grace is ashamed. She returns
it by smiling back at Miranda. "I know what you mean." She
gives Miranda her hand, though she can't bring herself to return the little squeeze with any pressure of her own. After
Miranda sweeps out, Grace sits silently. Then she says, "I'm
sorry. I just don't know where I am, you know?"

"Shall we start over?" her father says. "We're here together,
just the two of us."

"For the first time," Grace says.

"In twenty years. More."

Then Grace says, "Since she left me."

He lowers his head and shuts his eyes. "I used to feel that
way too." He reaches over the table and takes Grace's hand.
He strokes each finger, looking at her knuckles, her ragged
nails, her skin dry and red like his.

"They spend too much time in the dirt."

After a minute, he looks back up. "Your mother died. I'm
the one who left."

Grace keeps her eyes steadily on his; a little smile starts in
the corners of her mouth. In her chest, behind her eyes, nothing, nothing she can let herself feel. She could stop herself,
but she doesn't. "Only because she didn't have the chance to
go first."

His whole face clenches, and he turns his head away fast,
as if by reflex. When his face unknots, his wrinkles follow
exactly the creases of that expression.

Grace is surprised to know so exactly how to hurt him. She
softens. "I'm being a pig."

Still looking across the room, he says, "For years it was like
living in a dark room. Every morning, waking up, feeling okay.

Then it would all come back when I opened my eyes. It was like she died all over again, every single day. I almost stopped sleeping."

"I know exactly," Grace says. "It's like that with Pascal. But I sleep too much."

"All that time, I felt I'd failed her. Like I'd never quite got it right."

Grace lays her hand over his. "You loved her. How could that be a failure?"

"And then Miranda came. It wasn't exactly like starting over. Some things you can't just set down and leave behind. But it was the next best thing." He holds the ends of her fingers tightly in his hand. "Do you remember you were the apple of my eye? I always wanted to come back."

Grace is almost speechless. What she remembers is her mother, present, vivid, and her father in the background, looking on. "But you didn't."

He rubs the back of his hand across his eyes. "It wasn't a matter of how badly I wanted it." He twines his fingers with hers. She lets her palm rest in his palm. He seems never to stop moving; she is watching his every twitch, and her eyes on him make him jumpier. Something in her chest begins to shift. She doesn't want this to happen; once things start moving, they'll fly out of her control. The iceberg behind her breastbone has begun to break apart as if under the pressure of some great heat, and she can feel both the cold and the burning. Behind her eyes the surface of ice is smooth and blue and glittering like glass, and from its center the orange glow grows stronger. Grace thinks of stars in collapse—as if the pressure of the ice itself could cause the heat at its core. For the fire to be visible at all through that blue, opaque surface, it must be raging.

Her father says, "I'd know that look anywhere."

"I've always been a little melodramatic. So Imo would say."

"I was thinking more of something unmovable."

"Imo always says, 'Your mother had trouble with her ego, too.'"

Grace's father says, "There's always the chance your mother and I would have lasted. I believed we would." He smiles. "With me, she knew what she could get away with."

The room begins to tremble, and they hear a far-off rumble. Grace's father looks with a practiced California eye at the lights beginning to sway. "It's an earthquake," he says. "Under the table."

"What?" she says, looking around.

"Now." His voice has all its old paternal authority. Together they drop to the floor. People in the booths around them do the same. Grace and her father huddle together. Byron puts his arms around her shoulders, and she leans into him, the smell and feel of him both strange and familiar. The room shakes gently for perhaps half a minute, plates vibrating off the tables around them and shattering on the floor, then the motion subsides. Everyone stays put for another minute, then they begin to emerge, looking around. Grace and her father slide back up onto the benches of the booth. Grace starts to laugh, and he joins in. From the kitchen they hear a crash of dishes. Whatever somebody dropped, it was big—the residual tinkling of glass keeps on.

"I know," he says. "It's going to be all right."

When someone is murdered, not randomly but out of somebody else's necessity, however momentary, the death gains a meaning another kind of death can't achieve, not without some unlikely heroism, perhaps, on the part of the dying. What must be accomplished is an absence—palpable, complete. What a killer gets, usually, is an obstructive presence. Those who haven't yet imagined themselves with their fingers not just against the trigger but active on it think of the murder and its solution as an intrigue, a complex but tidy puzzle to be pieced back together through dispassionate logic and passionate heroism: untangle the emotional progress of a person into a monster and you'll have in the palm of your hand an irrefutable answer and the seed of absolute, unquestionable justice. This is what science and Arthur Conan Doyle have done for us—though we expect, on the other hand, that soldiers and the police will be able to lay down their guns at the end of a day, of a war, and lie with perfect bliss, unchanged, in the peaceful arms of their lovers.

Grace tells her father, "It was as clear as that." Dan was riveted by rage. He turned the gun, fired. She can see it in her mind's eye, which lights the dark space under the freeway. She hasn't dreamed this, but she knows it is true. Grace thinks of the delicate mottle of bruises, like a bracelet, on Bliss's wrist—another emblem of Dan's anger, a sort of power, of loss. The metaphors our media and mythologies give us.

"How can you know what he meant?" her father asks.

"There's the result." Desire and action: Dan lifted his hand in the shape of a gun, and for a second, flesh and metal became one. It's this or believing there was accident involved. If she is as culpable as anyone in what led up to the shooting, she won't know what to do with her anger. She will be set into a motion that might be dangerous. If she concentrates on her own hand in the matter, and on Ralph's, on Rita's and Bliss's, so, as responsibility multiplies, it diminishes, Pascal's death loses its meaning. Pascal is vanished into the earth; they are the ones left behind on the surface to burn for him, their cells daily combusting into air.

"You've got to think about this," her father says. "What if Dan's dangerous?"

"That's the question. He is dangerous. That seems, at the moment, to have nothing to do with what will happen to him. The issues all seem to be legal ones, made of paper."

"Will you be careful?"

Grace thinks of Dan's hand on hers, his finger tracing the

lines in her palm. "I was at first. Too careful. Now I'm just angry."

Her father looks through the restaurant window down at the street. "Here she comes," he says. Miranda's carefully blonded head bobs above the crowd. She is laden with shopping bags, though on this stretch of road, besides the Broiler and seven student burger and pizza joints, there are only one New Age paraphernalia store, a record store, a bookstore, and a store that sells knitting needles and wool. Watching Miranda, Grace's father looks younger, petulant, the way he used to when his plans had gone awry—a look Grace doesn't remember until she sees it.

Miranda appears at the table. "Did you feel the quake?" Grace looks around at the busboys sweeping up fallen plates, but Miranda doesn't wait for an answer. She sits down, turns to Grace as if there's something she's been saving up. "If you think it's been easy for your father," she says, "you're mistaken. You were too young to know."

"I'm sorry," Grace says to Miranda. "I can tell you're very nice. But we were talking about something else."

Grace's father says, "At first, we argued."

"Excuse me?" Grace says.

"Your grandmother and I. She thought it would be best this way."

Grace thinks what this means. "And you just went along with it?" Imo, the little grandmother, even smaller than Grace is, with bones that look as if you could break them if you so much as touched her.

Rita once said, "Yes, but the woman has a steel rod up her ass."

Grace doesn't want to believe what her father is saying, but she knows her grandmother, the names that were never spoken in her house. Grace knows there's more. "Did she pay you to stay away?"

Byron looks at Grace with what seem like tears in the corners of his eyes. "It wasn't that we agreed on anything. She just helped out."

Grace just looks at him, shaking her head, then lifts her shoulder helplessly.

"I couldn't work afterward," he says. "I still take nitroglycerin for my heart. But it wasn't only that. Or the night terrors. Hell, day terrors." He looks at her bleakly. "I didn't remember you. My heart stopped with your mother's. Hers stayed stopped. Mine started again, but my life was gone. I had to leave my job with the Survey, and then for years nobody would touch me."

Grace will not meet his eye. For a moment, listening to him, she has vanished to herself. She turns to the window, fixes her almost transparent image in the glass.

He says to Miranda, "I'll be right back." He runs his hand through his silver-red hair, then he tugs at his jacket as if to tidy it. "I'll take you home," he says to Grace. "I'd hoped it wouldn't come to this. But when you asked, I had to tell you, didn't I?"

She follows him to his rental car. She unlocks her bike, pops off the front wheel, and slides it into the back seat. While they wait for the traffic to clear, they don't talk at all. Grace's hands resting on her knees look blue and ill-defined, as if they are under water. It takes all her effort, it seems, to lift one through that medium—it must be very deep, since the weight is so enormous—and lay it on her father's leg.

"I guess I'm not quite ready for this," she says.

He looks over at her, then he puts the car in gear.

CHAPTER 12

■ ■ ■

A Breath of Air

Grace is not surprised to see what she assumes is Pascal's Colt lying in front of Detective Flint on the scarred interrogation room table. The detective rises, waves his hand at the chair opposite. "You said you were careful not to touch this?"

"Yes. I closed the lid of the box and put it in my pannier. Then I gave it to you." Grace looks at it, its blue sheen. She imagines the scent of burned powder on the air and waits for Flint to say what comes next.

"And you recognized it, as soon as you opened the box?"

"I thought so. We already know it's not the only one of its kind." She looks at it more closely. "It looks the same."

"When was the last time you saw it?"

Grace lifts her eyes to the ceiling. "If it's Pascal's? The day of the shooting."

Flint lets her sit and think for a minute.

Then she says, "He came to the condo. I considered shoot-

239

ing him with it myself." She smiles. "Briefly. But I told you, he took it with him."

"Ah."

"I didn't think of shooting him in any conscious way." Grace describes again how she took the gun from its drawer, loaded it, kept it between them while Pascal kissed her.

He purses his lips. "Well, that would explain why your prints are all over the barrel. Yours and his."

Grace thinks this over. "It was a cold night, when Pascal was shot. Probably everybody was wearing gloves of some kind. I was."

"We've considered that. And it can be hard to lift prints from a gun anyway, especially the butt." Flint shows Grace where the handle of the Colt is textured, grainy. "Almost impossible to get anything worthwhile. When you loaded it, you must have touched the barrel. But we still can't account for its appearance in your garden."

Grace nods. "In the annuals bed next to the lilies. Whoever buried it didn't want to disturb whatever was already coming up."

Flint sighs. He looks even more tired and crumpled than usual. "Ah. Considerate." He rubs his eyes with a thumb and forefinger. "How likely was it that you would find it there?"

Grace thinks. "Inevitable. After separating the perennials, I always prepare the annuals bed first thing. As soon as the soil can be worked. But only a gardener would know that."

"We have to start with what we've got." Flint pauses, drums his fingers against the tabletop.

He couldn't be much older than forty, she realizes, though his face has so much of another kind of wear.

He says, holding her eyes with his powdery gray ones, "And at the moment we haven't got Bliss."

Grace sits up in her chair. "What?"

"Vanished. She didn't return to the house last night. We

wanted to question her. We can't hold Dan much longer without talking to her."

Grace runs the possibilities through her mind. There are a few she doesn't want to think about. "Do you even know if she's okay? What does Dan say?"

"He says he doesn't know. He doesn't know about the gun, about where Bliss is, nothing." Flint turns his ballpoint pen between his fingers. He pauses. "Right now, the only sure connection we have is you."

"Rita was with me the whole time. We paid the bill and left the bar. We were never out of each other's sight."

"And Ralph?" Flint asks again, this time leaning toward her over the table.

Grace sighs, looks away. When she looks back, she says, "I don't know. When Rita and I left, we couldn't find him. We figured he was probably in the men's room."

"Cowboys'?" Flint smiles briefly and leans back again in his chair. "That," he says, "is exactly what he claims."

"I wish I'd let Rita go in and check, but it's too late now. He was there right after the shooting, but I didn't see him before. Are there any witnesses?"

"At two in the morning, in a bar?" Flint looks at her sideways. "I have to ask you this. For the record."

Grace sighs. "I know."

"Why didn't you tell me in the first place?"

"I'm not really sure." Grace studies the flesh-colored wall above his shoulder. "I didn't really know what had happened, I was so confused." She drops her eyes to his. "I hadn't eaten since breakfast, and I'd had a couple of beers. Then there was all that blood. Everything was mixed up in my mind. Ralph said he had been there, and I halfway believed him."

"And the other half?"

"I convinced myself. I could even picture him walking out with us." Grace sighs again. She can't meet his eyes. "I guess I was afraid."

"For you, or for him?"

"I don't even know. For both of us." With effort, she looks him straight in the eye. "Detective, I needed him. I needed to believe him."

"What made you remember?"

"It came back slowly. For one thing, I was dreaming about it. And then, when I thought I knew, I asked him."

Flint leans back and folds his arms with a sigh. "There are no real witnesses."

Grace thinks for a moment. She says, "I don't know if this will help you. I don't even know if it's related."

"We need to know whatever there is."

"It's just that there were footprints in my border. Right next to the lilies. I thought they belonged to my dad, but now I'm not sure. It looked like whoever it was just walked in through the mud, stopped, and went back out again." She holds his faded eyes with her own. "It hasn't rained," she says. "But I'd get there soon if I were you. This time of year, you never know."

The first thing Dan tells Grace on the phone after his release is that he forgives her. Then, he wants to talk about flowers. "Fall," he says. "My mother planted mums."

"I'm thinking more in terms of blues. Salvia. Some white and purple cosmos. Balloon flowers." Grace has her eyes shut. She's letting the colors soothe her, but suddenly she sees Bliss's delicately bruised wrist. "What you want is a tangle, a riot. Blossoms escaping."

"The kind of flower that sort of floats free of its foliage," he says.

"Exactly."

"I wouldn't know. That's what Bliss says."

"The painter's eye." Grace tries to make her voice as casual as possible. "So, you've talked to Bliss? Where is she, exactly?"

"I don't know. She calls sometimes, but she doesn't say

from where. She's been keeping up on her sketching, she says."

"Spring," Grace says. "Lilacs, delphinium, iris, cornflower, chives in the herb garden, phlox. What is Bliss running from? You?"

"Grace. I just want you to know, I didn't shoot Pascal. Did not."

"Highlights, depending on the season, of yellow or pink or red. Some roses. Some coreopsis. Moonbeam." With this garden on her tongue, Grace can find hope for them. She says, "You're free. What do you care what I believe?"

"You may have more in common with Bliss than you think."

She shivers. "I might."

But Dan isn't free for long. Grace reads in the morning paper about his arrest, about the prints in her garden that belong to a pair of his shoes. She is not surprised. She watched Flint's men from her bedroom window while they took plaster casts of two prints dried perfectly into the dirt. She tries calling both Ralph and Rita, but neither answers. She leaves messages on their machines.

Grace spends the rest of the morning in the arboretum greenhouse. Later, she and her father walk in the arboretum tucked up against the foothills just above campus, along paths lined with beds of flowers that Grace herself has propagated and nursed. They are sweating lightly in an unusually warm sun. From some of the paths the shrubbery opens and you can see nearly the whole city through branches of exotic and native trees. The flowers on the cherries are full out now, and the air is heavy with their fragrance. From the right spots, they frame the city in white blossoms. Grace wants her father to see this, this thing she has become apart from him, though she keeps her eyes away from his face, nervous about exposing herself to him. She stops at each bed and names the new plants to him, common and uncommon.

She says, "Creating a whole garden is like making a painting, except it changes from hour to hour. You have to be able to imagine it in time as well as in space. In six weeks, that flax there"—she points to where the barest feathery foliage is breaking through the earth—"will bloom in the morning, a cloud of blue, and then in the afternoon the blossoms will be gone. You have to plan for both. I used to be interested mostly in the science. More and more, I want to make something beautiful."

Her father waves his hand in front of his face as if he's brushing something away. "You're not what I remembered, either," he says.

"I was a child."

"I thought of you as staying just the same, but bigger. I knew better. But it was what I could imagine."

She runs her hand over her hair. Its new length still surprises her. She feels it waving at the nape of her neck. "Are you disappointed?"

He looks from the little bridge down through the hollow of the garden. "Yes and no." He waves his hand. "That's the way the world is. I mean, so are you."

Grace is hurt. "It's a father's job to lie about things like that."

Byron says, "We're adults, Grace. The rules have changed." He shakes his head, looks out over the city. "We don't have that history of deception between us."

"Don't you regret it?" Grace says. "In a way, Pascal was the only father I knew." Byron wipes the corner of his eye with a gesture Grace remembers. Just there, his face has gone rough and ruddy with age. "I've been an adult for a long time," she says. "Technically, anyway."

"Grace. What I'm sorry for is not who you are but what I've missed. To see you like this, grown up—it's a miracle, just as wonderful. And as disturbing. As if I have no right to be proud of you."

The knot in Grace's stomach begins to go soft. She touches his arm. "All my life, since I've been grown, I've looked for what you and Mother had between you." This is not only a compliment. "I must look like a failure to you."

"How so?"

"I'm alone, living with my mother's mother in a big, dark house filled with furniture bought by people who are dead."

He looks at her, his mouth slightly open, his eyes narrowed.

"Really." She thinks, Now he'll put his arm around my shoulders and walk me over the bridge.

He waves his hand at the newly blooming beds at their feet. "You helped make this. I can't even imagine it." Then, "Things weren't always that good between your mother and me."

There's so little Grace really remembers, and what she does recall has been coming only recently, first in a trickle and lately in a steady stream. She has no idea what's true. "At the end?"

"Any time after the beginning. There were moments"—he shakes his head and smiles—"I wouldn't have traded for anything. But most of the time." He leans his elbows on the bridge railing. Below, lily pads float like rafts. Grace watches his reflection in the water, tries to find his expression, but his face is fragmented by the golden coins drifting on the surface, the thalia growing through his reflection and into the air between his two faces, the one turned to water and the solid one next to Grace, which she can't see at all unless she turns to him and he to her. She watches the water face. It's more familiar anyway, its surface and edges blurring like memory.

"I think I knew," she says. "But until recently I've always pretended otherwise."

"I would have stayed. I thought if I just kept giving her a home to come back to, she always would come back. And eventually"—he laughs—"she would tire enough to stick around."

Grace pauses. She can find no way to say this tactfully, but it's the only fact that will explain their conversation, and she wants, for once, to have all the eddies and currents working on the surface instead of underneath. Finally, she says, "Mother was unfaithful. Even I knew it." It's the word "mother" that feels unfamiliar in her mouth, not "unfaithful." It feels like an apology.

He leans on the rail of the bridge, almost his whole weight on the palms of his hands. His face ripples over the water. "Perpetually. It made me miserable, but I never blamed her. Whatever it was in her that made her do it—I don't know. It's as if that was what I loved. A sort of wilderness. I thought the pain and the passion had the same source. I couldn't tell which was which. It was as if the pain of it made everything more real."

"I think I know what you mean."

He smiles. "I was afraid of that." He reaches out and touches her hair where it curls over her ear. "A father wants his child to be happier than he is. And wiser. I thought if I left you'd have a better chance. Imo had so much to give you."

"Pascal and I didn't exactly repeat your marriage, but that's not to our credit. We couldn't figure out who was supposed to be the stalwart one."

He smiles, as if Grace is trying to be funny.

"Just when I decided he was, he turned out not to be. And when he found out I was unfaithful, he didn't care."

"Are you sure?"

"Let's just say he was adaptable." Grace taps out a rhythm with her foot, and the little bridge trembles. "He could forgive." Grace stops tapping, but the bridge keeps shaking gently. She reaches to her father, says, "Do you feel that? Another tremor."

He takes her hand. "There are worse things than being adaptable." This is a plea in his own defense, not Pascal's.

"I know that now. I blamed you for everything. I was wrong, at least partly."

"You will have other chances. Miranda has been a wonder to me." Slowly, the bridge stops swaying. A crack spiders through the wood railing. Byron looks away, up toward the mountains. "It's funny how much can change. This winter, watching the war. It wasn't like last time—shots of bodies, people bleeding and dying. It was machines against concrete."

"A hundred thousand people."

"I didn't see them. The whole strategy worked. I was happy to let it. To me, the protesters on the television screen were enemies. It was uncomplicated. I don't know if I'm just old, or if this one really was different."

"Maybe it didn't matter." Grace doesn't want to believe it, that everything is as faded as it feels to her. "What did you expect? Our two heads knocking over a photo album while we reminisced about all the happy, lost years?"

His short, dry laugh sounds as if it comes from the middle of his throat. "Maybe I did." He shakes his head, still smiling. "I never prevented Julia from doing anything. So I guess Imo was right, and you could say I played a role in her death."

"Everyone has bad days."

"I loved her."

Grace smiles at him. Suddenly, her mother leans down to her; she can feel a breath of air, as if someone has opened a window in a close, hot room.

He says, "But I'm happier without her. That's what I'm trying to say. Now the passion's gone, things are easier. With Miranda, everything is comfortable, clear. There aren't always complicated undercurrents."

"I know what you mean." Grace forms her words carefully, shaping her lips around them as if they were small, hard candies. "In a way, I was glad when she died. That's why it was so terrible. It was like her death was the only thing that could release you." Grace is looking away from her father. "And once you were free, you left. I wanted to go too, that's all." When she turns back, she sees a pallor around his lips.

"I know," he says. "I thought I couldn't talk about your mother with you."

"Whatever it is, I have a right to know."

He smiles, a little weakly. "You've forgotten how to be a child. They have no rights." He laughs, and Grace looks at him for a second, then laughs too, but through closed lips. She supposes if her mother had lived the two of them would have gone through what other mothers and daughters do— that time of trying to find out who is who. Grace would have begun to judge her mother, might have pushed her to settle down, to grow up faster than she wanted to, would have wanted her to remain always older, always ahead, urging Grace on, cautioning and encouraging. Grace might have wanted her mother to have become placid and stable and true.

But now, from this distance, Julia emanates a smoky halo in the center of a darkened room, or stands bright as Moses ahead of Grace on a trail somewhere, in her outstretched hand a small chip of stone. To Grace, Julia was all the glamour and mystery of her own future. There's still a sense in which she prefers violent death—her mother's, who kept making a dare she must have been surprised to have taken up, or Pascal's, who walked out into the night looking for another, maybe less painful, way to be—than the sort of ordinary life her father has chosen.

After the arboretum, Grace's father takes her back to Imo's. He turns off the car and comes around to open her door.

She says, "Are you sure you want to come in?"

Imo sits at the window looking out, a pair of socks in her hand, waiting for Grace to make her way home. "Through the ruins," she says when they walk in, arm in arm.

"What are you talking about?" Grace says.

"Didn't you feel it?" Imo points her darning needle at the floor.

"It was only another tremor," Grace says.

"Well, I've lived through worse." Imo presses her lips together, and her chin bunches up in that way that means she's remembered Grandpa really is gone. It's not any damage to buildings that bothers Imo, so much as knowing the earth could shake someone else she loves right off it, that we all have potential disasters ticking inside us, waiting to be jarred loose by the ordinary convulsions of life.

Grace puts her arm around Imo. "I'm sorry," she says. Since coming back from the hospital, Imo seems even smaller, as if something's whittling her away from the inside. But her wig—auburn today—is as jaunty as ever.

"We can skip your walk, if you aren't feeling up to it," Grace says.

"You're looking none too fresh yourself," Imo says, standing upright under Grace's arm. She still ignores Grace's father. "You go upstairs and get cleaned up."

Grace looks at her father.

He says, "Maybe I'd better check the house. If it would make you feel better."

"Imo," Grace says.

Imo puts her hand over her heart. "This house will be here for you after I'm long gone, that's for sure."

"I'm sure it's fine." Grace feels helpless. With her father standing next to her, the house looks a little dingier than she remembers just from this morning. The hall needs paint. In fact, there is a new crack in the plaster of the stairwell wall, and as Grace watches, it inches up toward the ceiling.

Imo's chin unbunches. "We're sitting right on the fault. The ground could just open up, and we'd be gone." She points at the door to the foyer, which shares the cracked wall. On the other side, the old convex mirror has fallen and shattered, the frame too with its fat, gilded cherubs splintered into irretrievable pieces on the marble tile. The littered floor reflects in fragments the dim glitter of the overhead light, their own faces.

Imo says, "I've always told your grandfather a nail wasn't enough to hold it. He'll be on one for sure when he gets back."

"Yes," Grace says. "For sure." She doesn't want her father to see Imo this way.

"It belonged to his mother." This is wrong: it came from Imo's side, carried by wagon over the Plains. Imo makes a little moue with her mouth. "Just don't tell him. I always thought the thing was monstrous. Naked babies indeed."

Grace sweeps up the fragments of broken glass while Imo sleeps. After her nap, Imo doesn't seem much revived. "You're an adult," she says to Grace out of the blue. "Make up your own mind." This is the first time she has admitted Grace into the grown-up club. She's sitting in the living room in her own mother's green velvet chair, which she has had recovered over the years, always in green but in progressively more brilliant shades. Now, it is the color of the very earliest leaves.

"About what?" Grace says. "What are we talking about here?"

Imo's mouth purses. "You may be grown, but you are still not to speak to me that way."

When Grace is not looking at Imo, she sometimes wants to shake her. There are things she is on the verge of saying, accusations she wants to make. But when Grace looks, she thinks how thin Imo's shoulders are. Even Grace's small hands could snap something in her.

Imo says, coming down with precision on each syllable, "Your father made his own decision."

"There was never any question."

"In whose mind?" Imo looks up at Grace, her eyes hard and blue again, not the gray they keep fading into as if there's a dimmer switch behind them. Grace can never tell when Imo's going to turn it up or down.

"In mine," Grace says.

Ticking the list off on her fingers, Imo says, "Her body had fallen three hundred feet. It was bruised and broken beyond recognition. It had been carried out tied underneath a helicopter, for heaven's sake"—Grace actually likes this image, the body of her mother spinning in the sky under the whirling wings—"Like some animal." Imo gives "for heaven's sake" and "like some animal" each a finger of its own. She presses her mouth shut again. She's holding the five ticked-off fingers of her left hand in her right, and she shakes them at Grace as if they were material evidence. "Her boots had been blown open. There are things I remember like yesterday."

Grace kneels in front of the green chair, takes Imo's face in her hands and looks into her eyes. They are watery, not only with tears but with age. Grace can feel Imo's skull directly under the skin. If Grace could only keep Imo's eyes focused on her own, maybe Imo would stop fading. Grace says very slowly, "You have to listen. It was inevitable."

Imo's eyes widen. She just keeps looking.

"There was nothing she wouldn't do."

"He was her husband. He should have controlled her."

"Like Luther controlled you?"

Imo looks at the ceiling over Grace's head. "I'm still here, aren't I?"

"Byron's selling insurance now. He's got a swimming pool. He's exactly what you wanted him to be."

"It's a little late for all that, isn't it? After he just left her there." Imo looks right into Grace's eyes. Grace can see no reason in her face.

Grace says, "Imo, no."

"Who was there for her? Who?"

Imo's daughter is dead. Grace's mother. Nothing but ash, mistaken memory refusing to reduce to human size. Grace no longer needs to say what she thought she was going to, that Imo has it all wrong. Which of them doesn't? Grace reaches for Imo, stands and brings her grandmother up into her arms. She puts her hand behind Imo's head and presses the small face to her shoulder and kisses Imo's hair. It is very soft, dry, an old woman's hair. It could dissolve under Grace's lips. Grace has to keep herself from holding on too hard. They stand there together and sway, both crying.

Imo keeps saying, over and over, "How will we ever know?"

"Shhh," Grace says, until at last Imo lifts her face from Grace's blouse.

She looks into Grace's eyes. "What is happening to me?"

Grace rolls her own eyes upward, trying to catch the new tears. "It will be okay," she says. She leads Imo to the couch and lays her down and puts the afghan over her, the one Imo's own grandmother crocheted square by square under candlelight in the little house attached to the store. Where, Grace wonders, did they keep that awful, fancy mirror? What dream had provoked Imo's grandmother to bring it here, where there would be no wall to hang it on for generations?

When Imo is settled Grace puts her finger to her own lips and then to Imo's. "Now sleep," she says, and Imo shuts her eyes and is instantly gone.

After Imo's asleep, Grace goes out into the garden. The sudden spring is just as suddenly nearly over, and she's running behind; the roses she hasn't yet pruned have already leafed out around their dead canes and formed buds; everything, especially weeds, grows up through last year's uncleared debris, stopping for nothing. She can't believe it has so quickly got the better of her. A few short, unseasonably warm weeks. She tries to think what she's been doing instead of this. Nothing. Watching the weather, holding herself to sleep.

Grace gets out the bamboo rake, pulls it gently through the beds wherever there's space, moving the old mulch aside. Then she gets down on her knees and clears dead foliage from between the plants. She waits to feel the reliable lift in her chest, the physical swelling she gets every year when she sees how the earth shows forth, but there is still the dull, heavy tightness she has felt there for months, the familiar ache of dirt under her nails. The only change: a restlessness, a need, whether motion can satisfy or not, to move. When she looks up, Imo is standing there in her sneakers and an old cardigan of Grandpa's, hugging the sweater closed over her breasts though it must be eighty-five degrees in the sun.

"How does it look?" Imo says.

"All I can see are weeds." Grace takes off her gloves. The bindweed is already taking over—to get it she'll have to follow its roots barehanded through the soil, from plant to plant to its bitter end. "I never know where it all comes from."

"All those degrees for nothing?"

"Why not?" Grace says. "You paid for them."

"Smarty pants." Imo puts her hand on Grace's arm. "I've always loved you." She looks out toward the back fence, her chin quivering. "I may not have been right, but I tried. You're all I've got. I wanted to protect you."

"Not all." Grace is small, but next to herself Imo must look tiny, absolutely breakable. Grace puts an arm around her. "You did the best you could."

Imo looks up at Grace sidelong. "Shall we divide the lilies this year?"

"It's already done."

Imo smiles her little smile, the one that looks like a triangle. "I wanted to pull something apart, is all."

"We'll find you some weeds."

"Not weeds," Imo says, shaking her head. "Flowers. Something beautiful."

Grace looks at Imo closely. The conversations are getting harder and harder to navigate. Imo's still got that smile on, but her eyes are misty. After all, what does it matter? Flowers grow, wherever you put them. Grace waves her hand. "Whatever you want. This is all yours."

"And yours," Imo says.

"No," Grace says. It's a favor she's asking. "Not yet."

"But almost."

"I'll let you know when I'm ready."

Imo pulls herself up. She says, "You don't have a thing to say about it."

CHAPTER 13

■ ■ ■

Overlooking Eden

When Grace first sees the postcard, she doesn't realize what it means. It's not slick like a photo card; rather, it's pebbled, heavy, torn-edged. The picture on the front is a watercolor, a delicate wash in a style familiar to Grace, though it's not until she looks closely that she realizes the painting must be Bliss's. It shows a low green house with a rough-built stone chimney, a deep front porch, a front yard shaded by aspen and willow, the lawn constellated with wildflowers. Bliss's renderings of the papery trunks of the trees are perfect. Grace runs her finger down one of them. On the back of the card, Bliss has written, "Wish You Were Here."

"So do I," she whispers. Again she tries to call Ralph and Rita. All day from the greenhouse, she dials each of their numbers on the quarter-hour, hanging up when their answering machines click on. After she gets home in the late afternoon, she phones her father's hotel to tell him she knows where Bliss is, that she'll pick him up in thirty minutes.

"Why?" he asks. "It sounds like her reasons for going away are good enough."

"I don't think she knows Dan has been arrested."

"Should she?"

"Wouldn't you want to know, if you were in her position?"

He says, "What about Imo?"

Grace hasn't thought of Imo. She leans her head against the foyer wall where the mirror used to be. She doesn't know if it's happened only in the last couple of months, or if she has just finally faced it, but she knows Imo can't be left alone. Her legs are shakier and shakier. If she fell, she might break in two, Grace thinks. She will have to come along.

"You're right," Grace says. "Make it forty minutes."

"Where are we going?"

"I'll tell you on the way. Pack an overnight bag, will you?" Grace hesitates, then says, "Look. Tell Miranda I'm sorry."

"Thank you," he says. Then, "I'll tell you what. Why don't we leave Miranda with Imo?"

Grace starts to laugh. "It would serve Imo right. But I could hardly do that to Miranda."

"Miranda used to be a registered nurse. She can take care of herself."

When Grace hangs up the phone and turns around, Imo is standing in the doorway with her lips pressed together and her arms crossed tightly over her chest. "You can't make me stay with her," she says.

"Imo, listen," Grace says. "This is important. This is life and death."

Imo uncrosses her arms and holds them out, looking down at her shrinking body. "And this isn't?"

Grace feels a give in herself. Of course Imo is afraid. She takes Imo into her arms. "I know. It is. You don't have to talk to Miranda if you don't want to."

Imo looks out toward the kitchen window, the dapple of green leaves on the other side. "I won't, then," she says. "And

I trust you'll hurry up." Her voice sounds childish, petulant.

"A day, maybe two. I promise."

An hour later, Imo, wrapped in sweaters like an old lady but swearing like a film star, looks over Miranda in her boutique cowboy hat and jeans with suede chaps sewed on. "My," she says. "Some people will wear anything for a little attention."

Miranda winks at her. "You ought to know. I don't understand how Grace talked you into those little-old-lady clothes."

"Imo," Grace says. "Remember, it will be a couple of days at most. No more."

Imo waves her hand. "Don't mind me. I'm just a senior citizen."

"We'll have a wonderful time," Miranda says. "Maybe we'll do some shopping."

Imo bunches up her mouth as if she's just bitten into a lemon and found it even more sour than expected. She says around her teeth, still small and pearly, "Lovely."

"You can give me some advice on evening wear. I read all about you in *People* magazine."

Imo pulls her sweater closer, but she can't hide that she's pleased. "I don't eat fresh fruit, just so you know. It upsets the digestion. And I like my sweets. You can't take them away."

"Imo, nobody's going to take away your cookies." Grace looks at Miranda so Miranda will take this seriously. "They're about all she'll eat anymore."

Miranda says, "Of course not. We can bake some right after Grace and Byron leave. I have a recipe for Sweet Mollies that will break your heart. Then maybe you'll give me your autograph."

"If you don't poison me first," Imo says. She squares her shoulders. "But if you insist, you might as well get started. I'll show you where the kitchen is."

Grace drives the pickup north on I–15. From the foothills on their right, Ogden Canyon opens into a haze of green.

They roll down the windows. The river is high enough with the runoff that they can hear it over the sound of the engine.

Grace's father says, "Like the old days." He has a sketch pad on his lap. He's already drawn in the Salt Lake Valley and the road north to Ogden, the new green leaves and rushing water of the canyon, Grace's red pickup with their arms and legs sticking out the windows.

Grace takes her eyes from the winding road long enough to glance at the map. "I'm not a child anymore," she says.

"How do you know this is for you?"

Then, just at the reservoir, the valley opens up and they can see, all the way up on the other side of the bowl, the grove of trees that shelters the ranch's guest house. The valley between the reservoir and the ranch looks like a soft green blanket. In its center, they turn at Eden's general store, drive past the town's few houses, and curve with the road past the Mormon wardhouse. They pull south through the ranch gates onto the dirt road that runs between the house and the barn of the working ranch and then on up.

"This is where it all went on," Grace says.

Grace's father says, "What all?"

"If you wanted to know that, you should have stuck around." Grace looks around again, says, "My childhood. This is where it happened."

"There was more to it than this," he says.

As soon as they open their doors, Wendy is out the front door of the house, sniffing Byron, and Elvis and Paint, the ranch dogs, are growling at him. "They don't much like men," Grace says. "Except Ralph, of course."

They lean against the truck and wait. In a minute, the screen door opens and Bliss steps out onto the porch. She's wearing her short cutoffs and a man's ribbed undershirt beneath a straw hat trimmed with cloth roses. She shades her eyes with her hand. "You got my card," she says.

Behind her, a shadow moves, then the door opens again

and Rita says, "What are you doing out there?" She squints into the sunlight where Grace and Byron stand. "Oh," she says.

"You haven't changed," Byron says to her. He grins. "A little taller, maybe."

She lifts her lip at him, but good-naturedly. "Aren't those the same shorts you were wearing the last time I saw you?"

"Like I said," he says.

Grace hasn't been in the ranch house since her marriage. Though the buildings of the working ranch, where the hands live, are modern, Ralph's uncle, and now Ralph, have left the original house intact. Except for electric lights, plumbing, some 1940s furniture, and appliances from the same era making a sort of kitchen at the fireplace end of the common room, it all looks as it has since before the turn of the century, when Ralph's family homesteaded the valley. Against the bare log walls, under the east windows across from the door, an old couch is pushed up, and in the center of the room two green leather recliners flank a table. Ralph is sitting in one of them, reclined all the way back, his eyes shut. Over his head, enormous log beams cross under the roof, and from them stuffed pheasants and a bobcat, his back arched and paw raised, peer down through glass eyes dazed by dust. Under one window, Ralph has a desk stuffed with papers and, sitting among them, a computer, compatible with the one in his office in the Hole-in-the-Wall. Tacked to the wall above the desk are a life-size head shot of the Dalai Lama and a Grateful Dead poster festooned with skulls and roses.

Without opening his eyes, Ralph says, "What are you doing here?"

"You said I was welcome anytime," Grace says. "And anyway, Bliss sent an invitation. A formal one." Grace holds out the postcard for Ralph to see. "You can't protect somebody who doesn't want protection."

Ralph leans forward in the chair, and it creaks back into

upright position. He looks at the card, then at Bliss. "You did that? After everything?"

Bliss walks over and stands right in front of him. "It's all this I've worried about. I don't really understand what we're doing."

"*We*," Ralph says, "*we*, meaning Rita and I, have risked our necks to save you, that's what." He stands up, so that he is looking down at her. "We have rescued you from a maniac who would have killed you either sooner or later, and we have brought you to this idyllic place for your own protection. Remember that."

Grace is watching both Ralph's face and the set of Bliss's shoulders, which drop a little. "Don't be pedantic, Ralph," Grace says. "Not everybody wants to settle down with horses. Bliss is a city girl."

Bliss shakes her head. "It's not that."

"Do they let you see the paper?" Grace says. "Dan's been arrested."

Bliss turns around, her eyes wide. "What?"

"Let her? We're not holding her prisoner, Grace," Ralph says.

"His footprints were in my garden," Grace tells Bliss. "Where the gun was buried."

Ralph lowers his face into his hands, then raises it. "Thank God."

Rita goes to Bliss and wraps her in a hug that, Grace realizes after a moment, is not entirely platonic. She's knocked Bliss's hat crooked. "It's nearly over," Rita says.

Bliss straightens her hat, lifts her head, and kisses Rita softly on the lips. Then she says, "No. It's not."

Rita tightens her grip. The hat tips again. "What do you mean? He's off the streets. He can't hurt you anymore. Or anyone else. That's justice."

Bliss opens her mouth, but Ralph interrupts. "Bliss. I have to agree with Rita. It's justice. What more do you want?"

"I want some food. It's almost dark, and we haven't started supper yet." Bliss turns to Grace and Byron. "I take it you two are staying the night?"

There are four bedrooms, two with double beds off to the left, and two smaller rooms, each with a single bed, off the kitchen area on the right. A month ago, Grace thought, she and Rita would have been assigned to share a room, and she would have asked, joking, "Can you be good?" But Bliss and Rita have taken one double bed, Ralph the other, so Byron and Grace make up the two singles.

After the beds are made, Byron and Grace light a fire in the big fireplace, built by hand, stone by stone, by Ralph's great-great-grandfather. The evening air is chilly, but what they really want is light, to be able to see each other's faces flickering in and out. Ralph, Rita, and Bliss take Ralph's Cherokee to town to stock up on food for dinner and breakfast.

When they've gone, Grace shakes her head. "I read that one wrong. I had Bliss paired with Ralph, not Rita."

Grace's father passes her a bottle of rum and a ceramic mug. "So much for your assumptions." He takes a drink of rum. His voice is too casual. "Are you sorry?"

Grace looks into the fire. "I don't know. Probably a little." She smiles. "It's mostly vanity, I guess. I really do want Rita to be happy."

Byron puts down his mug and looks at her. "She couldn't be happy with you?"

Grace shakes her head. The fire flares, then settles. "Why does Imo think you killed my mother?" Grace no longer wants to do this, but the cold years of curiosity push at her back.

He wipes his fingers over his eyes. "I don't know. Because it's all she can think. She needed somebody to blame, and I was there."

Grace whispers, "Not for long. I needed somebody, too. Not to blame."

Her father won't look at her. "I kept waiting to hear from

you," he says. "Then, when I thought I'd almost forgotten, Ralph tracked me down. He told me about Pascal and you. He said you needed me."

"Ralph?" Grace looks at him sharply. Then, "It didn't feel that way when you called. It felt like an intrusion."

"Miranda finally persuaded me just to come."

"You know," Grace says, "I spent a whole year searching for Julia." She is weighted down with love and anger. She makes herself look, unblinking, at his face, at the cheeks roughened by age. "I was eighteen. I went around the world. There was everything to see, but all I wanted was her face."

"For *her*," he says.

"The Alps. Nepal. The Sahara. I thought for sure I'd find her." In the lamplight he finally looks familiar to Grace, smoothed out—shadow and flickering forehead, clear eyes, the oddly squared lips. She pushes on through what feels like a thickening air. "I followed your postcards. But it never crossed my mind to look for you."

"I was looking for her, too. After the accident, I was a wreck." His eyes hold hers.

"I was nine years old."

"Your grandmother had a home, a roof. Money. She wanted you."

"And you didn't."

He hesitates. "Sometimes, what we can manage has to become what we want."

This is familiar. Looking into the fire, Grace sees her life. She leans back in her chair and folds her arms. "The hard part is over."

He says, "Doesn't it just keep getting harder?"

Grace shakes her head.

He waves his hand. "After all this, I'm surprised to hear that."

Grace's father and Ralph are already awake, and Grace can smell coffee brewing. When she comes out into the common room in her jeans and T-shirt, her father pours a cup for her and two to take to Rita and Bliss. Bliss heads for the shower, but coffee only slows Rita down. In ten minutes she steps out of the bedroom, still in cotton Jockey bikinis and bra, and stretches, as luxuriously immune to cold as she's always been. Grace picks Ralph's Polaroid up off the table and snaps a picture. Her father looks Rita over. Grace feels a surge of jealousy, and is surprised. Didn't she freely give up on her father? Isn't she the one recalcitrant about mending the past?

He says to Rita, "It *has* been a long time."

On backpack trips, Grace's father would get up first, light the Coleman stove, and heat water for coffee, washing, breakfast. He'd bring hot chocolate to her and Rita in their tent, singing out, "Up and at 'em. Time's a-wasting." Now, she can't imagine him talking that way.

"Yeah, Dad," she says. "A long time." The "Dad" comes out with a spin on it.

Rita says, "Grace. Behave." She's still in her underwear, rummaging in the cupboard for the granola.

"Would you rather call me Byron?" he asks.

"That might not be a bad idea," Grace says.

"Ralph has to ride to the upper pasture to bring down the horses," Rita says. "I thought we could head up the canyon on foot today and see what we find."

Bliss emerges, fully made up, with a towel around her head. She removes it and begins scrunching her curls in its folds. "I don't think I've ever been hiking before. Will I need my aerobics shoes, or can I wear these? They're Aerosoles."

Rita looks at Bliss's feet, on which she's wearing her silver gladiator sandals. "There will be snow," she says. "But we won't go far."

After breakfast, the four of them hike up the little canyon behind the ranch. Soft hills give way to granite cliffs down which runoff from the high peaks falls in long, dark ribbons. Elvis and Paint have gone with Ralph to fetch the horses; Wendy circles the hikers, splashing in the water and search-

ing the underbrush for signs of life. In the shade, the air is
cold, and even down this far there are places the sun doesn't
touch where the snow is still deep enough for Wendy to sink
in up to her belly. Grace is glad she's thrown her sweatshirt
on over her T-shirt.

Rita hikes in front, setting the pace, slower than usual so
Bliss can keep up. This is a concession she has never made to
Grace's shorter stride. Grace would never have asked her to.
After a couple of miles of scrambling over boulders and pushing through brush, Bliss is panting. Rita turns from the narrow trail to examine the rock wall running next to it. There's
a sunny ledge twenty or so feet overhead.

Rita raises her hand to the rock, begins to climb. Grace
turns to watch, and when Rita's nearly at the top Grace starts
up after, stopping every few feet to remind herself what holds
Rita found, which better ones she spotted from the ground.
She finds a rhythm and the concentration she needs to stay
close to the rock. It's been a long time—her fingers, cold
against damp granite, are stiff by the time she reaches the
ledge and Rita puts her hand down to help. At the top, Rita
ties herself into a rope. Byron ties Bliss in at the bottom, using
the knot Grace remembers from childhood, her mother's
voice talking about the rabbit coming up from its hole, hop-
ping around the tree, returning to safety.

When the knot has been tied and tested, Byron shouts,
"On belay!"

"Climb!"

"Climbing!"

Grace hears her father's voice from below, directing Bliss
where to reach for holds, how to move her feet against the
rock, patient and calm, exactly the way he was with Grace
twenty-five years earlier. After Grace and Rita have helped
Bliss over the top, he starts up, breathing hard, grunting gently as he pulls himself onto the face.

Wendy sniffs around below, then lies down against the cliff

in a patch of sun. They sit down on the ledge, their backs against the rock. Just a few feet over, water snakes down sheer granite slicked green with moss. Grace can feel the slightest mist on her cheeks, but up here the sun is enough to warm her. She pulls off her sweatshirt. They listen to the sound of water echoing off the canyon walls.

Then, after a long time of not knowing she was thinking about it, Grace says, "Why didn't she stop?"

Her father lifts his arm from over his eyes. He must have been thinking about the same thing. Grace believes he must think about it much of the time.

"When did she ever? She climbed the last hundred feet or so alone." He shakes his head as if to clear it. "Bill and I waited below her on the ledge. Usually, I would have been first on the rope. But when I wouldn't climb, she took the rope from me and started up. All around us the lightning was cracking. We'd been in bad spots before, but this was the worst by far." He gazes up the canyon. "She always was braver than anyone."

"Or dumber," says Rita.

Byron says, "I kept yelling for her to come down. Then she was too far gone to hear. She vanished over the top and tossed the rope down for the belay. Neither of us was about to use it. We waited. Then I could feel my hair stand up, could feel where every follicle on my body entered the skin. For some reason, I grabbed the rope. A kind of anchor, I guess. As if I could help. The air around us filled with light, then it opened. Light snaked along the rope, and just as I let go my body seemed to blow up. The doctor says it's impossible, but I swear I saw the fire leap up from my hand to meet the fire coming down. I don't remember anything else."

"Up?" Rita sits up straight and opens her eyes.

This is the first time Grace has been willing to listen, to believe what her father might have to tell her about his responsibility or lack of it, what he may have paid that afternoon or over the years since. All these weeks, he's listened to her. Her father opens his hand, which Grace realizes now he's always kept almost closed, curved around the scar burned into his palm and halfway up four fingers. The skin is shiny and mottled. She takes his hand and looks at it, then she rubs the scars under her fingers. "In a way," she says, "you did kill her."

"God and I between us, anyway." His smile twists. "It happened so quickly, I don't know what I really saw and what I've invented. The important thing was, she was waiting for me, and I failed her."

"There are some things you can't expect from people," Grace says.

"No. But you can from yourself." He puts his head in his hands; whatever he sees is behind his own eyes. "When I woke up, Bill was doing CPR, slamming into my chest. I was flat on my back on the ledge, six or seven feet away from where I'd been. I'm lucky it kicked me sideways instead of over the edge. She was all I remembered. Bill told me she hit the ledge next to me. It was like a reflex—I reached out to catch her, but she was long gone."

The bones of Grace's own hand are tiny under the skin. Julia's must have been the same, though the last time she touched Grace's back her hand covered all of it. She says, "You couldn't have caught her."

"Imo wouldn't wait the funeral," he says. "I was still in the hospital. It was a few days before I even remembered I had a child. All that time, Imo had never said a word about you. My heart—the charges were messed up. Interrupted. But the brain gets the worst of it." He looks down into the canyon. Below, the path and the creek are almost invisible under shadow. "That may be the thing I can't forgive."

"Imo had her troubles too," Grace says. "She had me."

He reaches over and grabs the back of her neck. "I couldn't move. Bill climbed down alone. They brought in a helicopter and took your mother and me out on stretchers. They had to lower us with ropes to where the helicopter could land. I looked over, still thinking I'd be able to catch her eye, ask her to forgive me, but they'd covered her. Still, it took me years to understand she was gone."

Grace says, "I can hardly remember any of it. What I do remember is wrong. Were you burned?"

"Arborescent erythema."

"Like trees," she says.

"The electricity traces the moisture on your skin." He turns to her. "Grace, please believe me. I tried to call your mother back, but she kept on going."

"It was just like her."

Bliss's eyes are very wide, her face pale. "Did she scream?"

"If she did, I couldn't hear her. You wouldn't have believed the wind." He looks across the canyon. "I never knew how much of it was my fault." He shakes his head. "The other climbers always called her crazy, but they admired her. The men were all in love with her. But from a distance it's always different."

Grace pauses. "Not from a distance. That was the problem." Her voice sounds hard.

He waits, too, before answering. Then he smiles a tight smile. "There are all kinds of distance, my child. Anyway, she wasn't sleeping with all of them."

Rita says in her driest voice, "Well, that's a blessing."

"That's enough, Rita," Grace says.

After all, Byron hasn't forgiven Julia everything. He takes Grace's hand. "You're right. Am I stupid to want to try again?"

"I don't know," she says.

He puts his arm around her, his cheek against her hair. "The worst part was, it was as if she knew it would happen. She was laughing when she started up. Like she wanted it."

Grace is surprised to find herself settling in under his arm, to find she fits there. "Pascal, too," she says, though she's only testing the idea, and she can't tell if it feels quite right on her tongue. What she remembers is nothing like what was real.

After what seems a long time, Bliss says, "You shouldn't

blame yourself. Taking responsibility for something that's not your fault is as bad as not taking responsibility at all. It lets somebody else off the hook."

"That's exactly right," Grace says.

Bliss takes a deep breath. "Pascal didn't scream either."

Rita and Byron both open their eyes and look at her.

"I knew it," Grace says. "You were there."

Rita says, "With Dan." A warning.

"I've made up my mind, Rita," Bliss says, and Rita puts her arm around her. Bliss nestles in next to her, her face buried in Rita's armpit. After a long time, without lifting her head, she says, "No. Dan was there with me."

It takes Grace a second to sort this out. She remembers Jemma by the hospital elevator. She says, very gently, "Pascal tried to tell Jemma. When he was dying. Not happiness. Bliss."

"What?" Rita says.

"What Pascal said before he died. I knew he couldn't have been talking about heaven."

Rita's smile is tight. "It wouldn't have been like him."

Bliss's voice has almost lost its airy whisper. "Pascal was trying to help. I'd gone to his office to ask him to tape a broken rib." She touches her rib cage lightly. "I didn't want to go to the emergency room. They were getting to know me."

"Jesus," Grace says.

"He told me to leave Dan. He said I could stay with him at the cabin until I got set up." She opens her eyes and looks at Grace. "Nothing between us. Just that."

"I know. It wouldn't have mattered. Not at that point."

"He made it clear. He said all he wanted was you. I want you to know."

"Thank you," Grace says. She shakes her head, as if she can clear it.

Bliss takes another deep breath, but her voice still sounds firm, not windy. "We had just reached Pascal's car when Dan caught up. We were inside, but Dan grabbed the handle on the driver's door before Pascal could shut it. He pulled his gun out of his waistband and pointed it at Pascal's head. I didn't know what to do. Pascal's gun was sitting on the passenger seat when I got in. I didn't even know what it was pressing against my legs. It was hurting me, and I reached down and found myself with a gun in my hand."

"Pascal was outside the car when he was shot," Grace says.

"I was scared. I knew Dan might really shoot. And the look on his face—I wasn't thinking. I just grabbed Pascal's Colt from the seat and jumped out of the car. There was nowhere to run but under the freeway. I thought if I could get to Dan's bus on the other side it would be okay. Pascal would be okay. Dan wanted me, and if I could stay ahead of him I could start the bus and get away. But I could hear him running behind me. He was too much faster."

Grace closes her eyes and pictures it. Pascal under the freeway. Bliss. Dan between them with his gun raised.

Bliss's hands are shaking, but her voice is even, her eyes dry. "He told me to stop. He said he was going to shoot. So I stopped and turned around. I took off the safety. I knew how, because Dan taught me on his gun, so I could protect myself." Bliss smiled. "Dan was a few yards away. Pascal was behind him, a little to the side, but I wasn't looking at Pascal. I'd forgotten he was there. All I could see was Dan, the gun in his hand. I lifted Pascal's gun and closed my eyes and shot."

"You shot twice. It was the second shot that killed him." Grace wants to make sure everyone remembers what's at stake here, what the issue is.

Bliss nods. "I wanted to be sure. I wanted Dan dead. And I opened my eyes and saw Pascal fall. Then Dan had me by the arm. He said, 'We've got to get out of here.' I stood still, but he pulled at me. I didn't know what else to do, so we ran."

Rita has her hand in Bliss's hair, and Bliss curls up more tightly against Rita's chest. Rita says, "You can see we had to get her away. Everything was just getting worse. She was a prisoner. He would have killed her."

Grace leans over and puts a hand on Bliss's shoulder. She realizes the hand is shaking. "I'm sorry. But, Rita, what happened to justice?"

Rita buries her face in Bliss's hair and rocks her. "What about love? She didn't mean anything."

"That's just it. What *about* love? He was my husband." Grace is crying now, as much out of rage as grief. "Don't you see? This is worse. It was an *accident*. How could you hit the wrong man *twice*?" She doesn't know if she can bear it—that there was no passion to give Pascal's death shape or meaning. Nobody to hate, whomever she may blame. She closes her fist and beats it against her thigh.

Bliss says into Rita's armpit, "You're right. I know."

Grace stands and grabs Bliss by the arm, tries to drag her to her feet. "We're going to the police. Now. Get up."

Bliss presses into Rita's side, hiding her face.

Rita holds on to Bliss's other arm. "Don't *handle* her. She's pregnant, for godsake."

Grace lets go, presses her hands to her mouth. "You let her climb?"

Byron stands up, steps forward, steps again. He has an odd look on his face—his eyes are on Grace, but she can tell he doesn't see her. She doesn't know if he's going to help her or pull her away. She tightens her grip on Bliss's arm. The ledge narrows just where she stands, and when Byron steps again there is nothing under his foot. His arms beat the air. For a second he seems to hang, as if he'll be able to recover, to fling himself back onto the ledge, but the moment passes. He turns in the air and goes over. He hits the cliff once before he lands at the bottom.

At first, Grace can't look. When she does, she can tell from how he's squeezed his eyes shut with pain that he's not dead. Wendy whines, then she licks his face.

Byron bats at her muzzle and says, "Ouch." He's done a full somersault down the cliff face, and now his leg is bent under him at an angle that can only mean damage. He opens his eyes. "At least I didn't land on my head." But he's breathing hard and it's obvious talking's not easy. "I didn't feel anything snap," he says.

Grace looks down what they've climbed up. It's not a bad descent, and if Rita and Grace were alone they would have climbed the cliff ropeless without thinking about it. But there's Bliss; there's Byron at the bottom, and anyway going down, moving with gravity instead of against it, has always been the hardest for Grace. For one irrational moment, Grace thinks they could leave Bliss here on the ledge. She couldn't escape; she'd never make it down without help.

"I'll belay you both," Rita says. "You first, Grace. You can help Bliss at the bottom. Hurry." She loops the rope around her waist and settles behind a low boulder, bracing her feet against it.

Grace ties herself in, using carabiners front and back so the rope will run freely. She says, "Climbing," and backs down the cliff, her body perpendicular to the rock. In three sliding leaps backward, she's down. She releases the rope, and Rita ties her day pack on, lowers it to Grace, then loops a harness between Bliss's legs, tying the rope carefully so her stomach bears no weight. Once Bliss has been safely lowered, Rita unties and free-climbs down, turning her hips in the crack to brake, taking it, it seems to Grace, slower than usual, pressing her hands and feet against the nearly sheer walls.

At the bottom, Byron lifts each of his arms and moves it according to Rita's instructions, rolls his shoulders, his head. "I think it's only the leg. But if you could get my nitro out of my pocket?"

"I knew I did pre-med for a reason," Rita says, her hand in his trouser pocket, "but if I imagined feeling you up, it was never like this."

Grace crosses her arms over her chest. "How do we get him out of here?"

Bliss says, "We have to go for help."

Grace feels panic well up in her, remembering the last time Byron had to wait alone in the mountains, his wife's broken body on the mountain below him, his heart firing erratic charges. "No," she says. "We can't leave him."

Rita looks at Grace as if she's about to argue, but then she stops, lifts her hands. "Okay. Let's get to work." She has Bliss and Grace take off their spare clothing while she uses her pocketknife to strip two sturdy branches from a young cottonwood. She ties the sticks to either side of Byron's leg with their bandannas and sweatshirts. Then she stands back and folds her arms over her chest. "Not much of a splint, but it will have to do. What's the plan?"

Grace crosses her wrists. "We can carry him if we take shifts. Can Bliss help?"

"Looks like I'll have to," Bliss says.

Rita nods and helps Byron to his feet, and she and Grace make a basket for him out of their crossed and woven hands, the way they and Ralph used to carry each other as children. Bliss watches how they do it, then Grace ties on the day pack.

He says, "I'm too heavy." He's very white. He closes his eyes. "I can wait."

"Grace is right," Rita says. "Even if we leave you and hike out, we'll never get a horse up over those boulders. A helicopter would take hours, and there's no place to land, much less in the dark. This is the only way."

"We aren't leaving," Grace says, and nods at their clasped hands.

Her father sits down on the basket. At first he seems lighter than Grace expected, but the perception of lightness lasts only a few seconds. They tighten their grip and lift him. They carry him fifty steps—Rita counts them off—then they set him down and rest. Then Rita and Bliss take a turn. When it's

time for Grace and Bliss to take their shift together, they look
at each other for a moment. "I want you to know I'm sorry,"
Bliss says. "I want to do the right thing."

"Why didn't you in the first place?" Grace asks.

"Why didn't you?"

Grace sighs. "It's a little late now." But after a moment, she
holds out her hands and Bliss takes them in hers. Bliss loses
her grip before the fifty steps are out, so they shorten her
shifts to twenty-five steps. Even so, though she says nothing,
the tears are in her eyes before her turn is over.

Wendy, in front, whines for them to hurry. Boulders that
were trivial to scramble across on the way up become serious
obstacles. Once, Bliss, in her pink-and-white aerobics sneakers, slips and falls to her knees, jarring Byron's splinted leg
into the ground. Grace cringes for both of them; Byron only
gasps, then says, "It's okay. I'm fine." If a boulder is too big to
carry him over, they set him down, go around, help him lift
his legs over the top, then pick him up again from the other
side. Grace's hands go numb; her ankles and calves are barked
and bruised by rocks. Wendy has long since run ahead and
out of sight.

By the time they have carried him out through the rough
canyon and onto the dirt road leading down to the house, it
is late afternoon, but the days have been lengthening toward
the equinox and the sun is still pretty high in the sky. They
stop to rest with a view of the valley. Bliss is silently weeping.

Rita says to Byron, "Can you stand for a minute? We could
use a break." Her voice is light and firm, but Grace can tell
that even she is on the weaker side of tired.

Byron is pale and sweating, but he nods. Bliss and Rita set
him down on one leg and shake out their hands. Rita still
looks okay, a little hot, but Grace's hands are sore and swollen, her arms twitching, numb from effort. She wonders how
they can make it the last mile or so to the cabin, even over
the relatively smooth dirt road. Her father leans heavily on

Grace's shoulder. Rita puts her arm around Bliss. They all look out over the valley.

Rita points at some still-snowy peaks to the north. "Do you think that's in Idaho?" Grace is sweating hard, and when she turns back to the view she can see light shimmering, pooled in the grasses below. Rita says, "A mirage."

Byron's eyes are shut. Grace touches his forehead. It feels warm even to her hot fingers. She says, "Father. It's beautiful."

He opens his eyes and looks first at her and then at the horizon. He breathes in, says, "I can see why someone would follow such a thing." Then he shuts his eyes again. He shivers.

Rita says, "It's only a little way more to the house. Don't worry."

Grace has forgotten about Bliss, about calling the police. She and Rita join hands and heft Byron up again between them, and Grace's fingers begin to slip immediately. Rita tightens her grip and Grace winces but lets Rita hold on. She looks down the road just as Ralph rounds the bend on Jude, Wendy running in front of them, barking to urge them forward, and Elvis and Paint herding them from behind. He pauses to look at Grace and Byron and Rita, Bliss trailing behind, then kicks the horse toward them in a gallop.

On the ranch house's front porch, in those canvas sling chairs that fit themselves exactly to the shape of your body, Grace sits next to Ralph. Rita is inside washing the dishes from last night's soup, humming, as always enough off-key that Grace can't tell what she means the song to be. "The Wabash Cannonball," she finally decides: a song from her childhood. She remembers her father's fingers on the banjo, his slightly nasal tenor. Bliss is also inside, turning breakfast bacon in the big iron skillet. Grace is amused that Rita, though she will not eat the bacon, has neither commented to Bliss about animal slaughter practices nor made her usual faces. Wendy is stretched out in the shade at Grace's feet. She looks very satisfied with herself. Grace is considering how to get Bliss back down to Salt Lake and the police, but right now she's in no hurry. Though Byron's leg isn't broken, they've rested here two days longer than they planned. Grace can hear him inside, hobbling around in his elastic brace, helping Rita put away the dishes. Grace wants to watch the sun on the valley for a while. She shakes her head and looks up toward the mountains in the north. Their highest peaks are still barely snowed in. By late summer they will be parched and yellow, but now they look tender, as if a touch could bruise them.

"I think it is Idaho," she says.

Ralph says, "It is."

"I don't want to move from this chair. Ever. I don't want to do what I have to do."

He closes his eyes and lifts his face to the sun. "You don't have to move. Not if you don't want to."

"I've made a promise to Flint. I have to keep it."

He opens one eye at her. "That's a change."

"Anyway, it will get cold soon. You'll have to use the snow-mobiles to get to the house."

"I wanted you to be here, at the ranch, when I told you," he says. "I'm moving back."

"For good?"

"I'll be going down to the city long enough to sell the bar and pack. But I've strayed too far from where I started. I don't know what I was thinking."

"You thought you could make a little justice in the world."

"I'd rather raise cattle. I'll be running the working ranch myself." His eyes are still closed. His face looks smooth, peaceful, as if he were sleeping but not dreaming. "Mostly, cows aren't complicated. I can understand them."

"Can I visit?"

He opens his eyes. "Is that your answer?"

"For now, I've got only questions."

He closes his eyes again, stretches. "That's fine with me. I know what I've been missing. You're welcome here, anytime."

Grace takes a breath. "You saw it, didn't you?"

"I saw them leave, and I was worried. I followed them out."

"You *knew*. The whole time." She pauses. "I should slap you."

Ralph rolls his head on the back of his chair. "Rita knew, too, eventually. She figured it out, then got Bliss to confess. What about that?"

"Rita has an excuse. She's in love, and she never believed in justice anyway."

"Grace," Ralph says, "it was an accident. Bliss was afraid for her life. And her baby's." He covers his eyes with his hand.

After a moment, Grace reaches over and takes his fingers, lifts his hand from his face. "She has you to say that for her."

"I'm so afraid I won't be able to help her. This"—he waves at the ranch, the valley—"is all I'm sure of anymore."

Grace objects, but after breakfast Byron insists on riding. Ralph uses a stool to mount him on Isadora, a gentle elderly mare with what looks like a simper, though when the chips are down she'll get you out of anything. Byron swings his hurt leg up over her back, and they take off at the kind of slow walk they think the occasion deserves. At first Ralph rides next to Byron on Gunter, and Rita and Grace take up the rear on Jude and Marley, now a little gray around the fetlocks. Bliss stays back at the house to cook lunch, but she comes out on the porch to admire them as they go. Grace can see dark circles under her eyes even through the makeup.

Marley's getting old. It takes him a few minutes to work the stiffness out of his gait, but he stretches his neck forward, eager, when Grace chucks her tongue at him and says his name. They ride through the sage over the foothills. Below, the reservoir glints as the breeze comes up. The valley is green and fresh.

In front of her, Grace's father begins, "I ride an old paint," and she chimes in without thinking, "I lead an old dan." By the time she's reached the second line, it's too late to choke on the words. She smiles and keeps going. Ralph nods, then he and Rita raise their voices too, into the verse about the daughter gone to Denver, the son gone wrong. Or maybe it's the other way—the song doesn't specify.

Rita says, "Brings it all back, doesn't it?" Then Rita, Ralph, and Grace take turns galloping out in pairs, giving the horses their heads, while the other rides at a walk with Grace's father. The dogs run between the two groups and keep track of everyone.

Grace has almost forgotten what riding feels like, as if rider and horse share legs, will, enormous pounding heart. A body open to wind. At last they reach the other side of government land and turn around. Rita and Ralph take off at a full-out gallop, and Grace rides at a walk with her hurt father beside her and the morning sun behind her. It occurs to her that this is the opposite of what she has envisioned. She can feel a tickle of something like comfort, like happiness, moving over her skin, a sensation she has almost forgotten. She savors it. Her father starts singing again, the old songs he and her mother used to sing, and Grace pipes in with what was once Julia's part, lyrics and harmonies she thought she had forgotten. Byron keeps stopping in midsong and asking, "Do you remember this one?" And so they make their way back toward fenced land, Marley and Isadora under them picking up speed, the smell of their stalls and oats drawing them home.

Once the animals are brushed, fed, and watered, dozing placidly in their sweet-smelling stalls, the four head back to the house for lunch.

Bliss has left the ranch house door unlocked. She's taken

Grace's truck keys off the hook by the door. She's left a note on the kitchen table saying, "Rita, I love you, but there are things I have to do." And, weighting the note, she's left a plate of cheese sandwiches and a stack of empty bowls for the left-over vegetable soup coming to a boil on the stove.

At the house in town, Imo and Miranda stand over a pot of chili with their heads together, Miranda's arm around Imo's waist. Imo is wearing dove-gray satin trousers, a sweater stitched with silver sequins, and a silver wig on her head, all new.

First, Imo still won't look right at Byron, but she keeps stealing little sideways glances at his crutches and leg.

Finally she says, "What happened?"

Now that he's all right, Grace is angry. "Good question," she says. "Why don't you tell us, Byron?"

"It's been a long time," he says.

Rita says, "He just misstepped, is all."

"He didn't *mis*step," Grace says. "He *stepped* right into the air. He might as well have done a swan dive."

He looks over Grace's shoulder, toward Miranda, gives a sideways smile. "What can I say? At that moment, it looked like it would hold."

"It was your heart, wasn't it?" Miranda hands Byron a fistful of spoons. "Set the table for eight, please."

Byron counts heads. There are only six. Miranda puts her finger to her lips, but he says, "Company coming?"

Imo flares her nostrils and tucks in her chin. "Now you're here, you may as well sit down. You and Miranda." She still doesn't look at him. She waves her hand at the table, says to Grace, "Your grandfather and Pascal will likely be late."

"Imo, we can't stay," Ralph says. "We have to find Bliss."

Rita says, "Ralph and I can go."

"Where?" Grace says.

Ralph pushes back his chair. "Where we've been trying to keep her from going. The station. It's the only reason she would leave without us. It was her way of keeping her nerve."

Grace cocks her head. "Why should I believe you now?"

"You can hardly blame her for not wanting you to haul her in like a prisoner," Rita says. "Let her do this."

"You're right." Grace sighs. She wanted to humiliate Bliss, to punish her. "She'll have a hard enough time without my help."

Ralph leans over and kisses Grace on the cheek. "She could have an easier time with it. I'll call you later."

After they leave, Imo puts her hand over Grace's and looks at Byron. "I must say, I never thought I'd see him sitting at my table again. But he keeps marrying the right women."

Byron says to Imo, "I owe much of my success to you. Wanting to prove myself." He shakes his head. "Lord, how I hated you."

"Well." Imo looks hard at the window. It is edged with a froth of green shadow from the trees outside.

"I just think it's time, is all. We're her only family." Byron's voice lifts a little at the end.

"There are some things you don't get over," Imo says.

Byron looks at Grace. "That's exactly it."

"Exactly." Imo sniffs.

He says, "You and I aren't the only people involved here, you know?"

Imo's face seems to soften second by second, the flesh loosening. She shuts her eyes and takes a deep breath.

Grace reaches out and touches her father's arm, then she gets up and puts her arms around his neck. She is forcing herself into her body. She can smell his cologne, Old Spice like before, and feel the scratch of his beard against her cheek. She can feel his presence not only on her skin but inside, where her heart is. It hurts like nothing she can imagine.

He is holding her tight. She feels the bruises forming on her skin, as though they haven't been there already forever, just under the surface. He pulls up a chair, then she is sitting on his good knee and he is rocking her.

Imo sighs. She takes the cozy off the pot and pours them each a cup of strong, black tea.

CHAPTER 14

■ ■ ■

The Problem with Distance

Sometimes at night, to put herself to sleep, Grace still dreams about packing up and going to exotic places—places north, where the skies are gray and she walks with her hands in her pockets along a pier, bending her head to the wind. Places where she rides her bike for miles on a beachfront road, waiting for the sun to set over the water. Nobody there, just Grace and the birds, their cries raised against the hushed sound of water moved around the entire earth by great tides, a slow-beating heart. The breeze rippling its surface, wind blowing waves to fury. Still, intruding on both visions is that old one of herself on horseback riding easily through the high late-summer grass. The grass, too, moves in waves under the wind, so tall the gold stalks brush the horse's belly. Always, at least until now, Grace is riding away, never toward anything.

This cannot be the movement of her life, even if almost everything is too large for her to understand. Maybe because it's too large—she keeps getting new pieces, though the picture is never finished. Will she ever fathom how the physics and biology of her brain, the interaction of one cell with another and with perception, make her who she is? How time is only a series of arrivals and departures? Real time, at least, that human invention. Imaginary time, more authentic, doesn't distinguish between past and future—it all exists at once. No question of where things begin, where they end. Sorting it all out is a human need, fueled by our fear of finishing, of death.

Grace shoots another Polaroid of her garden, the colors beginning to come out, and imagines, in the sun, what May and June will look like. Pink and white peonies. And behind them, delphinium, showy and poisonous, a whole bank. Roses in front of the yews, floating against the dark green. She can picture anything, now that the yard's flattened out hand-size in front of her. But really she shoots the photos for Bliss. She lays them out on Rita's kitchen table.

Grace points to a photograph, summer flowers drawn in. "Predictions," she says. "Like the cards."

Bliss smiles, wraps her hands around her belly. She's begun to show. "Now you're getting it. Though I hadn't thought of it quite that way."

"A project like this takes a while. It keeps changing." Grace is warming to Bliss. Bliss tried to plead guilty, told Ralph she wanted no bargains. But the prosecutor's office, at Ralph's urging, and, to everyone's surprise, Flint's too, has arranged a complex of pleas involving accident and self-defense, a long parole. Rita and Grace have persuaded Bliss to go along.

Bliss says, "I have something for you." She presses a package into Grace's hand. It's wrapped in the Sunday funnies. Grace's name is written across it in gold glitter; silver glitter stars and crescent moons dance around it. "The cards go into stores next month. I have orders already, mostly from California. But I wanted you to have this deck. It's hand-done, and signed."

"They're just what I've needed," Grace says.

Bliss nods at her, not smiling. "I had a call from Dan."

Grace loosens the tape from the end of the package.

"He wanted to let me know he picked up another Colt. Just like those others, you know. At a gun show."

Grace stops unwrapping. "Is that legal?"

Bliss shakes her head and looks away. "Does it matter? I'm afraid. He doesn't go to trial for a couple of weeks, and even then—"

"Surely he'll go to prison?"

Bliss shakes her head again. "I'm not much of a witness, at the moment. I killed a man." She's looking at Grace now, at Grace's eyes.

"In self-defense. Sort of." Grace hesitates, fiddles with the wrapped deck. "Why did he tell you?"

"Why do you think?" Rita says.

"That's harassment." Grace sighs, closes her eyes to think. "Okay. Tell me where he keeps the gun."

Bliss touches the tabletop between them. "You don't have to do this. I know what it would take."

"It's okay." It doesn't feel okay, but Grace can't figure out what else to do.

The next week, Bliss asks Dan to meet her at the Broiler. Grace locks her bicycle around the corner from their bungalow, then watches from behind the chain-link fence, the Concord grapes now in full leaf for camouflage, while Dan climbs into his Volkswagen bus and chugs down the street. Grace is wearing her winter bicycle gloves, not the warm-weather ones with no fingers. She finds the house key where Bliss said it would be, on top of the back door frame, and she lets herself into the mud room. The house smells damp and moldy, and the floor in the kitchen is tracked with dirt. The ticks and creaks of the house have an unfamiliar rhythm. Grace keeps looking over her shoulder.

The bedroom is down the little hallway on the right. There are clothes scattered everywhere. The room smells of stale sweat. Grace opens the closet door, pulls the chain that turns on the light. Nothing. She stands on her toes and gropes around on the closet shelf, until her hand hits the box. Nike aerobics shoes. Bliss must have bought them in bulk, she thinks, or else she saves boxes. White letters on the red-orange cardboard say, JUST DO IT.

Grace opens the lid. Inside is Dan's Colt, blue-black, dull. Wrapped separately in newspaper are a loaded magazine, extra bullets. Grace checks the magazine, then slides it into the handle of the gun and begins to put the whole thing in the pocket of her anorak. She leaves the spare bullets where they are.

Behind her, Dan says, "I was going to take her some clothes she left here, but I forgot them. I had to come back."

Grace's hand is still on the gun. She spins, the Colt lifted in front of her, her heart leaping with the motion of her arms. "They wouldn't fit her now anyway," she says.

"I should have known she didn't really want to see me." Dan is leaning against the door frame, casual, his arms crossed in front of him. He holds out his hand.

She remembers Pascal, his hand held out like that, and how she put the gun right into it. "You don't really think I'm going to give it to you, do you?"

"All I have to do is lift the phone and call the police."

"I have permission to enter this house. Bliss owns it, just as much as you."

Dan purses his lips. "Bliss has moved out, and it's my gun in your hands. I have others, but that one has sentimental value."

"It isn't even the same one." Grace looks him over, trying to decide what he might do, what she is capable of. He looks relaxed, almost happy to be where he is. She takes a deep breath. "So call the police." She jerks her head toward the phone at bedside. "I'll still be here."

He smiles at her. "I always liked your brains. On second

thought, why don't you just put that down and go on your way?"

"Dan," Grace says, "think how much trouble this gun has cost you. Guns like it."

He shakes his head. "Not guns. It's always people. Guns are reliable. You always know just what they'll do." He lifts his hand in the shape of a gun, points it at Grace. "Bang," he says.

"That's true. You know. So why not let me take it?"

"I need it. If I thought you'd shoot me, I'd tell you to go ahead. But you won't."

Grace is shaking, but, she realizes, with fury, not with fear. She says between her teeth, "Don't you count on it. Just don't. You killed my husband."

He won't stop smiling. "The person who pulled the trigger is living a life of luxury in your best friend's house. She's carrying my child."

"Yes, she is. And you're lucky things didn't turn out just a little differently."

"So is she. It goes to show what happens when you put guns in the hands of amateurs." He nods at the gun in Grace's hand. "I tried to teach her. That thing has a little kick to it. You have to lock your wrist, hold it steady." Dan lowers his head, runs his hand over his forehead. "I tried to protect her. I tried. But I couldn't make her see. I was the only one who cared enough. And she screwed me."

Grace says, softly, "She did what she had to do." Grace looks again at the phone on the bedside table.

"Don't think about it," he says. "Not unless you're ready to shoot me."

"Why not get some help?"

"It's too late." He looks at Grace flatly. He says, "Get out. Before you really piss me off. Put the gun on the kitchen table on your way. I'll stay here until you're gone."

This may be her only chance. "Don't do anything," she says. "Wait here. I'll come right back." She slides her back along the wall, stepping over piles of clothing, aiming the gun at him so that he stays against the wall opposite. Briefly, she wonders what Flint will have to say about this. She sighs. When she reaches the bedroom door, she says, "Sit down on the bed. Count to one hundred. Slowly."

He grins at her. "You've been watching TV. You know how the tough guys act." She knows he's going to move, but she's still not fast enough; he takes two long steps and is next to her, his hand on her hand, and he's right, she doesn't pull the trigger. He raises her hand, the gun in it, and presses the muzzle to her cheekbone, so that she can feel both metal and the flesh of his hand against her face. She is acutely aware of her gloved finger trembling on the trigger.

"Dan," Grace says. "I'm sorry. About all of it."

"The world is full of grief," he says. He lets her hand go, walks over to sit on the bed. "We have a deal. Get out," he says. "Do like I said: leave the gun."

Grace turns out of the bedroom and runs down the hall. She hesitates in the kitchen, glances once at the table. She doesn't know if Dan was telling the truth or not about other guns. It wouldn't surprise her. But she slams out the back door with the Colt still in her hand. Hands shaking, she clicks the safety on and puts the gun in her pannier. She thinks of knocking on doors, asking to use a neighbor's phone, but it's midweek, and the driveways of the nearby houses are empty. There's a 7-Eleven at the bottom of the hill. She listens all the time, but she hears nothing from Dan's house. Under her breath, she counts. Sixty-one. Sixty-two.

She gets on her bike and coasts fast downhill. She has no quarters for the pay phone; she gets change from the teenager behind the counter before she remembers she doesn't need it to call 911. She tells the dispatcher to get Flint, to hurry. Then, she sinks to the pavement, buries her face in her hands, and waits for the sirens.

By the time she's recovered her nerve and pedaled back up the hill, the police have arrived, but it's too late. She paces behind the yellow police tape, her arms crossed over her chest.

Flint comes out of the little house and walks over the weedy lawn to where she stands. "They found him in the bathroom. You don't need to go in; I've identified him for now." He shakes his head. "It's pretty messy in there."

"Oh, God," Grace says. "Isn't enough enough?" She looks up at the sky to keep her eyes from tearing over.

He looks down at the pavement, then follows her gaze to the watery blue sky. "Sometimes it's not," he says.

Grace unzips her bicycle pack and hands him Dan's Colt. "You'll need this for evidence, I guess. What's going to happen?"

"I can't be sure. But as I see it, you were trying to prevent"—he waves his hand toward the house, then drops it. "It was a hostage situation."

"Yeah." Grace shades her eyes and looks up at him. "I was holding him hostage. I should have kept the gun on him and phoned from there." She wonders if she should tell him she was breaking and entering.

"He would have made you shoot him. Or he would have shot you."

"That's what he said." Grace looks away, into the valley. "But somehow I think he was kinder than that. Anyway, the result was the same."

"Not the same," he says. "What happened to you is not the same." He touches her arm. "To him, it doesn't matter anymore."

He's not being nearly tough enough on her. Grace has the feeling he wants to take her hand, but he stands still.

She says, "I wanted to prevent it. In the end. But you should know that's not why I went inside in the first place."

She is thinking about the feel of the gun against her skin, about Dan at the end, sitting in the bathroom with cold metal in his hand.

"I don't think it matters anymore," he says.

Here's how a small city brings you back to yourself: in Pascal's cabin, which Grace hasn't entered since before she stood in the snow on the outside watching him fumble, framed in the picture window, is Willem's last painting, finished years before and in her absence. It hangs on the wall next to the window, in the space where his eyes were fixed that night. Grace is here, finally, to go through Pascal's things, and she is stricken almost still again to be reminded in such a material way how much of her Pascal owned—a piece of her own past. The painting strikes in her a flint of sadness, another of anger. She always thought of it as incomplete. Now she has to think of its presence in Pascal's home as a coincidence not only of observation and creation but also of memory. She takes in her breath. He must have taken it down after their first meeting so she wouldn't see it.

She tries to look at the painting with the eyes of a collector. The figure that was Grace sits in the same green chair she remembers, but instead of painting the window in behind her, Willem placed the chair in a grove of trees, a canopy of green light above and, around her, closing in, trunks straight and shaded black as prison bars. Now, looking back through the paint, she can't quite believe in this evidence that Willem existed, this sign that Pascal looked through Willem's eyes at her past and the marks it made on her skin, before he even met her. Did he take the painting as a kind of omen, an inevitable vision? There was something there he thought he needed to know: the spread legs mottled with bruises—surely they weren't as bad as all that?—the thrown-back head, the pale eyes and slightly open mouth. Willem called it *Still Life, With Grace*. For the first time, she fully realizes that out in the world, on the walls of strangers, are three other versions of her younger self. What, she wonders, would compel somebody to buy such a work?

She is glad he never showed it to her, never asked her to explain it. And that he didn't sell it, didn't send that version of her out into the world to join the others.

Out of the habit of this long winter and spring, she has turned on the radio, though, unlike so many, preparing to turn out for ceremonies and ticker-tape parades, she is sick of Iraq, the Kurds, America's small-timeness. For this, she blames not individual soldiers but something larger about the country. Rita has been arranging local donations for the Kurds, badgering businesses and the clergy, but she says it's like dropping a penny into a deep well, hearing your wish echo back at you. On the radio, the president says we will not abandon them, though he feels no direct responsibility for their fate. The problem with distance: eventually, you are far away from even yourself.

In the painting, the figure that was Grace, or for which she served as model, seems to blur around the edges, going ghostly as Willem knocked on her apartment door and she sat as quiet as she could on the other side so he wouldn't know for certain she was there, stillness as another form of flight. Just another recalcitrant muse, offering herself as blank canvas. Now, she would open that door, invite Willem in, speak to him, as she never did at the time, of herself, of what she believed and wanted, of how she didn't love him but loved the abandonment he saw in her. She had never wanted to be stirred where Pascal stirred her; it's easy to be brave in the absence of danger. She mistook danger for love, and so asked Pascal for the wrong thing.

She reaches to the surface of the painting, what she offered them both. She touches the bruises on that girl's thighs. The paint is rough against her fingers. The figure is just pigment on canvas, not flesh. Still, if it is what Willem wanted to see, it is also what Grace showed him. She can see her own fault now so clearly, how she wanted to take care only of what didn't belong to her. She would pose for Willem again, or for someone else, but this time she would like to take her own stance, assert herself as revelation rather than mask, the subject as well as the object of the gaze—though that was never what either Willem or Grace wanted at the time. For Pascal.

She says out loud, "Darling, that was never it," talking to all of them, and herself. How did Pascal interpret those bruises? As metaphorical, or as specific to a moment in the past? Grace never spoke to him about Marcus, about Willem, and in spite of the painting he never asked. With the painting in front of her, firm evidence, she can see he knew how much she had withheld.

Grace lifts the painting from the wall and wraps it in the comforter from Pascal's bed. She wonders how long she will have Imo's attic to hide things in, all the snapshots, the windows into a figured past—how long it will be before the attic, too, belongs to Grace, and everything left of Imo, of Grace, and of Julia, the missing link, is there for her to unfold from dusty boxes. What to keep, what to throw away.

"I never made a hard decision in my life," Grace says. She is answering a question of Ralph's, and though her answer is not quite accurate, like the painting it is true enough under a certain light. She says again what she said to her father: "This is only a start." She moves, then, from room to room, opening drawers and closets, the medicine cabinet. There is nothing here to surprise her—prescriptions, the same black underwear, a pair of cowboy boots plainer and more worn than the ones Grace knew.

Last, she goes to Pascal's desk. Everything in it is hers, but she still looks over her shoulder as if she's entering somewhere she's not welcome. As with Rita's dresser, she may find things she doesn't want to see.

Looking through his check stubs, Grace sees that he contributed, from just before their wedding, to every cause Rita was involved with, and she feels a rush first of anger over the old betrayal, then of love for both of them. She holds the checkbook for a few minutes. Then she finds a pen, balances the checkbook—something Pascal apparently never did— and writes out a check to Rita for the full amount in the account. Though everything belongs to her now, she holds Pascal's private savings passbooks and a pile of investment statements a minute without looking into them, then, still without opening them, she puts them in an envelope with the check, writes Rita's name on it. It will take more than this—lawyers, papers to sign—but the gesture feels true and final.

In the last drawer is a manila envelope stuffed with photographs: Pascal with a man who must have been his father standing on a beach—Galveston, Grace thinks—squinting into the camera; more family shots; and, finally, in a separate envelope, photographs from the *Coral Sea*. A group of men poses on deck with no rail to keep them from going over the edge into the water, which is indistinguishable from sky, a washed-out blue. In another shot, a figure it takes Grace a second to recognize behind its goggles and helmet pushes two bombs on a wheeled cart across the deck. On the back, in Pascal's writing, it says, "Snake eye, five hundred lbs. per." Even behind the goggles, his face looks young, tender and raw.

Grace puts the photographs in her purse. She closes up the desk and lifts Pascal's model ship from the mantel. She runs her hands along its scarred sides, the chipped black lettering that says *Coral Sea II*. She takes the boat out the back door to the creek, still swollen with runoff. The flow is nothing— only about eight feet across, three feet deep—but to the model boat it is a raging torrent. She sets the ship in the water. It holds for a second in an eddy, then it shoots over the lip of a rock and downstream. She watches it until it catches in some twigs, then pulls free and rounds the bend out of sight, rocking and swaying. She doesn't follow.

She leaves her truck at the cabin. She leans the painting in the passenger seat of Pascal's Jaguar and drives back down to the condo. She never once drove Pascal's car while he was living, has been afraid to drive it all these weeks.

At the condo, she stands in the hall, listening at the door as if she may find somebody there after all. But when she walks inside, the living room is almost as she left it, a little cluttered from the police search, though they must have been careful to put things back as neatly as they could. She feels a sudden warmth for Detective Flint, a sweet hopefulness, though everything is dulled by a thick film of dust, and the air feels, still, like February, cold and with the vague after-smell of ice. There are cobwebs in all the corners.

Grace goes down to the storage room. She gets out the collapsed moving cartons, brings them up, and begins to unfold them, to toss things into them at random—books and knick-knacks, the telephone answering machine, whose message light is blinking before she pulls the plug. She avoids opening the study door, imagining behind it a frayed and withered jungle, her neglected orchids dying back to air.

Instead, she goes into the bedroom and begins to pack shoes, jeans, all the wispy lingerie Pascal bought her. She sits on the floor and shuts her eyes and runs teddies and night-gowns through her fingers, silk and lace, a kind of softness available to Pascal in no other way. She lifts a slip to the light and looks through it—how it both reveals and obscures what is beyond it. And for a moment, maybe a moment she can build on, she is glad he could find in more than one place what he must have been looking for, maybe some sense of give in himself, though he worked against it all his life—or at least could work it into his life only as a kind of irony. Grace sits with one of the more ridiculous pairs of panties in her hand—pink chiffon ruffles across the back, with little pearl bows tying the hips—then she lies back on the carpet and closes her eyes and begins to cry. In her chest, something is breaking. She's a scientist and she knows it cannot be her heart and that this is only a metaphor anyway, but the sense is there and real, of cracking open at the ribs like a hinged box. She lies there long enough to fold back around the pain and fall asleep.

When she wakes up, she feels lighter, emptied, though she has no recollection of having dreamed. She goes into the kitchen and makes coffee, then returns to the boxes, almost ready at last to decide what will go into them. Leaned up against the living room wall is her guitar, which Rita or Ralph must have brought back from the Hole-in-the-Wall. She opens the case and rubs her hand along the neck. When she strums it, the sound is arbitrary. Without thinking, she begins to tune and then to pick. It's all there in her fingers, automatic, as if the notes are coming through her from somewhere else. But the calluses on her fingertips are almost gone, and in a few minutes the strings have left deep welts in the fingers of her left hand. She keeps playing anyway, moving from old licks to variations and, finally, new ground.

When she can no longer press the strings with her raw fingers, she lays the guitar back in its case. She cuts the tape on one of the boxes and digs the answering machine back out. She plugs it in and hears voices from last January—the condo association president wondering about her maintenance fees, then calling back after reading the newspaper. Jemma, her voice uncertain, saying, "If there's anything I can do to help," then trailing off, sounding less comforting than in need of comfort. The odd student. Newer messages from clients.

Grace rewinds back to the first message: Ralph phoning after she'd left the bar and gone out into the snow toward Imo's house, like some instinctive animal making a seasonal return. His voice, preserved as if the message were left yesterday, says, "Are you all right? Let me know if I can do anything. Give me a call?"

"Okay," Grace says, and she dials the ranch. When there's no answer, she tries the bar. Ralph answers.

"I got your message," she says. "I think I *am* all right."

He hesitates. "I don't think you've ever told me that before."

"I wish I could come back to work."

But Ralph has signed the papers this morning, selling the bar. He tells her the buyers are putting in an upscale restaurant for tourists, with free bowls of shrimp and mass-produced entrees named after wilderness and western themes. But he's having a farewell party, and he wants her to sing. "I've always liked your voice a little rough around the edges," he says, and she can hear that he's smiling.

Grace sings into the phone, something about going home. She's made it up, but it could be any song. "One last time," she says. They both pause. Then she says, "The problem is, I haven't been a friend to you."

"Not always. Though you've always been good for some entertainment along the way."

She says, a little sharply, "Or vice versa, for that matter." Then, "If we could manage simple friendship, would it be enough?"

"I don't know. It would be a start."

"When you know your moving date, let me know. I'll help out."

"Darlin', I will," he says very softly.

She hangs up, opens the drapes on the floor-to-ceiling windows in the living room, and watches the sunlight fall in over the walls and floors. She takes a deep breath and walks back toward her study. She is ready now for disaster: orchids withered down to bare medium, evidence of Rita's fruitless but sustained devotion.

Grace opens the study door to a blaze of color. The curtains are open, the blinds adjusted for the perfect filtering of light, and afternoon sun diffuses, bright but gentle, over the orchid cases onto the carpet. Under the cases' glass, a riot of blossom—more of the flowers are in bloom than Grace has ever been able to manage at one time. It's as if Rita has planned for just this moment. Only a few rare bloomers, the flowers on the most delicate and complicated schedules, are closed, though their foliage is green and lustrous. The rest turn their blossoms to the light, musky and full of sex. Before she's had a chance to think, Grace has cupped her breasts in her hands. She opens the glass doors and breathes in the orchids' moisture. With the sun on her back, she could be in the tropics. She touches the delicate, threadlike petals of the *Cirrhopetalum medusae.*

"Way to go, Rita," she says.

Grace boxes the flowers and loads them into the back of the car. The Jaguar is not made for people who move their own things, and it won't hold much, but it's a start. She lays the painting in on top of the boxes and, finally, leans the guitar like a stiff-backed child in the passenger seat. As an afterthought, she pulls the seat belt around it. On the passenger side of the windshield, the sun throws into relief bare footprints, the curve of arch and five round toes—her own from the summer before, when she kicked off her sandals and rested her feet on the dash while Pascal drove. She leans over with a tissue and smears the prints into an unrecognizable blur.

She drives up to the mortuary. Rita's in the front yard, clippers in her hands. Wendy roots at the grass with her nose. "Bliss is inside," Rita says. "Go touch her stomach."

Grace smiles at the idea of Rita courting her on behalf of another woman. She points to the car. "I'm getting my stuff out, before it's too late. I have something for you. And the Kurds." She hands Rita the manila envelope.

Rita opens it. She reads the amount on the check and glances up at Grace before opening the passbooks and looking inside. "My God." She opens her other arm to Grace. "But I'm refocusing my efforts. I'm working with the ACLU now. Prison stuff."

"I should have guessed." Before Rita can start talking about overcrowding, Grace opens the hatchback and pulls out the painting, still wrapped in the comforter. She opens the boxes of orchids so Rita can see them, strange petals luminous in the light.

"You'll have to show me a thing or two," she says. "I would have thought this was impossible. You'll have to write it up."

Rita says, "I had nothing better to do. Wendy and I visited every day." Wendy wags her tail and looks from Rita's face to Grace's. Rita points at the painting. "What's that?" Grace unwraps it and stands it against the Jaguar. Sunlight washes through the trees, blurring even more the lines between the body and the green chair, whose color ripples like lake water over the skin and into the bruises.

Rita reaches out and touches the bruises with one finger. "I never knew Willem was so good." But a bright spot of color flares on each cheek. "This morning, Bliss and I took out my old photographs. Shots of us from six, seven years old. Ralph, too. And I just wept."

"Why?"

Rita leans against the Jaguar, her broad forehead in sunlight, her eyes and mouth shaded by a curtain of red hair. "I love Bliss. I want to make a life with her. And the baby. But I didn't know how hard it would be to give up on you. Even though you were just an idea."

"Because I was an idea." Grace puts her arm around Rita's waist. "I take it you aren't joining the Peace Corps?"

"I'm needed here. With Bliss—it's all I ever wanted. I only planned to go because there was nothing for me where I am."

Grace ducks in under Rita's hair, lifts her hand up to take Rita's face. "There are so many kinds of love." She hesitates. "I want to be welcome in your house. And Bliss's."

And finally she feels Rita lean into her, lay her cheek on Grace's hair. They stand there in the late spring sunlight, summer building against their backs.

By now, by Grace's watch, her father and Miranda are sitting in the wide seats of first class, drinking sluggish champagne and winging their way over deserts and mountains back to their suburb, which, if they fly low over it, will look like looped necklaces of green lawns and blue swimming pools. Or so Grace's father would draw it. Suddenly, seeing in her mind those orderly jewels mapping out his life, Grace believes her father hasn't really changed so much, has not abandoned who he was but has only discovered a more bearable version of himself, one he can live with until the end.

What Dan failed to do, perhaps. When she thinks of him, a lump of grief rises in her, grief mixed with anger and, she admits, relief.

She will visit her father for a week or so at a time, in the ordinary way of an adult child. They will sit next to the pool sipping gin and tonic, making small talk, riding currents and undercurrents. Grace looks forward to it, though the idea also takes her with a shiver of nerves.

Driving back up under the old trees to Imo's, in the back of her throat, to the rhythm of the engine, she's singing old cowboy songs about happiness right under the same sky where she is, as if the words and melodies joined can create a truth. She's choosing songs with hardly any longing in them. She sings, "We don't have cold weather, it never snows or rains," wobbling her voice in a parody of a yodel. Just a test. The words form like ideas in her mouth. At a stop sign, she tries it louder: "This is where the sun shines best, out on the western plains." Her window is rolled down, and a man out mowing his lawn with a push mower stops pushing and joins in.

Back at Imo's, Grace pulls the Jaguar under the porte-cochère. She gets her shovel from the shed and digs a hole at the base of the big lilac, fragrance now practically flaming from its dying flowers. It's so old it must have been put in when the house was built. She goes to her closet, to the box she hasn't opened since she received it back from the evidence room. Back outside, almost as an afterthought, she takes the painting from the car. With a razor knife, she cuts it from its frame, rolls the canvas, feeling the paint crackle and give under her hands, and lays it in the bottom of the hole. She drops Pascal's gun in next to it and shovels dirt over it.

The gun will be safe here, out of reach but with its location precisely marked, blooming. She will have to stay in the house herself as long as it's there, but that's a decision she's already made without knowing how. As long as Imo needs her. She taps the patch of sod back into place over the gun. She pulls out her camera and shoots the lilac and then the house from every possible angle, the elaborate gables and the garden beds growing fast like small daily miracles, then she goes in and photographs the foyer, the phone, the white round space on the wall where the mirror used to hang. She runs upstairs and pulls the roll of maps and the box of postcards out from under her bed, and then she climbs up to the attic, where she wipes the dust off the tops of boxes of magazines and photos and sheet music before she carries them down.

Imo sticks her head in Grace's bedroom door. She takes off her reading glasses and says, "What the hell are you doing?"

"You'll see. Go get ready for your walk."

Then Grace goes to work. She runs her fingers over the wall where the old pinholes still are. She opens the box of postcards and takes them out, beginning with the Rockefeller Center all lit up and ending in Indonesia. It's the first time she's read the messages—usually just a description of the place, the things most tourists don't see, in her father's precise hand, ending, all of them, with those blacked-out "loves." Starting in the upper left corner of the wall, she puts the cards back up. She can remember exactly where each one goes.

But she is not finished. At the top, she pins her father's last map, beginning with the drive up to Eden and ending with the drawn-in horses, a table set for eight, and, finally, a figure meant to be herself but disproportionately small, childlike even, curled in the lap of a figure meant to be him. In the drawing, his hurt leg juts straight out, and the balloon over his head reads, "Ouch." Next to this, Grace pins pages torn out of the *Pete Seeger Songbook,* then Julia's obituary—the yellowed photo of her dark cloud of hair. Grace's own travels. The color photos of women's lit-up brains from *Omni,* pressed flowers, Pascal and Grace's wedding photos, Grandpa's funeral notice—she's run out of wall and turns the corner toward the door where Imo is standing—Imo pursing her deep-red lips and cocking her muled foot below the hem of that evening gown pouring like liquid gold from her body, Pascal pushing two 500-pound bombs in front of him, Baggies with small pieces of iron pyrite and snowflake obsidian picked up off trails, clippings of Rita with medals shining against her breasts, torn-off pages from botany texts and Pascal's books on the heart, poems by Rimbaud, pages out of *Middlemarch,* Pascal's canceled checks to Rita's charities, posters for the Hole-in-the-Wall with black-and-white pictures of Grace and her guitar next to Imo's movie posters showing Imo in poses of manufactured distress, Bliss's precise drawings of the vascular systems of plants, Pascal's green shirt with bleach spots on the placket.

Imo watches over her glasses, her eyebrows raised. "Do you think you have everything?"

There will be more. Bliss, Rita, Ralph, and herself meeting on the veranda for tea, passing a baby from one set of arms to another. Imo. Flint, too—why not? Eating a sugar cookie. Taking her hand, after all. Flint. She pauses and shuts her eyes. Wendy digging under the lilac, sniffing out the gun and the painting, the past.

Why not, indeed? Though they have such a long way to go. Grace doesn't want to think about what else—the way Imo's heart barely whispers now, when it used to roar. Pascal in the ground, and Dan. Even Wendy, middle-aged and slowing down.

Grace reaches out her hand, and into it Imo puts one of Grandpa's darned socks, which Grace tacks up next to Bliss's drawings. She says, "Enough, at least for now," though she keeps remembering more: Imo's *People*, Pascal's medical charts with the final stamp over them in red. She writes in black Magic Marker at the end of what she's done, right across the curved arms of the Degas ballerinas, "Part 1." She says to Imo, "There may be some sense to be made of this."

"It may just be you're going off your bonnet," Imo says. "Which you're a little young for, at least if you want to do it with any charm." She fingers the photo of herself on horseback. "I'd forgotten what a knockout I was."

"No, you hadn't. But if charm isn't everything, neither is beauty." Grace closes the lid to the box of pushpins.

Imo shuts her eyes. "A lot you know about it."

Grace stands on Imo's front porch with her guitar. The car is still parked under the porte-cochère, its front seat and hatchback loaded with boxes of orchids. She has many more trips to make. She's trying to figure out how many empty cartons she will have to take up to the cabin, wishing she'd brought down the pickup instead of the Jaguar. She never even thought of it. She is tempted to hire a mover, to put all Pascal's things in storage somewhere on the edge of town, but there's a part of her that knows she needs to touch it all, to put it away herself in her own attic.

Imo looks into the back of the Jaguar at the cartons. "Are you moving out?" She is trying to keep her voice steady, pressing her hand against her throat. As usual, she is wearing perfume, but after the first wave of it breaks behind Grace's nose, Grace can smell the unmistakable, sharp odor of age, the body decaying. "I'm not going into any geezer home, if that's what you're thinking," Imo says.

Grace stops short for a second. She sets down her guitar

and puts her arm around Imo. "I forgot to ask," she says. "I'm sorry. I wondered if I could stay here." Then, when Imo doesn't answer, "It's time for your walk."

Imo pauses, and Grace feels her mustering something—clarity, strength. She says, "It's time for you to grow up, Grace. You can't live with me forever. You don't want to move backward, not at your age."

"No. I can't live with you. But we can live here together. We just have to give things a different emphasis."

"Words." Imo waves her hand in front of her face, as if she can clear the air of them. "You can't even figure out your own heart."

"Imo." Grace takes Imo by the shoulders. "You're right. I'm hoping to begin. As long as you know where you are, even for ten seconds a day, you'll be here. So will I."

Imo looks Grace in the face with her bluest, sharpest eyes, trying to read her. "Maybe I'm not right. What then?"

"We have to go in," Grace says. "Rita's coming to tea. With Bliss."

"So that's it." Imo grins. "I knew all about it, those two, a hell of a lot earlier than you did. But who can tell you anything?"

"Don't mistake me," Grace says. "It's only tea."

"Of course, that Bliss is easy on the eyes. I saw her picture in the paper. There's a girl who knows how to make the most of herself."

Grace laughs. "Even in a mug shot. You always had a talent for the obvious."

"Somebody has to point it out, or nobody sees it. You know, you can have anybody over that you want. Things have changed since my day." She nods. "It will be nice to have a baby around. Not that I ever expected to get one out of you."

Grace puts her arm over Imo's shoulders. "Next week, we'll go to Ralph's party. I'll sing some dirty songs. Would you like that?"

Imo says, slow, "Of course, in my day they could have lived

together. Nobody would have thought twice about it. A couple of spinsters, is all. But I'm a little old lady. We didn't dare think about those things then, and so people were safe. Now, they could cause a scandal." She flashes her teeth at Grace, all of them white and sharp.

"You're a little behind. They're hardly scandalous now."

"A shame. Nothing like a little scandal." Then "Is Miranda coming?"

"Miranda's gone. Maybe another time. You can come to California with me when I visit."

"We'll go shopping on Rodeo Drive." Imo clicks her tongue. "And you?"

"I haven't made up my mind about everything."

Imo shakes her head. "Still? You know, that detective is an interesting fellow. He could stand a heavy pressing. I wonder where my old mangle is. But he's not without his appeal."

"You've always had a good eye," Grace says. "But for now, I'll just stick with you." This time, Grace can see Imo's eyes blur over right as she's looking into them.

Imo looks out at the street. "What do you think happened to your grandfather?"

"There are some things you can't forget." Grace feels this urgently, but against hope.

Imo says, fretfulness slurring her voice, "Forget? Why should I?"

"If you don't feel like walking, why don't you come in? I'll tell your fortune." Grace picks up her guitar. "I've been learning all about it from Bliss."

"That would be fine. You just make it a nice one," Imo says. "Tell me about your grandfather. How it was."

Grace steers Imo toward the door. "Why not? I suppose it's just as chancy, predicting the past." Over Imo's shoulder, Grace sees a blue sedan pull up at the curb. The door opens, and Flint gets out. She waves.

Imo says, her voice firm, "You've got it right there." Imo

opens her hand and touches its palm with her other index finger, then she closes it into a tight fist.

"We'll set Grandpa a place," Grace says, "and Mr. Flint. But not Pascal."

"Whatever you want."

"By the time Rita and Bliss get here," Grace says, "we'll be ready."

"What do you mean? We're ready now, if you ask me."

"I do ask you," Grace says, and she helps Imo over the door-jamb, leaving the door open behind them.

Western Literature Series

■ ■ ■

Western Trails: A Collection of Short Stories by Mary Austin
selected and edited by Melody Graulich

Cactus Thorn
Mary Austin

Dan De Quille, the Washoe Giant: A Biography and Anthology
prepared by Richard A. Dwyer and Richard E. Lingenfelter

Desert Wood: An Anthology of Nevada Poets
edited by Shaun T. Griffin

The City of Trembling Leaves
Walter Van Tilburg Clark

Many Californias: Literature from the Golden State
edited by Gerald W. Haslam

The Authentic Death of Hendry Jones
Charles Neider

First Horses: Stories of the New West
Robert Franklin Gish

Torn by Light: Selected Poems
Joanne de Longchamps

Swimming Man Burning
Terrence Kilpatrick

The Temptations of St. Ed & Brother S
Frank Bergon

The Other California: The Great Central Valley in Life and Letters
Gerald W. Haslam

The Track of the Cat
Walter Van Tilburg Clark

Shoshone Mike
Frank Bergon

Condor Dreams and Other Fictions
Gerald W. Haslam

A Lean Year and Other Stories
Robert Laxalt

Cruising State: Growing Up in Southern California
Christopher Buckley

The Big Silence
Bernard Schopen

Kinsella's Man
Richard Stookey

The Desert Look
Bernard Schopen

Winterchill
Ernest J. Finney

Wild Game
Frank Bergon

Lucky 13: Short Plays about Arizona, Nevada, and Utah
edited by Red Shuttleworth

The Measurable World
Katharine Coles